REDEMPTION ROAD

A SMALL TOWN ROMANTIC THRILLER

AMANDA MCKINNEY

HH TISEVICH

Paperback ISBN 978-1-7358681-4-1
eBook ISBN 978-1-7358681-3-4

Editor(s):
Pam Berehulke, Bulletproof Editing
Nancy Brown, Redline Proofreading
Cover Design:
Steamy Reads Designs
📷: Michelle Lancaster Photography

https://www.amandamckinneyauthor.com

DEDICATION

For Mama

ALSO BY AMANDA

BESTSELLING STEELE SHADOWS SERIES:

Cabin 1 (Steele Shadows Security)

Cabin 2 (Steele Shadows Security)

Cabin 3 (Steele Shadows Security)

Phoenix (Steele Shadows Rising)

Jagger (Steele Shadows Investigations)

Ryder (Steele Shadows Investigations)

Her Mercenary (Steele Shadows Mercenaries)

BESTSELLING DARK ROMANTIC SUSPENSE SERIES:

Rattlesnake Road

Redemption Road

AWARD-WINNING ROMANTIC SUSPENSE SERIES:

The Woods (A Berry Springs Novel)

The Lake (A Berry Springs Novel)

The Storm (A Berry Springs Novel)

The Fog (A Berry Springs Novel)

The Creek (A Berry Springs Novel)

The Shadow (A Berry Springs Novel)

The Cave (A Berry Springs Novel)

The Viper

Devil's Gold (A Black Rose Mystery, Book 1)

Hatchet Hollow (A Black Rose Mystery, Book 2)

Tomb's Tale (A Black Rose Mystery Book 3)

Evil Eye (A Black Rose Mystery Book 4)

Sinister Secrets (A Black Rose Mystery Book 5)

And many more to come...

LET'S CONNECT!

Text **AMANDABOOKS to 66866** to sign up
for Amanda's Newsletter and get the latest
on new releases, promos, and freebies!
Or, you can sign up below.

https://www.amandamckinneyauthor.com

REDEMPTION ROAD

Redemption: The act of being saved from sin, error, or evil.

Antiques dealer by day, secret painter by night, Rory Flanagan arrives home to find a man, battered and bruised, sprawled out on her newly upholstered Victorian sofa. The brash, six-foot-four stranger takes an unusual interest in Rory's vintage gold pendant—given to Rory by her mother the day she was killed.

They say Christian Locke is a loner, an orphan, a mysterious cowboy the small-town gossips deem an outsider. They tell her to stay away. But Rory can't ignore the connection she feels to the mulish recluse, or the interest he has in the cursed necklace she wears around her neck.

Christian says he doesn't believe in fate, but every twist and turn of the pendant's story seems to lead her to the same place...

Welcome to Redemption Road.

Fair Warning: Due to serious subject matter and mature content, please be aware that this book might be an emotional trigger for some readers.

*T*hey say there are five stages of grief: denial, anger, bargaining, depression, and acceptance.

I'm quite familiar with two.

The first is denial. Some refer to it as isolation. It's widely accepted that denial is our greatest defense mechanism to the shock of loss. It serves as a buffer to the pain, therefore numbing us to our emotions.

Denial may come in the form of questioning test results, such as *this terminal diagnosis can't be mine; the test had to have gotten mixed up.* Or in the form of blatant rejection. *My daughter wasn't just killed by a drunk driver; you've got the wrong person. I just talked to her an hour ago.*

Often the shock of losing someone is so extreme that it shakes everything you know to be true. And for a society that bases fact on tangible things—things we can touch, see, hear—this is usually the catalyst for a monumental shift in one's life.

This is the beginning of my story.

For me, the experience of loss manifested in a physical state of emptiness inside my body, as if organs had been removed and replaced with, simply, nothing. I literally felt a space of *nothing* inside me, in a specific location on the left side of my chest. Nothing was there. My heart, and my soul around it, were gone. Vanished.

I felt a disconnection from the world around me. I had no grounding anymore. Just . . . nothing.

The second stage of grief is anger.

Once denial is no longer possible—maybe you saw the body of your deceased loved one, or received confirmation that the lab didn't mix up your tests with someone else's, and the results do, in fact, suggest a terminal timeline— reality begins to take hold.

Emotion triggers a vulnerability in us, and in turn is redirected and expressed as anger. This anger may be directed toward objects—like throwing your cell phone across the room, or lashing out at strangers, family, or friends. *This isn't fair. Why me? Why now? Why them? I don't deserve this. My beautiful, innocent three-year-old boy doesn't deserve this diagnosis.*

The anger then funnels into blame. *Who did this? The drunk driver deserves to die for killing my daughter. I'm the reason for my son's diagnosis because my body failed him in utero. Why?*

Our pain is so extreme, so unprecedented, that in order to cope, we must hate something, because we're literally incapable at that time of processing the anger. The emotion has to be directed from our bodies onto someone else, something else, or maybe onto the ultimate else—the creator of all things.

Why.

Why.

Why?

This is where I seem to be stuck. A swinging pendulum

between absolute vacancy of life, and raging anger that's usually directed toward myself. Maybe if I'd done this, done that, didn't do that. Maybe if I'd reacted like that, maybe, maybe, maybe. Maybe I could have changed the course of events.

Maybe if I hadn't loved so much, so hard.

The Buddha said, "The root of suffering is attachment." He also said, "You can only lose what you cling to."

You see, I immersed myself in a sea of books and step-by-step workbooks about loss . . . how to cope with it, and how to accept it. Each served a purpose, but nothing permeated the fog of my brain like the theory of detachment, the idea that pain can be remedied by letting go of our attachment, our obsessive love of certain people or things.

Basically, if we never love, we never feel pain.

This sounded like a solid plan. Easy. Something I could *do*.

Years ago, a high school teacher delved a little in philosophy by asking our class if, given the option, would we prefer to live in ignorant bliss, a calm state of nothingness, not knowing the pain and suffering around us. Or would we rather live in heightened awareness, where nothing is hidden and everything—good and bad—is exposed and must be dealt with.

As a naive teenager, I'd said *heightened awareness*. On this day, though, the start of my story, I chose the nothingness. I made a decision to release myself to it—whatever that may be, accepting this nothingness as pure and simple as the rain streaking down my naked body.

I was just a shell on that cold night, not really myself as I walked slowly from tree to tree, running my fingertips along the rough, wet bark as I passed. Each touch was a connection to the nature around me, something we often overlook and pass by without so much as a second glance. That life around us is taken for granted, mainly because it isn't us but only a silent being. It's still a being, nonetheless.

With each step, my bare feet sank into the cold mud, thick brown sludge squishing between my toes, wilted grass tickling my ankles. I remember the scent of the damp earth . . . musty, ripe with fertile soil and budding plants, and the sound of the waves pummeling the rocks far below. The feeling of each raindrop as it hit my bare shoulders, then slid between my breasts, down my stomach and then my legs. My wet blond hair hung heavily around my shoulders, a few strands sticking to the side of my face.

I don't remember being cold, or feeling the cuts from the rocks below my feet. Instead, I remember being numb.

The headaches were gone, as was the anxiety, the pain, the fear, the hunger. I was nothing. Blessedly, I'd finally stopped feeling.

A flash of lightning lit the black sky, gnarled witch's fingers pointing to the jagged cliff in the distance. My destination, Devil's Cove, the chosen spot to accept my place in the nothingness.

Thunder boomed, and sprinkles of rain became a pounding deluge. The drum of the drops against the trees turned into a deafening buzz, drowning out the sounds of the woods at night.

A branch cracked in the distance, the sound echoing off the trees as I pressed on, slowly, steadily, my gaze locked on that cliff. The lightning came every few seconds now, flashes lighting up the alabaster skin covering my skeletal body.

I must have looked horrifying, an image that I know now still haunts not only me at night.

If only I had known then.

The mud thinned and the ground became rockier, my

path interrupted by boulders spearing up from the ground. Rain blurred my vision as I maneuvered easily around the large rocks, as if I'd done it a hundred times.

As if someone else were guiding me.

My pulse quickened—the first sensation of life in me— as I climbed the rocky path, the tree line fading behind me. Below my feet were only rocks now, dark and slick with rain.

I stepped onto the cliff, one foot, then the other, my gaze dropping to the churning black lake below. Angry whitecaps ripped as waves crashed against the rocks, swirling circles atop the ice-cold water.

Another bolt of lightning lit the sky, followed by a crack of thunder.

I slowly crossed the large rock, each flash of light drawing me closer to salvation. My heavy hair was lifted by the wind, whipping around my face, momentarily blinding me as I stepped to the edge.

I looked down at the water with a distant curiosity of what I might feel at that moment.

Nothing.

Inhaling deeply, I tipped my face up to the rain and closed my eyes.

Nothing.

I spread my arms, opening my palms to the sky.

Nothing.

Leaning forward, I let go.

I don't remember the fall. I do remember hitting the water, a million pinpricks of ice piercing my skin. There was a moment then when fear spurted through me. A split second of panic. Of fear.

But it wasn't enough.

I was done. Done with it all.

Water engulfed me, pulling me down. A stream of

bubbles escaped my mouth as I opened my eyes and stared at the colors waving above me, the pops of light.

Take me, I thought, allowing myself to sink deeper, deeper into the water.

Take me.

I miss you, I miss you, I miss you.

Take me.

2

Four months later...

a bead of sweat rolled down my temple as I swatted away a mosquito the size of a Volkswagen. The little monster zipped out my window and joined a swarm of gnats swirling in front of my dented hood as I slowed my truck, their tiny little bodies reflecting like specks of gold under the scorching July sun.

Rolling to a stop at the four-way, I eyed the rusty, crooked pole that I assumed was once a stop sign. No pickets or road signs could be seen, simply four pitted red-dirt options disappearing into miles and miles of wilted trees in different directions.

Contemplating, I glanced in my rearview mirror, the view blurred by the cloud of dust spun up from my back tires. Despite the open windows, the humidity was stifling, the air still, as thick as molasses.

It was a hell of a time for your vehicle's air-conditioner

to break—if you were accustomed to such luxuries, I guess. I wore sweat proudly, like a badge of honor gifted to me after being raised in a one-bedroom cabin without central air and heat. I wore each droplet like a big *screw you* to a generation of self-entitled pricks who considered e-cigarettes and golf frisbee necessities for survival.

I wore it to remind me of those I loved the most. To me, it was just another summer in the South. Definitely not for the faint of heart.

Glancing at the clock on the dash, I cursed. I was late.

Cricket, my thirteen-year-old collie/shepherd/hound mix, raised his furry head from the passenger seat, reminding me to watch my language, one of my many habits he seemed to disapprove of.

"Sorry, buddy."

The dog yawned dramatically, as if knowing I didn't mean it, his long pink tongue flipping out and curling back in. Then, passive-aggressive point made, he closed his eyes and lowered his head with a huff, resting his nose against a brand-new rip in the upholstery I hadn't noticed before.

Biting my tongue, I refocused on the road ahead of me, pretty sure I was lost at this point.

I unclicked my seat belt and began searching for the directions I was sure I'd tossed into my truck before leaving the hotel earlier that morning. My purse was buried under Cricket, whose head was now lolling against the mismatched suitcase and duffel bag on the floorboard.

Deciding to search everywhere else first, I used my arm like a street sweeper, pushing through the random papers, receipts, gum wrappers, dog toys, and treats that littered the bench seat, and deftly reached through my window and tossed a trio of empty water bottles back into the bed of my truck without looking.

Finally, I found the napkin I'd scribbled on. Coffee and something green smeared the bottom half of the directions —which were illegible anyway. I tossed it out to join the empty bottles in the back.

Shrugging, I hung a right, pulling onto an even narrower dirt road, this one riddled with potholes. A cloud of dust trailed me, coating the thick brush and trees that lined the ditches, their dry, brittle leaves sagging in the Southern heat wave.

I leaned forward, squinting at the break in the tree line just ahead.

A blinding-white mailbox with a thick, ornate golden base glimmered in the late afternoon light. *Gaudy* was my first thought. My second was that the owners must be imports, because in the small hillbilly town of Berry Springs, gold was only used for bargaining and fillings.

My gaze shifted to the spotless silver sign with gold-leaf letters that screamed *yes, I have money, and plenty of it*. It read:

RUTHERFORD ESTATE SALE – INVITE ONLY

"Well, buddy. I guess this is it."

Cricket thumped his tail, expelling the most energy he had all day. Clumsily pushing up from the vinyl seat, he stuck his head out the window, his nose wiggling with sharp, quick inhales.

"Smell that? It's called money."

He snorted.

"Yeah, tell me about it."

I leaned over and repositioned the stained, ripped-to-hell bags on the floorboard so that they leaned securely against the passenger seat to cushion a potential fall—

although based on the wet circle darkening the paisley print, maybe I should be more worried about another kind of spill. The poor guy had recently started medication for incontinence, and I'd since replaced two rugs, my comforter, and a brand-new sundress I'd picked up at the local thrift store, tags still attached.

I gently pushed the old dog's body against the seat, careful to avoid the still-healing wound above his amputated back leg.

"Steady boy, steady."

After a quick glance in the rearview mirror, I slowly accelerated through the wide iron gates. A pair of obnoxious stone pillars secured the sides, topped with stone horse heads holding lanterns between their teeth.

Cricket growled.

A tall, lanky older man in a three-piece suit—despite the heat—emerged from a covered checkpoint just past the gate.

I rolled to a stop.

The man cocked a furry gray brow as he rounded the rusted hood of my Ford, a long beak-like nose turning up at the bungee cord securing my left headlight.

I hung an elbow out the window.

"I'm sorry, miss, this is an invitation-only event," he told me in a tone as snotty as the Rolex around his hairy wrist.

Noticing the dog for the first time, the man jerked his chin back in revulsion—at the fact that I had a dog in my passenger seat, or the fact that the dog was missing a leg, I wasn't sure which.

I glanced at Cricket, then at the open duffel bag that had tumbled next to the suitcase. A sweaty thong and a pair of bleach-stained gray socks peeked out from under mud-spattered running shoes.

Okay, maybe that was the source of his disgust. I decided I didn't like the man.

Flashing him a toothy smile, I flipped up the gold-glittered postcard. "My invitation. Here you go, Jeeves."

"It's Pendleton," he said with a sneer. "Will Pendleton."

With the scrutiny of a post-9/11 airport screening officer, he scanned my invitation.

"Rory Flanagan," I said impatiently. "With the Black Butterfly."

"The Black Butterfly what?"

"The Black Butterfly," I deadpanned.

"Never heard of it."

"An antiques shop. I own the Black Butterfly in town, as you can see right there on the invitation." I tapped the card with my chipped fingernail, and he recoiled. "My partner here," I glanced at the dog, "and I, have just returned from an antiques show in Dallas. We're tired and would like to move this along, so, would you please step aside before my truck overheats? I'm leaking antifreeze—and a few other liquids I'd rather not discuss."

Jeeves scowled at the old dog and then took a quick step back, checking his shiny wingtips before lifting a red velvet bag. "One more thing," he said, his tone obligatory. "The Rutherford estate will be collecting additional donations for the Breast Cancer Research Foundation." He shook the bag and cocked a brow.

"Oh." I looked at the bag, then back at him, who was clearly waiting for something.

Oh. Money. Clearing my throat, I yanked my purse from underneath Cricket, sending a tuft of his fur flying into the cab.

Jeeves took another step back.

A tampon—half-opened—tumbled onto the floorboard

as I pulled out my beaded wallet and flipped it open. After checking for the cash I knew I didn't have, I zipped open the change purse and tipped everything I had into my hand.

Sixty-seven cents.

That's what I donated, that day, to breast cancer research. Not even enough to supply a Coke to a thirsty cancer survivor.

Jeeves shook his head, not bothering with a thank-you.

Can't really blame him.

With a flamboyant wave of his hand, he said, "That way. Try to stay on the driveway."

"Thanks." My back tires spun as I hit the gas, the *ping, ping, ping* of rocks against the metal gate more satisfying than I'd intended.

God, I'm a bitch.

Cricket released an excited yip at the jerk of the cab.

"The Black Butterfly what," I said, mocking the man, then sighed. "Not surprised you've never heard of it, Jeeves. No one has."

Rubber-necking, I drove up the long paved driveway. Acres of pristine fields enclosed in white fencing stretched as far as I could see. Vibrant green grass, thriving, glistened under the sun, in sharp contrast to the dry brown forest just beyond the property line.

It was as if I'd driven into another dimension, a bubble secured by wealth and privilege. Apparently, the Rutherford family was unaware of the county's outdoor watering ban that had been issued earlier that week. Or they simply didn't care. I assumed the latter.

The driveway took a sharp curve, and I immediately slowed. Shiny sports cars and fancy imports lined the driveway. At the end was a massive Southern plantation-style home, complete with white pillars, a wraparound deck, and matching weeping willows on either side. It looked like something out of *Steel Magnolias*.

I lifted a finger from the steering wheel in greeting as I passed a couple walking toward the entrance, a man in his late seventies, and his Botoxed Barbie wife in her late twenties.

His gaze didn't make it past the hood of my truck.

Rolling my eyes, I whipped my vehicle into a tight spot between a BMW and a Tesla. I turned off the engine, surprised by the flutter of nerves in my stomach.

I couldn't remember the last time I was nervous. Money tended to have that effect on me. Lots of money, anyway.

"Okay, buddy." I turned to Cricket. "Be on your best behavior here, okay? No jumping up, no pooping, and no licking your balls, got it?"

Cricket whined.

"I know. But you can do it. Just for an hour. In and out, then home."

When he didn't protest, I flipped down the visor to check my reflection in the cracked mirror. I blinked, momentarily jarred by my own reflection. There had been a few times over the last six months that I'd startle at the face—the body —staring back at me in the mirror. But this day took the cake.

My stomach did that little dip.

Frowning, I traced the bones of my face, once concealed under a pair of chubby, ruddy cheeks now sharp, distinct angles. My cheeks were sunken, my skin sallow, the dark circles under my eyes giving me a ghostly appearance. My eyes were a little too buggy, my mouth a little too toothy, my ears a little too forward.

My long blond hair, once highlighted with golden streaks, lay limp and stringy over my shoulders and down my arms, tangled and frizzy from driving hours with the windows down. The shine was gone, I realized. The strands were as dull, dry, and cracked as the ground below my tires.

I look like a skeleton.

It was as if I'd aged twenty years overnight. Over a matter of months, I'd gone from a healthy, glowing sun-kissed thirty-year-old to a post-Cobain Courtney Love, sans the boobs and red lips. Come to think of it, I was beginning to look more like Kurt Cobain himself than his train-wreck counterpart.

When did I stop wearing makeup?

Staring in the mirror at the woman I didn't know, I slid my fingertips down my neck to my collarbones and pointy shoulders. I lifted the pendant away from around my neck, noting my sharp breastbone.

My gaze shifted to Botox Barbie with her long legs, perfectly sculpted calves, round ass, and voluptuous cleavage under a yellow dress as bright and beautiful as the sun. I, on the other hand, resembled the wilted, dying dandelions that sagged in defeat.

Cricket nudged my shoulder, nestling against me. But I couldn't take my eyes off my reflection.

"When did I get so old, buddy?"

Thirty-one, going on sixty.

I'd once been told I looked like Claudia Schiffer. Now I looked more like her X-ray. I looked sick, like a mental patient who'd escaped her padded walls.

Wondering how true that comparison was, I took a deep breath. "Hang on."

I yanked my handbag from the floorboard, flicked off the dog fur, and unzipped the top. The makeup bag I was searching for wasn't readily visible, so I poured the contents onto the seat—a toothbrush, floss, sunglasses, eleven nail files, a phone charger, a dozen crayons, dirty paintbrushes, a sketchbook, an Agatha Christie paperback, balls of receipts, old airline tickets, a bag of dog treats, caffeine pills, a bottle of Pepto, three bottles of aspirin, four packs of gum, four tubes of Chapstick, three sleeves of tissues—and a teeny-tiny makeup bag.

I smeared concealer under my eyes, turning the purple to a haunting green—but better, I decided. Added mascara to my opaque eyelashes, blush to remove the paleness, and a swipe of sparkly pink lip gloss to quench the cracked lips.

"Better?" I looked over at Cricket, flashing him a child-like smile, and his tail thumped. "Good. Okay. Let's do this. No licking, kid. Got it?" He blinked at me, and I cocked a brow. "Seriously. No licking."

Why am I so nervous? And when was the last time I went to a public gathering?

The truck door creaked as I cracked it open, careful to avoid nicking the paint on the six-figure thrill ride next to me. I squeezed out, then carefully lowered Cricket to the ground and hooked his leash to his collar. A smile cracked my face as he wobbled excitedly to the back tire.

My little hero.

I closed the door, once, twice, the third time finally catching the latch. It had broken months ago, and I hadn't bothered to get it fixed.

With a deep exhale, I smoothed the white silk tank I'd tried on three times before settling on it. Wrinkles creased the bottom, but there was nothing I could do about that. I yanked up the waistband of the gray slacks I hadn't worn in months, now a size too big—maybe two. One by one, I kicked out my wedges, shaking the too-long baggy hem back into place.

I need to get new clothes.

Ignoring another ripple of nerves, I pulled in a deep breath and yanked back my shoulders, focusing on the event. The purpose.

Get it done. Make it count.

"Let's do this, buddy."

Cricket and I made our way up the driveway, toward the smooth instrumental jazz carrying on the heavy air. Laughter and muted voices mingled with the music from inside and the shrill of cicadas from the bushes.

A sheen of sweat broke out under my clothes. It felt at least ten degrees hotter all of a sudden. I looked to the sky, where a line of dark, brooding clouds gathered in the distance.

A summer storm was moving in.

A woman stepped out of the mansion's double doors and onto the porch. She was on her phone—very busy and important, in case you were unaware—in a black power suit that hugged curves that needed their own caution sign. The woman sidestepped Cricket, frowning at him while not even noticing little old me.

Breathing heavily from the hike through the rainforest, I stepped through the doors and into an air-conditioned wall of cool air scented with fresh flowers and designer perfume. Women in flowy summer dresses and heels clung daintily to men in pastel dress shirts and khaki sport coats. Everyone looked perfect. And no one was sweating. Not a single shiny forehead or pit stain. How was this possible?

"Oh. Um, excuse me . . ."

A brunette in a skintight cocktail dress missing half its neckline came out of nowhere. Below her cleavage was a name tag that read Chastity.

Of course it was Chastity. A virtue the young twenty-something had given up long ago to get the baseball of a diamond hanging off her ring finger.

"Ma'am . . ."

Ma'am?

The skin on her face barely moved as she spoke, gesturing to the three-legged creature sniffing her heels. "We don't allow—"

"He's a service dog."

"Is he?" She frowned down at the mangy mutt who was clearly in no position of authority. "No. I'm sorry. The rules are—"

"The rules under the ADA prohibit discriminating against individuals with disabilities and allow their service animals onto premises, as permitted by federal law. Failure to do so can result in a fine—or even time in the county jail." My gaze flicked to her breasts.

"Oh, really?" She cocked her hip with attitude. "What's your disability?"

"Intermittent explosive disorder. Excuse me."

Grinning, I strode past the glowering brunette, aiming for the exit, deciding a root canal would be more enjoyable than mingling with the likes of Robo-Tits all evening.

But I was stopped by a voice I hadn't heard in a very, very long time.

3

"*R*ory?"

I kept going with my head down and teeth clenched, my arms pumping as I speed walked like the tracksuit-wearing geriatrics every morning at the local mall.

"Hey! Rory."

As he called out to me, people began to take notice of the man chasing the woman with a three-legged dog.

Inwardly cursing, I turned toward the voice that used to whisper sweet nothings to me under my sheets, otherwise known as the last man I'd had sex with. The man I hadn't seen since the funeral.

Simon Goodwill.

His eyes rounded as he scanned me from head to toe, inciting a rush of insecurity through my system. I knew I looked different. I didn't need anyone to emphasize the point. Especially him.

Simon looked as impeccable as usual in his Brioni suit and matching silk tie. Lean and tanned, with a swath of sun-kissed blond hair combed perfectly to the side, as usual.

With bright blue eyes and blinding-white teeth, the man looked like he'd just stepped off the cover of *GQ* magazine. While I, on the other hand, looked like the alien featured on the cover of the *National Enquirer*.

"Rory," he said, his voice tinged with thinly veiled concern. "Wow, it's . . . been a long time. You look—"

"I've taken up running," I said, a bit too quickly and much too defensively.

"Right." He nodded, those blue eyes scanning me again. "So. How are you?"

"Good, I'm good." Again, too quickly.

"Yeah?"

"Yep."

Righto. One hundred. Totally fine.

He nodded to the dog at my feet. "Who's the mutt?"

"His name's Cricket."

Simon crouched down. Cricket hobbled back a little, eyeing Simon with hostile curiosity as he awkwardly patted the dog's head.

"What happened to him?"

"Cancer."

Simon's gaze shot to mine, and I looked away.

He stood, wiping his palms on his slacks, which insulted me. "So—"

"How have you been?" I cut him off, regaining control of the conversation.

"Busy as usual. Thanks for responding to my email. I'm glad you made it back in time to come to the event. What were you doing in Dallas?"

"Visiting an art show."

"Pick up anything interesting?"

"A few pieces."

"Do anything fun while you were in the city?"

"Well, I spent the mornings hitting up the local garage sales, and the afternoons, the flea markets. So, yes—fun," I said somewhat defiantly.

Our definition of fun had always been different. While Simon was a social butterfly with a large group of friends, I was a homebody with a wall of books. It was one of the many reasons I knew we'd never work out, one that I expressed in detail when I ended it with him.

Which was why I'd been confused to receive his invitation to this event. Was he hoping to corner me with a well-practiced synopsis of *Gone with the Wind*, lure me back with eloquent prose of courage and passion?

"You go alone?"

And there it was. The loaded question.

I reached down and scratched Cricket's head. "Just me and my dog."

"Oh."

An awkward silence passed between us.

"Well, I'm still working for Pops," he said, despite the fact I hadn't asked. "Flipping houses."

"You thinking about buying this beauty?"

We stepped under the massive crystal chandelier that hung from a vaulted ceiling. The house was nothing short of extravagant, with sparkling black-and-white marble floors and a mahogany double staircase that served as the focal point of the foyer. Contemporary furniture with sharp angles, sleek accents, and bright colors filled the house, mixed with the occasional antique. Large sculptures, one of a lumpy naked woman, loomed in the corners, ensuring every inch of the house announced how much money the Rutherfords had in their checking account.

Thick velvet curtains draped from sweeping windows that overlooked the mountains. Bright gold fixtures twinkled under recessed lighting. Colorful artwork splashed like paint against the blinding-white walls. The house was opulent. Loud. Obnoxious.

Simon shrugged. "Depending on how much they'll come down on the price, I'm thinking about buying it."

"It's overpriced?"

"Oh yeah, as is everything in here."

My gaze landed on a small crystal angel centered on a small table under the stairs. She was holding a bouquet of daisies.

I looked away.

Simon continued. "Let's just say I hope you're still as good at wheeling and dealing as when I first met you." A soft smile crossed his face, along with something else that looked like sadness.

I cleared my throat and dropped my gaze, willing the floor to open up, suck me under, and remove me from this awkwardness.

Eight unreturned calls, fourteen unanswered text messages, and four dozen roses are the last memories I have of my short fling with a man who, on paper, was Mr. Perfect.

I met Simon while house-hunting years earlier. He'd just listed a small two-bedroom house he and his father had flipped, not far from my mother and father's home, and I wanted to buy it. The problem for me was that Simon wanted significantly more than the old house was worth. So I did what I do best. I bargained.

One Mexican dinner and thirty thousand off the sticker price later, I had a new home and a new significant other. One much easier to mold to my liking than the other.

Son of a self-made millionaire, Simon was one of Berry Springs' most eligible bachelors. Just shy of thirty years old, his California-beach-boy look stuck out like a sore thumb in a town filled with burly corn-fed rednecks. Add his bank account into the equation, and Simon had his pick of nearly every woman in town—single or married.

Yet the guy chose me . . . the old me, I should say.

"Who are these people?" I changed the subject, nodding at the groups of men and women dressed in their Sunday best, despite the fact that it was Wednesday.

"Rich people. The owner of the house, Clement Rutherford, hired some big-shot New York real estate firm to handle the sale of his estate after he died, which happened a month ago. The wife passed of breast cancer years ago. Money goes to the Southern Baptist Convention—after the Realtors get their cut, of course. They invited everyone with a seven-figure W-2 within the tri-state area to come today. Everything you see is up for sale—the furniture, cars, tractors, house, the horses and cows out back. They've even got a small plane for sale. The place comes with a lot of land that backs up to the lake. Lots you can do with it."

"The Rutherfords didn't have children to pass things down to?"

"Nope. Which is good for you, right? I figured there would be at least a thing or two you'd find for your fancy new shop."

You have to have customers first, I thought, but bit my tongue.

"Congratulations, by the way."

I forced a smile and nodded, assuming that he—that everyone—knew the business I'd so hastily opened a few months ago was already one missed payment away from being shut down. Which reminded me of the early morning I had the next day.

"Why are they having this event so late in the day?" I asked.

"Encourages drinking." Simon nodded to the waitress offering flutes of champagne adorned with ripe strawberries. "And the windows in the great room face the west. Stunning views at dusk, apparently. Not today, though, not with this thunderstorm coming in." He pushed back his hair, and it flipped effortlessly back into place. "Haven't felt this kind of humidity in years."

Always humid before the storm.

"Thanks again for inviting me," I said.

He smiled. "Glad you came."

"When does the auction start?"

"There isn't one. The reps are dealing with the items on a case-by-case basis. If you look, there are information cards and numbers on each item."

"Who's running the show?"

"Two people the real estate company hired." He leaned closer, and a waft of spicy cologne tickled my nose.

I recognized it as the same cologne Simon wore when we were together. Memories flooded me. Good ones. Lighter ones. When I was happy. Had my shit together. And for a moment—a split second—I considered one more roll in the hay with Simon Goodwill, an escape to a time when things were so much easier.

"The woman standing by that gold-leaf mirror," he said, pulling me out of my absolutely *insane* thoughts. "She's a New Yorker named Aveda. She's handling the main furniture—tables, chairs, beds, things like that. Over there, by the grandfather clock, is some local guy named Arny. He's handling the decor and fixtures. And somewhere is the main real estate agent, trying to sell the house and the big stuff."

The New Yorker named Aveda stood as rigid as a stone in a couture suit as black as her hair. Hyperaware, she scanned the crowd with a gleam in her eye that suggested she knew exactly whose bank accounts to exploit, and whose to avoid. The other man, Arny, wore an ill-fitting suit over a thick body better suited for security than sales. I guessed he was just over seventy, but no less savvy than the New Yorker.

"Aveda reminds me of the owner of that B&B we went to that one time," Simon whispered. "Remember? The place on the lake. The owner had that weird cabinet filled with naked dolls and whips." He laughed. "Fun times."

His laughter quickly faded, though, his brow furrowing as he looked over what was left of me. A look of worry—pity —flashed in his eyes.

I reached desperately for Cricket, remembering that night very well. It was the first night we'd had sex.

For reasons unbeknownst to me, Simon had worshipped the ground I walked on. This always annoyed me. He did as I asked, when I asked it, and where I asked it to be. He was always there, always available. He rarely questioned me or challenged me, and maybe that was the problem. I needed more in a partner. A teammate to call me on the carpet when needed. One who would stand up to me. A man who would take control—in the bedroom and out of it.

The day Simon mentioned an engagement was the day I ended our relationship. It was also the only time he ever stood up to me.

"Not every relationship is going to be like your parents', you know?" he'd said. "Not everything is perfect at first. You have to give someone a chance. You have to stop being so damn independent. You can't control everything, Rory."

Yes. I know that now.

Simon had trouble letting go, but considering the way he looked at me now, I guessed he wasn't so upset anymore.

I wanted to get away from him. From the past.

"Well, I need to . . ." I gestured to the room. "Thanks for inviting me."

"Anything to support our local small businesses." He winked, flashing a perfect row of pearly whites. "Have fun."

Pretending I belonged, I perused some of the furniture, running a finger along the finish and pulling open a drawer or two. Tugging at his leash, Cricket led me to a long table topped with fancy hors d'oeuvres. Mini beef tourtieres, honey-mint lamb skewers, shrimp tartlets, crab tapas. For dessert, chocolate-covered strawberries, cheese-cake cups, caramel-pecan cookie bites, and other assorted goodies.

My mouth watered as we passed, my heart pumping double-time. Feeling as if everyone were staring at me, I picked up a meatball, and a pink macaroon with purple sprinkles.

My pulse roared in my ears.

Turning my back to the crowd, I stepped away, feeding the meatball to Cricket. The macaroon, I balled up inside the napkin and tossed it in the trash.

I exhaled. "Okay, Cricket-boy, let's just find what we're looking for and get out."

Cricket's tail wagged at the mention of leaving. Two peas in a pod, we were.

We wove our way through the cologne and diamonds to the wall of art at the back of the foyer. Unlike everything else in the Versace mansion, the paintings were tasteful and timeless. Abstract. Striking colors blended into a cacophony of shapes that reminded me of midnight dreams. No beginning, no end. Just dreams.

I paused at a trio of framed wildflowers. Vibrant, delicate blooms against an angry sea of blended color. Their bright petals were a burst of life compared to the bleak, muted background.

I thought of a lotus flower, its roots submerged in thick, muddy water, where it retreats in the night only to bloom flawlessly clean every morning. A symbol of life after death, rebirth, spiritual enlightenment. I wondered what happened to those that submerged and never found their way back to the surface in the morning.

Scratching the top of Cricket's head, I pressed on, drawn to a picture hidden in the corner. This one was different from the others.

The painting featured a close-up of a woman's face, showing only the left side. A rainbow of vivid hues colored the woman's skin. Her eyes were closed, her long lashes downcast, her brow drawn in emotion. Red drops under her eye resembled tears of blood. But the slightest upturn of her orange lips made you question what emotion she was feeling. Blue cheeks, yellow and green nose, all blended seamlessly into a rainbow of colors.

I felt her.

I knew her.

"Beautiful, isn't it?"

I turned toward a gruff, gritty voice. Arny stepped beside me in his ill-fitting suit, a subtle scent of aftershave and motor oil following a second later.

"Yes, very. Who is it?"

"An artist named Aaliyah Buhle." He pulled a card from a sleeve hidden behind the frame and handed it to me. "An up-and-coming Southern artist. Lives in Louisiana."

"The painting is different from the others. A different taste."

Arny nodded. "Story is, Clement and his wife met Aaliyah

in New Orleans years ago at a street fair. Claire took a liking to this painting, and Aaliyah gave it to her, no cost. If you ask me, it was probably a genius business move more than anything. Free marketing in the circle of Southern elite."

"Smart girl."

"Talented girl."

Turning the information card over in my fingers, I met his gaze. "I want it. I want the painting."

"Four-hundred seventy-five dollars, and it's yours."

Inwardly, I cringed, not sure if I had enough credit left on my card. I'd recently entered that harrowing place where you simply quit checking your balance because you know you can't pay it anyway.

I shook my head. "Nope. You and I both know that's as overpriced as that reproduction Hepplewhite table over there you're trying to pass off as period."

Arny looked at the console table, then back at me. "What makes you think it's a reproduction?"

"The joints. Period Hepplewhite furniture was made in the late seventeen hundreds. Back then, dovetail joints were handmade. The joints on the drawers on that table are machine-made."

"How do you know?"

"Handmade joints are cut by a hacksaw and a chisel; they're uneven and each is different—unlike modern machine-made joints, which are perfect. Although, I'm sure you knew that."

Flinty eyes narrowed as he regarded me in an entirely new light.

I grinned. "I'll give you a hundred bucks for the Buhle painting, Arny."

"One fifty."

"One twenty-five, and I'll throw in a signed first edition of *The Old Breed*."

His brow arched. "And what makes you think I'd be interested in the Pacific War?"

"That EGA and American flag tattoo you've got peeking out from under your cuff."

Arny glanced down at the Marine Corps eagle-globe-anchor tattoo on his wrist, only visible when he moved just so. He widened his stance and crossed his arms over his chest. "What's your name, lady?"

"Rory Flanagan. I know my antiques and art. And books, for that matter."

"Impressive, Miss Flanagan."

"Thanks. One twenty-five and *The Old Breed*."

"First edition print? Signed, you say?"

"Yep and yep."

"At Peleliu and Okinawa?"

"One of the first published copies in 1981."

His eyes narrowed. Arny liked to play hardball.

"Fine," I said. "One hundred twenty-five, *The Old Breed*, and a case of Bud Lite."

"Bud heavy."

"Done.

"Fine. Done."

I winked. "Nice doing business with you, Arny."

Arny and I exchanged contact information and mailing addresses. As I turned away, I collided boobs-first with none other than Robo-Titty herself.

"Oh," I blurted as I bounced off the silicone. "Sorry."

I blinked, noticing Simon at her side.

He grinned, scrubbing his hand over his mouth as if to hide a smile. "My associate here was just asking about your dog and your, uh, intermittent explosive disorder."

This is when I noticed the wedding band—a circle of commitment on his ring finger.

To say that my reaction to his ring shocked me is an understatement. It felt like a punch in the gut. Simon hadn't invited me here on the off chance that we'd rekindle what we had. Simon was *not* still in love with me. In fact, Simon had quickly moved on, met a woman and married her, and was probably working on starting a family.

And look at *me.*

Suddenly, I felt like I was suffocating, my heart skipping beats, heat rising up my neck.

"I . . . uh," stammered like an idiot. "We're about to leave, anyway."

Chastity rolled her eyes.

Simon nodded with that same worried expression as he looked me over for the umpteenth time. "All right. Let me know if you need anything, okay, Rory?"

"Yeah. Thanks." Heat licked up my neck. "Good to see you."

"You too," he said, although I'd already walked away.

Beelining it to nowhere in particular, I wiped my palms on my slacks, very aware my bra and panties were drenched in sweat.

Focus, Rory, focus.

With my fingertips on Cricket's head, I pushed my way through the crowd to a narrow door marked powder room. Once inside, I leaned my back against the cool wood door and closed my eyes, taking a few deep breaths.

One, two, three.

One, two, three.

Once my pulse slowed, I opened my eyes and lifted the back of my head from the door. I sighed, stroking Cricket's head. "Let's get out of here, huh?"

He whimpered.

"Yeah, okay. Just a quick drink."

Inhaling, I gripped the edges of the sink and stared into the mirror. My face was beet red, my chest and arms flushed.

God, I *hated* that reflection.

A knock sounded at the door, and I called out, "Just a minute."

I turned the water to cold and ran my arms under the stream. While drying my hands, I stepped back to check my full reflection, twisting at the side.

I gasped. "Oh . . . my . . ."

My voice trailed off as I gawked at two sweat marks on my slacks under the folds of my butt cheeks. The moisture had darkened the light gray fabric, leaving a pitch-black half moon under each ass cheek. As if I'd pissed myself.

Embarrassment engulfed me.

"Oh my God, oh my God, oh my God. Cricket, look," I whined, wincing.

In sheer panic now, I shoved down my pants, grabbed the fancy embroidered hand towel, and blotted the fabric.

No luck.

How many people had seen it? All the rich well-to-do pricks and perfect women in their designer duds—and Simon.

I was *humiliated*. This was easily in the top ten of my most embarrassing moments. In my entire life.

Cricket whined, confused as to why I was suddenly so upset.

Another knock at the door.

"*Shit.* Shit, shit, shit."

I returned the hand towel to its proper place on the rack. My pulse roared in my ears, beating drumsticks against a brain that felt like it was being squeezed like a vise. I knew this feeling all too well—the beginning of another damn migraine.

My hands trembling, I searched for my pain medicine but couldn't find it in the trash can that was my purse.

"Hello?" came from outside the door.

"Just a minute!" I snapped back.

There was nothing I could do. I had to face the music.

Gritting my teeth, I yanked open the door and pushed past Chastity and all her glorious cleavage. "I'm leaving, I'm leaving," I muttered, sounding like an insolent preschooler.

Frantically, I searched for a back exit. A single ray of sunlight pooled on the floor beneath the staircase. There had to be an exit somewhere past that light. With laser focus, I beelined toward it, Cricket hot on my heels.

The light shifted, sparkling off the crystal angel I'd noticed the moment I entered the house. The angel with the daisies. The light around it seemed to brighten as I drew closer.

Anger spurted through me, raw and hot.

Running my fingertip along the table, I flicked a wing of the angel as I passed, sending it teetering on the edge of the table.

I strode outside, the sound of the crystal exploding against the marble like a thousand little angels crying their last breaths.

4

*T*ears welled in my eyes as I half shuffled, half jogged around the house and down the paved driveway. Cricket hobbled next to me, keeping pace.

"Come on, buddy." I sucked back snot. "You can do it."

"Rory!"

No.

I pushed myself faster, ignoring the voice behind me. My vision started to waver with the pain in my head. Cricket stumbled, trying to keep up, nearly tripping me. I spun around and dropped to my knees in front of the panting dog.

"Rory, wait!"

"Dammit," I bit out, turning my face as Simon jogged up.

"Is everything okay?"

"Yeah." I kept my face low, willing the tears away. "Cricket needs to get home. He needs his meds."

I felt Simon's gaze burning into the top of my head.

"Rory . . ." Simon drew out each syllable in my name, as one might approach a hormonal teenage girl. "I mean *with you.* Is everything okay with you? Is—"

"Yes," I snapped, surging to my feet and meeting his eyes, showing him the ugly tears.

It was the first time the man had ever seen me cry. Soon to be a day of many firsts.

"Rory, talk to me," he begged, stepping forward.

"I did. I'm fine. And now I have to go. Cricket, come." I pushed past Simon, continuing down the hill. I was so close to my truck. So close to escape.

His hand gripped my arm. "Wait. *Wait*, Rory. Talk to me. What's going on? Please."

I stopped and turned. The look in his eyes was genuine, an expression I hadn't seen in quite a while. He wanted to help me. To be there for me.

"Rory, just talk to me. I can tell something's wrong. You've . . ." He faltered but forced himself to continue. "You've really lost some weight. It's—"

"Shut up." I glared at him, yanking my arm away.

"No." He reached up and cupped the side of my face. "Let me take you home. I can stay for a while and talk. I want to help with whatever you're going through. You're not alo—"

I grabbed his face and crushed my lips against his, threading my fingers through the back of his hair so he couldn't move. Couldn't pull away.

So he was there.

So *someone* was there.

His body stilled with shock. But then he wrapped his arms around me like he used to and kissed me, pulling me back in time. We stumbled backward to my truck, out of view of prying eyes.

A sudden hunger gripped me, an insatiable need to be loved. To feel that connection to someone else, another human being. I wanted to *feel* again, the closest thing to the love that had been so viciously ripped from my life.

My hand fumbled with the door handle. Once the door opened, I pivoted and shoved Simon inside.

"Rory . . ."

"I said shut up."

I quickly swooped down and lifted Cricket into the bed of the truck.

A second later, I was on Simon, kissing him as if my life depended on it. Messily, frantically, begging him to make me feel better about myself, about my life. Buttons clattered to the floorboard as I ripped open his dress shirt.

Rays of the setting sun cut through the windshield like fire against my naked skin. I shoved Simon against the seat, then straddled him like a ten-dollar hooker at a truck stop.

"Wait." He grabbed my hands, pushed them back and pinned them against my chest. "*Shit,* Rory. Wait. What the fuck are you doing? I'm married."

I stilled, embarrassment mixing with a wave of nausea washing over my slick skin. Chests heaving, we stared at each other—my expression one of mortification, and his filled with regret.

Wishing for death to take me at that very moment, I lifted off him and retreated to the passenger seat.

No words were spoken as he quickly rebuttoned what buttons were left on his dress shirt. The door slammed, punctuating his escape.

His regret.

His value of me.

The moment Simon's silhouette faded into the house, I crawled out of the truck and scooped my dog into my trembling arms.

I couldn't even look at him.

5

a bolt of lightning split the pitch-black sky, pulling my attention from the dirt road ahead. Slanted rain pummeled my windshield, the fat drops coming down too fast for the wipers to handle. I remember actually noticing how dark the night was, like you could reach out and touch the color.

As I tightened my grip around the steering wheel, I shifted in my seat, wincing at the replay of my ex's face after I kissed him, running on a loop in my head.

Thunder boomed in the distance.

It was late. Time had gotten away from me again, as it seemed to more and more lately. Day and night blurred together. Weeks. Months. All the same.

Cricket slept soundly in the passenger seat. Dead to the world, he let out a symphony of snores that resembled the mating call of a dyspeptic bullfrog. Smelled about the same too.

The windows were up because of the rain. Between the lack of air-conditioning and the wind of a dog who'd eaten three chili dogs for lunch, the cab of my truck was as humid and pungent as an Iranian brothel.

Cursing, I pushed the guilt away, the memory of pity on Simon's face.

My hand drifted mindlessly to Cricket, smoothing his matted hair, slowly dispelling the anxiety inside me. He pressed into my touch.

It had been a long day for him too. We'd awoken with the sun and had breakfast on a picnic table outside our motel. I'd moseyed through a few garage sales before driving the seven-hours back home to Berry Springs, straight to the Rutherford estate sale.

Travel was becoming difficult for Cricket. Something that I had to remedy; I just wasn't sure how. Because travel was the only thing keeping me sane.

Sane: a person of sound mind; reasonable, sensible. Healthy in mind. Healthy in body.

For a few seconds, I meditated on the concept of sanity. That lingering moment of contemplation only verified its absence in my life.

Thirsty, I plucked the lemon water from the console and took a deep sip, mentally counting the hours until I could take another pain pill. The headache had eased but the effects were still there, lingering like a baseball cap squeezed too tightly around my head.

I felt like shit.

Almost sex without an orgasm was enough to ruin anyone's energy level, but this was more. I was tired. Weak. I needed sleep. Needed something.

But being the glutton for punishment I was, I didn't go straight home after ripping my ex's shirt off in the front seat of my truck. *Nope.* I'd voluntarily added two more hours to the hellish day by taking a detour to the cemetery. There, in the comfort of my usual place under the pines, I'd sat and watched the thunderstorm roll in. Watched darkness replace the light.

And come it did, with gusto, chasing Cricket and me from the shadows and back into the truck.

As I drove, I tried to think of somewhere else to go, something I could pretend needed to be done at that very minute. Anything to keep me from the place that was once a refuge, but now a prison of memories.

But Cricket had grown impatient. I needed to get him home.

My truck bumped over a pothole I didn't remember being there as I steered onto County Road 3228. Squinting, I leaned forward and clicked on my high beams—and hit the brakes.

Cricket jerked at the sudden jolt of the cab and joined me in staring at the small river rushing under my headlights where a dirt road had once been. Twigs and leaves rode the waves of muddy water, washing away the gravel and clogging the ditches.

Otter Lake was less than a mile from my house, and Shadow River was even closer. The surrounding creeks flooded on occasion, but nothing like this. Then again, we'd never had a heat wave like this. The ground was so dry that the water simply washed over it.

"Well . . . shit, buddy."

Cricket looked at me, at the road, back at me, then grunted.

"I know. You're right. There's no other way to our house."

I chewed my lower lip. "Okay, then." I shrugged. "Here goes nothing."

Holding my breath, I accelerated slowly through the water, my truck bouncing over potholes deepened by the washout. A gust of wind blasted the side of the truck, spinning rain and leaves against the windshield. The storm was intensifying, stealing both my confidence and visibility.

My back straightened with anxiety. I couldn't see more than a few feet ahead of the bumper.

Just get home.

Between the sheets of rain and debris from fallen limbs, a road that usually took five minutes to drive took twenty that night. I slowed as my headlights bounced around the final sharp curve before my house—I'd been *so close* when I saw it.

I hit the brakes. Using the palm of my hand, I wiped madly at the condensation on the windshield. What was once a low-water bridge was now whitecaps of swirling water.

That's when something in the ditch caught my eye, just beyond the pool of my headlights. It was a bright white that didn't match the bleak surroundings.

I filed away the trickle of fear that slid down the back of my neck, like cold fingertips tapping against my skin.

Am I seeing things?

I rubbed my dry, stinging eyes, mentally counting the number of hours I'd slept in the last few days. The count didn't take long.

After wiping the windshield again, I stared at the white object sticking out of the flooded ditch. It was a tennis shoe. I was sure of it.

"That's a shoe, right?" I asked the dog. "Is that a shoe?"

I shoved the truck into park and grabbed the paper-thin

umbrella I'd gotten for free with a tube of Chapstick at the local drugstore. Unwrapping the bungee cord from it, I paused, focusing on the shoe again to verify that I hadn't totally lost my mind.

Not yet, anyway.

A little warning bell went off in my head as I gripped the door handle, heavy rain pounding the roof of my truck like a chorus of drums.

Should I ignore it?

Go home?

Should I stay in the car and call the police?

No time, I decided, something in my gut telling me that whoever was laid out on the side of the road in the middle of the woods during a thunderstorm wasn't simply taking a nap. They very likely needed help.

And here I was.

Stalling, I turned to Cricket. "Stay here, okay? I'll be right back."

I shoved open the door, cursing the deluge that dropped into my lap, soaking both me and the inside of my door. When the umbrella failed to open—*shocker*—I tossed it aside, took a deep breath, and hopped out into the rain. I was so concerned by the shoe that I didn't think to ensure the door latched. I should have.

Wind and rain whipped around my face as I stepped in front of the headlights, my silhouette stretching eerily across the road, disappearing into the woods.

"Hello?" I called out, my decision on what to do next warring in my head.

There was no answer.

Lightning burst through the sky, illuminating the shoe with a flash of light.

I called out again.

I was stalling.

Grinding my teeth, I dipped my head and strode across the road, careful to stay in line with the headlights at my back, my knees stiff, my pulse picking up. The dollar-store wedges I had on sank in the mud, so I kicked them off. My first order of business the moment I got home was to throw the entire sweaty outfit in the trash—and maybe burn it first.

I squinted through the rain, now more certain than ever that a body was attached to the shoe.

I was faintly aware of the sudden barking behind me, muted *yips* from the cab of my truck, but I dismissed them. Nerves twisted in my stomach as I stepped onto the small mound of dirt that marked the edge of the ditch.

My breath caught in a garbled gasp.

I stumbled backward, bile rising into my throat, the scene at my feet something out of a grotesque horror flick. Somewhere through the haze of fear and panic, my instinct told me two things: One, I didn't need to check for a pulse because there was no way the girl attached to the shoe was still alive. And two, I needed to avoid contaminating the scene, because whatever happened to this woman was no accident.

The next few seconds were a blur.

The barking behind me was no longer distant. It was loud and vicious, a panicked bark I'd never heard before. I didn't hear the truck door creak open or the sound of Cricket throwing himself onto the ground.

It was then that I noticed a pair of beady golden eyes just beyond the tree line, fixed on me, and the mouthful of sharp white fangs below them.

Coyote.

Blood and skin dripped from its snarling jaws, its muddy

feet planted in the mud inches from the dead girl. The wild animal must have been eating the body before I approached. I'd apparently intruded on its dinner. *Not good.*

The barking behind me suddenly registered as Cricket. I spun around, catching the dog in midair as he awkwardly leaped toward the coyote, his jaws snapping and spit flying.

I spun back around just as the coyote recoiled to lunge at me.

"No!" I yelled, struggling to contain a thrashing, frantic Cricket in my arms. "No!"

Viciously, I kicked my leg into the air toward the beast, trying to seem bigger and scarier than I was, squeezing Cricket against my chest in a death grip.

The coyote lunged toward me, its paws landing on the bloated stomach of the woman.

"Get awaaaay!" I roared in a guttural, monstrous voice not my own. I kicked again, wildly, as if I were kicking through a door. "Get away! I'll kill you! Get away!"

I lunged forward, my bare toes sliding into the ditch.

"Away!" I kicked mud and rocks into the air with the other foot, hitting the coyote in the face.

With one final snarl, the coyote slowly retreated into the darkness until its haunting eyes disappeared.

My chest heaving and my pulse roaring in my ears, I held my ground until I was sure the beast had skulked away. Cricket stilled in my arms, his barks fading into a whine.

"Good boy. Stop. Calm down. Stop." Gasping, I tried to pull in a breath. "Stop, stop . . ."

I refocused on the body at my feet.

"Oh my God," I whispered. "Oh my—"

The girl—in her mid-twenties, I guessed—was naked, wearing only a single white tennis shoe on her left foot. Purple veins ran like a road map over gray, papery-thin skin.

Her head was cocked at an abnormal angle, her neck obviously broken. Only holes remained where her eyes once were—eaten or removed, I wasn't sure which. Jagged lines sliced across her cheeks as if someone had carved her face. Her body was grotesquely bloated, her stomach, legs, and arms thick like sausages. Long, wet, matted auburn hair snaked across lips so swollen, they looked like they were about to split open.

Memories slammed into me, blurring the past and the present.

The rain, the ditch, the death.

One arm was tucked under her body, the other splayed out to the side. The leg that wasn't wearing the tennis shoe was bent awkwardly, the flesh shredded from the shin down to her ankle. By the coyote, I assumed.

As if the destruction of her face and body wasn't enough, slashed across each breast was an X, puffy flesh bubbling open to reveal the bones beneath. Her vagina was shredded, gaping open with more angry slashes.

Vomit expelled from my mouth with no warning.

Clutching Cricket, I turned and stumbled toward the truck, slipping on a patch of mud and tumbling to the ground. Cricket flew from my arms. Mud splattered my face, my neck, my hair, the cool sludge seeping under my clothes.

"Cricket!" I crawled forward, gathered the three-legged dog into my arms again and scrambled up, pitching forward into the hood.

Calm down, Rory.

My hands trembled as I shoved Cricket inside the cab, the door already open. "Passenger seat. Go."

With trembling hands, I grabbed my purse and dug through it for my cell phone. I dialed 911, and after ensuring the door latched closed, jogged back through the rain to the body.

"Nine-one-one. What's your emergency?"

"This is Rory Flanagan. There's a body—a woman—in a ditch on the side of the road." My voice shook as the words tumbled out. "I need someone out here. Now."

"Ma'am, are you hurt?"

"No."

"Are you alone?"

"Yes."

"Are you in any kind of danger?"

"No." My gaze shifted to the woods.

"Can you tell me your location?"

"County Road 3228, about three miles in. Just beyond that sharp curve."

"Yes, ma'am, I know the one. Okay." After a brief pause, the dispatcher said, "Someone is on the way. Is the woman breathing?"

"No."

"What condition is she in?"

The dispatcher's voice faded to a distant buzzing in my ears as I looked down at the body, flashbacks clouding my vision. The phone dropped from my hands, my body shaking in palsied shudders.

One side of my brain was telling me to turn, to run. The other side told me to calm the hell down.

But I couldn't.

It was the third dead body I'd seen in less than six months.

6

*B*lue and red lights spun against the trees like an eerie discotheque, sparkles of rain like blood falling from the sky.

An hour had passed since I dialed 911. Sixty minutes of being asked the same question by every officer who had shown up to the scene—every officer in the entire Berry Springs Police Department, it seemed. Apparently, not much went on in this small Southern town.

Berry Springs was the kind of place where people still called each other sir and ma'am, regardless of their age. Traffic consisted of jacked-up pickups, logging trucks, and the occasional family on horseback going to and from their business. Main Street was the center of town, the home of the only stoplight and the hub of all things, Donny's Diner —an all-you-can-eat Southern eatery complete with blue-and-white checkered curtains, red leather booths, and the latest gossip on tap, 24/7.

I lived just outside the city limits down a quiet, lonely road, now loud, chaotic, and illuminated by harsh fluorescent lights. A fire truck, an ambulance, and the county medical examiner joined the party shortly after I made the call. Klieg lights had been erected, and a blue tent now shielded the body of the girl I'd found in the ditch.

The lightning and thunder had shifted west, but the rain lingered, despite the investigation unfolding in front of me. The air had turned electric with the buzz of a potential murder in Berry Springs.

I was formally interviewed by two men in uniform. The first, Tommy Darby, the town's newest detective. He was tall and lanky, and despite his young age, carried an innate authority to him. The other officer was older, with deep-set frown lines, thinning hair, and a hard look in his eyes that suggested he'd spent decades dealing with the scum of society. Though he didn't formally introduce himself, I heard Detective Darby refer to him as Chief McCord.

In hats, raincoats, and full uniform, both men regarded me closely, in a way that made me feel like they were dissecting *me* as much as the events of the evening. I knew my eyes were swollen, my skin sallow, my mud-streaked clothes hanging like wet blankets from my body. One officer asked if I'd been drinking.

After the interviews, I was given an umbrella and guided under a scraggly oak tree that did little to shield the rain. I was advised to wait there until they released me, in case they had any other questions. I didn't mind this when I realized I was close enough to eavesdrop on their conversation.

"Jesus, Mary, and Joseph." Detective Darby crossed himself as he looked down at the body.

Chief McCord studied the gaping slits between the girl's legs. The smoke from his cigarette curled into the rain as he blew out a long, unsteady stream. "Recognize her?"

"Nope."

"What about you, Heathrow?"

The medical examiner, a short stocky woman with fiery red hair under a hooded yellow raincoat, snapped on a pair of blue latex gloves. She had an air of competence, and from what I'd seen so far, little patience for bullshit. Looking up from where she squatted next to the body, she shook her head.

"What can you tell immediately?" Darby asked.

"Besides the obvious?" she said, and three pairs of eyes shifted to the woman's vagina. "She's been submerged."

"Submerged?"

"Yep. That bloat isn't from a Mexican dinner, I can tell you that. I won't be able to give you details until I get her on the table, but she's definitely spent some time underwater. That's the cause of this swelling. She's also got the worst case of washerwoman's hands I've seen in a long time."

"What's washerwoman's hands?"

"Look here." Heathrow pointed to the hands, then crab-walked to the feet. "The wrinkling of the skin—like when you're in a bath for too long. Number one sign of submersion. She's also got a wicked case of vascular marbling, also common in submersion."

Darby glanced into the woods. "Could've been washed down from the lake or river."

"You'll be the one to determine that, but it's a good guess. The shallow contusions and bruising all over her body support that theory too. Looks like the poor thing went through a washing machine."

"Can you determine cause of death? Did she drown?"

"Before or after someone sliced her to shreds and dumped her?" the chief asked.

"I can't say at this moment."

"But you can say someone cut her up."

Heathrow sighed. "I can say this. It's highly unlikely the

lacerations on her breasts or vagina are a result of being washed down the mountain. The incisions wouldn't be so deep or exact. In the rare event she would have been caught up in boat propeller blades—say, in the lake—the injuries wouldn't have been at such precise angles and locations, and much deeper."

"What's your estimated TOD?"

"Again, I won't be able to tell you specifics until I get a closer look at her, but I'd say she's been dead no more than forty-eight hours. But that's extremely preliminary. The warmer the water, the faster the decomposition. This damn heat wave is working against us, for sure, along with whatever obliged themselves to her while she was under."

"Dammit." Chief McCord shook his head. "Any trace evidence she had on her will have been washed away. How soon can you get a profile workup on her?"

"Well, she's got no purse or wallet on her. I'll check more thoroughly when I get her on the table. Maybe we'll get lucky and she's got a tattoo somewhere on her that can help identify her. The obvious is that she's Caucasian, auburn hair, I'd say five foot nine, guessing a buck-thirty in weight. I'll do a dental workup on her. Maybe we can get an ID that way. Or if she's had any fillings or implants, we'll possibly get a hit that way too." Heathrow looked up. "Has anyone reported a missing person that matches her?"

"No, but I'll double-check."

She nodded. "I'll look closer under the lights. Inside and out."

Detective Darby stared at what remained between the woman's legs. "Any chance semen could survive inside her for that long?"

"Not underwater, sorry to say."

"You seen anything like this before?"

"No." The medical examiner examined the vagina closer. She stilled, then pulled a magnifying glass from her pack and knelt closer. Finally, she pulled away and looked up, pausing as if choosing her next words carefully. "There are several striations on her pelvic bone. More than a few just from what I can see right here."

"Scavenger marks?"

"No." She pointed to the leg, where the bone was exposed. "These are scavenger marks. Look here. There are two types of scavengers, carnivores and rodents. With rodents, you'll see multiple perfectly parallel small striations made by teeth. But see here, these small dots?"

The men leaned closer.

"These are puncture marks from a carnivore. Based on the size of the marks and the rapidly spreading population in these damn mountains, I'm guessing a coyote."

"And I'm guessing these marks are different from the ones you're seeing between her legs."

"Exactly. The striations between her legs are shallow and funnel to a V, resembling those made from a knife. They're also close together." She cleared her throat. "It appears our victim here was repeatedly penetrated with a tool."

"Are you saying some sick son of a bitch fucked this woman with a knife?"

"I'm saying a sharp object repeatedly penetrated her vagina, nicking her bone. The narrative is on you to figure out. But I will say, off the record . . ." The ME pushed to her feet, the first sign of emotion in her face. "The way the wounds have been inflicted, over her breasts, inside and around her pubic region, suggest an emotional killing. An extreme disrespect. Not some drug deal gone bad, or a mugging gone wrong."

"Boyfriend or a significant other, maybe," Darby muttered, deep in thought.

The chief pulled another cigarette from his pocket. "Until we get an ID and are able to work our way out from there, we need to get a list of all the sex offenders in the area, assault and battery, domestic abuse reports . . ."

"And do it fast, before the gossip spreads like wildfire." Heathrow looked down at the body. "Nothing wets the lips faster than a sadistic murderer running around Berry Springs."

Their words sent chills running over my skin, and all I could think was that I wanted to get the hell away. Away from death. Push it away. Forget about it. Forget about the girl. I didn't want to be a part of it.

No more shit in my life.

And the ME was right. The gossip would ignite overnight, a mutilated dead girl quickly replacing the late-breaking news of a pair of local goat snatchers, the conspiracy theories that the mayor's new girlfriend was really a distant cousin, and the rumors of a recent Sasquatch sighting. The "girl found in the ditch"—as she would undoubtedly be dubbed—would be the topic on everyone's lips while sipping their morning coffee from behind their double stacks and cheese grits.

I was plotting my escape when a bright red sports car pulled up. A tall blond woman in a red raincoat ducked out of the car and jogged to the scene. A flicker of recognition tickled my brain, although it was too dark to get a good look at the woman's face.

The officers exchanged words with the woman. When all faces turned in my direction, I shifted my weight.

The blonde said something to the men, then jogged over, her hood hiding her face. "Rory Flanagan."

I recognized the voice immediately. Becky Davies was a six-foot-tall former Berry Springs basketball champ, known to everyone in town as Dunks, a nod to her ability to consistently dunk a basketball at age sixteen.

Dunks was two years older than me, and had been the most popular girl in school. Smart, athletic, good at everything, including taking everyone's boyfriend. She was the girl everyone wanted to be. To me, though, Becky Davies would always be remembered as the first girl to bully me, setting off a snowball effect that made me a target until the day I graduated.

I remember the day like it was yesterday.

It was lunchtime, seventh grade. Location, the girl's restroom, where I discovered blood on my Wonder Woman panties for the first time ever. But not just on my panties, also on my skirt—as well as the neon windbreaker I'd had tied around my waist.

I was in the middle of a panic attack, sitting on the toilet, desperately thumbing through one of the three books I'd stashed in my backpack that my mother had gotten me when I'd noted hair growing in funny places. The book I was madly searching through at that moment was titled *So you got your period, now what?*

It came with a free pad and tampon.

The paisley-print skirt that mom had made me was around my ankles, a circle of blood in the middle. I was so upset that I'd ruined her skirt. Tears streaked my face, smearing the mascara I'd recently started wearing.

The door to the bathroom opened to giggling voices. I

sucked in a breath and froze, every muscle in my body stilling like a statue.

Becky "Dunks" Davies and her little squad gathered around the mirrors to do what the popular girls did best—gossip.

My pulse roared in my ears as I prayed to the gods that the girls wouldn't notice me.

Suddenly, the bathroom went quiet, immediately followed by low whispers.

My heart raced as the toes of a pair of new brand-name tennis shoes appeared in front of my stall. Somewhere in the stall next to the left of me came a giggle. Then to my right.

My eyes rounding in horror, I quietly closed my book and placed it on my lap.

A singsong voice called to me from the other side of the door. "Rorrrrry . . . Need something?"

Then from above me—

"Say cheese!"

I looked up just as the camera clicked.

Laughter exploded. I blinked, little dots sparking in my vision, just as Dunks jumped off the toilet of the stall next to me.

"Oh my God, you guys," she squealed to her friends. "It's like a murder scene in there! Gross, so *gross*, Rory. You are *so sick*. Come on, girls."

They left in a chorus of giggles that faded as I sat alone in the bathroom, where I remained the rest of the day until the final bell.

The next day, a picture of me sitting on the toilet, with a book that read So you got your period, now what? on my lap and a blood-stained skirt at my feet, was posted on every pole in school. My face was pale with black mascara running down it, a look of shock in my eyes.

Everyone saw that picture.

From that day forward, I was known as Gory Flanagan.

And here she was, Becky Davies, on one of the worst nights of my life. Seeing me again at my absolute worst.

Lowering the umbrella, I tilted it to cover as much of my face as I could. I hated that she could still make me feel like that, all over again.

Her brows drew together as she looked me up and down in the same way the cops had. "Wow. It's . . . been a long time."

"Yeah." I swiped a clump of mud from my face. "What are you doing here?"

"I'm the new journalist at NAR News. Heard the commotion on the scanner." Her gaze dropped to my body again. "Wow. It's been a *really* long time."

You are so freaking skinny, she might as well have said in that stupid valley-girl voice.

Anger began to replace the insecurity, that hot rage I'd felt after my encounter with Simon, right before I'd straddled him in my truck.

"You, uh, doing okay?" she asked, pursing her lips.

"Fine. I've already given my statement to the cops, so . . ."

"Yeah, well, I have a few questions. What were—"

"I don't have anything more for you," I said firmly, and her brows arched at the attitude in my voice. "I'm just waiting to leave."

"Got a hot date to get to?" A catty smile crossed her perfectly made-up face, and I felt like I was right back in school.

Heat flew up my neck and face. "I'm not talking to you, *Dunks.*"

"Yeah?" Her mouth pinched with disgust as she looked at my arms. "Looks like you need to talk to *someone.*"

"I'm *fine.*"

She went on, continuing to needle me. "The cops over there think you've been drinking or using. Is it true?"

"It's none of your damn business what I have or haven't been doing."

"Well," she cocked her hip, "they're thinking about giving you a Breathalyzer, or taking you to the mental health clinic on Main." Her brown eyes slitted. "You know, the one your mom went to."

I don't remember the next few seconds.

Only snippets of the shouts, the bouncing flashlights, the hands pulling me off the muddy ground, my bloodied knuckles.

I remember being cuffed and thrown into the back of a police car, screaming for Cricket after breaking Becky "Dunks" Davies' perfect little nose.

*a*fter being thrown into the back of the police car, I was asked if I had any friends or family that I could call to pick up Cricket while I was in jail.

I had no one. Not a single person in my life to care for my dog. It was a monumental moment for me. Jarring.

I'm truly alone in this world.

What if something happened to me? Who would the hospital call? Who was my "in case of emergency"? What if I needed a routine surgery at some point—who would drive me to and from the appointment? Who would stay with me if I were temporarily incapacitated?

Who would care if I died?

Despite my protests, Cricket was taken to the local animal shelter, where I was told he would be cared for while I was booked into jail and bail was set.

I was given a Breathalyzer and consented to a urine and blood sample to test for illegal drugs. Then I was tossed into a jail cell with a tweaked-out forty-something who pissed herself, then proceeded to pick infected scabs from her face and arms while muttering incoherently to a tattoo of Tweety Bird on her inner thigh.

Two hundred fifty dollars later—otherwise known as half my mortgage payment for that month—my checking account had been emptied and I, Rory Flanagan, age thirty-one, was released from jail. I left with a pending criminal record for assault that would be forever attached to my name.

It was one thirty in the morning by the time Cricket and I were dropped off at my truck, feet from where the murdered girl had lain hours earlier. A favor from the tall officer who was on his way home for the evening.

The moment his car disappeared around the corner, I fell to my knees, doubled over, and began dry heaving onto the ground, the lingering rain wetting my already damp back. With one violent retch after another, my empty stomach cramped painfully in an attempt to empty itself, but there was nothing inside. My body shuddered beneath the rain, my migraine pounding with each heartbeat.

Exhausted, I crumpled to the muddy ground, rolling onto my back like a beached whale. As my chest heaved, I stared up into the raindrops spearing me from the darkness. The blackness.

I thought of my mother. My father.

I thought of the look of pity on Simon's face. On Becky Davies' face.

I thought of the glass angel with the daisies—the symbol of faith I'd shattered on the cold marble floor.

My hand drifted to the pendant around my neck. And for the hundredth time in the last six months, I wondered what was beyond that blackness above me. Beyond the clouds, the rain, the stars, the universe. I wondered if my parents were there. Together, holding hands, smiling, happy.

Watching me? Proud of me?

No, they wouldn't be proud of me. I wasn't either.

I thought of the girl in the ditch and wondered if she was there now too.

There. Where was there?

Where are you, I wanted to scream into the wind.

Cricket whimpered from the driver's seat, pulling me from the beginning of a train of thoughts that I knew from experience wouldn't end well.

I rolled my head to the side and sighed. I'd left the truck door hanging open—again.

"Hang on, buddy. Stay. I'm okay. Stay." My voice was hoarse and rough like a chain-smoking trucker's. And in addition to the migraine, my throat also hurt now from dry heaving.

I'd never had a migraine before the funeral—the first one. Since that day, I'd been getting them almost daily, driven to bed for hours at a time. Not to sleep but to wallow in pain, hating my broken brain, until I could see straight again.

Nothing helped.

Cricket whined again, this time louder.

"Don't jump. I'm fine. Hang on. I'm coming."

I rolled onto my side. With my head lolling like a rag doll, I pushed up onto all fours, mud dropping from my back in clumps. I squeezed my face, the pounding in my forehead intensifying with the movement. My stomach muscles burned from the attempt to vomit, and so did my sides and lower back.

I felt like death.

Focusing on the patter of the rain like an anchor, I

slowly pushed to my feet and poured myself into the cab, which was now soaked again, as well as mud-spattered.

We looked pathetic, Cricket and me, as we drove down the muddy road, now passable since the water had receded. Like two homeless wanderers . . . one missing a leg, the other her soul.

I cringed, wondering what the EMTs thought when they laid eyes on this dirty, mascara-smudged train wreck in her rusted red Ford with her three-legged dog. What a motley crew we were.

Thunder rumbled in the distance as I rolled to a stop in front of my postage-stamp-size house. Dropping my hands from the wheel, I released a deep sigh, staring at the rain dripping from the edges of the shingles.

I didn't want to go inside and face the memories, face another sleepless night.

Cricket nudged me and I sighed again. I needed to move. For him.

After carrying my dog to the porch, I stalked back to the truck and fumbled with my duffel bag and suitcase, yanking them from the cab. I kicked the door shut and dragged the suitcase through the mud and toward the front door, where Cricket was waiting patiently under the protection of the pergola that the former owners had erected over the small front porch.

Blooming vines of clematis grew like a thick canopy overhead, weaving in and out of the wood slats. A poor man's roof. It provided shade from the sun, warmth from the cold, and a shield from the rain. The beauty and uniqueness of it was one of the reasons I'd been drawn to the house. It felt whimsical when I'd first laid eyes on it, like a home for a faerie or a magical little gnome.

"Come on, buddy, let's get inside."

Cricket tap-danced on the wood porch, his usual routine when he needed to do a number two and wanted privacy. Licking balls was an acceptable thing to do in plain sight, but pooping? *Nope.*

"Take your time."

The dog disappeared around the corner of the house, headed to his designated pooping spot in the backyard.

Fumbling with my keys, I hefted the strap of the duffel bag higher on my shoulder and dragged my suitcase past the front window, not noticing the television glowing from inside.

With my head pounding, I unlocked the door and shuffled inside. And froze instantly. My duffel slipped from my shoulder, hitting the floor with a loud bang.

I wasn't alone.

8

*D*umbstruck, I stared at the man sprawled out on my couch, naked as a jaybird and sound asleep.

The room was dark, with only the glow of the muted television flickering across his naked body. He was massive, tall, the sheer size of him dwarfing a full size couch that both Cricket and I usually slept on together comfortably. This was no boy or teenager, but a man. A big, hairy grown man.

One hand was flung over his head, and the other dangled to the floor. One leg stretched the length of the couch, its ankle propped on the armrest. The other foot rested like dead weight on the floor. The man was spread-eagle—right there on my newly upholstered couch.

With a full-blown *boner.*

My brain short-circuited. I stared, instantly hypnotized by the erection between the man's legs, pointing directly to the ceiling at full salute. While the size of his body was impressive, the length of his manhood was nothing less than shocking.

I was pulled from my trance by a sudden jerk of his body. The man wiped his nose as a snore like a thousand bumblebees caught in the backfire of a diesel truck rippled from his throat. Cricket's snoring had nothing on this guy's.

A chorus of rabid barks suddenly sounded behind me.

Shit.

"No, Cricket," I muttered, grabbing the dog's collar and pulling him back. "No. *Shhh. Stop.*"

The man's eyes slowly drifted open. He turned his head toward the door, his face darkened by shadows.

Our gazes met like a clap of thunder and something electric flickered between us. My stomach did a tingly flip-flop.

Do I know him? I don't think so.

His gaze shifted to the barking dog at my feet.

You'd probably assume at this point the man would jump up, horrified by the situation, and cover himself—not only from my view, but from the dog's snapping jaws as well.

Nope.

Instead, the intruder slowly scanned me from head to toe, taking in every inch of me, as if we were standing in the middle of Frank's Bar during the last song on singles night.

A clump of mud fell off my chin. Heat rose to my cheeks, and I was instantly thrown off. Derailed. Confused.

And then I remembered this was *my* house.

What the hell is going on?

"W-w-who the hell are you?" I squeaked out, stuttering like crazy while attempting to avert my gaze from the man's penis. Which was *still* a raging boner.

He winced at my tone, displeased at how he was being awoken—*in my home.*

With a low grumble, the man ran his fingers through his mussed greasy hair, then slowly unstuck himself from my couch and shifted into a seated position. It was obvious he wasn't going to attack me—immediately, at least. And it was also obvious that he wasn't scared of me or my dog, or embarrassed by his nakedness. If anything, the man seemed annoyed at my panic, which meant I was overacting.

Although common sense was telling me I should be scared, every bit of my instinct was telling me this man wasn't a threat to me. Something—a feeling—pulled at me like a distant memory, confirming this, although I didn't know why.

His erection—otherwise known as the most beautiful penis I'd ever seen in my life—was now out of my line of sight, thanks to a perfectly placed table lamp. Kryptonite out of view, my powers instantly returned.

Regaining my composure, I squared my shoulders. "I won't ask you again. Who the hell are you?"

He slowly surveyed the room as if trying to recall the answer to that question.

This is the moment I noticed my house, which no longer looked like *my* house at all.

The furniture had been rearranged. The litter that had once covered my living room—empty soda cans, cups, plates, tissues, magazines—had been removed, the hardwood floor polished and gleaming under the glow of the television. The rugs were now vacuumed and free of dog hair. My well-loved wall of books had been dusted and organized, no longer haphazardly stacked with overstuffed sections. Cricket's yellow dog bed was now white. Bleached, or was white its original color? I couldn't remember.

The windows, walls, and floorboards had been scrubbed. The blades of the ceiling fan and the box fans that had once sat in the windows had been wiped clean. A faint trace of Pine-Sol hung in the air—which was the temperature of an ice box, I suddenly noticed.

I *never* turned on my air conditioner.

Fury mixed with confusion. This intruder had gone through my home, my stuff, and disinfected my life. The only thing that wasn't immaculate was an empty bottle of wine on the coffee table, next to a half-eaten bacon-and-egg burrito.

My lip curled to a snarl. I released Cricket's collar, and he took off like a bullet.

In the most energy I'd seen from the man, he grabbed a pillow and shoved it over his penis.

My hands shook as I frantically searched for the phone in my purse, uncaring that Cricket might seriously attack the man.

"I'm calling the police," I yelled over the rabid barking.

"How 'bout you call this dog off me first." His voice was gritty, deep enough to shake the windows, and slow and lazy enough to confirm that he definitely wasn't an immediate threat to me.

Finding my can of mace first, I grabbed it, aiming it at him like a gun.

"Whoa," he said in a slow Southern drawl. "Just a minute there, Annie Oakley."

His puffy eyes slowly flickered between the mace and the dog, and it was then that I realized he was drunk. Very drunk. I doubted the man could get off the couch faster than I could spray my mace. This gave me back my footing.

He shifted his weight, eyeing the dog, his now flaccid penis flopping onto a thigh as thick as a tree trunk—and back into my view.

I cleared my throat. "I'll shoot you if you don't tell me who you are."

"Not with that aim, you won't."

The mace in my hand was now pointing two feet to the left of his body.

Damn that penis.

I repositioned. "Name?"

"Christian Locke." He observed the dog. "Guy's missing a leg."

"How about you use that eagle eye of yours to locate your freaking pants?"

"What's Tripod's name?"

"Cujo. What are you doing in my house, Christian?"

"Dog's. Name?" he said again, enunciating the words as Cricket snapped dangerously close to his fingertips.

About to lose my shit, I pulled in a harsh breath through my nose. "Cricket."

"Cricket?" He jerked his chin back with disdain. "Hasn't the guy suffered enough?"

"It's how I found him. A cricket jumped on my windshield—" I snapped my mouth shut, shaking my head. Why was I defending myself to this strange man?

"Cricket . . . Hey there, nice doggy."

He shifted, and there was a slight wince in his voice, giving me the impression he was in some sort of pain. Hung over was my best guess at the moment. I watched him curiously as he shoved his hand between the couch cushions. A moment later, he produced a piece of bacon and slowly offered it to the dog.

Cricket cocked his head, sniffed, took the gift, and with a wagging tail, sauntered over to his rug next to the fireplace.

I rolled my eyes. *Traitor.*

Refocusing on the insanity in front of me, I shouted, "What the hell did you do to *my* house? And why is it so *cold* in here?"

"Hot out there." He flung a hand toward the windows.

"Well . . ." I grabbed my phone with my other hand. "It'll be a lot hotter in the back of the police car in about two minutes. I'm calling—"

"Relax. I'm leaving. Just had to crash here for a minute." Christian pushed clumsily off the couch, and once again, my gaze dropped between his legs, his balls like two ripe beefsteak tomatoes cushioning a jumbo squash. I squinted, but still couldn't get a clear picture of his face through the shadows.

"Where the hell . . ." He stumbled, scratching his head and searching the floor.

I squeezed my eyes shut. "You realize you're naked, right? Can you just put some damn clothes on?"

"Trying, sweetheart."

I covered my eyes, peeking through my fingers. "They're right there. Dammit, man. Your freaking pants are next to the empty wine bottle that I was saving for my birthday—thank you very much."

He grunted as he picked up the pants from the floor. After dropping back onto the couch, he began working his legs into the denim.

"Wine wasn't worth ten dollars, if you ask me," he grumbled to no one in particular.

"This coming from the drunk, naked man in my house with more grease in his hair than the griddle at the Waffle House."

"Those weren't good, either, by the way."

My hand dropped from my face. "You ate my waffles?"

"No, I definitely did *not* eat the cardboard that was labeled waffles. The birds didn't even eat them."

"They're cauliflower waffles. Two carbs each," I said, defending myself again. "You wrecked my home—"

"I cleaned it."

"*Wrecked* it. You're in *my* home—"

"You had a colony of ants living in your sink, and a hair-ball under your hutch that I'm pretty sure was growing hair and teeth." He tugged the pants over one leg.

"That's my business."

He was right, though. The house had been a wreck. Cluttered, dirty, laundry strewn about. Dishes uncleaned, empty tissue boxes everywhere. Yes, my place had been in dire need of a cleaning, but it hadn't always been like that.

Six months ago, I was normal and had my shit together. I wasn't this shell of a person who didn't give a shit anymore.

"What temperature do you have my AC set on?" I snapped.

"Sixty-eight."

"Sixty— Are you *serious*? For how long?"

Ignoring the question, the man sucked in a breath as he attempted to shove his other leg into the pants. I realized then that whatever pain this man was in was more than a hangover.

Trusting my instinct, I slowly crossed the room, mace in hand, leaving the front door open for a quick escape if I needed it—and to defrost the walls.

Rain ticked against the windows.

Christian didn't notice I'd left my post at the door, or didn't care. His focus was centered on getting his foot through the leg of his jeans.

I gasped at his disgustingly swollen, red, oozing ankle. "What happened to your ankle?"

"A rock." He grimaced, pushing harder against the fabric.

"Stop." I cringed as I watched him try to shove a watermelon into the top of a straw. "Stop. I think it's broken. Good Lord, *stop doing that.*"

Christian released his vise-like grip around the waistband.

Careful to keep my distance, I leaned over and flicked on a lamp. My heart dropped as the light washed over him.

*A*lthough a million questions flooded my head, the words caught in my throat. I stood, frozen, the swollen ankle and generous penis no longer the most shocking thing in my view.

His eyes, a shocking clover green framed with inky black lashes, looked up from under deeply hooded lids that gave him a mysterious, brooding vibe. His hair, as dark as his lashes, was mussed and shaggy, licking just below his ear. His skin was darkly tanned, with speckled bruising under days-old scruff. His lips, full and pink, had a downward tilt that made me want to nibble on them, despite the deep gash in one corner of his mouth.

I stared back, those eyes drawing me like a beacon through the rain. Alluring. Magnetic. All-consuming.

Butterflies awoke inside me.

In contrast to the flawless emerald irises, dark circles ringed his eyes, the result of sleepless nights and excruciating pain. I noticed the beginning of crow's feet at his eyes and fine lines around his mouth, which somehow only added to the rugged sexiness that rolled off this man in waves. He was a kind of unkempt handsome that only belonged to those who have no interest in exploiting it.

How old was he? Fortyish?

My gaze shifted to his body, chiseled like stone but covered in angry red cuts. A deep gash marked his shoulder.

Remembering the girl in the ditch, I took a step back. "What happened to you?"

"I told you. A rock."

"Christian—right?"

He grunted.

"I'm going to need a bit more here. I see that you're drunk, but I need you to pull it together."

"I fell."

"Into the seventh circle of hell?"

"Close. A ravine. About a mile east of here."

I knew that ravine. I'd almost tumbled down it myself several times.

He reattempted to push his ankle through the leg of his jeans.

"*Stop.* That turns my stomach." I scrubbed my hand over my mouth, my mind racing. "Okay. Here's what's going to happen. I need to know that you aren't about to murder me, rape me, or slice me up and cook me in a frying pan."

"You mean the frying pan that's covered in egg droppings or the one coated in rust?"

"You're an ass. I'm serious. If you make one move, I swear to God, I'll spray you with this mace." I clicked the tip to emphasize the point. "Do you understand?"

"Yep."

"Okay. I'm going to kneel down now . . ."

"I'm not going to hurt you."

"I believe you. I shouldn't, and I don't know why, but I do." I slowly knelt. "And keep your penis covered, please."

A muffled snort sounded above me.

I rolled my eyes and carefully lifted his foot. He jerked, sucking in a breath.

"Sorry." I switched angles, lightly pressing my fingertips around the swelling. "There's no way you're getting this thing through the leg of those jeans." I scratched my nose, the mud on my face beginning to dry and make my skin itch. A few specks dropped onto his leg. I glanced up to see if he'd noticed, but his focus was fixed on the pendant dangling around my neck.

It made me uncomfortable.

Tucking the pendant under my tank, I pushed to my feet. "Hang on. I'll be right back."

I scrubbed the dried dirt from my face as I crossed the living room, catching my reflection in the freshly washed window. I'd forgotten I was still wet, covered head to toe in mud, and had mascara running down my cheeks. I looked like Ozzy Osborne had stumbled onto the set of *Swamp Thing*.

After grabbing a pair of scissors from the junk drawer under the books—now alphabetized—I returned to my knees in front of Christian. Carefully, I punctured the thick fabric and cut off the hem of his jeans, then opened a slit up to the knee.

"There. You should be able to pull them on now." As he did, I looked away. "Your ankle is infected. You need to get to a doctor."

"It'll be fine."

"No, it won't. I'll call you an ambulance."

"No." He snapped at me, the first sign of energy in his voice.

"Listen," I snapped back. "I'm not going to go out of my

way to help you out here. I could seriously have you arrested right now."

Lord knows, I knew all about that.

I sat back on my butt, looking up at him. "Why are you here?"

"I told you, I fell. Hurt my ankle. Got to the point where I couldn't walk anymore, and this was the first house I came up on. You weren't home, so . . ."

"So you broke in?"

"I didn't have many options."

"Uh, yeah you did. Call someone. Have someone pick you up. Send out a smoke signal. Call for help. The cops, anyone."

"I didn't have a phone."

"Why?" I asked, and he frowned at me. Apparently, that was a crazy question. "Everyone has a phone."

"You don't."

"I absolutely do. Right here in my hand, ready to connect to nine-one-one if I need to. I always have my phone with me."

"I'm talking about a landline. I looked everywhere in here."

"A landline?" I scoffed. "Who the hell has a landline these days? I suppose you looked for a pager and a Black-berry too?"

"Who doesn't have a landline?"

"Uh, anyone in Gen X or Z, Pops."

He ignored the zing. "Landlines are important in case of emergencies." He gestured toward his ankle.

"Okay, I'll add it to my list of things to offer wayward hikers who break into my house. How long have you been here?"

"Two days . . . I think."

"Oh my G—" I shook my head, still unable to believe the situation I'd found myself in. "What were you doing in the woods?"

"Hiking."

"By yourself?"

"Yes."

"Who doesn't take a phone when they go hiking alone?"

"Anyone who wants to disconnect. You know, anyone *not* in Gen X or Z."

"Let me get this straight." I rubbed my temples, the headache piercing. "You go for a hike with no way of letting anyone know if you got lost or in trouble. You fall down a ravine, drag yourself to my house, and break in when no one answers the front door. Am I on the right track so far?"

He dipped his chin, regarding me closely now, his gaze flickering between the pendant and my face.

"And instead of figuring out how to solve this little pickle you've found yourself in, you simply make yourself at home. In *my* home." When he didn't respond, I surged to my feet and threw my hands into the air. "I could be a crazy person! I could have walked in and shot you between the eyes! I could have allowed Cricket to chew your balls off. This is crazy. Who does this? How did you even break in?"

Christian shrugged. "Picked your lock. You need better locks."

I looked over my shoulder at the cheap lock on the front door, then turned back around with a glare.

"I can't believe you." I shook my head again, looking down at his ankle. "You're lucky, you know that?"

Something flickered in his eyes that suggested he didn't believe it to be true.

"I think I have a first aid kit in my truck." I headed for the door, then called out over my shoulder, "Stay."

When I returned a minute later, Christian's head was tipped back against the couch, his eyes closed, his breathing shallow. My tampering with his ankle had put him in a world of pain. He'd concealed it well.

"Hey," I snapped curtly, reminding myself I had no reason to feel bad for this man.

His eyes drifted open.

"I know it hurts, but this needs immediate attention. Can you handle it?"

"Do you have any more wine?"

"No. You drank it all."

He groaned, repositioning on the couch.

I knelt back down. "Another day and you might have lost this foot, you know."

"I'd be in good company, then."

We both glanced at Cricket, now snoring on the rug.

"What happened to him?" he asked, almost as interested in my dog as the necklace around my neck.

"Abandonment." I looked down. "Okay, here we go."

Relying on instinct and faded memories from the first aid class I took in school, I cleaned the gash on his ankle the best I could, bandaged it up, and secured a splint along each side. Lastly, I wrapped it tightly in an ACE bandage.

"Normally, at this point, I'd say you should let air get to the wound. But it needs to close up, and stay clean while it does. Keep it wrapped until you go to the doctor—first thing in the morning."

He shifted his foot, attempting to roll the ankle.

"No. Keep it still. Have you taken anything for the pain?"

"Wine."

"Aside from wine?"

"No."

"I'll get you some ibuprofen."

I crossed the room and flicked on the light to the kitchen, not recognizing the room. Anger boiled in my veins, and I spun around. "Why did you clean my house?"

"I was bored."

"Well, I don't appreciate it."

"You understand there's an entire subset of our economy dedicated to people paying to have their house cleaned, right?"

"You're not getting a thank-you card from me."

"That's okay. Save the sixteen boxes of rainbow stationery you have for your next book club meeting."

I took in my living room, plain and drab aside from the rainbow candles and knickknacks, rainbow throw pillows, rainbow-painted planters that held dead plants, and a trio of rainbow-printed butterflies. Splashes of color to chase away the darkness. Trying to, anyway.

"You've got a problem with my rainbows?" I closed my eyes and lifted my palms. "Never mind. I don't even care. It's none of your business. Nothing of mine is any of your business. My house is—*was*—exactly the way I like it."

Lie.

"And I know where everything is."

False.

"And I don't like the fact you invaded my privacy."

He stared at me, not listening to a word I was saying, with an intensity that made me feel like he was staring into my soul.

"What's your name?" he asked.

"Rory."

"Rory." He nodded as if accepting this name. "Rory." His focus shifted to my bedroom. "The angel in the storm."

I frowned. "The what? What are you talking about?"

The man was *drunk.*

I didn't have the energy for this crap. I needed him out of my house.

Digging in my purse, I found my phone and thrust it at him. "Here. Call whoever you need to. To come pick you up."

Christian took the phone, dialed a number, and stared at me as it rang. My pulse quickened.

He handed it back. "No answer."

"Call someone else."

He shrugged. "There is no one else."

Squinting at him in amazement, I said, "You have only one person in your life you can call right now?"

I thought about my exact experience hours earlier—minus one.

When he didn't respond, I demanded he try again.

He did, to no avail. I assumed whoever he was calling was asleep, considering it was almost two in the morning.

"Call an Uber."

"There're no Ubers in Berry Springs. Or taxis, for that matter."

I snarled. He was right. Something that convenient and trendy hadn't been accepted in the small Southern town that clung to the old way of life when people still hid money under their mattresses because they didn't trust the banks. I had a feeling if taxis or ride shares ever became a thing in Berry Springs, they would come in the form of a horse-drawn carriage.

In a stalemate, we stared at each other.

There was no way I was allowing this stranger to sleep in my house, with me.

"Try again."

When he tried again and the call failed to connect a

third time, I heaved out an annoyed breath. My gaze shifted to the rain-streaked windows as I thought.

"Then I'll take you home."

"It's fine."

"What's fine? No, it's not. You're not staying here." I pushed past him. "Let me just grab my raincoat . . ."

Change out of these wet clothes is what I meant, but I wasn't about to tell this strange man I was going to be naked only fifteen feet away. I stepped into my bedroom. Thankfully, this room appeared to be undisturbed and as messy as always.

Thank God.

The four-poster king-size bed was still made, the rainbow throw pillows stacked haphazardly on the side exactly as I'd left them. The cream-colored net canopy draped on either sides of the bed, in its usual elegant position. My murder mysteries were still stacked on the nightstand, in the same place, next to the accent chair crowded with antique dolls. I was a bit embarrassed by that, but *oh well*.

Finally—and most importantly—my easel, stool, boxes of beeswax, bottles of dye, and stacks of canvases remained undisturbed next to the sweeping window that overlooked the woods. Resting on the easel was my latest creation, angry slashes of blue against a tower of brown.

Heat burned my cheeks at the thought that he'd seen my secret hobby. That he knew about it.

God, I hate him.

Groaning, I stepped to my dresser and noticed the jewelry tree had been moved. I always kept it angled so the tiny suncatcher at the top caught the sunrise, sending sparkles through my room every morning. My eyes narrowed, I touched each of the necklaces, rings, and bracelets. None appeared to be missing.

Then I stepped into the bathroom—the *only* bathroom in the house. The bathroom Christian had to have used during his free stay at Casa de Rory. Sure enough, the toilet paper was almost gone.

Men.

My eyes rounded in horror as my gaze shot to my vanity.

There are two places a man should never snoop in a woman's home—her vanity and her nightstand. Luckily, my nightstand only contained bottles of melatonin and Advil, and wads of used tissues. My vanity, on the other hand . . .

I dropped to my knees and flung open the cabinet doors that concealed my small but impressive collection of vibrators.

Oh. My. *God.*

Pink, purple, *bejeweled*—right there next to a pair of freaking anal beads I'd gotten for free with my last purchase. That I've never used—*to be clear.*

Mortified, I pushed to my feet and refused to look at myself in the mirror.

Gritting my teeth, I peeled off the muddy tank top and sweat-stained slacks, tossing both into the trash can in the corner. After wiping down my face, neck, and arms with a wet washcloth, I twisted my matted, nasty hair into a bun on the top of my head. As I hadn't done laundry in over a week, I didn't have much in the way of clothes, so I grabbed an old pair of cut-off shorts and my last clean T-shirt. I bypassed my flip-flops and yanked on a pair of rain boots.

Believe it or not, the look was an improvement. Not that I cared.

Just get him out. End this godforsaken day.

After grabbing a raincoat from the closet, I clomped like

a Clydesdale out of the bedroom, steeling myself for another confrontation. But I didn't need to.

Christian was gone.

I stared at the front door, his presence still lingering in the air.

His last words echoed through my head.

The angel in the storm . . .

10

*T*he next morning, I awoke with the sun, which was surprising considering I'd watched the moon slide behind the treetops not two hours earlier.

The whir of the box fan that I kept inches from my face, usually comforting, was now a category five hurricane. My swollen eyes felt like they'd been dipped in sand, and I was positive my head was squeezed inside the grip of a gigantic wrench.

Keeping one eye closed, I rolled over and clicked off the fan, accidentally knocking the alarm clock over, sending it tumbling to the floor.

A robin darted from its perch on my windowsill. The air was thick with the musky scent of a summer morning after a rain. Birds chirped loudly from the trees, hunting for worms that had risen from the mud.

Cricket lifted his head from under the covers at the foot of the bed. No matter how many doggie beds and blankets I got him, he insisted on sleeping next to me. Every night, the dog would fall asleep next to the fireplace. And every morning, I'd wake up to him burrowed under the covers, curled into a ball at my stinky feet.

I lifted the sheet—the only cover bearable that time of year. "Morning."

A minute slid by as I waited for a response that didn't come.

"I have to get up," I said to myself as much as to him.

Still, no movement from the lump under the sheet.

"You get to sleep all day. I have to go to work." I rubbed my eyes, wincing at the pain. "You know, go stare at the wall for eight hours and watch my bank account dry up? Yeah, I've got to go do that."

I pulled back the sheets, careful to keep them enclosed around the dog who had no interest in moving. The pulse in my head was a steady *whomp, whomp, whomp* as I flung my legs over the side.

Another night of no sleep, except this one was filled with night sweats. Visions of death. Memories of that day. They hadn't faded, but another body in another ditch made it feel like it was yesterday again.

It was too much. Renewed anxiety settled into my bones like a constant electrical current.

All night, my thoughts had ping-ponged between the woman found in the ditch and the woman whose nose I'd broken an hour later, and the shiny new criminal record that would come with that. I'd already accepted the fact that it was a very real possibility I'd serve jail time. I just worried about Cricket and what I would do with him. That's what bothered me the most. According to the officer who drove me home, my best-case scenario would be a misdemeanor and community service. Even then, I'd still have a criminal record.

Between that and my rendezvous with Simon, my

unstable state was reaching new heights. I was making bad decisions. Slowly unhinging, as I'd done months earlier, but this time was not only hopeless but reckless. Angry.

I regretted what I'd done with Simon. Becky Dunk Davies, though? *Nope*. Truth? I'd do it again. In fact, I spent a good hour of the night coming up with a new nickname for Dunks, settling on Broken-Nose Becky. Unoriginal, but accurate.

As much as I'd like to say *all that* was the center of my thoughts, I would be lying. The majority of the night was spent thinking about the strange man I'd found in my house.

After I'd discovered that he was no longer here, I'd checked for him in the front and back yard, by my truck, in my truck, and even in the small shed that housed the lawn equipment that I didn't own. No luck. The only thing that remained of Christian was a track of boot prints that faded into the woods.

The crazy bastard had walked home—on a grotesquely infected ankle. And for reasons I couldn't pin down, I was worried about him. Couldn't stop thinking about him.

Where the hell did he go? Had he made it home? Was he lying at the bottom of the ravine again, lodged between two boulders with his head in a coyote's mouth?

I felt oddly responsible for him. I should have ensured he had a way home.

Was I going to be responsible if he was found dead? Would they think I had something to do with it? Crazy old Gory Rory, losing it like her mom.

Another dead body tied to me. What kind of luck is that?

Last night, I'd considered following his tracks into the woods, or taking my truck out and looking for him, but reminded myself that I owed the man absolutely nothing. If anything, *he* owed *me* a couple hundred bucks to replace the food he'd eaten and the astronomical electric bill I was surely going to get at the end of the month, thanks to his turning my house into a sixty-eight-degree meat locker for two days.

Cold-blooded, indeed.

I'd vacuumed the couch where he'd slept and washed everything he'd touched.

After eating the last twelve almonds he'd left in my cupboard, I felt bamboozled. Shat upon. A laughingstock to the asshole who had zero respect for the home I'd worked so hard to pay for, and the groceries that I'd bought using the coupons I'd spent hours clipping from the Sunday newspaper.

Christian had literally made himself at home in my house, with no regard to the woman who paid for everything.

My fridge had been emptied, as well as my liquor and wine cabinet. The pantry was bare, aside from a few boxes of diet wafers and cans of SlimFast, which were apparently unacceptable to my unannounced houseguest.

And to top off all of that, my coffeepot had been destroyed. Literally dismantled, taken apart, and was hanging by wires. The condiments had been used, however, and my best guess was that he'd somehow made coffee with the pot and strainer he'd left on the stove.

Unable to go without my morning coffee, I tried this method, failing miserably and ending up with grainy, flavorless brown water. Cursing the man, I grabbed my rainbow coffee mug and filled it to the top, refusing to let him ruin my morning.

In my nightshirt and holey socks, I padded across the house, glancing at the blaze of orange streaking up from behind the mountains. It was going to be another scorcher.

I carried my mug to the couch, where I began my morning routine of exactly ten minutes of watching the weather channel followed by the morning news. Then it was off to shower, once the caffeine started doing its trick.

Clicking on the television, I sipped. As expected, the coffee was terrible.

I forced down another sip while watching the weather confirm another day of triple-digit temps. I clicked to the local news just in time to catch the morning headlines.

"... *our own Tabitha Raines is on the scene now. We want to warn you, the details you are about to hear may be disturbing. Tabitha, what can you tell us?*"

I recognized the scene immediately. The narrow dirt road, the low-water bridge, the ditch.

My stomach dropped.

"*As you can see behind me, the police have sectioned off part of the road and the ditch where the body was found late last night. I've been told they've yet to identify the victim but have confirmed it was a young woman, her age estimated to be between seventeen and twenty-one, around five foot nine in height, with shoulder-length auburn hair. It has been reported that she was found naked, wearing only a single white tennis shoe. Her breasts and pelvic region had been severely mutilated in what appears to be a sexual assault/homicide. Although not confirmed, it is assumed that last night's rainfall washed the victim's body down from Shadow River, possibly from Otter Lake. I'm told that a local dive team is there now, soon to begin searching Devil's Cove, which authorities believe is the most likely place a body that had been washed into Shadow River would have been dumped. I understand they'll search for the victim's clothes, jewelry, anything to help begin to put the pieces of this puzzle together. Authorities have yet to make an arrest, and the police are asking for information regarding this incident. If anyone knows who this woman could be, or has any information, please call the number on the bottom of your screen."*

I set my mug on the coffee table and pushed it away. My thoughts racing and stomach churning, I made my way to the bathroom, eager to begin the day and get out of the house. Get out of my head.

After an ice-cold shower, I pulled on a long olive-green sundress, slipped into a pair of beaded sandals, and paused at my jewelry tree.

I thought of Christian.

What had he seen that had interested him? Why had he left everything in my bedroom untouched, except for the jewelry?

I thought of the way he looked at my pendant.

I slipped on my many rings, an eclectic mix of gemstones and silver, then carefully lifted the old pendant from its perch next to the tiny suncatcher. A burst of rainbow sparkles danced across the walls as the sunlight shot through the window and reflected off the gems.

"Morning, Mom," I whispered.

Swallowing hard, I ran my fingertip over the gold, across the Celtic cross that served as the trunk of a large, thriving oak tree engraved on the front of the oval gold disc, and down the three tiny gemstones that were embedded in the center of the tree's trunk. Red, pale green, and blue.

I turned over the pendant and gazed at the faint, but familiar, etching of a black butterfly on the back, above the words:

from hate
from harm
from act

from ill

Below that, the numbers:

080481

My fingertip lingered on the black butterfly.

Exhaling, I slipped the chain over my head and tucked the pendant safely under the neckline of my dress.

11

Thirty minutes later, I squeezed my truck into the last parking spot along the busy street known as Tourist Row.

Just off Main Street, the narrow dead-end road was lined with mature oak trees, quaint Victorian-style specialty shops, bistro-type restaurants, bars, and bakeries that catered to tourists. Its eclectic, new-age energy was a far cry from the rest of the town's vibe, which proudly embraced Southern small-town stereotypes.

I grabbed an eight-dollar latte at a coffee stand on the sidewalk manned by a teenage girl with a gauge in her earlobe that I could stick my fist through. Mentally adding it to the bill I was going to pretend-mail to Christian Locke, I returned to my truck and lowered the tailgate.

"Heard you got arrested."

Cursing under my breath, I turned toward the raspy voice that greeted me every morning when I pulled up to work. "I see you've already been to Donny's this morning."

Wearing his usual short-sleeved plaid shirt, brown wool

hat, and matching slacks—despite the heat—my landlord, Mr. Abram, met me on the sidewalk.

"Broke her nose, huh?" The old man smirked, a trail of cigar smoke snaking out of ashy, chapped lips scented with brandy, his usual morning scent.

I closed my eyes and shook my head.

"Heard they had to pull you off her."

"Great," I muttered.

"Don't worry. I told everyone that I was sure you had good reason."

"I'll bet they believed that, huh?" I sipped my latte, needing the kick of caffeine to lift an already waning mood.

"Ah, forget about it. They've already switched topics to the girl you found in the ditch."

I forced the coffee down, my stomach instantly souring.

"Heard it was pretty bad?"

"Bad enough that if you ask any more questions, you're going to be wearing my breakfast on those new boots you've got on."

A proud US Army veteran, Cecil Abram owned the historic two-story brick building that housed my new business, the Black Butterfly. On the ground floor, the building was divided with my shop on one side, and his business, the Back Porch, on the other. Abram lived in the small apartment on the second floor of the building, where he moved after his wife of forty years passed away.

Although the Back Porch was advertised as a cigar shop, it was widely known among the locals that Abram offered not only illegal stogies, but free spiked coffee and a place to sit to all his customers, most of whom stayed for hours at a time—buying cigar, after cigar, after cigar. It was also rumored that the war vet traded and sold guns, knives, and ammo behind the closed doors of his office.

He was a popular guy in Berry Springs.

With craggy gray skin and veiny hands, the old man appeared to have one foot in the grave. But for those of us who pushed past the scent of cigar smoke and stale beer, Abram had a sharp wit and a keen eye that made you feel like he could see right through you. Not one to miss much, the man doled out unwanted advice almost as much as gossip in his shop.

The elderly veteran and I had formed an unlikely friendship when I'd wandered into his cigar shop after a solo two-hour lunch at the pizzeria down the block that consisted of one bottle of wine—and nothing else. It was a day I decided to give smoking a shot, otherwise known as the day I was laid off from my position as communication director at the local library. Budget cuts, they'd said.

I'd been immediately drawn to the bookcases that lined the back wall of his shop, packed with old books and classic movies. Within ten minutes, the old man and I were engulfed in a cloud of vanilla smoke and a heated debate about whether *Die Hard* was, or was not, a Christmas movie. Next up, an even hotter debate about whether romance novels were, or were not, responsible for the country's fifty-percent divorce rate.

Two hours later, Abram held my hair back while I vomited in his toilet. I decided I liked the old man—and hated smoking.

And that's how the town drunk and I became friends, and how he later became my landlord.

I handed Abram one of the three boxes in the back of my truck and carefully lifted the painting I'd bargained for at the Rutherford estate sale. Arny and I had exchanged loot in the Walmart parking lot ten minutes earlier.

Abram whistled. "*Wowie*, how much did that cost you?"

I tilted my head, avoiding the question while admiring the woman's colorful face. "Beautiful, isn't she?"

"She is."

"The artist's name is Aaliyah Buhle, from Louisiana."

He nodded sagely. "It'll sell quickly."

My fingertips tightened around the frame. I wanted it, but I also wanted money. No, I *needed* the money.

"Hey, where's Cricket?" Abram asked, peering into the truck's cab.

"Home."

"Not up to it today?"

I shook my head, carefully sliding the painting under my arm. "No. He didn't even want to get out of bed this morning."

"Should've added a shot of brandy to his breakfast. Try it tomorrow."

"Well, if I need any, I know where to go," I said with a wink.

The corners of the old man's mouth lifted into his wrinkles. Just as quickly, his face fell again. "So, how are you doing?"

I exhaled. "It was pretty bad, Abram. She looked . . . unreal, almost. Like something out of a horror movie. And again, I don't want to talk about it. I'm serious."

We dipped our heads at a young blonde in purple spandex as she passed us on the sidewalk, pushing a stroller with sleeping twins, their chestnut curls stirring in the breeze. My stomach rolled at the thought of the family of the girl I'd found in the ditch.

Did they know? Where were they? Could she have had children herself, young babies somewhere, crying for their mother?

Abram refocused on me. "Last question. Did you recognize the girl?"

"Not from what I saw—or could see, rather. Reports say she could be as young as seventeen. If that's true and she's a local, I'm not surprised I didn't recognize her. Big age difference."

"Ah, honey." He winked as I handed him a box. "Three years ain't that big of a difference."

"Abram, you know good and well that I'm a decade past twenty." I balanced the last box in my arms. "A couple more years, and this flirting you've got going is going to turn creepy."

"So, seventy?"

"Yes. Make a note to yourself, at age seventy you must stop all flirtatious commentary with younger women."

"Note to self, die at sixty-nine."

I snorted, and we fell into step together on the cracked sidewalk to my shop, as we did most mornings. Although barely eight in the morning, the air was already sticky with humidity. We stepped under the shadows of a maple tree that crowded the front of the building, shading its red brick walls, stone arches, and beveled windows. Although badly in need of restoration, the old building was beautiful and unique, with an old-world feel that made it perfect for an antiques shop.

"What have you heard about it?" I asked, referring to the girl in the ditch.

"That's about it, although I'm expecting to hear more as the day goes on. No one seems to know who she is."

"They think she was dumped in the lake, then washed down the river."

"Makes sense. Keep me updated with what you hear."

"You do the same."

Abram shifted the box in his arms. "Looks like your trip to Dallas was fruitful?"

I nodded. "Bargained for a table clock that I think is gold-plated, and a set of gorgeous blue Depression glassware that I'm excited about. I've already called Jeff. Said he'll come by to appraise it as soon as he can." I narrowed my eyes, cocking a brow at the passive-aggressive smirk that twisted the old man's lips. "What?"

"That guy's got a crush on you the size of old man Morrison's lip wart."

I wrinkled my nose. "That thing really has tripled over the last few months, hasn't it?"

"Told him he's going to have to start bringing his own mug for coffee in the mornings. Anyway, Jeff has stars in his eyes when he looks at you, Rory."

"I'm pretty sure that's called cataracts."

"I think that's called deflecting. He's not even forty."

I shrugged.

"Has he asked you out yet?"

"I'm not interested in dating." *Just screwing married men in the cab of my truck, apparently.*

"Guy's solid, all's I'm saying. I knew his folks. Good stock."

"Thanks for the approval."

"Hey, you need someone looking out for you. There's a lot of sickos running around this town. Just ask the girl in the ditch."

"That was an ass thing to say."

Abram shrugged. "Sensitivity has never been my thing, you know that. Anyway, what else is in the boxes?"

"A stack of books to add to the collection, a few pieces of

jewelry, and an obnoxious olive-green vintage fan that I'm probably going to keep."

He laughed. "I still don't know how you go through a night this time of year without air conditioning, sweetheart."

"I have air conditioning. And heating, for that matter. I just choose not to turn it on."

I thought of Christian. Those emerald eyes, those lips. The way he looked at me. And for the tenth time that morning, I wondered if he'd made it through the night.

We crowded the small stoop in front of the door. Balancing the boxes on my knee, I unlocked the thick wooden door and shoved past a wall of stagnant air perfumed with cigar smoke and whatever Mr. Abram had cooked himself for dinner the night before. Italian, if I had to guess.

Oblivious to the smells in the building, Abram sauntered into the shop, weaving between the display cases, and set the boxes on the glass checkout counter. I assumed the man had become desensitized to the scent of cigar smoke. Or simply didn't care. Either way, I kept a can of room spray under the counter.

The early morning sun streamed through the wall of beveled windows that lined the left side of the shop, pooling onto the scuffed hardwood floor, sparkles of dust dancing in its warmth. The right side of the shop was a brick wall that separated my store from Abram's cigar shop. I'd covered the wall with art. Dozens of wind chimes and sun catchers hung from the vaulted ceiling. In the back was an office and a tiny bathroom next to a door that led to the alley.

I carefully stacked my boxes next to his.

"I want this." Abram plucked an ashtray from the top box.

"That'll be fifty dollars off rent, sir."

"Twenty."

"Sold." I smirked.

He poked through the other boxes. "What kind of jewelry did you get?"

"Nothing that I'm too excited about in terms of making money off of, but the pieces were so beautiful, I couldn't pass them up. Handmade beaded necklaces and bracelets. A few brooches. And this . . ." I lifted a silver cross with a line of turquoise down the middle.

Abram's brow arched as he took it from my hands. "If that's real turquoise, you might get a couple hundred bucks for it."

I nodded, debating on keeping it for myself—a nasty habit I had after spending a weekend antique hunting.

"I think it is real turquoise." He examined it closer. "I also think this is a piece of authentic Native American jewelry."

"Really?" I leaned closer. "Talk money."

"A lot." He held it up to the light. "See these marks in the silver? Like slashes? I'm not one hundred percent, but I think that's the hallmark of Charles Loloma, a famous Hopi Native American artist and jeweler. Could be a knockoff, but if not, you've got something."

"I'll ask my crush when he gets here."

Abram snorted, still studying the necklace.

"I didn't realize you knew much about jewelry," I said.

"I was married for forty years, honey," he said, and I laughed. "You know, in Native American culture, turquoise is supposed to be good luck. A sign of good fortune. Some people believe that wearing Loloma's jewelry specifically is good luck, and that his knockoffs are cursed."

My hand drifted to the chain I wore, my thoughts to the

terrible random events that began happening the day I put it around my neck.

"Do you know of any artists who have a hallmark of a Celtic tree cross or a black butterfly?"

He looked up from under his sparse lashes. "Why? Got something else interesting?"

I hesitated, possessive of the necklace I held so dear, despite the bad luck that seemed to follow it.

Abram's gaze shifted to my fingers running along the long chain around my neck. Reluctantly, I pulled out the pendant I'd been so careful to hide from prying eyes.

He whistled. "Holy catfish, dear, that's a beaut."

"Thanks."

Frowning, he stepped closer and snatched the pendant from my hand. "Wait a sec . . ."

He yanked the chain, eyeing the gold piece. I jerked forward, tilting my head to avoid knocking noses as he pulled a magnifying glass from his pocket. I held my breath as he studied the Celtic tree, inches from my face.

"It's well made, for sure, but I don't recognize it, or know an artist that has that kind of hallmark."

"Look on the back," I squeaked out, trying to hold my breath. "At the black butterfly."

He looked at me. "Is this where you got the name for this shop?"

I nodded, considering for the first time that the place might have been doomed from the start.

He flipped over the pendant. "Interesting. There's words etched below it," he muttered, peering even closer. "Barely legible . . . faded. I can't quite make them out."

I gave the old man three more seconds before plucking the pendant from his hands and taking a step back, inhaling deeply, wondering if it was possible to get a contact high from cigar smoke.

The odd look on his face gave me pause.

"What?"

"A black butterfly is a sign of misfortune, bad luck. In many cultures, it's a symbol of impending doom . . . or death."

"Death?"

"Yes. An omen of death."

We stared at each other a moment, neither wanting to acknowledge the massive elephant that had just entered the room.

"Where did you get it?" he asked.

"My mom. Found it at a flea market." I blinked. "She gave it to me, right before . . ."

Something flashed in his eyes, and he took a step back.

I turned the pendant over in my hands, my heart racing. "What do you make of the gemstones down the middle of the tree-cross? Red, green, and blue?"

He shook his head. "Not sure. I have a section of books in the shop of folklore, fables, legends. Some Wiccan and curse books too."

Another moment passed as we both stared at the necklace.

"Anyway," Abram said in a tone meant to clear the air now suffocating us. "Let me look into that possible Loloma turquoise piece. Might buy it off you."

"Yeah. Sure," I said mindlessly, my thoughts racing. "Thanks for carrying the boxes for me."

"Always." Another beat passed. "All right. Well. I'm going to top off that latte, dear. Looks like you could use it."

"No," I said quickly, knowing my stomach couldn't

handle it. "No thanks. I'll swing in later to search through the curse books."

"Okay, hon. See you in a bit, then."

Abram crossed the shop, his heavy footfalls beating in time with the drum of my heart. I felt his eyes on me as he closed the door that separated our shops behind him, but I didn't turn.

I was too busy staring at the pendant in my hands.

12

"What the hell are you doing, you crazy-ass woman?"

First sign of insanity? Talking to yourself.

I glanced in the rearview mirror before turning onto a rutted dirt path that cut through the trees. It was a hidden road—if you could call it that—that only locals knew about, used mostly by hunters. I happened upon it while getting lost on my way home from the cemetery one night a couple of months ago, after polishing off a box of wine by the headstones.

The late afternoon sun slanted through the trees, casting deep shadows across the path. Clumps of brown grass and parched brush wilted under another hundred-degree day.

I squinted, peering into the woods ahead of me, imagining the route Christian must have taken the night before. The direction of his footprints had given me a general direction, suggesting three options.

One, Christian had trekked to the main road and hitchhiked, or two, to the trailhead of a popular hiking trail where he might have parked before setting out on his idiotic cell-phone-free hike. Or three, he'd dragged himself to one of the few houses I knew were on the other side of the mountain, less than a mile from mine. Having grown up in these woods, I knew every blade of grass like the back of my hand.

Shadow River cut through the middle of the mountain, with only one bridge connecting both sides and all three options. Common sense told me that was the path Christian would have taken, but I mapped out multiple scenarios just in case. There was something about the man, a recklessness in his eyes that suggested he preferred the road less traveled.

I pushed aside the stack of dusty old books I'd taken from Abram's shelves while he was busy refilling his customers' cups in the main room, and pulled out the map I'd spent all day creating in a shop that had zero customers today—not a single one. Not a single penny in sales, all day long.

The map was streaked with red, yellow, and green lines, marking the multiple paths Christian could have taken.

I was on the red one.

I want to take this moment to remind you that I'm not stupid. I wasn't totally oblivious to the coincidence that a mutilated girl had been discovered the same night I'd found a strange man living in my home. But I kept returning to the fact that Christian had many opportunities to hurt me while I tended to his ankle. And he didn't. There was also something about him, a distant memory that kept nagging at me like a whisper in the wind. I couldn't recall the memory, but for some reason, I knew in my gut that this man wasn't a stone-cold killer.

I also knew I couldn't get him off my damn mind.

A gnarled bush dragged its thorns down the side of my truck as I slowly drove deeper into the woods, scanning the surroundings. The path appeared undisturbed, with no sign that anyone had been down the road recently, on foot or on wheels. This also meant that the police hadn't canvassed that particular area the night before.

Although this was interesting, I pushed it aside. I wasn't looking for evidence to help the girl in the ditch. I was looking for Christian. I wanted nothing to do with the girl in the ditch.

I came to the end of the path where a thick line of trees marked the edge of the riverbank. I shoved the truck into park and turned off the engine. Leaving the keys in the ignition, I pushed out the door in my cotton jersey dress and sandals, swatting away a cloud of gnats. The humidity was stifling. I pulled a can of bug spray from the toolbox and saturated my arms and legs, already glistening with sweat.

Rounding the hood, I looked around, listening to the distant sound of the river rushing over the rocks, memories flooding me. My heart squeezed.

After knotting the bottom of my long dress at my knees, I pushed my way through the thicket. A trio of birds squawked and took flight as I emerged onto the riverbank, disappearing into the sunset. The far side of the river was lined with a rocky cliff, riddled with caves.

A pile of charred wood was on the bank where someone had built a small fire. Before the thunderstorm, based on the scattered pieces that were still wet. If this was Christian's fire, it verified his story that he'd been out in the woods for several days.

I poked around it a bit, then decided to follow the riverbank, searching for any sign of him.

I walked until the river took a bend, the rocky bank ending at a small cliff that blocked my path forward. Water rushed along the side, disappearing between the rocks. The only way to continue forward was to either wade through the water or make the climb.

Sweat rolled down my temples as I made my way up the steep, rocky hill, brushing myself off once I reached the top. I searched the river below, looking for a body. Nothing.

A butterfly flitted past my face, its inky black wings tipped in aquamarine. Abram's words echoed in my ears.

An omen of death . . .

Despite the heat, a chill ran along my arms.

For a while, I watched the butterfly dance and dip through the air. Long enough that my determination to find Christian Locke was replaced with that dead, hollow feeling that I'd felt so much over the last few months. The nothingness.

Time seemed to pause with the flutter of the butterfly's wings. I had nowhere to be, nowhere to go, no one waiting for me.

Just . . . nothing.

Tears stung my eyes. Gritting my teeth, I bit back those damn tears. So *sick* of crying, I tilted my face to the sky and cursed, though not knowing who to curse to.

Not anymore, anyway.

My mother and father had raised me to believe in good and evil, heaven and hell, and that there was more in this crazy world than only what you could see and touch. I was born and raised in the Bible Belt, reciting prayers every night, going to church every Sunday. We were back-row Baptists, though, a family of wallflowers who reveled in our own little bubble of happiness. We lived a solitary life that most would consider their own version of hell.

My parents, modern-day hippies, raised me deep in the woods, away from paved roads, cars, and people. We loved the water, my mother especially. No matter the season, if the weather allowed it, we'd go to the river or the lake to swim or fish or just read at the shoreline. My mom joked that she must have been a mermaid in another life. I believe that to be true.

In my family, money was required for survival only, nothing else. Money wasn't something to seek or hoard, or spend in excess, just simply something to use as needed. Most of ours came from my dad's occasional work as an on-call handyman.

For the most part, we lived off the nature around us, rarely going to town for anything at all. We ate fish that my father caught from the lake, and vegetables from my mother's garden. Not because we were weird survivalists or anything, but because my mom and dad were nature fanatics and total introverts. And so was I.

Growing up, I was terribly, awkwardly shy in school. I was the girl who had a borderline panic attack at the mere thought of the teacher calling on me. Most days, I ate lunch alone by choice, with an organic drink of sorts in one hand and a book in the other. On the rare days that I forgot my book, I'd join the only two friends I had. We'd hide in the corner of the cafeteria, away from the bullies and cool kids, and talk about, well, books.

I spent most of my school days hiding in the shadows, counting the moments until I'd see my mom, smiling from the front seat of her rusty four-door Chevy Caprice Classic, which was the size of a small fishing boat. The Gray Ghost, it had been dubbed by my schoolmates. I loved the damn thing.

But I loved the driver even more.

My mom, Charlotte, was my best friend. My hero. My everything. I truly believe our bond wasn't of this world. It was something special, gifted to us—only us—since the moment I took my first breath in her arms.

My mother was an angel on earth, the most selfless, caring, innately kind human I'd ever had the pleasure of meeting. She was a teacher, a creator, a dreamer, a pro at mending second-hand clothes and super-gluing boots.

She dedicated her life to me, her husband, and the twelve children she taught art to every week. Her passion was art, the expression of oneself through color. Aside from her family and art, my mother loved collecting antiques. When the weather warmed, no garage sale was safe. In the winter, we'd take the Caprice Classic to local flea markets and antiques shows. Most of the time, we didn't buy a single thing, as the family checking account wouldn't allow it. But that didn't matter. It was the experience we both loved. Our thing to do together.

The first picture my mom and I painted together was of a rainbow in a cloudless blue sky. I still have that painting. Mom loved rainbows and daisies, and I loved anything she did.

She was my entire life, and my father's as well.

Elijah, my father, was the yin to her yang. While Mom was an eternal optimist, my father was a realist and sometimes-cynic who would rein her in when she'd find herself dreaming too much, going too far down a rabbit hole.

My father passed on that realism to me, which manifested in more of a habitual pessimism. My mother passed her love of painting, of light, to me. Unfortunately, the darkness came with it.

It's accurate to say that I grew up dirt poor. No central air or heat, no name-brand clothes or frivolous snacks. Just enough food to fill our stomachs, and not a bite more.

I didn't have many love interests growing up. Mostly, I

avoided boys like the plague. I could never find the right words. Or the confidence, maybe. When I looked in the mirror, I didn't see the type of girl they wanted to date. I saw plain Jane with wild, untamable blond hair. Freckles below boring blue eyes that were a bit too big for my head. A long and curveless body. Barely there B-cups.

My mother once told me I had a timeless beauty, but when I looked in the mirror, I saw nothing more than a big-toothed blond Olive Oyl. Of course, my parents always told me I was beautiful. I was their only child, not from lack of trying. My mother had seven miscarriages before she had me.

They'd said I was their angel. I said they were my rocks. Turns out, even the strongest rock has its cracks.

For as long as I can remember, every few months or so, my mother would retreat to a place of solitude in which I was the only person allowed inside. During this time, my mother rarely spoke or ate. The laughter, the light behind her eyes simply faded.

I knew it was coming when I'd catch her crying in her bedroom for no reason at all. To cope, Dad and I had developed a routine. He would drive me to town, where I would rent bags full of books from the local library. Once we got back home, Mom and I would crawl into bed together, and Dad would retreat outdoors, giving her space.

Mom and I would burrow together under the covers and read book after book. It's funny—and terrible—that a part of me would get excited when I knew one of her episodes was coming. I reveled in those moments, nestled next to her side, listening to her breathe, smelling the fresh scent of laundry that was my mother. Safe with her, under the covers.

This would go on for days, neither of us leaving bed,

until my mother would suddenly snap out of it. No rhyme or reason, she would just roll over, kiss me, and with a smile, ask if I was ready to face the day now. I'd say yes, and that would be that. Life would be normal until the next episode.

It wasn't until my high school psychology class that I realized my mother suffered from severe depression. It was a turning point in our relationship. I no longer looked at her as only my mom, but as a human being, a woman. As someone I needed to protect now. I learned that she struggled with her medications, and sometimes simply stopped taking them altogether. It had been a lifelong struggle for her. And somehow, seeing this fault in my mother made me understand her, love her, even more.

We were unbreakable.

Until we were broken.

I remember the day like yesterday.

Six months ago, my mother gave me a gold necklace she'd secretly purchased during one of our recent flea market excursions. My dad said she sold all of her paintings to the parents of one of her art students to pay for it. The gift was supposed to be for my thirtieth birthday, but she said she couldn't wait.

Some days, I wonder if she knew then.

Six hours later, we went as a family to the hospital where we received the news confirming that my mother had stage-four ovarian cancer. Mom didn't say much to the doctor after that, and didn't ask any questions. Her calm acceptance of her death sentence was confusing to me, but I firmed my lips into a tight line and let her take the lead. When I glanced at my dad, I saw his face had turned pale, and I reached over to squeeze his hand.

On the drive home, it was raining. My father was in the passenger seat and my mother was driving, as she preferred to do. We were only a mile from the dirt road that led to our house. The speed limit on that road is fifty-five, although I'm not sure how fast we were going.

I remember my mom was drumming her fingers on the steering wheel, softly humming with "Let it Be" on the radio, as if we hadn't just received the most devastating news of our lives. My father sat stoically in the passenger seat, not a move, not a word. I was in the backseat, watching the rain while sobbing silently.

My dad shouted.

I looked up as an oncoming truck crossed the center line. I watched it, almost as if in slow motion, barreling toward us like a missile.

My mother screamed something to me. To this day, I don't know what she said.

The car swerved and tires squealed, followed by chaos and screams. Then blackness.

My next memory is waking up to silence. I will never, ever forget that lack of sound. I was upside down, my head on the floorboard, my legs on the seat. Dazed and confused, I scrambled up.

We were in the trees, or so it seemed. The car was wedged between two tree trunks, one large branch cracked over the hood, and another spearing in through the windshield.

I stared at the back of my parents' heads.

My dad was slumped over in the passenger seat, his forehead against the dashboard. My mother was sitting upright behind the steering wheel, her head resting against the door as if she were simply asleep.

I called her name softly, my voice small and shaking like a child's. When she didn't answer, I screamed her name.

That's when I smelled it. That metallic scent of blood.

And that's when I noticed the spray of red splattered across the driver's side of the windshield, like a painting.

Then she moaned.

Get her out of the car, was all I could think. I kicked out the glass next to me and shimmied out of the window, stumbling through the mud to the driver's side. When I finally was able to get the door open, my mother fell into my arms.

We tumbled into a ditch together, right there in the middle of the woods. The left side of her head was nothing but bloody mush.

I cradled her against my chest like a mother would a newborn baby, sobbing as I watched her take her last breath in my arms. Crying so hard I could barely see, I closed her eyelids.

The following week brought out the worst of humanity, the worst of small-town living. Gossip of my family's accident spread like wildfire.

After waking from his concussion, my father had no recollection of the entire day of the accident. It was as if his memory had been wiped clean. I had to tell him that he was now a widower. I was the only one who remembered seeing the old truck barreling toward us.

According to the police, the only skid marks on the road that day were from our car, which suggested another vehicle hadn't been involved. Basically, they implied the accident had been my mother's fault, impaired from either the multiple medications she'd been on, or the grief of hearing about her cancer, or a combination of both.

No one ever came forward to admit to their part in the accident. With each day that passed, I hated that faceless person a little more for tainting the memory of my mother.

It wasn't long until speculation began that I was covering for my "crazy" mother. No one believed my story that we were run off the road. And it was then that I—not my mother—started receiving sidelong glances in public, suggesting *I* was crazy, like my mom.

To be honest, there were times that I questioned my own sanity. Had I seen a truck cross the center line?

The weeks following my mother's death were a blur. My father was a shell of himself, barely speaking, eating, or sleeping. I didn't know this man. It was as if his soul had been ripped from his body. I didn't know how to take care of him, how to handle my own grief, how to navigate this new life without my mother.

So I painted.

Every morning and every evening, sometimes through the night, I painted. No plan, no outline, no preconceived notions. I simply grabbed my paint, sat, and began. Canvas after canvas, tear after tear, splattering paint, smearing colors, angry slashes against the white ecru background. In my mind, the paintings were nothing, meant nothing. They were simply waves of colors. The world, however, would refer to it as abstract art.

I thought of it as an escape. An ugly escape, but an escape, nonetheless.

Six weeks and hundreds of paintings later, my father died of a massive heart attack. To this day, I truly believe the man died of a broken heart.

Then the day after his funeral, I was laid off from my job at the local library.

Within a span of two months, I'd lost everything that meant anything in my life.

The following week, I jumped into the river in the middle of the night. I don't remember anything after hitting the water. My life was spared by a doctor who happened to be camping nearby with his family.

Looking back, I believe something broke in my brain during that time. Temporarily? The jury's still out on that one.

Then I found Cricket.

Driving home from the hospital the day after I was pulled from the water, a massive cricket jumped onto my windshield, drawing my attention. Beyond it, I saw a matted ball of mange and patchy fur hobbling along a clearing in the middle of the woods.

It was fate, I believe. He needed me, and I needed him.

Shortly after taking in the stray dog, I learned the large mass Cricket had on his back leg was osteosarcoma—bone cancer. The vet's best guess was that the dog had likely been dumped after the owner received the news. I emptied my savings account to have the diseased leg amputated in an effort to save the dog's life, and we've been a pair of lost, broken souls together ever since.

That was four months ago. And it's safe to say my life has taken a different path since then.

Grief manifests itself in many different ways, different for each person unlucky enough to experience it. For me, at first, it was days of not eating, drinking, or sleeping, followed by weeks of a weird dazed state. I still don't remember much of that time.

Within weeks, my grief morphed into a subtle constant of panic, anxiety, and anger coursing through my body in a vibration of waves that I didn't notice at first. All I felt was an amped-up, uncontrollable energy to do this, do that, find *something* to do—all the time. Never stop moving, planning, doing, because if I did, I'd have to face my new reality.

I became obsessed with silly things that really didn't matter. Like eating. Like calories.

After my mother's death, I lost weight . . . a lot of it. I

didn't have much to lose, but what remained was a (finally) flat stomach and skinny arms. I became obsessed with keeping this new body. It became my focus. I gave up carbs, gave up sugar, began counting calories, pre-packing my meals so that I didn't cheat.

All because *I could.* It was a false sense of control in this new world of chaos, a way to redirect my focus to something I could control.

If I didn't go to bed hungry, I didn't consider it a successful day, which was a totally screwed-up sense of achievement. And I craved that, I realized. My mother had always been the one to remind me of my worth. No more.

My weight became my fixation.

It happened slowly, so slowly. I didn't realize how skinny I'd gotten until the day I couldn't hold up my pants anymore. My face started changing. My bones stuck out a bit too much. I'd tell myself that I needed to eat more, but when I would, I'd feel so guilty that I'd run six miles an hour later.

Of course, I was constantly hungry, but to me, that meant I was doing a good job at controlling what went into my mouth.

I knew this behavior was abnormal, that my head wasn't right. But I didn't stop. Even when the migraines started, I didn't stop. It was a constant daily internal struggle, one that gripped me with bloody fingernails.

Eventually, I started not feeling well, constantly fatigued and light-headed, my body simply not getting enough calories. But instead of doing what I knew I should do—eat more—I simply pushed myself harder. Kept myself busy so I wouldn't think about it, dwell on it, feel the ickiness.

Think about anything else other than the real issue.

Exactly as I was doing on that day, in the middle of the

woods, searching for a strange man I didn't know. I became fixated on this new distraction in my life, like the calories. I had to know that he'd made it home. I had to know more about him. I couldn't let Christian go because I didn't know where it ended.

A crazy thought, isn't it?

13

I awoke with a scream, propelling myself off the pillow, my hair hanging in my face. Gasping for breath, I blinked wildly, my heart racing with fear. The room swayed, disorienting shades of black weaving in and out of my haze of sleep.

"Cricket," I croaked out, realizing he wasn't in bed with me. "Cricket!"

Ripping the covers off, I swung my legs over the side of the bed. Beads of sweat rolled between my breasts. I grabbed the bedpost as I stood, a wave of nausea washing over me. Stumbling through the room, I called his name again, my legs heavy, my brain a thick fog.

"Cricket," I called, my voice shaking with panic.

Pressing a hand against the walls, I stumbled into the living room. The cool evening breeze blew in through the windows, rustling through the bushes under the sill. The glow of a full moon streamed onto the floor, illuminating a little ball of fur, curled into a circle.

I staggered across the room and fell clumsily onto my knees. Lazily lifting his head, the dog yawned at me.

"You scared me, buddy," I said with a loud exhale. "You didn't hear me?"

Stroking his head and body, I took a few deep breaths. My gaze shifted to the windows, to the woods beyond the screen, bathed in an eerie silver light. Shadows swayed across the backyard like ghosts dancing in the breeze.

Aside from the whir of the box fan in my room, the world was silent.

I looked back at Cricket. "Okay. Don't want to sleep with me tonight, huh? That's fine. Go back to sleep, my baby."

I pushed myself off the floor, taking a moment to get my bearings. My T-shirt and panties were soaked, and my hair matted to the side of my face.

Another nightmare. They were getting worse.

I padded to the kitchen, yanked open the fridge, and downed a bottle of water. Resting the cold bottle against my chest, I leaned against the counter and stood still. A cloud drifted across the full moon, moving shadows along the kitchen.

I ran my fingers through my hair and glanced at the clock—2:03 a.m. Another night with no sleep.

On autopilot now, I began the routine of making a cup of chamomile tea with exactly one teaspoon of honey. I clicked on the stove light, reached up to the cabinet above—and froze.

A line of small purple bruises ran down the inside of my arm.

Frowning, I clicked on the overhead light, which revealed more bruises on the other arm. A few on my thigh. One on my rib cage.

What the hell?

As I ran my fingertips over my skin, I replayed the day before in my head. I didn't remember falling, or getting in another street fight, for that matter. Something deep in my gut twisted, that unsettling feeling that something wasn't right.

Forgetting the tea, I clicked off the light and made my way back to Cricket. Standing over him, I stared out the windows, fingering the pendant around my neck. The shadows curled like a finger, beckoning me to follow.

14

From my spot on the floor next to Cricket, I watched the clock tick to two thirty a.m. and to three a.m. The moment it clicked to four a.m., I pushed off the floor and headed back to the kitchen.

Four o'clock had become my acceptable time to start a pot of coffee. Not a minute earlier. Although, thanks to Christian, that morning I had to microwave instant coffee that I'd picked up at the gas station the day before. Buying a new coffeepot would have to wait until after I paid the electric bill.

After watching the pot boil, I fixed a cup, flicked on a dim light, and gathered the books I'd taken from Abram's shop earlier that day. I lowered myself to the rug, settling in cross-legged as I fanned out the books in front of the fireplace.

Cricket hobbled over, nuzzled into my hip, and after spinning four circles, snuggled as close to my thigh as he could without actually climbing into my lap. I smiled, scratching behind his ears as I studied the covers of the books. I'd searched blind, Abram too preoccupied with his buzzed customers to notice my perusal in the back of his shop. I left a note on the shelf that I'd return the books later.

I picked up a maroon leather-bound book and wiped the dust from the pentagram embossed on the cover. There was no title, only a list of seven authors—none of whom I recognized—in small script at the bottom.

Goose bumps prickled my arms as I opened the thick pages. Once white, they were now a dingy brown, crinkled and stained. Flipping through, I felt as if I'd gone back in time, the pages adorned with hand-drawn Wiccan and pagan symbols, images of demons rising from the ground, ancient deities, celestial beings floating in the clouds.

The book contained various rituals, curses, and spells, along with what appeared to be personal stories and experiences. None of which involved a black butterfly or a Celtic tree cross. I moved on to the next book, finding more of the same. And the same with the next.

After draining my coffee, I picked up what appeared to be an old leather-bound journal of sorts, wrapped tightly with a leather strap. Inside was a spiral-bound book and dozens of loose pages and index cards with handwritten notes, practically illegible. The cover read:

End of Life: A Collection of Short Stories

Inside were a mixture of both handwritten and typed pages. The handwritten stories were in barely legible script, the typed pages in manuscript format. Tucked in the back were dozens of sketches of spiders, most haphazardly drawn by someone with no talent whatsoever. At the bottom of each story and picture was a date, written in black marker, the script of the dates the same, but different than that of the stories.

A research folder for a manuscript? An anthology, maybe, or a horror novel?

Cricket shifted, startling me and sending my heart into my throat. I exhaled deeply and then took a few deep breaths to ease the drumbeat that was now my pulse. I glanced at the window, my reflection and the scene around me eerily distorted like a Picasso painting.

I picked up my mug. Remembering it was empty, I set it back down, then refocused on the notebook. I was stalling.

Why?

Swallowing the lump in my throat, I flipped the journal open to the first story, dated May fourth, nearly four months earlier, and began to read.

15

End of Life, Collection One – The Redhead

*I*t's getting warmer. I can tell by the humidity in the air, the growing number of bugs skittering along the concrete walls, moving quickly from one crack to the next.

It's been three days since I've seen the black one with the red hourglass on her back. The elusive black widow, I remember from science class years ago. Mr. Thompson even brought one into class, secured in a mason jar. The girls screamed while the boys flexed their pubescent courage by puffing out their hairless chests like wild turkeys during mating season.

I didn't scream, and sitting here now, I wonder if on some subconscious level, I knew.

She moves with less urgency than the other bugs, her long, skinny legs slowly stretching up and out as if testing the environment to ensure it's worthy of her approach.

I admire her, the fear she instantly instills in others simply by her presence. The other spiders eye her warily while retreating to the shadows to give her all the room she desires to roam. She travels alone. No need for friends or male companionship. She is a *queen among servants, and comes and goes as she pleases without restrictions.*

Without chains.

Without cuffs.

I'll bet she, a regal executioner, would never be tricked, lured into the shadows, and turned into a captive. No, she would have been the captor.

I still can't find her web, and I'm not sure where she nests. Either in the walls, or somewhere beyond the small hopper window just below the ceiling, teasing me, taunting me every single sunrise. It's the only window in the small eight-by-eight room in the cellar, the window he opens after switching out my buckets. The window that I stare at as I daydream and cry, thinking about what might have been. I can almost reach it, on my tiptoes. If only I was just a bit taller. Never thought I'd say that.

I can barely see past the shrub that grows in front of the window. It reminds me of my grandmother's. A witch shrub, she once called it. When he first brought me here, it was nothing but dead branches. Now it's orange and red, blazing colors of life as if mocking me, saying "look how beautiful and free I am."

I wonder if the black widow's web is in it. Makes sense. It's as bold as she is.

When she first started coming around, I, like the other insects in the cellar, scooted as far away from her as possible, recalling from science class that the venom of a black widow is fifteen times stronger than a rattlesnake's.

But as time went on, days bleeding into weeks, I stopped retreating. Or stopped caring, maybe.

Yesterday marked the last day of my fourth menstrual cycle in the cellar. This is how I keep count of the days I've been held captive.

Four months.

I remember being horrified when that first period started. As if being tied down at my wrists and ankles and repeatedly raped was somehow less humiliating.

I'll never forget the look on his face when he walked into the room, the beam from his flashlight stopping on the blood pooling between my spread legs.

I remember that spark in his eyes, the way his lips curved around his rotted brown teeth.

That's the day I realized he liked blood. The smell, the slickness, the taste. The look in my eyes when he lifts his face after feasting on me, the blood smeared on his lips and chin, on the tip of his nose. He loves to scare me. Like an evil child.

Sometimes I wonder if he chose me solely based on the color of my hair—deep red, like blood.

I vomited the first time he did it. Right there on the bed, I dry heaved until my stomach burned like acid. If I'd only known then what kind of fetishes he had in store for me.

They're getting worse. Toys have now been replaced with tools. What was once some sort of sadistic BDSM has now turned into a torture chamber. His pleasure is no longer derived from intercourse, but from how loud I scream. How much I bleed.

Each time he slices a bit deeper, watching me closely. Testing me. As if he's building to something.

I know this is my end. I've seen enough movies and crime shows to know that if your captor shows you his face, you're never meant to escape. I accepted that two periods ago. I often wonder what he'll do with me, or if I'll simply rot down here in the cellar where the spiders and the bedbugs will slowly dissolve me into nothing.

I let her crawl on me yesterday, the black widow.

From my seated position on the floor, my legs extended in front of me, cuffed and chained, my arms limp at my sides, also cuffed and chained, I stretched open my palm and waited, watching her draw closer and closer with interest.

I smiled as the tip of her long leg tapped my finger.

Bite me.

Poison me.

Kill me and put me out of my misery.

Bite me, *I silently begged as a single tear ran down my cheek.*

I closed the notebook, my stomach churning, wondering what kind of sick bastards wrote this kind of fiction, and what kind of people actually enjoyed reading it. Shoving the journal under another book, I vowed to never return again to that sick world, and prayed that the manuscript would never see the light of day.

With a shudder, I stood up and headed for the shower.

16

"*O*h, you have *got* to be kidding me."

Standing buck naked, my hair wrapped in a towel, I frantically searched the jewelry tree, tossing necklaces, bracelets, and rings to the side.

Cricket sauntered in, yawning, curious about the sudden outburst of emotion.

"No *way,* Cricket. No freaking way."

I stared at the mess I'd made on the dresser. The diamond stud earrings that my father had given my mother on their tenth anniversary were gone. I took a step back, my mouth agape as I tried to process the only scenario I could come up with.

There had been only one person, unsupervised, in my home in the last six months. One person who had access to every single thing I owned, including my jewelry. One person with absolutely zero respect for me or my home.

The mystery man named Christian Locke.

That son of a bitch stole my diamond earrings.

For a woman who grew up with nothing, stealing *anything* from me was like removing a finger. For better or worse, material things mattered to me. And when that thing held a memory of my parents? Hell hath no fury.

I'd let the groceries slide, the rearranging of my house, the fact that I would have to spend my entire next month's earnings on my electricity bill, thanks to Christian's demand to sleep in sixty-eight-degree air. But I wouldn't let this slide.

Not this. Not something that meant so much to me.

Furious, I grabbed my phone from the bed and glanced at the clock—8:14 a.m. I was going to be late for damn work.

I didn't hesitate while dialing, the burst of hot, angry adrenaline overcoming rational thought. Cricket left the room, bored with me now, and retreated to one of his many dog beds.

"Nine-one-one. What's your emergency?"

"Hi. This is Rory Flanagan." I stilled for a second, wondering if they remembered me. From calling in the girl in the ditch, and also breaking Becky's nose, I was becoming a regular with the local PD. "It's not an emergency, exactly," I said, my confidence wavering. "But I'd like to report a theft."

"To confirm, ma'am, you aren't in any danger, nor is anyone around you at this moment. Is this correct?"

"Yes. Uh . . . correct."

Holy shit, what am I doing? This was when the doubt crept in, coupled with instant regret and embarrassment.

"Can I get your current location, Miss Flanagan?" she asked, and I rattled off my address. "Thank you. Okay, tell me what's going on."

"A . . . a man," I stammered. "A stranger broke into my house—*lived* in my house while I was out of town. And I just discovered my diamond earrings are missing."

"Is the man there now?"

"No. He left last night after I found him."

"Did you report the break-in?"

"No."

"Did he hurt you in any way?"

"No."

"Threaten you?"

"No. Actually, he was hurt. Stranded. His ankle . . ."

Dear God, what am I doing?

"Do you know who the man was?"

"Yes. He said his name was Christian Locke."

You've lost your effing mind, Rory.

"Okay, I'm going to get you in touch with an officer to give a formal statement—"

"Oh. Wait. No. I don't want him charged with anything." *Oh my God, oh my God, oh my God.* "I just want my diamond earrings back."

The dispatcher paused. "You don't want the man who broke into your house to be charged with breaking and entering?"

My heart started to pound. "No. I just want my earrings back."

"Are you sure he took your earrings?"

My stomach dropped as I glanced at the dresser. Was I sure? I hadn't really looked around for them. I'd just freaked out and called the cops.

"N-no, I guess not. But he's the only person who's been in my house."

There was a brief pause, filled with annoyance from the other end.

"Ma'am, let me just get you in touch with an officer," she said, and I could practically hear her eye roll through the phone. "Please hold."

"Wait—"

The line went silent.

Panicking, I clicked off the phone and threw it on the

bed like a ticking bomb, as if the distance somehow erased the last sixty seconds.

Shit. Shit, shit, shit.

I paced the room, questioning my sanity. *Crazy Rory. Crazy like her mom. Crazy Gory Rory.*

I had *not* thought this through. No way did I want this attention, and I didn't want him to be arrested.

"Dammit," I muttered into my hand, staring at the phone, and it rang.

I froze, and it rang again, but I didn't move.

Two new voice mails.

"Oh my God."

I picked up the phone and sank onto the bed. Instead of listening to the voice mails of the officer calling me back about the break-in that I no longer wanted to report, I opened up the few social media apps I had on my phone, and searched for Christian for the hundredth time. The man was a phantom, a ghost, nonexistent. Nowhere on Facebook, Instagram, Google, nothing. Who doesn't have social media these days? Hell, I'd considered making Cricket his own page.

Not giving up yet, I browsed local hiking groups and blogs. The man was nowhere, unable to locate, and unable to call so I could demand my earrings back.

I looked at the clock. "Oh, dammit." I needed to get to the shop.

After slipping into a paisley midi dress and a pair of wedges, I hurried to the kitchen, refilled Cricket's food and water bowls, and knelt to tell him good-bye. My heart squeezed as he looked at me with his droopy eyes, his runny nose. His health was deteriorating.

I couldn't even think about it.

"Don't forget, buddy, you've got that fancy new doggy

door, right there." I pointed to the back door. "If you need to potty, just head that way. Not in here. No potty in here. Okay, buddy?"

He nudged against me.

Stroking his head, I smiled and then kissed his nose. "Sure you don't want to come today?"

He lowered his head back down to the bed.

"I don't blame you. Love you, buddy. Be back soon."

I grabbed my phone, my purse, and the lunch I'd packed from the fridge, and bolted out the door.

I scanned the woods as I drove, imagining what I would say if I saw Christian again, these thoughts dominating my entire drive into town. Thoughts of him.

I had to get my earrings back. Yes, I had to get them back.

I picked up the phone and made a call.

"Mornin', sweetheart. Everything okay?"

"Hey, Mr. Abram. Yes, I'm on my way in. A bit late this morning. Hey, how about a cup of coffee before work?"

"With or without Baileys?"

I smiled. "A wise man once told me coffee isn't coffee without Baileys."

"That's my girl. Where?"

"Donny's. Ten minutes."

"See you there."

Fifteen minutes later, I pulled my truck into the only open spot on the town square. Berry Springs was a buzz of activity, everyone trying to get their business done before the temperatures climbed to triple digits again.

I stepped onto the sidewalk, directly into the leashes of a

pair of goldendoodles, their oblivious owner gossiping on the phone, something about a paternity test and the captain of the football team.

After karate-chopping my way out of that mess, I waved at Mrs. Jackson, my fifth-grade math teacher, sitting in the window of Bonnie's Bouffant with curlers in her hair. The disapproving squint she gave me suggested she'd heard about my recent arrest.

Of course she had.

Outside, her husband, in starched Levi's and a pearl-snap shirt, waited patiently in one of the rocking chairs, staring at the yoga class that had taken to the grassy knoll by the fountain for morning salutations.

I glanced at my watch and picked up my speed.

The scent of fresh—not instant—coffee and bacon made my stomach growl as I stepped into Donny's Diner. Mr. Abram was seated at a booth in the back, reading the morning paper. Curious eyes followed me as I strode over the black-and-white checkered floor.

Keep your chin up, I heard my mother's voice say in my head, and jerked my shoulders back. She'd repeated those same words many times throughout my childhood, especially after the other kids started calling me Gory Rory.

"Morning, boss." I slid into the red leather seat across from Abram as he neatly folded the sports section of the paper.

"You look like shit."

"You look like a leather belt."

"Well, mornin' there, Miss Flanagan," the waitress said as she walked up holding a pot of coffee.

I greeted Mrs. Booth, bracing myself for the onslaught of questions and pity surely to follow. Pity about losing my parents, my job, and questions surrounding my involvement with finding the girl in the ditch, and with Becky Dunks Davies' new broken nose.

Born and raised in Berry Springs, Mrs. Booth was a local legend, having worked at Donny's Diner since it first opened its doors a half century earlier. The woman hadn't changed much. Her long gray hair was coiled in a bun on top of her head, pierced with the same yellow number-two pencil she took orders with every day. Wide-rimmed glasses framed a ruddy face and pink lips that matched the poly-blend dress under her white apron. Mrs. Booth knew everyone in town, their grandparents, their cousins, their dogs—and all their gossip.

"You've made quite a splash around here lately. How you doin', hon?"

"Just fine, thanks." I responded quickly, praying she wasn't going to extend her condolences about my parents for the third time.

This was exactly why I avoided going out in public.

"I'll take a refill, Mrs. Booth," Abram said, breaking the sudden tension.

"You got it. For you, Rory?"

"Just coffee."

"Comin' right up."

As the waitress sauntered away, I pulled a mini-bottle of Baileys from my purse and slid it across the table.

"Sorry I'm late. Had to run by Banshee's Brew."

Abram picked up the two-ounce bottle, unscrewed the cap, and poured it into what was left of his coffee. "You're forgiven."

Mrs. Booth delivered my coffee and topped off Abram's, jabbering about the scorching weather. She lingered, probably hoping I'd suddenly spill my guts.

Sorry, sister. Not happening.

When she left, Abram took a deep sip of his coffee. "You get your court date yet?"

I shook my head.

"Davies is coming after you—already filed charges, so I hear. Wants the book thrown at you."

"Not surprised."

"Yeah, she's that type. I can talk to the judge, if you'd like. We used to hunt together."

"No. Please. I'm going to plead guilty and take whatever comes."

"You won't get jail time, kid, don't worry. You'll get a misdemeanor, maybe a fine and community service. Hell, that's street cred around here."

I rolled my eyes, spinning my coffee cup between my fingers.

He stared at me a moment, and reading my body language correctly, changed the subject. "Saw you took some books from the shop."

"I left a note."

"Keep 'em as long as you want. Find anything about a black butterfly?"

"Nope. But some pretty creepy stuff, Abram. Where did you get them?"

He lifted a shoulder. "All over. Locals bring books in to donate for a free cigar. Some are mine, or my wife's, picked up from the discount bin in the library or garage sales. Hell, I couldn't tell you where half came from. Sorry they couldn't help you."

"It's all right. I've got a few more to go through, then I'll bring them back."

"No hurry. So, anything on the girl in the ditch?"

"Why do you assume I'd be on the forefront of that news?"

His brow cocked, his gaze shifting to the other diners still staring at me.

I rolled my eyes. "No, I haven't heard anything." Not that I would, considering I don't speak to anyone aside from my dog. "You?"

"Word on the street is that there's still no ID on her yet. Police are following up on a bunch of random anonymous tips since the report hit the news yesterday, but nothing concrete. Figure with something as heinous as that, something would link. People don't just go around sexually mutilating women with knives. Especially around here."

I shuddered. "Abram, this is not breakfast conversation."

"So you didn't invite me here to talk about that, then."

"No."

He leaned back, his eyes narrowed. "You closing up shop and leaving me?"

Surprised, I blinked. "What makes you think that?"

"There have only been two times you've asked to meet for coffee. Once, to discuss the rental agreement, and the next time, to tell me you broke a window while trying to hang one of those blasted sun catchers."

"No, this isn't anything to do with work."

"You need some money?"

I laughed. "No."

"You sure?"

"Yes."

"Let me know if you need an extension on rent. Or anything at all."

"Thanks, Abram. Really."

"I like you, Rory. Have since the moment I held your hair back while you vomited in my toilet."

"Thanks," I said with a snort.

"Spill it. What's up, young lady?"

"You were born and raised here, right?" I asked, and he nodded. "And you seem to know everyone, right?"

"I know what I need to know. What do *you* need to know? Spit it out."

"Do you know a guy named Christian Locke?"

Something flashed in the old man's eyes. "Why?"

"Do you?"

"Why?"

"We had an interesting encounter a few days ago."

The old man squinted, his lighthearted sparkle fading to loaded curiosity. "What kind of interesting encounter?"

I leaned in. "Listen. I don't want this to get out, okay? I've already . . ." I rubbed my forehead. "God, I've already made a mess of it. But the guy broke into my house—"

"*What*?"

"*Shhh.*"

"Did he touch you?"

"No. No, no, no. Nothing like that. He got hurt, hiking by himself, and needed shelter and my house was it. We had a weird encounter, nothing bad happened, and he left that minute. Anyway, now I think some things are missing from my house and, well, I just want to know . . . who is this guy?"

"He stole from you?"

"I'm not sure, but I think so."

"Did you call the cops?"

"Yeah, and I shouldn't have. I regret it. I don't want any more gossip around me. But I want to know who he is."

A moment passed as Abram stared at me, and I got the vibe that he was weighing whether to believe me or not. Finally, he grunted and looked down at his coffee.

"Christian Locke is a nobody."

"What do you mean?"

"Guy keeps to himself. A loner. He's not active in the

community, barely leaves his house. He's not one of us. No one really knows a lot about him."

"But you do." I jabbed my finger in the air. "I can see it in your eyes."

"Hearsay."

"Tell me."

"I don't spread hearsay."

I snorted, this huge lie sending me into a coughing fit.

Abram chuckled.

"Yes, you do," I croaked, then took a sip of coffee. "Tell me."

Abram slowly sipped his spiked coffee, eyeing me over the rim.

"I'll give you another Baileys," I said sweetly.

"Two."

"Fine." I reached into my purse and removed two mini-bottles from the four-pack I'd bought, then set them next to his coffee.

He winked.

"Talk, old man."

"Christian's an orphan. He was adopted by a young woman when he was a baby. A few years later, she passed, and he was left with Arnold and Anne VanCamp, who eventually adopted him. They've also recently passed, by the way."

My jaw dropped. Processing what Abram just told me, I stared at him, too many questions flooding my head.

"Hold on—did you say *VanCamp*? As in the rumored founders of Berry Springs, the multimillionaire VanCamps?"

"Yep." Abram nodded.

I blinked rapidly. "How the hell don't I know him?

Everyone knows the VanCamps. They couldn't take their dog to the vet without the town gossiping about it."

"They've been estranged a long time. He and the VanCamps had a falling out, long ago. I don't even think they consider themselves family anymore."

"Really? Why?"

"Don't know."

"Did he get any of the VanCamps' money after they passed?"

"Not a single penny. He was cut out of the will."

"Wow." I sat back. "So, they were his second adoptive family, right? Who was the woman who adopted him before the VanCamps?"

"A young widow woman named Maria Martinez. Not native to Berry Springs."

"Where did he get the last name Locke?"

"Don't know."

"And she died shortly after adopting him?"

"Yep."

"How?"

Abram's gaze met mine. "Car accident, I think."

I glanced away, taking a quick sip of my coffee. "And that's how he ended up with the VanCamps? Why them?"

"Maria, his adoptive mom, was one of the VanCamps' housekeepers. Not sure of the details, but there was no one else to take him. She didn't have family or anything."

"So this guy has had three sets of parents in his life. His real ones, his first adoptive one, and then the VanCamps." I sat back. "Does he have brothers or sisters? Any family at all?"

"Nope."

"Who were his real parents?"

Abram scratched his chin. "No clue. I don't think anyone knows. He'd been in the system since he was an infant."

"That's sad."

Abram shrugged. "Anyway, the guy lives in the woods. By himself, is the rumor, surviving on not much more than peanuts. Whatever he did, it's long forgotten, along with him. He made sure of that."

I thought of my earrings, and for just a second wondered if he'd stolen them because he needed money to pay bills. "Where does he live?"

"In the old John Stafford manor, on the other side of Summit Mountain."

"You're joking. Last I heard, that place was abandoned. In shambles."

"Like I said, peanuts."

I looked out the window at the mountain soaring in the distance, not far from my house. "Where exactly on Summit?"

Abram looked at his coffee.

"Tell me."

"I don't want you going out there."

"I won't. Just tell me."

His sharp gaze met mine. "At the end of Redemption Road."

17

*L*ater that day, I slowed my truck to a stop at the fork in the road.

To the right, the wide dirt road continued, lined with barbed-wire fencing and trimmed brush. A herd of cattle dotted the horizon, slowly emerging into the pasture from the sanctuary of the shade trees to bask in the late afternoon sun.

To the left, the dirt road narrowed, climbing upward and fading into thickly shaded woods. The sign read REDEMP-TION ROAD.

My brain told me to turn around. Forget the earrings, forget Christian. Go on with my life.

So I hung a left. The earrings were irreplaceable to me. I wanted them back, and there was only one way to make that happen.

Near the top of the mountain, the road came to an end, with a driveway leading off to the left that was marked with a private property – NO TRESPASSING sign. A mailbox was erected next to it for the only home on Redemption Road, exactly two miles west of mine.

I came to a stop, studying the driveway that seemed to disappear into the sky. Chewing my lower lip, I glanced at the clock. It was just after five in the afternoon.

I stared at the NO TRESPASSING sign and laughed at the irony. The man who broke into my house, ate all my food, drank all my wine, and stole my mother's earrings had a no trespassing sign on his property.

"Well, here goes nothing."

I turned and accelerated up the driveway, noticing the freshly laid gravel and the newly refinished wood fencing along it. Several stacks of lumber sat inside the fence, indicating someone was actively restoring it. The brush was trimmed, and although the woods were dense, they appeared maintained.

A pair of squirrels darted across the gravel. I drove up the driveway for what seemed like five minutes before suddenly, the trees broke, and the old John Stafford manor came into view.

My eyes rounded as I slowly drove forward, taking it all in.

The large square stone structure sat at the top of the mountain, resembling an old schoolhouse, as tall as the oak trees that surrounded it. Lush green vines snaked up the dark stone sides, all the way to the red-shingled roof. A brightly painted red door centered the structure, with a horizontal row of four windows above it, and two flanking on either side. Red shutters to match. There was no porch, just manicured shrubbery lining the front of the house on either side of the door.

What was once in shambles had been fully restored and well taken care of. As had the grounds, thriving green grass under massive shade trees. A free-standing wood porch swing sat under one of the trees, seemingly new and handmade, with a trio of red pillows tucked against the armrests.

A detached one-car garage sat to the side, nestled against the woods. The door was closed.

It appeared that the back of the house opened up to a larger backyard, based on the lack of trees.

The home was unique and inviting, like something out of *Southern Living* magazine. To say I was shocked was an understatement.

The driveway split, one side leading to the front door, the other continuing past the house. I wondered where that road went, but reminded myself that exploring wasn't the goal of this visit.

Get the earrings, and get out. And with that thought, I slowly pulled the truck to a stop next to the front door.

The woods were silent as I quietly closed the door. Once, twice, until the damn thing latched. A warm breeze swept past, making strands of hair that had escaped my ponytail tickle my nose. I tucked them behind my ear and smoothed the front of my dress as I crossed the small driveway. Nerves tightened my stomach.

A large rectangular stone served as the stoop at the front door, which had a large brass knocker. Lifting it, I knocked and waited.

Knocked again. Waited.

I took a step back. A sheer curtain covered the window, slowly swaying, either from air vents or a fan.

I knocked again, this time louder. The door swung open to a burst of voices, and I stumbled back.

"What?" the woman yelled over her shoulder as a pair of big brown eyes met mine.

From somewhere deep in the house, a man shouted, "The apricot jelly, woman. Where the hell is it?"

The scent of homemade bread baking met my nose—along with a hint of sawdust. Something warmed inside me. It smelled like the perfect home.

Keeping her eyes on me, the woman—mid-sixties I guessed—yelled back to the man who was shouting to her from somewhere in the back. "In the cabinet, in the exact damn spot you left it yesterday morning!"

The bells on the bottom of her gray dreadlocks jingled with the shake of her head. The woman towered over me with a tall, eye-catching figure you see in upscale fashion magazines. Hell, she looked like she could be on the cover. Her skin was the color of ebony, her flawless skin as smooth as chocolate. She wore an African-print silk muumuu over curvy hips and breasts the size of melons. Despite the ethereal aura that seemed to float around the woman, the bark that came out of her was nothing short of a foghorn. Combining that with the thick Southern drawl, I liked her instantly.

Addressing me now, she said, "The man wouldn't find his hands if you sewed them to his head."

She shot a contorted look over her shoulder that resembled something from *The Exorcist*. "You mutter one more word, Earl, and the only thing you'll be screwing is that light bulb I've asked you to replace fifteen times."

"You bought the wrong bulbs, woman!"

"They don't make lanterns anymore, you old goat. LED's all they got these days, Earl. And don't call me woman!"

"Damn hippies. All I want is apricot jelly on my damn toast . . ." The old man's voice faded to an inaudible grumble.

Curious, I glanced over her shoulder.

Bright beams of golden sunlight shot through the windows, pooling onto gleaming hardwood floors covered in Navajo rugs. The walls were exposed stone, with thick mahogany beams running throughout. A brown leather couch centered the large open space, with a few matching armchairs and a flatscreen TV on a low console. A massive fireplace stretched along the far wall. Dining room on the left, and kitchen in the back. A beautiful wood staircase led upstairs. A hum came from somewhere in the back that I recognized instantly—window air-conditioning units.

Stunning.

Everything was made of wood, intricate and hand crafted. The place was warm and welcoming. Totally opposite from the man I knew as Christian Locke.

The six-foot firecracker turned back to me with a roll of her eyes. "Stubborn bonehead won't go to the damn doctor for his arthritis. Got walnuts for knuckles, he does. Can barely open a door, let alone a jar of artificially flavored high fructose corn syrup. Anyway . . ."

She blew out a breath and waved her jeweled hand in the air to dismiss the last ten seconds. Then, as if seeing me for the first time, she tilted her head to the side.

"How can I help ya, young lady? You lost?"

I cleared my throat. "I must be at the wrong house. I'm looking for Christian Locke."

Her brows popped. "You sure?"

I smirked. "Yes, ma'am."

"Well, there's a first time for everything, I guess. You're in the right place."

"I am?"

"Yep. Name's Fatima Bradbury."

When we shook hands, a tingle ran up my arm like a weird déjà vu or something, momentarily stealing my focus.

"And that bullfrog you heard from inside is my husband, Earl," Fatima said in a strong, husky voice that suggested she wasn't unaccustomed to yelling orders. "We rent from Mr. Locke. Lived here going on seven years now. He lives down in that dreadful basement below."

Well, that made more sense.

"What's your name, dear?" She squinted at me with interest and curiosity.

"Oh, sorry. Rory Flanagan."

There was no mistaking that there was some sort of recognition from my name. I didn't think we'd met before, just as I was sure I hadn't met Christian.

She took a step back and her entire demeanor seemed to shift. The friendly warmth was gone, replaced with a wariness. "Nice to meet you, Rory Flanagan. You a friend of Christian?"

"I can say with all confidence, Mrs. Bradbury, that no, Christian and I are definitely not friends."

She didn't smile, just stared at me with an intensity that made me want to take a step back. "Why don't you come on in and tell me how y'all met. I just brewed a fresh pot of coffee."

I hesitated. "I'd love to, but I've got to get home pretty soon."

Just then, a shadow emerged from the arched doorway that led to the kitchen.

"What've we got here?"

With footsteps as subtle as a Clydesdale's, Earl hobbled across the hardwood floor in a battered pair of snakeskin cowboy boots. An American flag baseball cap with a net back balanced on the tip of his balding head. He wore a beige button-up tucked into Wranglers. An unlit cigarette hung from the corner of his lips. The man was much shorter than his hippie wife, and at least ten years older.

From their outward appearance, they were polar opposites, and I had to bite the inside of my cheek to keep from grinning.

"This here's Miss Rory Flanagan."

He looked at his wife, at me, then back to his wife. "She lost?"

"Came to see Christian." Fatima cocked a brow at her husband, verifying that Christian rarely, if ever, had visitors.

She noticed my attention flicking to the unlit cigarette in the man's mouth. "The man quit smoking ten years ago, but has yet to remove the cigarette from his lips."

"I'll remove the cigarette from my lips when you remove those godforsaken bells in your hair."

"If I do that, how will you know where your food is?"

Earl snorted. "What does she wanna see that ol' snolly-goster about?" he asked his wife, although his eyes remained on mine.

"Not sure," Fatima said, eyeing me coolly.

Suddenly feeling lower than the woman's ankle bracelet, I withstood their scrutiny. I really didn't want to get into the whole breaking and entering and stolen earrings issues, so I stayed strong and stared right back.

"The basement's around back." Fatima jerked her chin to the left. "Just take the path along the side of the house. If you need anything, just scream out."

"Scream out?"

"We'll be ready."

"Thanks?"

She grinned and winked. "Good day to you, Miss Flanagan."

Earl grunted.

I felt their gazes burning into my back as I found the footpath that led around the side of the house, which was as manicured as the front, with blooming forsythias brightening up the side. I glanced up at the second-floor windows. Someone was there, a dark silhouette watching me from the shadows behind the glass.

A chill shot up my spine.

My wedge sandal caught on a tree root. I stumbled, but I didn't break the stare. The figure was tall and lean. As I brought my hand to my eyes to shield the sun and get a better look, the figure disappeared.

Hmph.

Ignoring the knots in my stomach, I pressed on and rounded to the back of the house. The lush backyard was enclosed in a beautiful white picket fence. A large, newly constructed barn sat between a thicket of pines. Beyond the fence, the yard sloped sharply downward, fading into a field where a large man rode on horseback with two black dogs loping beside him.

Christian.

I recognized the dark hair, broad shoulders, and thick build. He and his horse were headed away from the house, toward the woods.

Determined, I turned and jogged around the house to my truck and pulled slowly away from the manor, watching as the horse and dogs disappeared into the trees. Throwing rational thought out the window, I veered to the side of the road and parked the truck, then hopped the fence and hurried into the woods, careful to keep my distance.

I spotted him through the trees, dismounting the large black horse in front of a dilapidated doublewide. He landed on one foot, favoring the other, and took a moment to get his balance. His injured ankle wasn't wrapped, or in a cast. If I had to guess, he hadn't gone to the doctor as I'd suggested.

Frowning, I crept closer, keeping one eye on the furry

mutts that were thankfully preoccupied with something in a garbage can nearby.

Christian limped to the trailer's door. He didn't knock, simply left a brown paper sack on the doorstep and lumbered back to his horse. I moved deeper behind the tree, catching a glimpse of his face as he mounted the saddle. My heart fluttered.

Pressing my back against the tree, I held my breath as he and the dogs passed by. Then I turned back to the trailer just as the door creaked open. An elderly man poked his head out, sending a menacing glare into the woods. He lifted the bag from the porch, opened it and sniffed, then disappeared inside.

A tinkling chime pulled my attention to a metal wind chime hanging from the awning. The base was a Celtic tree cross with three gemstones centered down the middle.

Red, pale green, and blue.

18

Climbing into my truck, I pulled the door closed as quietly as possible as I watched in my rearview mirror as Christian and his dogs crossed the field, returning to the manor on the hill. My mind raced as I pulled my cell phone from my pocket and stared at the pictures I'd taken of the wind chime.

It was an exact match to the image etched on the front of the pendant my mother had bought for me days before she died. Right down to the number of branches and leaves. Same color of gemstones. And on the back of the base of the chime was a butterfly—exactly like my pendant. The omen of death.

What are the odds?

I looked up from my phone, peering over my shoulder at the old mobile home through the trees. *Who was that guy?* Then I looked back at the man on horseback.

I had three options.

One, go home—undoubtedly the most sensible option.

Two, focus on my original plan to confront Christian about my earrings. Then *forget about the guy.*

Or, three, knock on trailer-home-dude's door and ask where he got a wind chime that looked exactly like the pendant hanging around my neck.

My pulse quickened, a swirling instinct festering somewhere inside me. Something was here. Something that was meant to be found. I was sure of it.

With narrowed eyes, I refocused on Christian and fired up the engine.

The old man could wait. I had a pair of earrings to get back.

Giving myself a mental thump on the chest, I pulled a U-turn in the road and hit the gas, returning to the manor. A cloud of dust enveloped me as I parked in the same spot, hopped out, and slammed the door. I glanced up at the windows as I walked around the house, searching for the mystery silhouette that had been watching me before. No luck.

By the time I reached the back of the house, I was damp with sweat. No man, no dogs, no horse.

Cracked stone steps marked a narrow staircase that led to a wood basement door underground. No window, no peephole. It reminded me of the entrance of a dungeon where evil lurks in dark shadows.

Fatima's words echoed in my head as I glanced over my shoulder. *Scream if you need anything.*

I slowly descended the stone steps. Cool air tickled my ankles. Squaring my shoulders, I took a deep inhale and knocked.

No answer.

I knocked again. Still, nothing.

Feeling daring, I tried the doorknob and found it unlocked.

A loud creak echoed through the silence as I slowly

cracked the door open. A gust of cool, damp air rushed past me, reminding me of my first job as a tour guide in Cosmic Cave. The scent of earth mingled with cedar and a fresh, piney musk that sent every sexual sensor in my body on alert.

My eyes widened as I scanned the space.

When Fatima informed me that Christian lived in the basement, I assumed she meant a fully finished apartment-like space with all the amenities.

Nope.

Christian Locke literally lived in a dark, cold stone basement.

The walls were stacked mismatched stones the color of river rock. No windows, no decor whatsoever—not a single picture or painting. The floor was stained concrete. Centered between thick support beams was a brown leather recliner and matching loveseat over a boring beige print rug. An empty beer bottle sat next to a remote on a wood end table that reminded me of the furniture upstairs. Hand-made, at first glance. A modest television sat on a table in the corner.

And that was *it.*

My gaze shifted to the only light in the room, pooling from an arched stone hallway that disappeared under the house.

I stuck my head inside. "Hello?"

I stumbled back at the sudden flurry of claws clicking against concrete. Two black Labs barreled into the living room, ears perked, tongues hanging out of their mouths. I froze, every muscle in my body locking up, bracing for the attack. Instead, I was trampled by muddy paws, wet tongues, and wagging tails. The dogs were identical, except for a small white dot on one's nose.

The moment they picked up Cricket's scent, they went wild, their noses snorting over every inch of me. Guard dogs, they were not.

"Okaaaaay." I swatted the eighty-pound fur balls away. "That's enough. Get down."

Claws dragged down my legs, leaving streaks of mud and shredding the bottom of my dress. I clenched my jaw.

Ruined. Add it to the list of things Christian Locke owes me.

"Where's the beast of this castle, huh?"

White-Dot instantly retreated down the arched stone hallway, its tail wagging. The other continued to sniff at my sandals, leaving drips of snot on my toes.

Trying to push the dog away, I stepped further inside, emboldened by the Labs' friendly greeting.

White-Dot emerged from the hallway with a whine and a shimmy, then turned and bounced back down the hall.

"He's down there, huh, Lassie?"

As I slid a rock under the basement door to ensure it didn't close behind me, a loud bang sounded from down the hallway, so I called out again. "Hello?"

Still nothing.

After a glance over my shoulder, I slowly crossed the concrete, the large dog still sniffing my foot.

A shadow passed the light from the tunnel. My eyes narrowed, I stepped to the archway.

A dark silhouette backlit by sunlit windows passed by the end of the hallway, then again, either oblivious to my presence or not caring. White-Dot followed closely on his heels, sparing me a glance and a tail wag each time he passed.

"Hello?" I called out sharply, irritated now.

He passed by again.

"*Christian*," I snapped out.

The silhouette stopped and turned toward the tunnel. A moment ticked by.

"Lost?" the deep gravelly voice finally barked out.

"Yep, I'm lost," I said, my tone laced with sarcasm. "Looking for food, shelter, a sixty-eight-degree meat locker, and anything else of yours I can take."

With a slight shake of his head, he disappeared again. White-Dot whined.

I squared my shoulders. "I'm here to get my earrings back, Christian."

No response.

With a huff, I stepped into the stone tunnel, nudging Black-Dog off my snot-soaked foot.

"I *said*, I want my earrings back, Christian." His dismissal of me angered me even more. "And you should also know, I called the cops on you."

He slowly stepped into view. His once pale, sallow skin was now sun kissed with color, his green eyes clear, his beard thicker. While the cut on his lip had been tended to and the bruising less purple, he still oozed that sexy mountain-man vibe that made me want him to toss me over his shoulder and carry me into the bedroom, calling me Jane.

He sneered at me. "You what?"

I cleared my throat. "I called the cops. On *you*."

A second passed as we stared at each other, my expression one of forced defiance, his as cold as the stone around him.

"What do you mean, you called the cops *on me*?"

"For stealing my earrings."

"What the hell are you talking about?"

"I want my earrings back."

"What earrings?"

I shifted my weight. "The ones you took. From the jewelry tree in my bedroom."

Another moment passed as he blinked at me, sheer confusion pulling at his brows. "You're crazy, woman."

"Says the man who broke into my house, went through my stuff, ate all my food, and stole my earrings. And your dogs just ruined my dress."

"I didn't steal your damn earrings."

"Where are they, then?"

"Probably next to your Burp-Me Brittany doll."

My cheeks flared with embarrassment. "Those dolls are antique."

He shook his head and disappeared, dismissing me again.

Oh, hell no.

Fuming, I strode down the tunneled hallway and stopped under the doorway, the dogs dancing at my feet.

Christian stood with his back to me, busying himself by washing dishes in a large copper sink. It matched the copper cookware hanging from the ceiling in the middle of a large stone kitchen with sweeping arched windows that over-looked the fields below.

My jaw dropped.

Chestnut-colored cabinets and counters lined the walls of the half room, recently refinished, their light color playing well against the dark stone walls. In the center was a large island beneath the hanging cookware, with a cutting board, knife, and basket of vegetables on top. In front of the windows was a small dining table that matched the cabinets. A cup of coffee and a newspaper lay next to a pair of tortoiseshell reading glasses. Much like the living room, the kitchen was barren, with only the bare necessities for survival, and immaculately clean and organized.

I noticed again—no pictures.

To my left was another stone archway that framed a room darkened with shadows, containing a large four-poster bed with a white comforter. His bedroom.

A narrow door led to the side yard. Next to it was a stack of lumber and a few tools.

"Did you make all this furniture? The cabinets?"

Christian dried a plate and slid it into the cabinet, continuing to ignore me. He stood slightly cocked, and I noticed a bulge at the bottom of his jeans that suggested his ankle was wrapped.

"You shouldn't be walking on that ankle, you know."

"How did you find out where I lived?"

"Lucky guess. Did you go to the doctor?"

"I had some old antibiotics. Working like a charm."

"You need to go to the doctor."

A painstakingly slow minute ticked by—literally, from a ticking clock somewhere in the house— as he ignored me. The dogs, bored of me now, retreated to their doggy beds under the sunlight streaming from the window.

Christian glanced over his shoulder at me. "Why are you still here?"

"I told you, I want my earrings."

He grabbed a dish towel, wiped his hands, then turned to me. "Listen—Tori, right?"

"Rory."

"I didn't steal your damn earrings."

"Well, they're gone, and you're the only person who has been inside my house."

"Maybe your girlfriend took them."

"My . . . my *what*?"

"Your girlfriend," he deadpanned.

I blinked. "What makes you think I have a girlfriend?"

"The rainbows."

My jaw dropped. "You think that because I have rainbow decor in my house that I'm *gay*?"

Shrugging, he grabbed another plate.

"You are something else, you know that? That's *asinine*."

"No, asinine is accusing someone of stealing a pair of earrings."

"Why wouldn't I think you took them? You lived in my house for days with no respect for my things. Just ask my coffeepot. Thanks for that, by the way."

"Your coffeepot was broken."

"It wasn't before I left town. You destroyed it."

"The water didn't get hot."

"Yes, it did. I had coffee the morning I left."

He sprayed bleach in the sink, then grabbed a paper towel from a rack secured to the side of a cabinet. "Lukewarm."

"So what?"

"So, that's disgusting." He began wiping down the sink.

"Oh, I'm so sorry my *free* house and all *my* stuff wasn't up to your usual standards. So, what, you got mad and destroyed it?"

"Took it apart, cleaned it out, put it back together. Still didn't work. Like your pepper grinder."

Annoyed, I crossed my arms over my chest. "That pepper grinder is an antique. It's worth fifty bucks."

"In US dollars?"

"Yes, smartass."

"Who says?"

"I say. I collect antiques, remember?" I felt my defenses creep up. "How about I ask you about your life, your house, why you do this or that. How about my first question is this: Where are my earrings?"

"I don't steal, Tori."

"*Rory.* And you stole all my food."

"Not true."

I opened my arms and dramatically looked around. "I'm sorry, have I entered another dimension where fact and fiction no longer have distinct definitions?"

"I didn't steal all your food. I left the boxes of Flab Fader prepackaged meals in the cabinet, the Lean Cuisines in your freezer, and the powdered detox shit on top of the fridge. And the black licorice." He shuddered. "I despise black licorice."

"I'll make sure to have some strawberry in stock for you next time you decide to break in."

"Cherry. And why don't you just eat raw food?"

I glanced at the veggies on his counter. "I prefer my food cooked."

"What you eat isn't considered food."

"Are you calling me fat?"

He tossed the paper towel in the trash and turned fully toward me, his eyes narrowed with intensity. "I didn't say that."

"You're telling a woman she should eat more vegetables. There's only one way to take that."

"Maybe for a woman looking for someone else to validate her own neuroses. I'm simply saying fresh, unprocessed food is healthier than packaged stuff."

"Now I'm crazy?"

"Far from it, I think, despite your obvious delusions."

He stared at me with a hard expression that I couldn't quite read. Again, I wondered if we'd somehow crossed paths before. In a previous life.

And if I'd pissed him off.

"I didn't take your earrings, Rory." He crossed his arms over his chest. "And that's the last time I'm going to say it."

"Fine. I guess I'm wasting my time here." I shook my head. "But you should know, those earrings mean a whole lot to—"

I choked up. Right there in the middle of the beast's basement, a lump formed in my throat. I was humiliated.

"Dammit." I turned to leave and the dogs jumped up, tripping me as I did my best not to run out of the room like an emotional basket case. Crazy Rory.

I was halfway down the hall when three booms vibrated the basement door. The dogs stilled, then took off like a rocket, barking ferociously.

From the other side of the door came, "Christian Locke, BSPD. Open up, please."

I froze and turned toward Christian like a ballerina on a spindle, my eyes the size of golf balls. Unbeknownst to me, he had left his position by the sink and was standing under the stone arch of the hallway, watching me. Our eyes met.

"Oh my God," I muttered pitifully.

"You weren't joking, were you. You seriously called the cops on me."

Slowly, I nodded, biting my lip.

He shook his head. "Wow."

"I . . . I am so sorry."

"Are you?" His head tilted to the side.

"I didn't mean for them to come here. I was mad and . . . God, you're an asshole, do you know that? Just tell me where my damn earrings are."

More bangs sounded on the door, making my heart start to pound.

"I think it's time for you to go, Tori." Without gracing me with a look, he strode past me, and I wanted to die.

Christian opened the door, allowing a blast of light into the dark room. At his sharp order to stand down, the dogs whimpered and sulked into the shadows.

Christian was *pissed.*

"Officer . . ." I attempted to push myself past Christian, but the man stood like a brick house, rooted to the floor. So, like a little girl, I peeked around him. "I'm Rory. I made the call about the earrings. I was wrong. I didn't mean for you to come here."

A burly officer with a handlebar mustache and ruddy cheeks looked down at me. I recognized him as one of the responding officers from the car accident six months earlier. "So you do *not* think this man stole your earrings after breaking into your home?"

"Yes. I mean no. He broke in because he was hurt and needed shelter. I know that now. I think there's just a misunderstanding."

The officer looked at Christian for a long moment, who stared right back, then he refocused on me. Studying me closely, he said, "Are you requesting I dismiss your call, Miss Flanagan?"

Embarrassed beyond words, I forced myself to maintain eye contact. "Yes."

"Okay. We'll dismiss that call. If there's nothing else, I'd like to speak to Mr. Locke alone."

Frowning, I looked at Christian. When he opened the door wide, I slipped past, making my escape, and jogged up the steps into the hot summer sun. My head dipped in embarrassment, I hurried around the corner, slammed my back against the house, and released a breath with my hand over my heart.

What have I done?

Voices carried through the still, humid air. With no shame at all, I shifted my weight and eavesdropped.

"You heard her," Christian said, his tone as cold as ice. "She was mistaken about the earrings."

"Noted. But I'd also like to talk to you about something else. Were you in the woods near Devil's Cove, three days ago?"

"Yes."

"May I ask what you were doing out there?"

"Hiking."

"Alone?"

"Yes."

"Did you happen to see anyone else while you were hiking?"

"Hunters, a couple of hikers."

"Was one a young woman, auburn hair, tall, about five-nine?"

My heart sank. The officer was talking about the girl in the ditch.

"Not that I can recall. What's this about, Officer?"

"Mr. Locke, does the name Jessie Miller mean anything to you?"

"No."

"You're sure?"

"Yes."

"Would you be willing to retrace your hike—"

"What's this about, Officer?"

"It was reported you were in the area at the time Jessie Miller was allegedly dumped into the lake. I'd like to know if you saw anything, anyone, vehicles, anything that might help us in this investigation."

"You'd like me to verify I had nothing to do with it."

"If you'd be willing to retrace your steps—"

"Miss Flanagan."

I squeaked and spun around.

"Your car's this way." Like a pissed-off mama bear, Fatima stood with her arms crossed over her chest and flames shooting from her eyes. The woman was protective of Christian. Or protective of something.

"Oh. Sorry. Thanks."

Her narrowed gaze sliced me like a thousand knives as I hurried down the footpath to my truck and jumped inside. My heart raced as I barreled down the driveway.

Jessie Miller. The girl in the ditch had been identified. And because of me, the cops knew Christian had been in the woods during the time she was reportedly murdered, and therefore was probably considered a person of interest.

As if the man needed any more reason to hate me.

Were there more reasons? I had to know.

19

*P*aintbrush in hand, I leaned back in the chair and exhaled, judging the canvas in front of me.

Thick gray clouds faded into angry slashes of blue—various shades blending together in churning chaos, marked with whitecaps and deep scores of indigo.

Mindlessly, I swept a wisp of hair from my face, transferring a dab of warm wax onto my forehead. I halfheartedly rubbed the spot, doing nothing but smearing it and causing it to crumble down my face. I didn't care. I was lost in my creation, assessing the colors, the feel.

I concentrated on the smear of brown teetering on the tip of a slash of navy. A small fishing boat on the water. It was the twenty-second time I'd painted a fishing boat in the last six months.

I pondered the boat and its place in my life from behind the small partition I'd added to the office in my shop, to shield prying eyes from the easel and canvas I'd set up in the corner. My hobby to pass the time while waiting for customers who never showed.

I'd had four human interactions that day. Four . . . in an entire eight-hour workday.

The first was my daily morning chat with Abram, where we discussed the latest news of the girl in the ditch, Jessie Miller. According to the latest headline, they'd identified Jessie by a tattoo on her lower back, given by a local artist who confirmed her identity. She was rumored to be home-schooled by a God-fearing widow who lived off the grid. Other than that, her story was still a mystery.

The second interaction was a phone call ordering a large pepperoni pizza with extra ranch. Wrong number.

The third came in the form of a lost tourist needing directions to a local bed and breakfast, while her bratty four-year-old asked me why my shop smelled like Grand-dad's breath. This question was followed by a sneeze that blasted the front of the olive-green sundress my mother had sewn for me.

The fourth and final interaction was with a fellow art shop owner I'd met while in Dallas. I called to see if she'd ever seen the image depicted on my pendant, and if she knew where it could have come from. *Nope.*

Around noon, I began my daily panic about lack of business, and in desperation, I emailed the up-and-coming Southern artist Aaliyah Buhle, inquiring about the possibility of selling her paintings in my shop. It was a stretch, but I was desperate.

And out of money.

I leaned forward again, careful not to knock over the hot wax warming at my heel, and a wave of nausea rolled over me, making my pulse spike. I exhaled loudly, doubling over in my chair. A cold, clammy sweat broke out over my body, and for a moment I thought I was going to throw up.

I couldn't do this today.

With a press of my palms to my knees, I willed myself off the chair, the room spinning around me. Squinting and holding on to the wall for support, I stumbled into the office and fumbled through the drawers, finding an old pack of peanut butter crackers stuffed in the back. My hands trembled as I ripped open the pack that I was sure was out of date. I didn't even remember putting them there.

After grabbing a bottle of water, I sank to the floor and stuffed the food in my mouth. My stomach rolled in protest, but I kept forcing the crackers down, chasing each bite with a swig of water. Ten minutes later, the shakes were gone, replaced with a headache. My arms and legs were limp like a rag doll's.

Everything was catching up to me. The grief, lack of sleep, no food, no money. It felt like a turning point.

Little did I know what was coming.

Sighing, I refocused on the painting from my spot on the floor, assessing the mess of colors. I wondered what Christian had thought of the painting in my room. He was now only the second person, aside from my mother, to see one of my paintings.

I plucked my phone from the counter and clicked it on, my last searches for Christian Locke on full display.

Facebook, nothing.

Instagram, nothing.

LinkedIn, nothing.

TikTok, nothing. That one was a stretch.

Google, nothing.

I'd even tried searching various forms of his name such as Chris Locke, Christian Lock without the *e*, Chris Lock without the *e*. I'd read every article available on Google of his adoptive family, Arnold and Anne VanCamp. Still, no mention or picture of Christian, though. I searched adoption records, criminal records, and voter registrations.

No luck.

Christian Locke didn't exist, not even in the darkest corners of the internet. Only in my every thought.

At 5:01 p.m., I flipped the OPEN sign to CLOSED and secured the locks. The sidewalks were bustling with tourists, meandering through shops before hitting happy hour at one of the bars. Not a single one looked in the Black Butterfly's direction.

Sighing, I turned from the door. If I didn't come up with a plan to save my business—or get it off the ground at all, I should say—I'd be locking that front door forever.

And then what? What would I do with my life? The thought made my stomach dip.

Then what?

My gaze shifted to the paintings for sale on the walls, none of which were mine.

Could I make a few bucks selling the paintings I had stacked in my bedroom? Maybe pay a bill or two a month? Would anyone even like them, or would I be a laughingstock?

I decided I needed a run, to stretch my legs and clear my racing thoughts before going home to stare at the walls all night, so I grabbed the gym bag from under the counter and squeezed into the bathroom next to the office. The postage-stamp-sized room had a toilet, a standing sink with a cracked mirror overhead, and a small window. I'd added a medicine cabinet for things like a toothbrush, lip gloss, and tampons—the necessities.

Kicking out of my wedges, I yanked the tie out of my

hair, and the long, boring blond strands fell over my shoulders. I removed my bracelets, rings, and hoop earrings, then tossed the handful of jewelry into the top drawer.

And froze.

Slowly, I removed every piece that I'd just tossed in, and stared down at the two diamond earrings twinkling back at me. My mother's earrings.

"Oh *no* . . ."

My words trailed off as I remembered taking a run the week before, removing my jewelry as I'd just done, and tucking the precious diamond earrings in the back of the drawer so that I wouldn't lose them. And then I totally forgot about them.

I closed my eyes and blew out a long, deep breath. Christian Locke hadn't stolen my stupid earrings.

And I had made an absolute *fool* of myself.

I braked at the tree line and squinted through the sun's last scorching rays before slinking behind the mountain. The Celtic tree wind chime swayed lazily in a breeze I didn't feel.

I glanced in the rearview mirror to ensure my covert mission hadn't been exposed. I'd driven up the opposite side of Summit Mountain, using barely there roads and trails that added a hundred new scratches to my truck, all to avoid tipping off Christian and his crazy renters of my arrival at their neighbor's house.

My *unannounced* drop-in.

I refocused on the rusty trailer home and the metal building next to it, almost as large as the trailer. I hadn't noticed the metal building from my hiding spot in the trees the day before.

My pulse quickened as I crossed over the dirt road and veered my truck onto the old man's small patch of land. I cut the engine and took a quick glance in the mirror. After my jog, I'd given myself a quick wipe-down in the bathroom before slipping back into the sundress I'd been wearing during the day. It was wrinkled and probably stinky, but it was better than my stained gym clothes.

I climbed out, scanning the front yard as I crossed it. The grass was brown and dead from the heat, but trimmed, as were the bushes and shrubbery that lined the trailer. The steps that led to the front door were swept clear of leaves and twigs. Despite the home's worn appearance, the owner took pride in their property. An old dually truck was parked under a shade tree.

With nerves bubbling inside me, I took the first step. As I raised my hand to knock, the door swung open to reveal a pair of narrowed eyes. The musty scent of an old window air-conditioning unit and freshly brewed coffee wafted out from behind him.

Instinctively, I stepped back onto the dirt.

Wearing a red T-shirt tucked into a pair of khaki overalls and worn boots on his feet, the man appeared to be in his mid-sixties, if not just past. He was tall and broad-shouldered with tanned, spotted skin and deep-set wrinkles from too much time in the sun. Thick hair, as white as snow, was combed perfectly to the side, not a strand out of place. A tattoo of a Navy ship colored his forearm.

The sharpness of his gaze on me suggested that despite his age, he still had his wits. The gun in his hand suggested he still had a brass pair between his legs.

I took another step back. "Hello, sir. My name is Rory Flanagan. I'm sorry to drop in on you like this. I just have a quick, hopefully easy question for you, if that's all right."

The old man scowled, glancing at my truck. When he realized I was alone, he slid the gun on the windowsill, out of view but not out of reach.

"I'm registered to vote, ma'am." His voice was deep and scratchy, as if it hadn't been used in a while.

I smirked. "That's great. So am I. But that's not why I'm here. I own an antiques shop in town, and I was just curious where you got that Celtic tree wind chime over there?" I nodded to the awning above the window.

Frowning, he took a step forward with a slight limp and looked at the wind chime, then refocused on me. "Why?"

I tugged the pendant from under the neckline of my sundress. "The exact image is on this pendant. Literally, exactly. A black butterfly on the back, and a Celtic tree cross on front. Same color gemstones. It's unique, and very special to me. I haven't found anything else like it—until I saw that wind chime the other day."

He stared at the pendant in my hands for a moment. "Where did you get that?"

"My mother bought it for me six months ago. She said she picked it up at a flea market." I flipped over the pendant. "Under the black butterfly, there are faded words etched in the gold. It's old, I can tell. And handmade, I believe."

"You looking to sell it?"

"No. God, no. I'm curious where it came from, is all."

"What did you say your name was again?"

"Rory. Rory Flanagan."

He glanced again at my truck, then at the wind chime. "How did you see the wind chime in the first place?"

"Oh. Sorry. I should have opened with that." I laughed, more of a nervous cackle, really. "Well, that's a funny story, actually. I was on my way to visit your neighbor, Christian Locke, and saw him delivering something to you yesterday . . ." I paused, hoping he'd tell me what that thing was. When he didn't, I continued. "I followed him, and that's when I saw the chime." I shifted my weight. "Just thought I'd ask where you got it."

He regarded me closely for another minute, then jerked

his chin toward the house up the hill. "The kid doesn't get many visitors. What brought you to the old John Stafford manor in the first place?"

"An emotional meltdown. Sir."

The corner of the man's lip curled up, a dim sparkle in his eye. "How'd the kid respond to that?"

"With about as much grace as a rabid hyena," I said. When this earned me a chuckle, I relaxed a little. "What's your name?"

"Walter Kelley."

"Pleasure to meet you, Mr. Kelley. Any reason why you're not divulging where you got that wind chime?"

"Pleasure to meet you too, Miss Flanagan. I'm sorry I can't help you. I've had that chime for ages. Don't remember where I got it."

I sighed, looking at the chime for a minute, then lifted the pendant from my chest. "Have you seen this design anywhere else? The black butterfly, specifically?"

He shook his head. "Sorry, ma'am."

"Okay. Thanks, anyway." I gave him an awkward wave as I took a step back and turned, then began making my way across the grass.

"Where you off to now?" he called out after me.

I took a few more steps before answering. "To right some wrongs," I mumbled over my shoulder.

"Good girl."

I halted at the comment, but pressed on.

Odd old man.

*a*s I shielded my eyes from the sunlight, I squinted at the large figure standing in the middle of the dirt road, blocking my path. I glanced in the rearview mirror at the trailer I'd just left, then at the silhouette in front of me, backlit by the setting sun.

Frowning, I slowed, a cloud of dust rolling up from my back tires. The figure didn't move.

As I inched closer, I noticed the thick arms crossed over his chest, his wide shoulders hugged in a thin gray T-shirt. A pair of khaki tactical pants covered a pair of narrow hips and long legs. A knife was hooked in his belt, and he had worn workman boots on his feet.

Christian.

I slowly rolled to a stop, six inches from his stomach, but he stood strong, wearing a scowl on his face I'd seen before. His natural resting face, apparently.

"What are you doing?" he asked.

I hung my head out the window. "Trying not to run you over."

"This is private property, you know." His chin jerked to one of the dozen signs that lined the road.

I looked at the signs, then back at him. "Feel free to call the cops. Pay me back."

"I don't call the cops for petty bullshit."

So he was still mad.

I cut the engine and climbed out. "Listen, I came by to say—"

"What business do you have with Mr. Kelley?"

My brows raised. "Nothing that's any business of yours."

"He lives on my land. Rents from me. His business is absolutely my business."

"Not this time." I crossed my arms over my chest, mirroring his stance.

His eyes narrowed. "I'm going to ask you to leave my property, Tori, but before that, I have two questions for you. One, why are you stalking me?"

"One, you know my name is Rory, you arrogant jackass, and two, I came to apologize."

"For calling the cops on me?"

"Yes, and for accusing you of stealing my earrings."

"I didn't steal your earrings."

"Yes, I know that now. I found them. I never meant for the cops to show up at your house—"

"And interview me about the woman you found in the woods?"

"I also wanted to make sure you know that I didn't intentionally tell the cops that you were hiking in the woods right before her body was found."

"Therefore implying I had something to do with her death."

Yep. Pissed. He was very pissed.

"I simply told them you'd been hiking, and they

matched the timeline and connected that fact to the body. I didn't link it for them . . . I want that to be clear."

He stared at me, a million words seemingly on the tip of his tongue. Foul ones, if I had to guess. Then, with a shake of his head—another dismissal of me—he turned and hopped the barbed-wire fence, favoring his injured ankle, and began crossing the field.

I blinked. *Seriously?*

"That's it?" I called out. When he ignored me and just kept walking, I jogged to the fence. "Wait. What was the second thing you wanted to ask me?"

I gripped the fence post and scrambled over, slicing my shin and the bottom of my sundress in the process. The dry grass scratched at my ankles as I took off after him, having to jog to catch up to his wide strides.

"Seriously, Christian, I'm sorry. I feel bad. It's just been a rough few . . . I don't want to feel guilty about this."

"Don't."

"Don't what?"

"Feel guilty. Life's way too short." His jaw twitched. "I forgive you. Forget it."

"Thank you."

We stopped at a structure that resembled a child's playhouse, next to the large barn that sat just below his house. Behind it was a long fenced-in run.

"What was the second thing you wanted to ask me?"

Christian opened the narrow door to the structure. Two black fur balls barreled out, tongues lolling, tails wagging. Having already been on the receiving end of Christian's dogs' welcome once, I strong-armed them.

"No jump," I warned in my best authoritative voice.

White-Dot sprang on his back legs, and Christian's voice boomed.

"T-Bone, *down.*"

The dog froze in midair at his master's command and then dropped to the ground. The other dog skidded to a stop. They were trained well—despite the horrific name.

"T-*Bone*?" I cocked a brow.

Christian picked up a stick and hurled it into the woods. "Fetch."

The dogs took off like rockets, disappearing into the thick underbrush.

"You could've used that authority when they mauled me yesterday."

"You were an intruder."

"I learned from the best. Why do you keep them locked in there all day?"

"Gonna call PETA on me now?"

I rolled my eyes.

"Coyotes. Bastards are starting to overrun the woods. I've never seen them so aggressive," he said, and I thought of my own run-in with a coyote when I found Jessie Miller's body. "And I don't keep them in there all day. Only when I'm not out here, close to them."

The dogs returned to our feet, their chests heaving and slobber flying. White-Dot had the stick in his mouth. The other dog carried a bloody groundhog.

"Ugh." I stepped back.

Christian picked up a handful of sticks and threw them into the woods. "They'll go all day."

"Note to the groundhogs."

We continued on the faded footpath that led to the barn, with Christian gathering the few twigs that littered the ground along the way, and me swatting at mosquitoes.

Frantic barks rang out from the woods.

"Tater! Hush!" Christian called out.

My mouth dropped open before a grin spread across my face. "I'm sorry, I'm sure I misheard you. Your dogs' names are *T-Bone* and *Tater*?"

"Yes, ma'am."

"As in *steak* and *potatoes*?"

"That's right."

"You named your dogs after the most cliché meal on the planet? Christian Locke, is there a sense of humor somewhere in there?"

He deadpanned, "There's nothing funny about steak and potatoes, Rory."

"Serious business, huh?"

"All grilling is serious business."

"Not at my house. Ever tried a George Foreman?"

He stiffened a second, with a break in his stride, clearly aghast at the comment.

I smirked. Christian was probably the type of guy who added hickory sticks to his three-foot, two-hundred pound charcoal grill/smoker combo while wearing grill goggles.

My gaze shifted to the dogs pummeling each other in the grass below a sapphire-blue sky dotted with big white fluffy clouds.

"I need to get Cricket a playmate."

"Get another shepherd. Good guard dogs."

"How do you know what breed he is? I can't even tell what mix he is. The vet only guessed."

"The hair. *Everywhere*."

"Oh, so you own the only two dogs on the planet that don't shed?"

"I brush them."

"Huh. Interesting."

Christian snorted and dropped the twigs in a spotless wheelbarrow parked under a tree.

"I'm going to go out on a limb here and say that you're a clean freak, Christian."

"I'm going to go out on a limb here and say you're looking for something." He paused, then repositioned the twigs in the barrow, the closest thing to nervous energy I guessed the guy experienced. "Why are you really here, Rory? Again."

"I told you. I came to apologize."

Christian straightened, looked out to the fields, and shoved his hands into his pockets as a beat passed between us. "You won't find what you're looking for here, Rory," he said softly, almost mindlessly, as if lost in thought.

Frowning, I stared at him a moment, wondering if the man was drunk again. What was he talking about?

What am I looking for?

The dogs barreled up to us again, breaking the sudden awkwardness.

"Well, I guess I'll be on my way, then."

He turned his back to me and began unlatching the locks on the barn doors.

"Before I go," I said, fisting my hands on my hips. "What was the second thing you wanted to ask me?"

He pushed open the thick wooden doors and turned to me. "I'd like to know where you got that pendant."

22

I was too awestruck to respond.

Ignoring Christian's question about the pendant, I pushed past him and stepped inside the massive barn, which was at least twenty degrees cooler than outside. Muted sunlight from a large window below the roof's peak pooled onto a concrete floor filled with furniture. Dust motes sparkled, suspended in golden rays over wood chairs, tables, chests, benches, dressers, and even a few clocks.

These weren't cookie-cutter pieces you'd see for sale in a big-box store. This furniture was rustic, perfectly imperfect polished pieces made from tree trunks, the surfaces marbled with swirls of ten different shades of brown, with knotted wood and brushed copper fixtures that made them appear as if they'd sprouted out of the forest floor.

They were unique and stunning. Just like the furniture in his house, I realized.

The left side of the barn served as a workshop with benches, rolling toolboxes, table saws, and machinery I'd never seen before. Stacks of lumber filled the corners.

Dozens of tools hung from pegboard that covered the walls. Wires dropped from the ceiling.

I spun around. "Did you make all this?"

"No. I stole it."

I rolled my eyes. "I said I was sorry about the earrings." I turned back to the room. "Seriously, these pieces are beautiful."

My focus darted from one piece to another, each more stunning than the last. I'd never seen anything like them. At a half-constructed end table, I stopped.

"Is this turquoise?" I asked and turned directly into Christian's chest. Unnerved, I stumbled back because I hadn't heard him come up behind me.

He nodded, looking down at me. "And rock from Shadow River down the hill."

"It's beautiful." I ran my fingertip along the edge of the table, lined with colorful pebbles and pops of bright blue. "You are extremely talented."

He grunted.

"Really. Everything is so unique. No two pieces are the same. Where do you get everything?"

He motioned to the front door. "The great outdoors."

"You get everything here? Locally?"

He nodded. "Most of this lumber is from the spot I cleared to build this barn."

"You built this barn?"

He nodded, surveying the slatted walls while scrubbing a hand over his mouth, mentally critiquing his work.

"And the pebbles, the rocks, and everything?"

"Yep. Otter Lake, Shadow River. Found a piece of quartz at Devil's Cove the size of a tennis ball. Everything is from my land or right around here."

"That's amazing." I stepped to the next piece. "Christian, this isn't furniture. This is *art*."

He shrugged.

"Where do you sell it?"

"I don't."

Shocked, I spun around. "What? You're kidding."

"Nope."

"Why?"

"Why what?"

"Why don't you sell it?"

He shrugged.

"Christian, these pieces . . . that table over there could go for eight hundred bucks, easy."

Looking at it, he scratched his chin.

"These are one-of-a-kind pieces. Handmade—*locally* handmade—using local resources."

And that's when the little light went off in my head. Exploded, more like.

"I want these in my shop. Yes . . ." My excitement building, I moved from one piece to the next, muttering my sales pitch. "One-of-a-kind pieces, locally sourced and made. Support your community by purchasing—"

"Hold on a minute there, Madoff."

"I'm not scamming you. I'm going to put your work—your art—out there for the world to see."

He cocked his head. "What if I don't want to sell?"

"I'd call you crazy."

"Not the first time I've heard that."

"Not surprised. You get forty percent commission. I take sixty percent of the sales price. I'll handle the stock, selling it, delivering it. All you have to do is make it."

"What shop is this?"

"The Black Butterfly, in town. On Tourist Row. I own it."

"Never heard of it."

I rolled my eyes and threw my arms into the air. "Exactly."

"Not doing well?"

I snorted, meandering through the furniture, reverently running my fingertips along each piece. "*Well* would mean it's doing anything at all."

I didn't hear Christian move, but I felt him following me, watching me as he mulled it over. When I reached the end of the barn, I turned. Christian had stopped midway, his gaze on me so intense, my stomach did a little flip. I blinked and looked away, but like a magnet, was pulled back.

"You're not fat," he said abruptly.

I blinked. A few times. "What did you just say?"

"You're not fat."

"Where the hell did that come from?"

"Yesterday. When I suggested you eat raw, unprocessed food. You thought I was implying you were fat. It bothered me."

"Is this an apology?"

"I have nothing to apologize for because I didn't say you were fat. I want to make that clear."

Squinting, I tilted my head to the side. "You're a strange man, you know that?"

"I do. Now, tell me about that pendant you wear around your neck. Where did you get it?"

My fingers trailed to my chest, as did his focus. "My mother gave it to me."

Something in his eyes darkened, and for some reason, I sensed Christian knew she was no longer with us. His eyes locked on mine, he slowly crossed the barn. My heart beat faster with each step.

"Can I see it?" he asked, and I nodded.

His fingertips swept along my collarbone, leaving a trail of heat on my skin as he lifted the pendant. With a gentle tug, he pulled me closer, inches from his face. My pulse exploded, heat soaring up my face, my body having an instantaneous physical response to his proximity and the feel of his breath on me.

The pendant seemed small in his hands, tanned and calloused from years of manual labor. His gaze lingered on the butterfly and the faded words etched underneath it.

"A friend of mine," I whispered, although I wasn't sure why I was whispering, "said a black butterfly is an omen of death. The end of something."

"Have you had many endings lately?"

"Too many." My throat closed up at my words. I pulled my gaze away from his and my pendant from his hands, stepping back for fear of revealing the weakness I felt inside. I felt small and vulnerable under his probing gaze.

What was it about this man that made me feel like he could see right through me?

"It's from the Caim," he said finally.

"The what?"

"The words on the back. It's an old Irish prayer of protection."

I looked down at the pendant. "A prayer of protection on one side, and an omen of death on the other? Makes no sense."

"Maybe you're looking at it the wrong way. Maybe the death isn't in the human form, but a representation of something dying and something else being reborn. Think of the butterfly itself—it starts out as a caterpillar, then dies in its cocoon and emerges as a butterfly. Death, transition, rebirth."

I studied the butterfly, then the tree cross. "Are you sure it's from the Caim prayer?"

"Yes."

"Do you know it?"

He dipped his chin, then recited the prayer slowly, his voice low, almost haunting. "The compassing of God and His right hand be upon my form and upon my frame. The compassing of the High King and grace of the Trinity be upon me, abiding eternally . . ."

My gaze met his.

"May the compassing of the Three shield me in my means this day, this night, from hate, from harm, from act, from ill."

The words lingered in my soul long after he'd closed his mouth.

"That's beautiful," I said softly as I stared at the etching on the back of the pendant—*from hate, from harm, from act, from ill.*

"There are many different forms of the prayer, but the meaning is all the same. It's a tradition in Celtic weddings and used to offer protection between loved ones."

"How do you know this?"

"You're not the only one who likes books."

I regarded him closely, a man of many surprises. "What does the word Caim mean?" I asked, refocusing on the pendant. "Is it Gaelic?"

"Yes. It means sanctuary. The prayer is an act intended to create a circle of protection around your loved one."

"Show me."

He stared down at me with a look that had me questioning his next move. If he were any other man, I would have thought he was about to kiss me.

A crow cawed from a nearby tree outside as we stared at each other.

Finally, he said, "Stand still."

"Yes, sir," I said in a mocking tone.

Christian didn't smile. Instead, he offered his open palm to me. When I slid my hand into his, goose bumps rippled up my arm.

With his other hand, he traced a small circle on the back of my hand with his fingertip. "Circle of love," he whispered. "Open my heart."

Then he gently placed my hand over my heart, and while trailing a fingertip around my waist, he circled my body, whispering in my ears.

"Circle of wisdom, enlighten my mind. Circle of trust, protect my path. Circle of healing . . ." He stepped in front of me, and our eyes met. "Grant me new life."

My cheeks burned with emotion, my heart beating like a jackhammer.

You won't find what you're looking for here, Rory.

Overwhelmed, I took a step back. When my heel hit a block of lumber, I lost my balance, my hands flapping in the air as my body fell backward. I hit the ground with a thud, surely cracking my tailbone, my dress hiked around my waist.

Strong arms wrapped around my body, and I smelled him. Fresh, piney musk.

I'm pretty sure he asked if I was okay, but I was too humiliated to hear a thing. Swatting him away, I scrambled up, yanking at the skirt of my dress, and forced out a laugh that did nothing but confirm how totally awkward and embarrassed I felt.

"Well, I think on that note, I should get going."

I cleared my throat and squared my shoulders. Pulling myself together, I lifted my chin.

"Thanks for hearing me out, and again, I'm sorry about the whole calling the cops and earrings thing. If you're interested in my business proposal,"—his lip quirked at this—"you can bring a few pieces by my shop tomorrow morning at nine. I'll get them priced and see how they do, and we'll go from there. Forty percent." I gave him my best bosswoman nod, as if closing a multimillion-dollar deal, and pushed past him.

Christian said nothing as I made my way through the barn, but I felt his gaze on my backside like a beam of sunlight.

At the doors, I stopped and turned. "Hey, Christian?"

He dipped his chin.

"Why did you ask about the pendant?"

"Just caught my eye is all. Good evening, Miss Flanagan."

As I walked to my truck, I was sure that would be the last time I saw Christian Locke.

23

*C*hristian never showed up the next day.

I'm embarrassed to admit how disappointed I was. And how I spent the entire day staring out the window, waiting for him like an obsessed, hormonal teenager.

Christian Locke was a mystery to me. The crude, shameless man I'd found on my couch was now a man who whispered a prayer of protection around me, soft and gentle, and sexy as hell. Despite his rugged exterior, Christian had the kind of suave swagger and confidence of a Fortune 500 CEO. He was controlling, stubborn, sure of himself, and didn't give a damn what others thought of him. Something I admired. And in maybe the most surprising twist of all, the mountain man was extremely talented.

I wanted that talent in my shop. His furniture would draw people through the doors, I was sure of it.

Christian Locke was a mystery I had to solve.

His words had rippled through my head all day. *You won't find what you're looking for here, Rory.*

What was I looking for?

Why did I feel like he knew?

Why did a small part of me feel like it was *him*?

I was becoming obsessed with Christian, his life and his story. But it was obvious this obsession was one-sided.

I closed my eyes and lifted my face to the sky, letting the last of the day's sun wash over my skin. The cemetery was still and quiet, as it always was. The only sounds were the rustle of the wind through the trees and birds chirping in the distance.

Cricket sighed on the grass beside me, deep in a dream that I assumed involved having four legs instead of three. Despite his protests, I'd taken him to work with me that day. His health seemed to be slowly deteriorating, and I was concerned the cancer had returned.

Taking a deep breath, I laid a single daisy on my mother's headstone. The bright white petals glowed against the dark stone. Around it lay dozens and dozens of wilted daisies, one for each of my visits. I decided not to remove them, even after they were dead. Instead, I allowed their beauty to fade into the earth, as had my mother.

You won't find what you're looking for here, Rory.

Emotion welled in my eyes.

"He's right, Mama. I'm lost, so lost without you." I placed my hand on the stone and bowed my head. "I miss you so, so much. I need something. I need *something*, Mama. Please help me."

Tears streamed down my face.

"I love you, Mama. I can't wait to see you again." I turned to Cricket, sniffed back the tears, and smoothed my hand over his head. "Come on, buddy."

The dog slowly rolled onto his back, his tongue lolling out of his mouth, and I smiled. Cricket was the only thing that made me happy, it seemed.

"Come on, old man, let's go home."

I helped Cricket off the ground, then stood, my knees popping in protest. Slowly, I made my way to the truck with my head bowed, feeling completely hollow inside.

24

*A*fter leaving the cemetery, I took my time, driving slowly down the long dirt road. When the sun disappeared behind the mountains, the light faded quickly, darkening the woods around me.

I wondered what Christian was doing.

The moment I pulled into my driveway, I knew something was off. Call it a sixth sense, whatever, something just didn't feel right.

Cautiously, I pulled the truck into my usual spot, cut the engine, and scanned the small yard. Shadows stretched across the grass. A cluster of dead leaves tumbled along the porch. A crow fluttered its black wings from its perch atop a pine.

"Stay here, buddy. For just a sec," I said to Cricket, and he whined. "Stay. I'll be right back, I promise."

I pulled my phone from my purse, hovered my fingers over the call numbers, and stepped out.

"*Stay*, Cricket. I'm serious."

Green vines fluttered around the pergola as I stepped onto the porch.

I paused at the front window, listening. The smell of my vanilla candles wafted through the open window. When I didn't hear anything inside, I quietly unlocked the door and pushed it open.

Beyond the dim light streaming in through the windows, the house was dark. Quiet. My heart pounded as I stepped inside.

"Hello?" I called out stupidly, as if an intruder would step out and introduce himself.

Clicking on the lights, I looked around. Everything appeared to be in its normal disarray. Nothing out of place.

Feeling neurotic now, I squared my shoulders, and with my phone in hand, walked from room to room, turning on the lights and checking every nook and cranny. After clicking on the box fans, I stepped onto the back porch. The light had faded quickly, the woods merging into one black mass in the growing darkness.

Frowning, I crossed the porch and knelt in front of a ceramic pot of elephant ear plants that I kept in front of the back window.

It had been moved. The pot was now a few inches from the brown circle on the concrete where it had previously sat for months.

My heart hammering, I surged to my feet and spun around.

The woods seemed to stare back at me, a menacing shadowy glare from the road where I'd found Jessie Miller, naked, mutilated, dead in the ditch.

A chill swept over me, and I rubbed my arms to warm them.

I looked back at the plant, then through the window to my house. Someone had been snooping around my house. I was certain of it.

But why?

After gathering my dog and things from the truck, I made a cup of tea to calm the subtle anxiety coursing through my veins. I watched the news, then clicked through an hour of mindless television. Bored, I turned it off, my gaze shifting to the books stacked next to the fireplace.

I thought of the manuscript about the redhead and the black widow spider, and wondered if anything else had been written about her. Reluctantly, I slid off the couch, picked up the leather-bound notebook, and settled onto the floor.

25

End of Life: Collection One – The Redhead (2)

his is it. The end of my life.

This will be my last note, I'm sure of it.

The infections from the cuts have grown worse, despite the pills he keeps shoving down my throat. I can't feel my left arm or my right leg anymore. The smell is almost unbearable. Despite the fact that he unchained my ankles, I can't move, even though he demands that I do. He's displeased with me now—not bored, just displeased.

I was displeased with myself long ago.

The black widow has even retreated from the cellar. The smell, combined with my screams and cries, must be too annoying, too weak for her liking.

I quit eating and drinking days ago. I'm too sick, can't keep anything down.

I'm done. I'm simply not myself anymore. As much as I don't want to die, I'm ready for whatever will end this pain.

He's coming now. I can smell him. His scent always precedes

him, lingering long after he's gone. A sweet, bitter, acrid scent that will forever be burned into my memory like acid on a rose petal.

It will be the knife with the red hilt, I'm sure of it. It's the only knife he hasn't used on me. That will be the knife that will take my life.

I welcome it.

I welcome it today.

And I pray that I come back as a black widow and poison him while he sleeps.

26

*I*n the middle of the night, I awoke on the floor, gasping for breath, certain I was drowning.

Frantic, I clawed at anything around me. A mug of cold tea tumbled onto my face from my bedside table, cutting my brow, the liquid stinging my eyes. A flurry of sheets and pillows fell onto me as I clawed the side of the bed, my chest heaving.

Cricket whimpered next to me again and again, slowly pulling me back to reality. Stilling, I blinked.

I was on the floor, next to my bed, which was now stripped bare. A shattered mug lay next to my foot. Behind me, the nightstand was on its side, the clock blinking from the floor and frozen on 1:27 a.m.

A rough tongue swept across my sweaty cheek.

"Sorry. Another bad dream," I whispered breathlessly to Cricket.

As I was digging my way out of the pillows and sheets around me, something shattered in the kitchen. Cricket popped up, his ears perked, then took off as fast as he could on his three legs, his claws scraping against the hardwood.

"No, Cricket!" I hissed, scrambling up, slipping on my own sweat.

Wild, frantic barks rang out through the house. My heart felt like it might explode as I darted into the kitchen and flicked on the light.

A drinking glass lay shattered in the middle of the floor.

I spun around. Cricket stood, his hair on end, barking at something in the middle of the room. At *nothing* in the middle of the room.

An icy chill crept over my skin as I stared at the empty space in front of the fireplace. At nothing. Keeping my eyes on the spot, I slowly crossed the room to Cricket and knelt next to him.

"*Shhh . . . Shhh*, baby."

As if a switch flipped, Cricket instantly stopped barking, his hair relaxing onto his back.

My breath was short as I stood and reached for the table lamp. And that's when I noticed a new set of bruises on my arm.

27

*J*uggling my purse, a box of knickknacks, and a brown paper sack that contained an apple and a stick of cheese I'd picked up at the gas station, I shoved my key into the lock of the Black Butterfly the next morning.

"You said nine o'clock."

Startled, I jumped, the apple tumbling out of the sack and bouncing down the stone steps. I turned, my already racing heart skipping a beat as I looked at Christian Locke.

Wearing a crisp blue button-up, a pair of khakis, and brown dress shoes, Christian leaned against a tree by the sidewalk. His dark shaggy hair was combed back, but still slightly mussed as if refusing to accept this new formal look.

Despite the obvious change in his appearance, there was a sparkle of interest in his eyes, like a hunter stalking its prey. Unlike the day before yesterday when he'd eyed me more like a termite he couldn't get away from. Something had changed in him, or had been decided, maybe. He was here to play. And I wasn't complaining.

"Uh . . ." I blinked. "I'm sorry, sir. We haven't met."

His lip quirked, practically dropping me to my knees with the simple tug of his mouth. My heart stuttered.

"You clean up nice," I said.

"I took the price tags off in the truck."

I laughed. "What's with the new look?"

"This is proper business meeting attire. Right?"

My gaze shifted over his shoulder to his truck, hauling a trailer packed with furniture that I hadn't even noticed when I parked. I'd been running late and was distracted.

"I don't think 'business meeting attire' is a thing. I think it's just business attire," I said with a grin.

"How about punctuality. Is that a thing?"

"No, no, no. *You're* late. You were supposed to be here at nine o'clock *yesterday*."

Christian pushed off the tree, swooped down, and picked up the green apple. He wiped it against his shirt, then bit into it, his gaze on mine.

I licked my lips.

Slowly, he moved along the sidewalk with a confident swagger that somehow instantly put him in control. A leaf fluttered down from the tree above him, joyfully dancing in a breeze not yet heavy with humidity. It was a beautiful morning.

He was a beautiful man.

"The ankle appears to be better," I said, nodding to his foot.

"Much." His Adam's apple bobbed as he swallowed the bite of apple. "Sorry for being a day late."

"You should know that reliability is the number one thing I look for in my vendors, Mr. Locke."

"I had higher priorities, Miss Flanagan." He took the box from my hands. "Where's Tripod?"

"*Cricket* is home. He wasn't feeling up to it today. He's . . ." I looked away.

"What?"

"He's not doing great. He's old, you know, and ever since the surgery, it just seems like his health is failing day by day."

"He's going blind."

"What?"

"I could see it in his eyes."

I snorted. "The last time you saw him, you were so drunk you wouldn't know his ass from his face," I said quite defensively.

"Take a good look at them tonight. His eyes are cloudy with little white spots. Also, they don't dilate. Your dog's going blind."

I blinked, my pulse kick-starting again with a gallop. "How do you know this?"

"I've raised eight dogs. Lost six. I know about it."

I shook my head, shaking his comment away. It was too much. "I'll see what the vet says. Anyway—"

"You need to accept that he's old and doesn't have the best quality of life, Rory."

"What the hell are you saying? That I should put him down?"

"I'm just saying you need to accept what's happening around you. His time will come, and you'll be okay with that."

"This is one *hell* of a sales pitch, Christian. First you stand me up, and now you're telling me the only thing I love —and that loves me back—is likely going to die on me soon."

"Just setting expectations."

"Well, thanks. Jesus, you really know how to kick off a gal's morning."

He reached forward and tucked a strand of hair behind my ear. "You'll be okay, Rory."

We stared at each other a moment, that spark of *something* passing between us. Our attention was pulled to a couple of gossiping forty-something power walkers in matching yoga pants.

"I heard her mother was nuts," one woman said to the other. "Never let her leave the house. Homeschooled." She snorted. "No wonder the girl got mixed up in drugs and alcohol. Had pot in her system, I heard."

The second woman nodded knowingly. "I heard she was recently seen with some boy from Berry Springs High School."

"They know who the boy is?"

"Don't think so. No arrests have been made."

"Well, they need to find this guy, and fast. Poor, poor girl. The things done to her with that knife . . . My Lord, they've got a special place in hell for whoever did it."

I turned my cheek from the gossips, muttering to him, "Don't say a word."

Christian raised a brow at me. "Oh, you mean, like, 'Here's the girl who found her. Wanna come ask her some stuff?'"

I scoffed. "Gossip in this town. It's traded like damn gold."

"Only the bad stuff. Good always gets overlooked."

I studied him for a second. "Hey, by the way, did you come by my place yesterday?"

"To steal more earrings?"

Frustrated, I rolled my eyes. "I thought you wanted to drop that."

"Why do you ask?"

"Oh, nothing. I just . . ."

"You just what?"

"I think someone was outside my house yesterday. Maybe looking in the windows. Figured you might have fallen down a ravine again," I said with a grin that he didn't return.

"Did you see anyone?"

"No." I shook my head. "It's probably nothing—"

"Your house was ridiculously easy to break into, Rory. You need new locks and a security system."

"Yeah, okay. I'll get right on that." *With all the excess funds in my checking account*, I thought but didn't verbalize.

Christian stared at me, assessing me like he always seemed to. I wanted to change the subject, mainly because I knew he was right that I should get new locks. Especially with a murderer on the loose.

"Anyway, did you bring the river stone table?" I asked.

"And a matching lamp. Finished it yesterday. That's what I was doing. I wanted to be able to give you the full set."

"You could have called, you know."

"I don't have your number."

"The Black Butterfly is listed."

The corner of his lip lifted slightly as he looked down at me. "Where should I unload?" he asked, changing the subject.

"You can loop around to the back of the building. It'll be a tight squeeze for your trailer, but we won't have to carry the furniture up these steps. The door is a little wider back there too."

"I'll meet you there."

He reached past me and opened the door, the scent of pine-fresh soap tickling my nose.

Damn that smell.

I dropped my purse and lunch on the floor and took the box from his hands. "Thanks."

"What's for lunch?" he asked, peering at the single stick of cheese in the sack.

I stepped in front of the open sack. "Normal lunch stuff."

Christian let out a little *hmph* as he looked at the sack, then back at me. An awkward moment passed.

He dipped his chin. "Okay, then. See you in a sec."

I watched him walk down the sidewalk, transfixed by the way the khakis hugged his high, tight ass. The man was drop-dead gorgeous. And suddenly nothing else mattered other than my appearance.

I dropped to my knees, frantically looking for my makeup bag. After emptying half my purse's contents on the floor, I yanked the makeup bag from the mess and darted to the bathroom for a quick fix-up. After adding a bit more mascara and lip gloss, I took a step back, surveying my reflection.

That day, I'd opted for a simple tank top, jeans, and sandals, the need to impress my nonexistent clientele no longer dictating my wardrobe choices. Frowning at myself, I repositioned my boobs, creating the illusion of cleavage the best I could.

Christian made me nervous. Made me want to impress him. And if I'm being honest, it felt good. Feeling anything other than sad or mad—or nothing at all—was a welcome relief.

The growl of his manly, vintage don't-give-a-damn truck pulled my attention. I took a deep breath and then went out the back door to see Abram approaching Christian as he climbed out of his truck. Wearing his usual newsboy cap and brown drab, the old man blew a long stream of cigar smoke in Christian's face.

Dammit.

"Morning," I said loudly, hurriedly crossing the gravel parking lot.

"This is private parking," Abram said to Christian, ignoring me and bypassing pleasantries.

"Oh, it's fine," I said, jumping in. "He's just dropping something off for the shop."

"Oh yeah? What's that?"

"Christian makes—"

"That door?" Christian asked, dismissing both Abram and the conversation.

"Yeah." I gestured to the back door I'd left standing open.

Christian disappeared to the back of his trailer.

"He makes what?" Abram asked, watching Christian with narrowed eyes.

"Furniture. He's really talented. I asked him to sell some pieces in my shop."

Unimpressed, the old man took a long drag of his morning cigar.

"Am I missing something here, Abram?"

"Probably not the only one." Without another word, he made his way back to his side of the building—without offering to help.

Frowning, I met Christian at the back of the trailer, who gave me a knowing look.

"He's possessive of you." The comment was ironic, considering the tone of his own voice.

"No." I grabbed a corner of a table. "That's just him. He comes off that way to everyone. He's the quintessential grumpy old man."

"He's possessive, Rory."

I looked over my shoulder. Abram was watching us from the window.

"Maybe just a bit protective, although I don't know why," I said as we began making our way toward the back door, me carrying one end of the table and Christian the other. "Is there something between you two that I don't know about?"

"You'll have to ask him."

"Why don't you save me some time and tell me what the deal is between you two?"

"Step," Christian said, guiding me backward. "Step."

"Thanks."

We squeezed the table through the doorway.

"Where is this going?"

"Fine. If you won't tell me, I'll ask Abram about it." I shifted, pulling the table through the short, narrow hallway. "Let's put it in the corner over there for now. I'll place it once we've got everything inside."

Thirty minutes later, I wiped my sweaty palms on my jeans and admired my new selection of one-of-a-kind furniture, locally sourced and handmade.

The pieces fit in my shop, I decided, the rustic earth tones playing up the antiques, as well as landscape art on the walls. The brass and copper fixtures reflected the wind chimes and sun catchers hanging from the ceiling. They were perfect for the Black Butterfly.

Christian and I exchanged contact information, scribbling the info on paper napkins, and then got down to business.

"Let's talk pricing," I said.

Christian shrugged. "That's your deal."

"It shouldn't be. How many hours did you put into each

piece? A lot, I'm guessing. You should have a say in the retail price—you should *want* a say."

"You're the business owner here."

I snorted. "My bank account says otherwise."

"Twenty-two hundred."

"*What*?"

"Twenty-two hundred for the dining table. Five apiece for the chairs, and a discount if they buy all together. Eight hundred for the end tables."

I blinked, staring at the table as I mumbled, "Well, that really turned around on me." I looked at him. "It's too much. No one in this Podunk town is going to pay that for furniture."

"And the lamp there, two hundred. No, three."

I laughed. "Christian, no offense, but it's too much."

"You asked me to price. Those are my prices. Let's see what kind of salesman you are."

"Saleswoman."

He snorted at this.

"Fine. I'll make you a deal. I'll price the pieces as you see fit. But if they don't sell within two weeks, I get to reduce the price to what I think will sell. Your cut remains the same—forty percent."

"Deal."

My brows popped up. "Really? Great." I rubbed my palms together. "Now, give me the specs so I know how to sell it. What kind of wood—"

The door opened, and an elderly couple wearing matching Hawaiian shirts stepped inside. Tourists.

"A good saleswoman doesn't need specs," Christian whispered into my ear. "Good day, Miss Flanagan."

"Wait. Christian, *seriously*," I hissed back. "I've never sold furniture before."

"I've got things to do."

"Wait. Where do you want me to send the money?"

"Bring it to my house."

"Christian," I whisper-shouted. "*Wait!*"

But the words faded behind his long, confident stride.

28

*A*fter a busy morning the next day, I glanced at the clock as I sped up my driveway—12:07 p.m.

Most days, I ate lunch at my desk in the shop. But that day, I wanted to check on Cricket.

I parked in my usual spot, jumped out, and jogged up the steps. The sun was searing, rays of fire shooting through the pergola. I decided I'd turn on the window unit air conditioner for the old guy.

I slid my key into the lock—but the key didn't fit.

Frowning, I took a step back, eyeing the brand-new lock and doorknob that had been installed on my front door. The knob was a long, ornate handle in beautiful brushed bronze. A teardrop flap covered the keyhole. It had an elegant antique look that matched the weathered wood of my door.

Christian.

The lock had been installed flawlessly, no scratches or marks on the wood. I noticed that a few nicks at the bottom of the door had also been touched up.

Grinning, I looked over my shoulder, waiting for him to

jump out from behind the bushes. Not that being playful was his thing.

No luck. But I knew it was him.

You need to get new locks. His comment from earlier echoed in my mind.

I refocused on the lock, realizing that I didn't have a key. Frowning, I searched the windowsill, the top of the door frame, the potted plants, and finally under the welcome mat, where a single bronze key lay in the center.

The door creaked as I pushed it open.

"Cricket?"

Nothing.

"Cricket?"

When I heard a faint shuffle, I dropped my purse in its usual spot on the floor and padded across the room. Cricket lay in a brand-new doggie bed, his tail thumping against the wood floor, a massive bone between his teeth.

"Had a little visitor today, huh?" I couldn't help but smile. "Brought you goodies?" I ruffed his ears. "Some guard dog you are."

Cricket pawed the bone, gnawing at the top, which was almost disintegrated at this point. Slobber covered his jaw and paws. He was the happiest and most lighthearted I'd ever seen him.

"I came by to check on you." I carefully lifted his face, peering into his eyes. Sure enough, they were milky and spotted, just like Christian had said. I took a deep breath. "We'll get you checked out, buddy, no big deal. Just enjoy that nasty bone for now."

I kissed his nose, then made my way to the kitchen and yanked open the fridge.

I gasped.

My once barren fridge was now packed with fresh fruit,

vegetables, lunch meat, cheeses, eggs, olives, milk, and a large jug that appeared to be filled with freshly squeezed orange juice. Tucked in the back was a stack of individually wrapped red meat—T-bones, of course—to grill on my George Foreman. Atop my fridge were four bottles of fancy French wine adorned with gold twine.

Christian. He'd replaced everything he'd eaten and drunk while crashing at my house.

"Cricket." I poked my head into the living room. "Did you see this? Did he bring all this?"

My dog gave me a thump of his tail before refocusing on his bone.

Thrilled, I opened each cabinet, now stocked with whole grain chips, rice, quinoa, beans, a jar of every nut imaginable, and a box of beef jerky—an entire box. Protein, protein, and more protein. Tucked in the back were three bags of pricey specialty coffee.

I spun around and gaped at the brand-new coffeepot tucked in the corner of my counter. The machine was shiny black with an espresso option, and more bells and whistles than my truck. Next to it was a ceramic mug with a rainbow painted on the front. A handwritten note was folded inside.

For you and your girlfriend.
Spare keys in junk drawer.

I laughed, staring down at the sharp angles of each letter. Even his handwriting was strong and manly.

Next to the coffeepot was a bright orange tracking collar and a large bottle of vision supplements for dogs. The note under it read:

Helped my dog. Give one pill twice a day.

I smelled the tiny piece of paper.

After sifting through my loot again, I grabbed a handful of grapes and padded to the bedroom to freshen up before heading back to work.

I paused at the jewelry tree on my dresser. It had been moved—again. Slightly, but definitely moved. I sifted through the jewelry, finding nothing missing, then turned and scanned the rest of the room.

My gaze landed on the painting next to the window.

I turned back to the jewelry again, my hand drifting to the pendant around my neck as I replayed our conversation from a couple of days ago.

"Why did you ask about the pendant?"

"Just caught my eye is all."

29

"Two thousand, three hundred dollars. *Cash.*"

I leaned against the door frame of Christ-
ian's barn, running my fingertip along the thick stack of bills
like an extra in a rap video.

Sunlight streaming through the loft window focused like
a spotlight on Christian, bent over a table saw, wearing only
jeans, boots, and a workman's belt—no shirt. He straightened and looked at me, slipping off the clear safety glasses
he'd been wearing before running a hand through his
shaggy dark hair. His wide shoulders flexed, his biceps
curling into muscles like bowling balls.

The butterflies. Again. Although this time with a little
heat. Okay, a *lot* of heat.

A bead of sweat dripped along his chest, snaking down a
shredded six-pack that faded into a worn pair of Levi's. Of
course he wore Levi's.

There was no questioning my attraction to the man. It
was like nothing I'd ever felt before. Visceral, down to my
bones, completely out of my control.

His clover-green eyes swept over me from head to toe,

leaving a trail of goose bumps on my skin. When he set down the tape measure he'd been using and crossed the room toward me, my pulse rate picked up.

"Good day?" he asked, grabbing a bottle of water from a nearby bench.

His chest flexed as he unscrewed the lid and chugged. My gaze shifted to a droplet of water that dripped from his chin to his chest.

"Good day is an understatement." I smiled. "My girl-friend thanks you for the food. And thank you for what you did for Cricket. And for the new locks. You didn't have to do all that."

"Someone needs to," he said with a hint of suggestion that *someone* needed to take the reins in my life.

Maybe he was right.

He glanced down at the money in my hand. "Nice stack."

"For you." I beamed, thrusting the bills toward him.

His brow cocked. "You sold some furniture?"

"I didn't sell *some*. I sold it *all*. I sold *out*, Christian."

"Knew you could do it. Come here. I'm kind of in the middle of something."

"It had nothing to do with me." I followed him through the barn to the table saw he'd been leaning over. "That's the thing. Your pieces sell themselves. I had only two customers all day, and between them, they bought every piece."

"Good." He slid on the safety glasses, then bent over the piece of lumber.

"What are you making?"

"Porch swing."

"Oh, I've always wanted one on my porch. Under the pergola."

"Step back."

I did as instructed. "By the way, I bypassed the front door and just drove down. Is that okay?"

"That's fine. I live in the basement, so that's my front door. You want to see me, that's where you go." He paused, giving me the side-eye. "You're not a fan of Fatima?"

"Oh, I am, just not a fan of her twenty questions. She's protective of you, and this place. It's extremely obvious."

"They've rented from me for years."

"They're a hilarious couple. Like Fred and Ethel. You know them well?"

"Nope. Step back further."

He didn't like talking about Fatima and Earl. *Why?*

The saw whirred to life, slicing through the lumber. The fresh smell of sawdust filled the air.

"Okay, come back," he said as he clicked off the saw. "Continue—about the furniture."

Not about Fatima and Earl. Got it.

"So, because the customers were so impressed with your furniture, they spent time browsing my shop and ended up buying a full set of china, a wall clock, two paintings, and almost every piece of jewelry I had. I'm going to have to plan another trip to restock ASAP."

The corner of his mouth lifted at my excitement. "Glad to hear it."

"No, I don't think you understand. Because of your furniture, I had the best day in sales since I opened the shop—tenfold."

He dipped his chin, a touch of pride in his eyes, so subtle that if I hadn't been tuned in to every twitch of the man, I wouldn't have noticed.

"And here's your cut." I waved the cash that he still hadn't taken from my hands. "Two thousand, three hundred smackaroos. Confession: I offered ten percent off for the second customer if they paid in cash. The woman had a brand new Louis Vuitton and more gold around her neck than Mister T. And the guy—"

Christian straightened and slid the glasses to the top of his head. "Hang on a sec. Did you just say Mister T?"

"Yeah. You know, the wrestler? B.A. Baracus from *The A-Team*? That show from the eighties."

"No, I know him as Clubber Lang in the 1982 third installment of *Rocky*, and excuse me while I adjust the raging boner that just popped in my pants."

I grinned. "Didn't know you had a thing for boxers."

"I have a thing for women who know anything about the eighties."

"Well, you'll be happy to know I have a drawer full of scrunchies and own a pair of high-waisted stone-washed denim, and a spandex exercise onesie."

"With matching headband and slouch socks?"

"Hot pink from head to toe, baby."

"Sold." He grinned, looking me over. "How do you know about this stuff? You look barely old enough to drink."

"My mom, dad, and I used to watch *A-Team* reruns almost every night. My dad loved anything involving former soldiers and special forces. He served in the Army before I was born. And my mom loved anything he did. And I loved Dirk Benedict. He was my first crush. I'm well beyond twenty-one—was that supposed to be a compliment, Christian?"

"It was actually your second from me."

"What was the first, because all I can remember—"

"That you're not fat."

"Ah yes, the world's most backhanded compliment. You're not fat, but you're not skinny."

"Not fat means you're skinny."

"I will no longer be skinny after eating all the food you stocked in my kitchen."

"Everything is healthy and good for you. Raw. Nourishing."

My eyes slowly narrowed. "Wait a second . . . did you stock my kitchen because you felt guilty about eating all my food, or because you think I need to eat more?"

"Both."

My brows rose at his curtness.

"One thing about me, Miss Flanagan, is that you're always going to get a straight answer. You don't want to hear it, don't ask. You're too skinny, Rory. Your body needs more nourishment."

"Yeah, well, I've had a rough few months."

"You're not the only one. Time to accept it and move on."

"Move *on*? Move on from losing my *family*?"

"Move on to your new life. Accept it, keep moving. Grab me that hand square over there."

"What's a hand square?" I snapped, looking in the direction he'd jerked his chin.

"Looks like a metal ruler. Triangle."

I found the tool and handed it to him.

"What I'm saying, Rory, is shit changes, constantly. You've got to adjust, adapt, and grow. Accept it."

I opened my mouth to fire off one of the dozen vile responses I had on the tip of my tongue, then remembered what Abram had told me. I wasn't the only one in this conversation who had endured great loss—and abandonment, for that matter.

"Now," Christian said, focusing on the piece of lumber he was measuring, "what were you saying about the second shopper?"

"I don't like you assessing me, Christian."

"Someone needs to."

"Stop saying that. And you need to work on your delivery. Your people skills, if you will."

"Noted." He grabbed a pencil and marked the wood. "And that's enough of that for now. Tell me about the second shopper."

"Are you going to quit analyzing me?"

"Are you going to stop being so damn sensitive?"

"I'm not—" I stopped, inhaling deeply. I didn't used to be sensitive. "Yes."

"Then, yes. Second shopper . . ."

I blew out a breath—and let it go. "All right. As I said, I offered Mrs. T and her husband ten percent off if they paid in cash. They bought everything the first couple didn't . . . and ordered more." A wicked smile crossed my face.

The hand square tumbled to the ground. "Ordered more?"

I nodded. "Yep. They requested custom pieces for a new house they're building on Otter Lake. They want you to come in and measure rooms and everything."

"Whoa, whoa, whoa." He straightened. "Just a second. I don't work for anyone besides myself."

"You work for me now."

"That's up for debate at this point."

"Relax, Emily Dickinson, I didn't commit you. I just told them I'd reach out to you and see what you thought."

"Why Emily Dickinson?"

"You know, the poet. The most reclusive celebrity in history. Never left the house, spoke to people through holes in the walls—*terrible* communication skills."

"So you're calling me a hermit. Look who's assessing who now."

"And who's being sensitive."

He cocked a brow.

"I'm calling you someone who's in dire need of human interaction, Christian. And you can start by accepting this job with the super-rich lake-house people. What do you think?"

"I think no." He pushed past me.

"Oh, come on." I followed him to the far wall, covered in tools. "Consider it, at least. Don't you want to profit from doing something you love?"

"I don't answer to other people." He selected a tool and returned to the table saw.

"Maybe you should. Maybe this is your calling. You could even create a website."

He snorted. "I'd rather swallow glass."

"I could create one for you." My eyes lit with an epiphany. "I could create my own—I never thought of that! Your furniture could be the feature. Special orders, free shipping. I even could include a 'suggested items' of my antiques that would pair with each piece of furniture. Oh my God, this is what I need. I mean, this is what you need. You have a talent. Do something with it."

He set down his tool and turned fully toward me. "Why don't you say that in the mirror, Rory?"

"What?"

"That painting in your bedroom, by the window. Why isn't it up on the wall in your shop?"

Heat rose up my neck. "I . . . it's not . . . it's not any good."

"It's exquisite, eye-catching, and it's unique. It's of Devil's Cove, right? The water and the cliff."

I looked down, wanting to crawl out of my skin. "Yes. It's of the lake during a storm."

"And an angel."

Frowning, I looked up. "What?"

"The angel. Above the water."

"What angel?"

His brows arched. "Are you joking? The angel above the water," he said slowly as if addressing a toddler. "The same angel you have in every one of those paintings you have stacked in that room."

"What are you talking about? You went through my paintings?"

He stared at me a moment, a slight look of disbelief in his eyes. "Rory, in your paintings, there is the outline of an angel hidden in the colors. In *every single one*."

"No, there isn't."

He shook his head. "Wow. Dude. You've got some things to work through. Take a look at your paintings when you get home. There's an angel hidden in every one."

The angel in the storm. His words from our first meeting replayed in my mind.

Frowning, I shook my head. There was no way he was right.

"They're beautiful paintings, Rory. Really."

"They're a mess. I paint when I can't sleep."

"Why can't you sleep?"

"Nightmares." I waved my hand, dismissing the confession I was surprised I'd shared. "Anyway, they're not professional at all."

"Hey." He lightly grabbed my chin and lifted my face to his. "They're beautiful. I don't lie."

I jerked out of his hold.

"What material do you use? It's not paint, right?"

"No. It's wax—beeswax. I create the base image in wax, and sometimes paint on top of it once it's dried. It's called encaustic painting." I heaved out a breath. "I can't believe you went through all my stuff, Christian. Did you go through everything?"

His lips curled into a devilish smirk with a flash of blinding-white teeth. It took me a second, but I finally read that playful look in those eyes—and I died a little inside of embarrassment.

"What's his name?" he asked, unsuccessfully trying to hide his grin.

"Whose name?" I barked out defensively.

"*His* name."

"Oh. My. God." I jabbed my fingers through my hair and turned my back to him, embarrassment scorching my cheeks. "You are such an asshole, you know that?"

"Asshole, huh?"

"No! Jesus, no. God, I *hate* you. Why the hell did you go through my bathroom?"

"I was looking for pain meds. Promise. What's the name, Rory?"

I closed my eyes and shook my head. "Daggins."

"As in *Dildo* Daggins?" Christian's unexpected burst of laughter sent a trio of birds scattering from a nearby tree. Hysterical, he doubled over, grabbing the barn door for support.

"Okay. All right." I nodded sarcastically. "Glad I could entertain you. Thanks, you *ass.*"

He finally straightened, dramatically wiping his eyes. "I'll never look at *Lord of the Rings* the same. Seriously, though, was that the biggest they had?"

"Don't question a woman's toys, okay? To each their own. Got it?"

He lifted his palms in surrender. "Got it."

"I really hate you."

"No, you don't. Okay. All right, all right, all right." He

took a deep breath, gathering himself. "Tell me how you got into encaustic painting."

"Are you going to make fun of anything else you snooped through?"

"No. There's no topping Dildo Daggins."

I slapped his arm, and he laughed.

"Tell me about encaustic. How long have you been doing it?"

"Since I was little."

"Why?"

"My mom taught art. And I got into it."

"Why wax?"

"Well, to be blunt, we were too poor for paint materials, so we'd buy used candles from garage sales for pennies, melt them down with crayons, and—bada-bing, bada-boom —poor man's paint."

"That's resourceful."

"That's my parents."

Christian's gaze trailed over me as if he were seeing me in a new light.

Eager to change the subject, I waved the cash at him. "Whether you agree to chat with the lake-house couple or not, you made a nice chunk of change today, and so did I. I hope you'll consider selling more items in my shop." I gestured behind him. "You've got plenty of stock."

"Three conditions."

"Shoot."

"One, you keep that cash to pay your utility bill next month."

"No—"

"Two, I set the prices for each piece. And no more discounts—for cash, gold, an eighteen-inch vibrator, I don't care. No more discounts. The furniture will sell itself."

"That's why you didn't bother telling me about the pieces before you left, isn't it?"

"Yes. They're quality, unique, and they tell a story; your customers will see what they want to see in them. People are drawn to the flaws. They connect with them. No discounts, let the pieces speak for themselves."

"What's the third thing?"

"You hang that picture on the wall in your shop. The angel in the storm—the cliff painting of the angel above the water."

"No. No *way*. I'm not going to try to sell that thing."

"I didn't say to sell it. Just put it on the wall. That's it."

I chewed my lower lip. The thought of anyone seeing my paintings made my skin itch.

"Those are my three conditions. Take it or leave it, Rory, right now."

I sucked in a breath and turned away, scrunching my face as I looked down at the money in my hands. With a deep breath, I turned back and squared my shoulders. "Deal."

"Good." He glanced at the clock. "Grab that paper bag over there. I'll meet you out front. We'll talk about the website."

I grabbed the bag and stepped outside into the sweltering heat. My heart was beating fast, my body riddled with nerves from the deal I'd just made with Christian Locke.

Putting my painting up for display felt wrong, like baring my ugly soul and forcing others to look at the mess of it. It felt like an intense invasion of privacy.

Regardless, I needed money. I needed Christian's furniture in my shop. And if displaying my painting would help pay next month's bills, I'd do it.

Because I had no other options.

30

Gripping a large grocery bag in one hand and a six-pack in the other, Christian stepped out of the barn. He'd pulled on a simple white undershirt that clung to his body like glue. The man was an Adonis.

As we fell into step together, I asked, "How's the ankle?"

"Nearly healed."

"You should have gone to the doctor. I still can't believe you walked home that night. I would have driven you."

We rounded the barn where a side-by-side all-terrain vehicle sat parked in the shade. Beyond it, the massive black horse I'd seen Christian on two days before grazed in a small fenced pasture.

T-Bone and Tater shot out of the woods, tails wagging, spit flying from open jaws. Christian turned on a spigot, filling a large silver bowl. The dogs beelined to the fresh, cold water.

The horse took interest in the commotion, meandering its way to the fence line.

"That is one huge horse."

"Don't worry. We're not taking her."

"I can ride."

He glanced over his shoulder, one brow cocked. "For some reason, I don't doubt it, but I don't feel like saddling her up right now. Too hot and too much to carry. Not you—to be clear." He lifted the drinks in his hands.

"Where are we going?" I asked.

"On an errand."

"Out here?"

"Yep." Christian secured the drinks in the trunk of the side-by-side and took the bag from my hands.

The horse snorted from the fence, eager to join us.

"Do you keep her penned in there all day?"

He laughed. "No, I don't leave her in there all day. She wouldn't stay anyway. She roams. She's a free spirit. Can't lock that up."

Christian stroked the horse's nose as she snuggled against him. He was gentle with her, and soft, which was surprising.

Whining, T-Bone and Tater circled his boots with their tails wagging, ready to go on an adventure.

I regarded him closely. He was in his element. At peace. That pain deep in his soul had faded. Christian loved nature and animals, I realized. And they love him back.

"What's her name?" I asked.

"Ishka."

"That's beautiful."

"It's Gaelic. They spell it u-i-s-c-e. Hop in."

"What does it mean?" I slid into the passenger seat of the side-by-side.

Christian lowered himself behind the driver's seat. "Water." His eyes flashed with something that sent a shiver of awareness up my spine.

"Why water?"

"She's drawn to it." He stared at me. "I found her wading in it years ago. She'd been dumped. She loves the water. If she doesn't come when I call, I know that's where she is. The water calls to her."

I understood that.

"Where does this Celtic interest you have come from? The Celtic prayer you seemed to know by heart, naming your horse Ishka . . ."

With a violent jerk, the ATV shot backward.

"Not sure."

Christian shoved the gear into drive and we descended down the hill.

I wondered what had set him off about that question, and then it hit me. Christian knew very little about his roots, other than his last name was Locke, a traditional Irish surname. Maybe in desperation to find his heritage, he'd studied the culture.

It was a sad thought, so I changed the subject as we entered the deep shade of the woods, a much-needed reprieve from the sun.

"How long have you lived here?"

"Twenty-two years," he said as he steered us up a narrow path that had been cleared of underbrush.

"You were the one who renovated it, then?"

He nodded. "Piece by piece, over two years."

"What do you do for work?"

"I don't."

"You don't work?" I scoffed. "Is there a money tree around here that I missed?"

"I own a few rental houses in town—bought them cheap and fixed them up. My house is paid for, the Bradburys pay me rent, my tenants pay me rent, and that pays to keep me living."

"And spending your days doing what you love, which, thanks to me, is now going to make you a lot of money." I winked.

Christian shrugged again. He was a simple man. Food, water, a roof over his head was enough for him. Just like my mom and dad, and I wanted to know more.

"College?"

"Military. Served five years before leaving and using my active-duty pay to buy my first rental house. The rest is history. Now your turn, Rory. College?"

I shifted. "No college for me."

"You regret this?"

"I'd say that's accurate. I always kind of felt like I missed out on that part of life."

"What kept you from going?"

"My folks didn't have the money, and I didn't want to go into debt for a degree when I had absolutely no idea what I wanted to be. The community college didn't offer a degree in tying fishing knots, so I was out of luck."

"Fishing knots?"

"Yep." No one could tie a Rapala like me. It's the only thing I was really good at. I mean *really* good at.

"That's kind of hot."

"BA-Baracas-boner hot?"

"Close."

"Well, tell that to the eleven scars I have on my fingertips."

"The sacrifice."

"For the perfect knot, yes. My dad would take me fishing almost every Sunday, in a little boat he'd saved months for. Years of tying knots, a lifetime of memories."

Christian squinted as if lost in thought for a moment. I wondered if he had any memories of his real family at all.

"They didn't offer an art degree?" he asked.

I shrugged. "My mom taught art classes. That was her thing."

"Yours now."

I stilled, blinking. Had I ever considered teaching art? Was I even good enough?

"What happened?" he asked quietly.

My hand drifted to the pendant, and he glanced over, not missing the touch. "Mom died in a car accident. Dad of a heart attack. The six-month anniversary of my mom's passing is tomorrow."

"I'm sorry."

I gripped the pendant and took a deep breath. Changing the subject, I asked, "Where are we going?"

"My neighbor's. I believe you two have met."

"Walter Kelley."

Christian grunted.

"What are we delivering to him?"

"Stuff."

I rolled my eyes, twisted in the seat, and yanked the brown paper bag from the back.

"Hey."

Ignoring Christian, I unfolded the top and peered inside.

A vine of ripe tomatoes and three green apples were thoughtfully arranged atop a plastic container filled with some sort of casserole. A pack of beef jerky—the same kind he got me—was tucked against the side.

I looked at him. "This is food."

"Nothing gets past you."

"You're delivering Walter Kelley food? What, are you a modern-day Robin Hood? He's too *skinny* for your liking?"

Christian grinned at my mocking tone.

"The old man has rented that piece of land from me for eight years. When he first moved in, I noticed a food-service van visited him every day. A kind of local Meals-On-Wheels for elderly folks on fixed income. Soon after, the deliveries stopped. Turns out the old man refused their charity, and they finally just stopped trying."

"Why'd he refuse free food?"

"Pride is my guess. The old man never leaves his house. He's got a small garden out back, and that's about it. I started delivering excess fruits and vegetables I'd pick up from the farmer's market, and then Fatima's leftovers here and there."

"Fatima brings you her leftovers?"

"Leaves them on my doorstep."

"And you do the same for Walter. Paying it forward."

Christian shrugged.

"How long has this been going on?"

"Seven years."

"Seven years? No kidding?"

"I don't really kid that much."

"What's his story?"

"No idea."

"You've been delivering food for the guy for seven years and don't know a thing about him?"

"He never invites me inside, which is fine with me. I've never even met the old man."

"What? But you're his landlord. How have you never met him?"

"One day there was a letter in my mailbox from him, asking if he could rent the land from me. I asked around about him, did a background check, and that was that. I've only seen a blurry picture of his driver's license and his silhouette through the trees."

"That doesn't sound like a responsible vetting process."

"The old man is a Navy veteran, and settled here after getting transferred to a base nearby decades ago. Widowed for about as long. No criminal record. And it's not like I was using the space anyway. He stays out of my way and takes care of the land, and that's good enough for me."

"And you feed him."

Christian huffed. "What he'll eat. For the first few weeks after I started delivering food, I'd step on what he deemed unacceptable in my previous delivery." A grin tugged at his lips. "The bastard would throw out what he didn't like, right where he knew I walked when I came by."

I laughed.

"No more radishes, cilantro, bananas, any casserole that doesn't involve some sort of meat, or anything pumpkin— which makes the holidays interesting. He hates pumpkins. Can even detect the spice."

"Yet you adapted and continued to deliver."

"Don't want to deal with the body of a starved old man on my land."

I regarded him skeptically. "I think there's more than that. I think you like the guy."

"Never met him."

"But you know him. Right down to his aversion to pumpkins."

"I want to know what *you* know about him. Why did you go by his place the other day?"

"To ask him something."

Christian glowered at me. "New condition."

"To what?"

"Me working for you. No secrets."

"This coming from the most guarded man I've ever met in my life."

"Had many men in your life?"

"You met Daggins, right?"

"That doesn't mean you don't have a boyfriend."

"That's exactly what that means, Christian. What about you? Girlfriend?"

"No."

"Ever been married?"

"No."

"Why?"

"I can't measure up to the Dagginses of the world."

"That was funny. Nice work."

"Thanks."

"Answer the question."

"I've had a few women."

I rolled my wrist, urging him along.

"I'm not very romantic."

"I don't believe that."

"Why?"

Because of the way my panties got soaked while you circled me in the barn whispering a prayer of protection in my ears.

"You're too thoughtful not to be romantic. Installing new locks on my door, replacing my food, helping my dog. It's in there. Not every woman's definition of romance is candle-lit dinners and roses. Sometimes it's just being there. I'll bet if you put the same amount of effort into romance as you do making furniture, you'd be the next Don Juan."

He shook his head, giving me an exasperated look. "Every man's ultimate life goal."

"Try it sometime."

"How about you try answering the question about why you went to see Walter?"

"Fine. I asked him about the wind chime that hangs from his awning. You ever noticed it?"

"I'm curious why *you* noticed it."

"It's the exact design of the pendant my mother gave me." I lifted the necklace from between my breasts. "I just asked him if he remembered where he got it."

"What did he say?"

"Not much. Didn't remember where or when he got it."

"Why are you trying to track down the origin of that pendant, Rory?"

"My life changed drastically the day my mother gave this necklace to me. Loss after loss after loss. It was her last gift to me. I just feel connected to it, like there's a deeper meaning of it in my life. I want to know how it came to be. I guess that's the antique-lover in me." I looked at him. "I answered your question, now you answer mine. Why are you so interested in it? I've seen you sneaking peeks at it since the first time we met."

"The first time we met," he repeated, his gaze on the trees ahead.

"Yeah. When I found you drunk and naked in my house. You stared at it."

"It just caught my eye is all."

"So you've said."

"And that's that."

"And that's that?" I rolled my eyes. "If Christian says *that's that*, then that *is* that."

We emerged from the tree line onto the rolling hill that led to Walter's trailer. I noticed the rutted pathway made from Christian's four-wheeler.

"Do you deliver food to him every day?"

"Pretty much."

"Yep." I nodded. "I think there's a heart in there somewhere, Christian, underneath all that armor you wear."

"Interesting observation coming from you."

"What's that supposed to mean?"

"What's under your armor, Miss Flanagan?"

"Nothing." I looked away. "Simply . . . nothing." Looking back at him, I asked, "What's under yours?"

"Scars."

31

"*N*ow, let's talk about this website." Christian slid into the driver's seat after leaving the food at Walter's doorstep.

As he reversed out of Walter's yard, I glanced back at the trailer. A shadow moved by the window. The curtain fluttered, then fell back in place.

"What do you have in mind?" he asked.

"Nothing too complex. Just a simple website, one page maybe, luring people to the shop."

We picked up the path through the woods. The sun was quickly fading, the shadows growing darker among the trees. The air was cooling.

"You don't want to sell products online?"

"I don't have the capacity to do that yet. I need to get my business off the ground first, get people inside my shop. Drive awareness."

"Have you done any marketing?"

"No." I looked down, a bit embarrassed. "The business just kind of fell into my lap, and I haven't really been in the right headspace, I guess."

"No time like the present."

"Exactly. That's why I'd like to feature you on the front page—"

"No."

"No?"

"No. I don't want my name or face featured anywhere."

"Why?"

"I just don't. I . . ." He shrugged.

"You're a hermit, as we've established. A behind-the-scenes kind of guy. I get it. Okay, fine, no mention of you, but your furniture is going to be the main feature. That's not negotiable, Christian."

He shifted uncomfortably in the seat.

"Listen, I'm not asking you to commit to back-stock inventory, or to be a partner or anything. As long as I have your furniture in the shop, I'm going to feature it. Yes?"

He dipped his chin in the closest thing to an agreement I was going to get. It was then that I realized that Christian not only had scars under his armor, he also had some aggressive commitment issues.

Of course he did.

"I've got a few mahogany bookends that would go with a lot of things in your shop—especially that painting you're going to hang." He slid me the side-eye.

"Hang on, you had me at bookends."

"I've only made four sets. Kind of happened organically when I had a few pieces of lumber and river rock left over. One pair has a turquoise pattern in the middle, earthy and bright, like your painting."

Bright.

Never in a million years would I have referred to my cliff painting as bright. I thought of the angel he swears is hidden in the strokes of color. It would be the first thing I checked when I got home.

"I love the idea of bookends, and I don't see many in the shops around here. You could make matching pieces to go with a chair or end table, or whatever." I gasped with an idea. "What about ashtrays? Do you do ashtrays?"

"Got a few of those."

"Oh my God, give them to me. I could advertise them in Abram's cigar shop. It would lure people over to me, help get them into my shop."

"On that note, I have some cigar boxes too."

My mouth dropped open, and I pressed my palms together to beg. "Please?"

His lips twitched as he looked at me. "They're yours."

"Done."

A shot of excitement, of hope, zipped through me, and I realized it had been a long time since I'd felt that.

"Just remember, I price them."

He sighed. "Yes, I remember."

The man didn't seem like he was hard up for cash, but I knew as well as anyone the financial struggles that went on behind closed doors. And if I could help him out, great. He was certainly helping me.

We emerged from the tree line into Christian's backyard. Atop the hill sat the manor, a bright orange glow from the sunset reflecting off the stone walls. A dark figure stood in a second-story window, the same that had been watching me the day before—and was watching me again now.

"Does someone else live in your house? With Fatima and Earl?"

"Jay."

"Who's that?"

"Fatima and Earl's grandson. Senior in high school."

"Why does he live with them?"

"Not sure. About a year ago, Fatima asked if it was okay if he moved in with them. I said yes, and he's been here ever since. Got the vibe there was some sort of family issue with his folks."

"And you didn't ask what that issue was?"

"Not my business."

"Do you know anything about the people who have been living above you for years, Christian?"

"I know the boy's been getting in some trouble recently. Sent home from school for fighting. Arrested for disorderly conduct a few months back. Got in a fight outside the Git 'N Split not long ago. Kid's a handful, I'm guessing."

"How do you know this?"

"Looked him up."

I glanced at the window as we pulled up to the barn, feeling the same uneasiness as when I first saw him in the window.

"I've got a few things I can load into your truck now if you want," Christian said, pulling my attention from the window.

"That would be great."

"Pull your truck to the barn doors. I'll get you packed up."

I glanced at the house again. The figure was gone.

Christian spent the next twenty minutes packing the cab of my Ford, while I perused his barn like the Black Friday sale at Nordstrom's. I tagged several pieces, laying my claim and demanding more to be made. This was met with grunts and nods and not much else. I'd take that.

A lamp in each hand, I stepped out of the barn. Stars were beginning to twinkle in the darkening sky as Christian secured an end table in the back of the truck.

"No more room in the passenger seat," he said as I reached for the driver's door. "We'll secure it back here."

I stepped to the tailgate and turned to assess the placement. Two hands gripped my waist and I was suddenly hoisted into the air. I yelped as I pulled my knees up, planting my feet on the bed of the truck, but remaining in a squat. His hands stayed on my waist and I cringed, knowing he was feeling my bones.

His grip tightened around me, and I wasn't sure why. I scooted out of his hold and crab-walked forward, my skirt trailing behind me. "I don't have far to drive. They'll be fine."

After securing the lamps, I turned to find Christian staring at my knobby knees. I yanked my skirt down my legs and avoided eye contact as I made my way back to the tailgate.

Christian grabbed me. Pulling me with a possessive, protective yank, he lifted me down like a feather. My breasts brushed over his chest, and I inhaled the scent that was him.

Breath escaped me as my sandals hit the ground, and failed to return when I noticed those green eyes were locked on mine. My heart skipped a beat.

"Rory," he said softly, and my grip tightened on his shoulders.

We stared at each other, and I was sure he could hear my heart pounding against my rib cage. His gaze shifted again to my lips. I closed my eyes, parted my lips, and leaned into him.

His hands dropped like lead weight from my waist. My eyes popped open as Christian looked away and stepped back, away from me.

I was speechless—*humiliated*—frozen to the ground, staring at the side of his face like a fucking idiot.

He stood still and rigid, angled away from me as he stared at a spot on the ground. His jaw was clenched, his shoulders tight, his hands deep in his pockets.

I gaped at him, unable to form a single word. *Say something. Make me feel like less of a total moron.*

But he didn't. Apparently, I wasn't worth that.

Completely mortified, I climbed into my truck and slammed the door. A part of me was expecting him to chase after me, but of course he didn't.

The engine roared to life. I shoved into reverse and turned the truck around, then peeled out with the furniture shifting and tumbling in the back, leaving a cloud of dust in my wake.

I dared a glance in the rearview mirror as I barreled down the driveway.

Christian was gone.

32

*H*ours later, I watched the darkness fade to a bleak, muted gray. A depressing dawn. I flexed my fingers, my arm numb underneath my pillow, my hip aching from lying on my side for hours without moving.

Or sleeping.

Scattered across the floor were my paintings, all of which contained the outline of an angel somewhere in the colors. Christian was right.

I didn't know what it meant. All I knew was that I couldn't get out of bed.

Maybe it was the fact that it was the six-month anniversary of losing my mom. Maybe it was finally acknowledging the weak shell of a woman I'd turned into, desperate for a kiss from someone who wanted nothing to do with me.

What a fool I was.

I expected to cry that day, but I didn't.

I expected thoughts of the last moments with my mother to plague me, memories of the wreckage, the blood, the last breath in my arms. The memory of her hand in mine as the warmth left her skin.

There was none of that.

On the six-month anniversary of my mother's death, I didn't cry, and I didn't reminisce. I just . . . didn't.

I hadn't lied when I told Christian there was nothing behind my armor. Since losing my family, my soul had been replaced by a dark, empty space. An emptiness that I'd never felt more than on that day.

Cricket nudged my shoulder from his spot on the pillow next to me.

"I'm here, buddy," I whispered, but I didn't move.

Cricket nudged me again. And again.

Slowly, I rolled over, squeezing my eyes shut at the dizziness that came with it. "Okay," I whispered, stroking his long white nose. "You're right. Let's get out of bed."

He whined excitedly and dropped out of bed, clawing his way to the door. Needing to pee, apparently.

"Buddy, I don't know why you won't use the doggy door," I grumbled as I pushed myself up, feeling a squeeze between my temples. The beginning of another damn migraine.

Cricket returned and barked at me, impatient with my sloth-like speed.

"Okay, okay. I just . . ." I ripped off the sheet, the early morning air cooling my sweaty skin. "Hang on."

The dog wriggling at my feet, I padded into the bathroom, turned the ice-cold water to blast, and stared at my reflection. My too-large eyes drooped above puffy bags of dark circles. My skin was pale and sallow, the only spot of color was the massive zit on my cheekbone that decided to make its debut sometime over the night. My boring blond hair was matted and flat, stuck to the side of my face. The gray nightshirt, speckled with sweat spots, had slipped off my bony shoulder.

I ran my fingertip along the tiny bruises over my collarbone.

Shaking my head in disgust, I splashed cold water over my face, allowing the droplets to run down my arms and neck. After wiping my face, I scraped my hair into a ponytail and stepped into the living room.

As I'd suspected from the dim light in my bedroom, the sky was blanketed by clouds. A thin fog floated above the ground, snaking through the trees. The morning was cooler than the day before, hinting at storms to come.

A large black crow perched on the windowsill, twisting its head toward me. He flapped his wings and dipped away, disappearing into the fog.

I opened the door for Cricket, then padded to the kitchen and set the coffee to brew.

My thoughts drifted to Christian, and the humiliation of throwing myself at him and being brutally denied. The single shred of pride I'd been clinging to with bloody fingertips was gone.

With that one idiotic move, I'd ruined the only thing that had taken my mind off death in the last six months. The only thing that had given me a shot of excitement. Made me happy, if only for a few fleeting moments.

I'd screwed it all up because I thought Christian Locke was about to kiss me.

Yeah, *right.* Me.

Gory Rory, Plain Jane, whose Friday night consisted of a box of Franzia and a tattered book. Me, the woman with no parents and a hole in her heart as deep and dark as the ocean.

Me, the Nothing Woman.

Tears burned, and despite my trying to sniff them away, they fell.

"Dammit." My lip quivering, I pushed off the counter. Without waiting for the brew to finish, I yanked down a mug, filled it to the rim, and strode into the bathroom.

Just get to work, I thought. *Do something productive.* But my thoughts were overridden by the weakness in my body.

I turned the water to ice cold, stripped out of my sleep shirt, and yanked the rubber band from my hair.

Numb inside, I stared at myself in the mirror—at my ugly, boring, nothing self. Tangled strands of hair fell like frizzy strings over my barely there breasts. My arms hung like twigs next to my body, limp and pale in the dim light.

Who was this woman? I didn't know, but I *hated* her.

I turned off the water and got back into bed.

I didn't get out of bed again that day.
Or the next.
Or the next.

My eyes fluttered open. I was dreaming. Aren't I?

The stale stench of vomit and urine forced its way through the haze of my brain.

I scrunched my face as pain from the migraine speared through my forehead. I felt the sweat of my body, the wetness of the sheets around me.

The smell. God, the smell.

It was dark. So dark.

I heard a sharp whine in the distance.

Cricket's face appeared behind my eyelids like an apparition that I could quite grasp.

Another whine came, and I forced my eyes open.

A black mass glided past the foot of my bed, disappearing into the dark corner of my room.

He's here, I thought. *He's finally come to take me.*

And with that, I closed my eyes and faded away again.

a bright light flashed behind my eyelids. Heinous screams pierced my consciousness, followed by desperate yelps and excited squeals.

My eyes shot open, the terrifying sounds from outside my door propelling me forward. Although I couldn't process anything in the thickness of sleep, I knew something was very wrong.

Dizzy, I forced myself out of bed, the world around me slowly taking shape as I scrambled across the floor, naked.

It was night. A storm raged outside. Pulses of light flashed through the room, followed by cracks of thunder that rattled my windows.

More screams.

A shout.

I must be dreaming. I'm in the middle of a nightmare.

But that terrible sound kept me moving.

It wasn't until I stumbled over Cricket's empty dog bed that I realized what the pained screams were from. Panic seized me.

I fumbled with the locks on the back door, my fingers

not able to squeeze hard enough. It was like one of those dreams where you're trying to run from the monster but your legs are like Jell-O.

Finally, the lock turned, and I threw myself out of the door, sending it popping on its hinges.

Lightning slashed through the sky, illuminated the horrific scene unfolding in my backyard. A coyote was dragging Cricket into the woods while another attacked his neck.

The scream that came from me was guttural, whipped away by the wind as I lunged across the deck.

There was a voice. Someone screamed at me. A man, but I couldn't make out the words. My focus was solely on Cricket.

More screams came before two blasts made me stumble to a stop. Suddenly everything was quiet.

I looked down at the river of blood seeping through my toes. Bile rose into my throat as I lunged forward again, stumbling through the rain.

Another flash of lightning illuminated a figure standing at the tree line next to three lumps on the ground. Two coyotes with bullet holes through the chest. Christian holding a pistol.

And Cricket at his feet.

36

*E*verything was white . . . white light, white walls, white sheets . . . as I emerged from somewhere between this world and the next.

My veins were cold. I registered a soreness in the crease of my arm and fumbled for it, finding a thin tube running along my skin. As awareness seeped in, goose bumps prickled over my body. Cool air entered my nose as I inhaled, expanding my lungs.

I'm alive.

Confused, I focused on the hypnotic beeping of the machines around me. Pulling in another breath, I noted a smell, the fresh scent of a summer rain mingling with musky pine.

I was in the past, four months ago, being pulled from the churning black water, my naked body curled against his chest as he brought me to shore.

Although it wasn't the past. It was him—*again.*

That smell.

Him.

My eyes opened to the silhouette of a man leaning over me.

Him.

Where am I?

"Where's Cricket?" I croaked out.

"He'll be okay." The deep voice from somewhere near me sounded distorted, as if I were underwater.

"It's my fault," I mumbled. "I didn't let him out for days. He used the doggy door. I didn't know, I didn't know . . ."

"Rest. He'll be okay."

I closed my eyes.

He'll be okay.

Thunder rumbled softly in the distance. The storm was moving out.

*T*he next time I woke, it was to darkness. My body felt heavy and weak, like a wet blanket.

A dim light pooled in from the doorway, the only light in the room. An oscillating fan whirred somewhere beyond the shadows. Rain ticked on the windows. I blinked, staring up at a ceiling that wasn't my own.

Him.

Turning my head, I made out a shadowy figure, leaning against the wall. At his feet was the outline of a dog, bandaged and sleeping soundly in a doggy bed I didn't recognize.

Cricket.

I was in Christian's house. I recognized the clean simplicity of the white bedding and the four-poster bed.

"It was you," I whispered.

Silent and unmoving, Christian stared at me.

"You were the one who saved me that day. When I jumped from the cliff at Devil's Cove, four months ago. It was you. I remember now. That's why I feel like I know you.

That's why I know that smell—your scent. Everything about you. You saved me from the water that day. Pulled me to shore where the doctor and his family were."

Christian pushed away from the wall and disappeared from the light. Heavy footfalls crossed the hardwood floor. A faint click sounded, and the room was illuminated in a soft golden glow.

Hands slid under my armpits. In one smooth movement, he pulled me up into a seated position against stacked pillows. There was no coddling, no *how are you doing?* When he spoke, his tone was stern and clipped.

"Eat." He lifted a wood tray from the end table, his expression tight, his eyes swollen and ringed with shadows from hours of no sleep.

Still trying to get my bearings, I stared up at the man who had saved my life once before, and now again.

"Eat," he said again, setting the tray onto my lap.

I looked down at a bowl of steaming soup, three whole-grain muffins, a bottle of water, and a cup of hot tea. Then I looked back at him, his arms crossed over his chest, watching me closely as one might their prisoner.

"Christian, I—"

"Eat, Rory. Please eat." There was a desperation in his voice now, a touch of panic as if he couldn't handle an argument with me at that moment.

I picked up the spoon and did as I was told. Christian stood stoically at my side, watching every bite, every move, every shift of my body.

Slowly, warmth began to fill my belly, a clarity chasing away the daze.

When I finished the last bite of muffin, I looked up. He dipped his chin in approval, moved the tray from my lap, and returned to the wall.

I closed my eyes and rested my head against the pillows.

"It's enough," he said finally.

I turned my head. "What's enough?"

"The grieving. It's enough."

I lifted my head, my jaw slack at his insensitivity. "Cricket was attacked—"

"It's *enough*," he said so harshly, his words rattled the windows and my bones. "Your mother, your father, your dog, your job. It's enough. It's time to accept what happened, pick up the pieces of your life, and use them to create one that's worth living."

I blinked, his words washing over me with the subtlety of a nuclear bomb.

"The doctor said you were less than a day from dying of dehydration. *Dehydration*, Rory." His eyes flared with anger. "You're also extremely malnourished."

"Christian, you don't get to tell me how to grieve—"

"Oh yes I fucking do," he bellowed. "Someone has to. You've been slowly killing yourself. *Everyone* dies, Rory. It's the circle of life. It's inevitable. There's a time to grieve, and a time to accept and move on. This didn't happen *to* you, Rory. You aren't the victim you've labeled yourself to be. It's life. Shit happens. You're in control of your reaction to that shit. And it's time you stand the fuck up."

I was too stunned, too shocked to respond.

"Rory, *hear* me. It's. Enough." Frowning, he pushed off the wall and took the tray. "Now, sleep."

My gaze shifted to Cricket.

"I'm watching over him. You sleep." With that, Christian turned and disappeared from the room.

Closing my eyes, I listened to the sound of the water hitting the sink, the dishes sliding into the rack. When he came back to the room and turned off the lamp, I peeked at him through my lashes.

He disappeared back into the shadows, returning to his perch against the wall, to watch over me while I slept.

"Christian," I whispered into the darkness.

"No, Rory. Sleep."

38

*M*y eyes flickered open to sunlight warming my face, soft sheets and a fluffy comforter tangled around my body. The room smelled like flowers. A flannel robe lay at the foot of the bed.

Peering at me curiously, a bluebird perched for a few seconds on the sill of the open window. Beyond him, the early light of dawn cast slanted shadows across the hill, the grass sparkling with morning dew.

The storm was gone.

I took a deep breath, then suddenly stilled. I could feel him in the room. Clutching the blanket to my neck, I rolled over.

Christian stood in the doorway. "Morning."

"Morning," I whispered, then focused on the empty doggy bed against the wall.

"He's sleeping in the kitchen, next to the windows. He likes the sunlight."

Wearing a fitted T-shirt, a pair of wrinkled jersey pants that clung to every curve below his torso, and bare feet, he crossed the room and repositioned the comforter around my body. His expression was softer than the night before, his demeanor less rigid.

"How are you feeling?" he asked, his voice low.

"Okay."

"I asked, how are you feeling?"

I sighed. "Weak. A bit of a headache."

He nodded. "Let's get you up, get you some breakfast and some water."

"I'm not hungry."

"You'll eat." That flash of anger I'd seen the night before lit his face again. "I know you like the fresh air, so I kept the windows open last night. I don't have much that will fit you, and assuming you don't want to wear my boxer briefs, I have a robe for you here."

He nodded to the red flannel as he rounded the bed.

I lifted myself to a seated position. "How long have I slept?"

"Most of yesterday and all night last night."

"Wow." I shook my head. "I feel like I haven't slept at all."

"You can go back to bed after you eat."

"How's Cricket?"

"He's stitched up and recovering. Being taken care of, twenty-four/seven. I've got him. Don't worry."

The gruesome images of the bloodbath in the rain flashed through my head. Christian had shot and killed the coyotes.

"What were you doing at my house?"

His jaw flexed. "Checking on you. I went by your shop to deliver more furniture. Abram said you hadn't been to work in a few days."

Realization hit me, and I shot up in a panic. "Oh my God, Christian. Your furniture. In the back of my truck . . . the rain."

"I'll make more."

"Oh my God, it's all ruined, isn't it? I wasn't even think-ing. I am so, so sorry." Blinking hard, I couldn't fight the tears that filled my eyes.

"Not right now, Rory. It's okay. It's no big deal. Now it's time for breakfast." He extended his hands, the emotion in his eyes making my heart skip a beat.

"I am so embarrassed. I'm so sorry."

"Not right now." He wiggled his fingers. "Breakfast first."

I slid one hand into his, then the other, and with surprising gentleness, Christian lifted me to my feet.

"Got it?"

I nodded, noticing for the first time I was in a hospital gown. Christian had taken me to the hospital after I'd passed out.

"Oh my God, everyone knows, don't they?"

He picked up the robe from the end of the bed and draped it over my shoulders while I slid my arms inside.

Christian frowned at me. *Not right now. Breakfast first.* He didn't need to say it.

With a strong, steady hand on my back, he guided me into the kitchen, where a chair was waiting for me at the table in the breakfast nook. A cup of coffee sat on the table, its steam swirling in the fresh morning breeze from the windows.

Under the table lay Cricket.

I stepped out of Christian's hold, hurried across the room, and fell to my knees. Cricket opened his eyes, the sunlight sparkling in his eyes. His tail thumped against the floor, and I swear the dog smiled. A tear slid down my cheek.

"He's been worried about you. Had to spend the night right next to your bed." Christian knelt beside me. "Guy's a trouper. He's on antibiotics and pain pills. Just needs to rest now."

I ran my fingertip next to the bandage around his neck. "What happened?"

"His throat was severed a half inch from his carotid artery. He's very, very lucky. His neck is going to be sore for a while, though." Christian stroked the dog's head, earning himself another thump of Cricket's tail.

"Where did you take him?"

Christian paused, shifting his weight. "I had Fatima take him to the emergency vet clinic while I took you to the ER."

I stared at him, the weight of this comment not lost on me. Christian had swallowed his pride and asked for help, so that he wouldn't have to leave my side, even after I was admitted to the hospital.

"Thank you."

He stood. "Up, now." He helped me stand and guided me back to the table, where I sat and gripped my coffee. He turned his attention to the stove.

The kitchen smelled like coffee and fresh-cut grass. It was a beautiful morning.

Christian added butter to a cast-iron skillet, then cracked several eggs into a bowl. I watched him move about the kitchen, preparing breakfast. Although his movements were graceful with the certainty of someone who'd cooked many a meal, his thoughts were a million miles away, a thin line of concentration running across his forehead, his lips pressed into a tight line.

We didn't speak while he cooked. I slowly sipped my coffee, allowing the buzz of the caffeine to bring me back to life.

Ten minutes later, my coffee was replaced by ice water

and a dinner plate overflowing with scrambled eggs, fresh fruit, and multi-grain toast.

"Breakfast." He stepped back, assessing my reaction.

"For a marching band?"

"For you." His brows lifted as if daring me to argue. "Eat."

"Where's your plate?"

"I already ate."

Christian filled a mug with coffee and slid into the seat across from me. A pair of reading glasses sat on the daily newspaper.

"I'll eat."

"Will you?" He sipped his coffee—black—eyeing me over the rim.

"Yes. You don't have to watch me."

"Can I not sit in my kitchen and read the newspaper?"

I narrowed my eyes, then dug into my breakfast.

Christian slid on the round tortoiseshell reading glasses —and damn if they didn't make him even sexier. Flipping open the newspaper, he settled in.

I sat in silence. I could tell Christian was making a concerted effort not to look at me. To give me some space, a bit of privacy. But there was no mistaking that the man was also ensuring that I consumed every morsel of food.

So I did. With gusto. Once I was finished, I pushed the empty plate away and leaned back in the chair.

"Done." When he peered at me over the top of his glasses, I grinned at the move that reminded me of my dad. "How old are you?"

"Old enough to wear reading glasses."

"Seriously."

"Thirty-nine."

I tilted my head to the side, regarding him. "I would've gone with forty-five."

His brow cocked. He slowly folded the paper and set it down, then took off his glasses and leaned forward, steepling his hands on the table. "And I would have guessed you were at least half your age."

"By the tone of that comment, I'm guessing you're not meaning it to be a compliment."

"You're at least twenty pounds lighter than when I pulled you out of the lake four months ago—and you were skinny then. You're not healthy, Rory. You've allowed your body to suffer as a result of your grieving, which, ironically, has only made your grieving worse because you don't feel well all the time. Hell, Rory." He sat back. "I'll bet half your mental state right now is simply a result of not nourishing your body."

I didn't speak, didn't argue. I needed to hear it. I knew I did.

"You've heard of hangry?" he asked. "You're way beyond that. Your brain is literally suffering and making you crazy because you're not nourishing it enough. The nightmares you told me about? Doc said no question it's related. He explained to me that when someone is malnourished, their breathing and heart rate slows. And sleeping decreases both even more, meaning sleep becomes a serious risk. You were *dying* in your bed. Three days, Rory. Three days you didn't eat or drink a drop of water."

I looked down, feeling so raw and exposed. This was it. My dirty, flawed soul, lying right there on the table for Christian to see. Emotions swirled inside me.

"And the little bruises on your body?" he said, and I looked at my arm, then at him. "The doctor said those are from malnutrition as well."

"He did?"

"Yes. Bump into the slightest thing—hell, just rub something the wrong way—and it'll bruise." He took a deep breath. "You've been slowly spiraling out of control."

"Yeah, I can see that, Christian," I snapped, my tone laced with irritation. Embarrassment.

It didn't faze him. He was here to set me straight, and nothing was going to stand in the man's way.

"Last night—the last few days—was it for you. It was your breaking point, the devil's final test. But you're here and you can decide the next step. Do you want to be happy?"

"Yes." I narrowed my eyes, grinding my teeth. "*Yes*, Christian."

"Good. It starts today, then. The first thing you're going to do is rethink how you eat. Eat more, eat healthy. You have control over this, Rory."

Control. That resonated with me. *That* felt good.

"Your focus now is to take care of yourself. The doctor recommended a list of local counselors and psychiatrists. We can filter through them and make appointments." He lifted the coffee to his lips. "Next, we need to—"

I held up a hand. "Just a *minute*, Christian."

His hand froze in midair at my tone.

"You have saved my life. Twice. And I thank you for that. And I *am* listening to you. I hear you. But I won't sit here and be treated and spoken to like I'm a child, or like I'm totally and completely helpless. I'm strong"—my voice cracked—"somewhere, deep down. My mom, my best friend, my hero, she had depression issues, I know that now, but she was strong. A strong woman. Fearless. I *am* my mother's daughter." My chin quivered as I pulled back my shoulders.

"Good." He dipped his chin, pleased with the fight coming out of me. "Let's make her proud, then."

The words hit me like a freight train.

Make her proud. Those three words changed my life.

And then the flood of tears came.

"Goddammit." I buried my face in my hands, unable to control the sobs now spurting out of me.

Christian rounded the table, wrapped his arms around me, and pulled me to the floor, into his lap.

"I'm so embarrassed." I cried into his chest, fisting his T-shirt. "I'm not this person," I whispered to myself, to him, to the universe. "This isn't *me.*"

"Then let's get you back."

39

"*W*hat do you think?" Christian asked me later that day.

I kicked up my heels in the standalone porch swing. "It's beautiful."

The sun felt good against my skin. It was that time of morning when the humidity actually feels good, right before it becomes unbearable. Christian had suggested a short walk after breakfast, although I think he just wanted to gauge my strength.

So, in nothing but Christian's smallest T-shirt, a pair of his tightest running shorts, and socks, I made my way down the hill with Christian at my side. I'd been wearing nothing but my necklace when Christian had taken me to the hospital, wrapped in a towel he kept in his truck.

Ishka was out of her pen, grazing next to the barn, where Christian had been working on the porch swing. T-Bone and Tater were in their pen, and if I had to guess, it was because the attack on Cricket was still too raw. It was horrific, apparently affecting even the manliest of men.

Christian had disposed of the furniture I'd allowed to

ruin in the rain while I ruined in bed. He'd replaced the stock with a few more pieces, this time packed in the back of my truck padded with multiple blankets and a tarp, if needed.

He never said another word about the furniture. I didn't have the energy to apologize again.

I tilted my head back to take in the sapphire-blue sky, fluffy white clouds floating slowly by. Christian was watching me closely.

"Do you believe in bad luck?" I asked.

"No." He stepped over to Ishka and stroked her head.

I reached up to touch the pendant. "I can't help but think there's a link between this pendant and everything going on, around me, in my life all of a sudden. My mom and dad dying, then finding the girl in the ditch, and then running into you, which leads me to your hermit neighbor who has the exact same symbols on a wind chime." I jabbed a finger at him. "And you've got some weird interest in it too, don't think I don't notice. Sometimes I feel like it's the only reason you're keeping me around."

"The necklace?"

"Am I wrong?"

He cocked his head. "It is a beautiful necklace."

I rolled my eyes.

He winked, then became serious again, his natural demeanor. "Are you saying you think Walter has something to do with the murdered girl?"

"I think Walter has something to do with this damn pendant, but I can't pin it down. I don't see how he would have known my mom, and he doesn't know where he got the wind chime. Just seems like a bunch of weird coincidences."

"That old man wouldn't hurt a fly."

"I'm not arguing that." Thinking it through, I chewed on my lower lip. "What about Jay?"

"Jay?" Christian's brow cocked. "As in the Jay who lives above me, the Bradburys' grandson?"

"Yeah. I know it's weird. But . . ." I blew out a breath. "The way he looks at me, he's watched me both times I've been here. Closely, from the windows. And someone's been to my house, I'm sure of it. I don't know . . . I just have a weird feeling about the guy. And we heard those women talking the other day that they'd heard Jessie Miller had been dating someone from Berry Springs High School. Isn't Jay a senior? And didn't you say he was arrested for aggressive behavior?"

"He watches you?"

"Both times I've been here, yes." I shuddered. "It's the kind of stare that just kind of makes my skin crawl. Like he knows something about me, or has some sort of beef with me."

Just then from behind us came, "*Yoo-hoo!*"

Christian and I turned to see Fatima shuffling down the hill, the bells on the bottom of her dreadlocks jingling against a hot-pink muumuu with bright blue piping. In her hands was a tray holding a jug of sweet tea and two icy glasses.

"Christian, I know this is your turf and I'm stomping all over it, but I saw you two outside and I just had to come and check on that precious little pooch."

Withering, I shot Christian a look. I wasn't even wearing a bra—not that it really matters to someone below a B cup. Catching the cue, Christian quickly stepped in front of me.

"That's just fine, Miss Fatima, and he's doing well. Sleeping inside."

Not one to be shut out of anything, Fatima nudged

Christian out of the way and handed him the tray. "Take this over to that beautiful table you're making over there, and pour us a glass. Assuming sweet tea is all right?"

"Yes, ma'am."

He shot me a pained *I'm sorry* look as he stepped away, and I forced a smile.

Fatima slid the small sack from her shoulder that I hadn't noticed. She leaned in to quickly whisper, "I know I'm no less than a dozen sizes bigger than you are, but I also know there are a few things a woman can't do without—her own clothes and toiletries." She shoved the bag to me. "My smallest house dress is in there, a toothbrush, tampons, and some makeup to cover those circles you've got under your eyes. Good Lord, girl, you look like a raccoon."

I took the bag, accepting the fact that apparently Fatima knew all the details of what happened, and also felt terrible for caring about the way I looked in front of her. Her charity was genuine.

"Thank you so much, Fatima." My lip quivered. God, I was a mess. "And thank you for helping my dog. Christian told me. Thank you, truly."

"Hush. You're welcome. Now, you stay here as long as you need to, you hear me? If Christian kicks you out, you walk right upstairs. I've already got a pot of my famous potato soup simmering in the kitchen. I'll keep Earl in the bathroom, where he spends half the day anyway. You just let me know what you need—"

"Everything okay here?" Christian asked, his return blocked by a bent-over Fatima and her voluptuous backside.

I smiled, peeking around her. "Yes."

We all turned to the sound of a door slamming in the distance. A blue Chevy reversed and peeled out of the drive.

"Finally got Jay a new truck?" Christian asked.

Fatima flicked me a glance before answering. And I caught it.

"Yeah . . . yes. Meant to ask you if it was okay. He'll just park it to the side of the garage, if that's all right."

"Of course. Same place he parked his old Ford a while back."

Fatima looked at me again, and I glanced at Christian.

"Anyway," she said, waving her hand in the air to dismiss the subject, then snatched one of the iced teas from his hand and gave it to me. "All right, well, I'll be on my way. Christian, you keep me updated on that pooch. Stole my heart, he did."

"I will. Thank you for the tea, Miss Fatima."

"Yes, sir." She looked at me again before she turned and huffed back up the hill.

"What's in the bag?"

"Girl stuff. That was weird—did you catch that?"

"How quickly she wanted to stop talking about her grandson? Yeah."

I ran my finger along the chain of my necklace. "I'm telling you, something is weird here."

Christian's gaze settled on the pendant, his lips pursed in deep thought.

"You really don't believe in omens or anything like that?" I asked again. "Curses, omens? Bad energy from inanimate objects?"

"I believe in the path."

"That everything is already planned out for us? We're just pawns in this thing called life, going through the motions? That there's nothing greater going on around us than what we can see and touch?"

Christian shook his head. "I didn't say that. Bad things

happen to everyone, as do good things. Each of our paths is different."

"Then someone upstairs despises me."

"There's that victim mentality again, Rory."

"Listen, you can't ignore the facts here. I lost my mom, my dad, a job that I loved. I had no control over any of it."

"Not true."

I shot up from the backrest of the swing, sloshing tea onto my bare legs. "Are you saying everything is my fault?"

"No, Rory." He laughed as he ran his hand over the top of his head. "God, you're difficult. You know that?"

"You're no walk in the park either, sunshine."

"What I'm saying is that you didn't have control over your mom, your dad, the layoff at the library, or the starving coyotes. But you do have control over yourself, like I said. You made the decision to crawl into bed and not come out. You didn't have to. You made the decision to jump that day. You didn't have to."

I looked away from him, and a moment stretched between us.

"Why didn't you tell me it was you that saved me that day?" I asked.

He shook his head. "Irrelevant."

"I disagree. Tell me the story. What were you doing? How did you see me?"

"I was out fishing."

"At night? During a storm?"

"Night fishing is some of the best fishing. Add a storm to it, and it doesn't get better. Something about the barometric pressure before a storm makes fish stir like crazy. I'd just pulled the boat to shore, on account of the lightning. Wouldn't have seen you if not for that lightning."

"You saw me where?"

"I saw a naked woman on the cliff." He kicked a rock. "I thought I was seeing things. Like I'd stepped into a . . ." He shook his head. "And then you just . . . jumped."

I looked down. He had to think I was bat-shit crazy.

"That must've been scary to see," I whispered, curling up a little from the shame.

"Scarier to think why this beautiful woman would think she had no other option."

"I didn't want to die."

"Could've fooled me."

"It's true. I know it sounds messed up. It's hard to explain. I just feel . . . nothing. Like I'm literally nothing anymore. I just didn't care anymore. I guess that's what it was. It's not that I wanted to end my life, it was just that I didn't care to live it anymore."

"The difference seems like a very thin line."

"I know. I don't expect you to understand. Hell, Christian, I don't understand what's happening to me."

"You loved your mother. She was your everything. Your whole life?"

"Yes."

He nodded. "That nothing you speak of . . . the feeling like nothing. Have you ever thought that maybe it's not nothing, it's simply that you don't know who you are anymore? You've lost your identity, not having your family anymore, and it manifests as this feeling of nothingness inside you. You feel like you aren't worth anything now because you have no one to validate you anymore."

When he looked away, it hit me. He spoke from experience, viewing things through the lens of abandonment. Yes, Christian and I were much more alike than I realized.

And he was so *right*. Everything I was, everything good that I was, was given to me by my mother. My confidence, my independence, my stability. When she left this earth, I'd been left with only myself to rely on. And I'd failed miserably.

Christian was right—it was enough. The pity party needed to end.

"I'm sorry you had to see me jump."

He looked away, his Adam's apple bobbing. A long moment stretched between us as he stared into the woods.

"I couldn't believe what I was seeing." His voice cracked in a feeble attempt to hide his emotion. "Your body falling through the air, the lightning flashing off your skin—and your pendant. That was the only thing you were wearing that day. I remember the gold sparkling—right at me, it seemed—and then the splash when you hit the water. And I just . . . dove in after you."

"And saved my life."

"I didn't save you. Doc Stafford did."

"Bullshit, Christian. You pulled me from the water and swam me to shore."

"Where Stafford and his family just happened to be camping a few yards away. What are the odds of that, by the way? Some might say you had *good* luck that night. That someone was watching over you."

I nodded. "I hear you." I took a sip of tea. "I think this last ordeal—"

"I wouldn't call the last few days an ordeal."

"Fine, this last . . ." I flapped a hand around as I struggled to find the words.

"Giving up."

"Yes." I sighed. "It's so freaking embarrassing."

"The woman I saw run out of that house to save her dog was nothing short of courageous—extraordinary, considering your health at that moment—and straight-up badass.

There was fire in your eyes, Rory. A fight. You've got it. You're good. Keep that fire, and you're going to be okay." He took a seat next to me on the porch swing. "When did you lose your dad?"

"Six weeks after Mom died." I took a deep breath, trailing my fingertip along the condensation of the glass of tea. "You know those couples you see and you think, 'Wow, they are so meant to be'? That one is not whole without the other? That was my mom and dad. They were madly in love. My dad worshipped my mom, and she believed he hung the moon."

Smiling sadly, I said, "They were so different, but they just fit. And when my mom passed away, it was like we fell apart. Not just me and my dad, but our family. The unit was destroyed. We both lost our best friend. It was like a darkness just kind of moved in and slowly spread everywhere, coating everything like a virus."

After taking another sip of my tea, I leaned back against the swing. "It was Sunday morning. Dad and I always had breakfast together on Sundays. I went to his house. For some reason, he'd gone above and beyond that day. Eggs, bacon, pancakes, fruit salad."

I looked down. "Sometimes I wonder if he knew. Anyway, that morning he told me how much I looked like my mom, and how alike we were. He never really talked like that, so it made an impression on me. Then we had breakfast together and talked about nothing in particular, just light, happy conversation."

I let out a hollow laugh. "I remember thinking how delicious the food was. Isn't that silly? After breakfast, he walked me to my car. I remember it was cloudy, with slivers of sunlight occasionally popping through the gray. He remarked that it was a beautiful day. He opened the door for me and paused, then looked up at the sky just as a beam of sunlight poured down on us. He closed his eyes and with the sweetest smile on his face, he whispered, 'The angel's light.' Then he looked at me and said, 'She's always with you. Keep an eye out. She's there.' It was so uncharacteristic of him to be so emotional. I didn't know what to say, so we hugged and I left."

Choking back a sob, I said, "That night, on my way home from work, I stopped by—I don't know why—and found him lying on my mom's side of the bed. He was dead. He'd had a heart attack."

Christian rested his elbows on his knees and looked at me with the most emotion I'd seen in his eyes. Understanding. Raw empathy.

"You know what's crazy?" I asked. "I truly believe that my dad died of a broken heart. That he literally couldn't live without my mom."

"And you can't either."

I stilled, considering the observation. "I guess that's right."

"I think your issue is that you haven't dealt with the pain. You need an outlet."

"Like shopping or booze or drugs?" *Or sex.* My cheeks warmed as I thought of shamelessly mounting my ex in the front seat of my truck.

Christian tilted his head thoughtfully. "No. Like something you love. Paint her. Paint your mother," he said. When I just blinked, looking at him as I processed his words, he explained. "Paint your mother in colors."

Taken aback, I stilled. *Why did I never think of that?*

"You've been subconsciously painting angels for months. Now *consciously* paint her. You're extremely talented, Rory. Believe in yourself. It's a lot of love you had. Paint it."

"Had."

"But you had it, Rory. Be grateful that you had it, and keep it alive through your art."

"I'm sorry. I know that you were an orphan."

"Do you? I guess I shouldn't be surprised." He shook his head. "Damn small-town gossip."

Together, we watched a pair of red birds flutter through the tree in front of us. A few leaves tumbled lazily to the ground in the warm summer breeze.

Glancing at him, I realized that a kinship seemed to be forming between us through our loss of family. In different ways, but it hurt just the same.

"Why didn't you stay that day, Christian? When you rescued me from the cliff?"

He reached down, plucked a handful of grass, and tossed it aside. "I knew you were in good hands. I didn't need to stay."

"Why didn't you tell me? We've been around each other all this time and you didn't tell me."

"When I realized you didn't remember when you saw me, I decided to leave it alone."

"You must've thought I was such a bitch for not seeking you out to thank you after it happened."

"I didn't need your thank-you."

"You saved someone's life, Christian. That deserves a thank-you."

"You can thank me by not jumping off a damn cliff again."

I smiled, appreciating the lighter tone, and took a deep breath. "Sorry. I guess I needed to talk."

"I might not be romantic, but I'm a good listener."

I jabbed a finger into his shoulder. "But not a good talker."

"I talk when I have things to say."

"Not about yourself."

"Not a lot to say."

"I don't believe that. I think you've got one hell of a life story. You've got clouds behind your eyes. I can see them."

Avoiding eye contact now, he plucked some more grass.

"What's your story?" I placed my hand over his. "Tell me."

"Another day." He jerked his hand away and pushed to his feet. Looking down at me, he extended his palm. "Time to get up, Rory."

Yes. It was time to get up.

40

"*I*t's beautiful," a low deep voice said from behind me.

I spun around on my stool, my heart leaping into my throat as my paintbrush tumbled to the deck.

Christian stood just inside my open back door, his gaze drifting over my bare legs, now splattered with yellow paint. His tanned skin glowed in the late afternoon light. He wore a fitted gray T-shirt, jeans with holes in the knees, and a pair of boots. He'd spent his day working, as had I. His hair was mussed to perfection, and a five o'clock shadow darkened his jaw. The man was a walking orgasm, no two ways about it.

Damn him.

I, on the other hand, had on a pair of cutoff jean shorts and an ill-fitting tank top. My hair was pulled into a messy topknot, my makeup sweated off from the heat as I worked on my painting on the deck.

"You scared me."

"Your front door was unlocked. You need to lock your doors, Rory."

"I did lock my doors."

"No, you didn't."

Okay, maybe I didn't. "I've been painting all day. Inside and outside."

"Lock it next time, okay?"

"Yes, sir." I winked.

He smirked, shifting his focus to the painting. "It's your mother."

I turned back to the canvas. "Yes. I took your advice." I tilted my head to the side, admiring the colorful bursts of blue, yellow, orange, and fuchsia. The painting wasn't what I wanted it to be yet, but it was close.

"It's her in the morning. She always woke up with a smile on her face."

"I see the angel outline in the bursts of yellow—in the rays of the sun."

"You've got a good eye. I didn't realize I was painting the shape until midway through—like the others. Now that it's intentional, it's brighter, right? My mother at dawn." I stared at the painting, lost in the colors. "She's caught in it."

"No. She's part of it."

I turned back to him and smiled.

"How's he doing?" Christian nodded to Cricket, asleep in his doggy bed bathed in sunlight at my feet.

"He's better. He ate well this morning."

"You're still giving him the meds, right?"

"Nope. Flushed 'em down the toilet. Yes, of course I'm giving him the meds. And doing everything else you demanded." I cocked my head. "If you're not careful, Christian, I might say he stole a little piece of that black heart of yours."

"He's a good dog."

"He is. Is this why you came by?"

"Among other reasons. I wanted to run something by you."

This is when I noticed the cardboard box in his hands. "Whatcha got?"

He shifted the box to one arm and pulled out the base of a lamp. "It's not done yet—"

"It's *gorgeous*." I gasped as I jumped up and padded toward him. The lamp sparkled in the sunlight, purple spheres of light dancing off the amethyst gems embedded into a river-rock stone base. I ran my fingertip down the side. "The contrasting colors are beautiful."

"I want you to paint it."

My gaze shot to his. "What?"

"Not *it*, exactly, but I want you to paint a picture using this as inspiration, however you creatives do that. Paint how it makes you feel when you look at it."

"Why?"

"I want to sell them together. Your painting and my lamp."

My brows rose.

"I'm thinking sets, maybe," he said. "For your shop. What do you think?"

"It's genius. But, *ugh*." Panic scrunched my face. "My work is nothing compared to yours."

He tapped my forehead. "Only in here."

Believe in yourself, Rory. Believe in yourself.

"Okay." I sucked in a breath. "I'll do it. When do you want the painting?"

"I'll finish the lamp tomorrow and bring it by. Then it goes in the shop, Rory. Hung proudly on the wall for everyone to see and want to buy."

Nerves ignited like fire inside me.

Not missing a beat, he narrowed his eyes. "Did you put your cliff painting on the wall?"

"Yep—yes, sir."

"You're a terrible liar."

I groaned. "I know. I will, I will. Tomorrow, I promise."

"You'd better. That was the deal."

"It feels like putting up a naked picture of myself on the wall—spread-eagle with Dildo Daggins."

Christian's eyes widened. "That one would be worth five thousand dollars—no, ten . . . fifteen thousand dollars." When I laughed, he added firmly, "Cash."

"Sold. Free magnifying glass included." I shimmied my small chest and grinned.

"You forget that I've already seen you naked. Twice."

I cringed. "Twice at my worst."

It still embarrassed me that Christian had pulled my naked body out of the water, and then months later, lifted my malnourished dehydrated body from the ground after I'd passed out.

"And still beautiful." He lifted my chin with his fingertip, and I smiled. His touches were becoming more frequent.

His finger trailed down my neck, his gaze devouring my beaded nipples though the thin tank. Goose bumps rippled over my skin, my insides tightening with a desperate craving—for him. A firestorm of energy crackled between us.

It was the same hungry look he'd given me standing by the trailer. The same look before I leaned into what will be forever remembered as *the kiss that never happened*.

And exactly as he'd done then, Christian abruptly turned away, stepping into the house and taking the heat with him. I knew then, with absolute certainty, I wasn't the only person with some major issues.

"Let's eat," he said gruffly over his shoulder, his demeanor completely changing.

I released the breath I'd been holding and stepped inside. "Eat what?"

"Dinner," he said, sliding the box that held the lamp base onto the kitchen counter.

"Oh. Well, thanks, but it's six o'clock. Who eats dinner at six o'clock?"

"Earl."

"Well, as much as I'd like to base my schedule on a man who sucks on an unlit cigarette all day, I prefer to dine after the sun goes down."

Ignoring me, Christian unloaded wrapped containers from the box and stacked them onto the counter. The smell of grilled meat filled the air.

"Let me guess—steak and potatoes."

"Rosemary rib-eyes, grilled potatoes, and green beans."

"You cooked?"

He ignored the question, either because *of course he cooked*, or because he didn't care to admit that he'd cooked for *me.*

It was a weird moment. The mixed signals this man was sending me didn't sit well.

"As delicious as all that sounds, I'm really not hungry right now."

"You'll eat."

I fisted my hands on my hips. "No, Christian, I'm not hungry. I ate lunch not long ago."

"What did you eat?"

Appalled at his accusatory, condescending tone, I jerked my chin back. "I ate," I snapped, purposely not answering his question in detail. Just to prove to him that I didn't have to.

"Fantastic. Let's eat again."

"I said I'm not hungry."

Our eyes met in a fireball of defiance. I didn't like his bossiness.

"Hey." I closed the space between us. "I don't like you coming in here and counting my calories, all right? Don't you understand that I'm embarrassed that you know that I have issues with food? That all my ugliness is out there for you to see? I'm *embarrassed*, Christian. And you keep forcing it down my throat. Literally."

"I'm trying to help you."

"You don't have to. I've never asked for your charity. Don't burden yourself by doing anything for me."

"I want to help you."

"Then change your damn tactics! Not everyone is as stone cold as you are. I'm sensitive—I'm *sorry*. I'm a woman. Treat me like one, dammit."

He blinked, his expression softening as the words dropped like a gauntlet between us.

"Why are you helping me, anyway?" I said sharply, my emotions barreling out of me in the form of anger. "Am I just some new project to you? Something to try to put back together and rebuild to your liking? It's obvious you want nothing to do with me beyond making sure I eat."

On a roll now, I kept going. "My God, do you know how you made me feel by the trailer that day? Leaving me standing there like an idiot? I thought you were going to *kiss me*, Christian."

Although his expression didn't change, I noticed the sudden heavy rise and fall of his chest.

"And I've got something else to tell you. Your rejection that day is part of the reason I couldn't get out of my damn bed the next day. There. I said it. That rejection, your cold dismissal of me . . . I was *humiliated*."

His lips parted in the closest thing to pure shock as I assumed this man got. "Why?" he asked breathlessly.

"Because I have fucking feelings for you, dammit!" I exploded, throwing my hands into the air. "You dim-witted, moronic jackass!"

Christian scrubbed a hand over his mouth, shifting his weight, obviously uncomfortable now. Assessing. Speechless.

"Listen, I don't need you to come by to make sure I'm eating more than steamed celery. I appreciate it, I do. But I'm not a lost pet that you have to take care of. I'm not your responsibility." I blew out a breath and began pacing. "Christian, you are so closed off, it's unbelievable. You are so . . . I don't get you. You—"

"You don't get me because there's not a lot to get, Rory," he snapped back.

"Tell me, then," I begged, stepping closer. "Tell me. Shit, tell *someone*. Why won't you open up to me? You know everything about me. All my faults, everything. I know nothing about you, but you keep snaking your way into my damn heart." I opened my arms. "You got me, Christian. This is me. The good, the bad, and the ugly. Now, who are you?"

With a groan, he jabbed his fingers through his hair and began pacing.

"Just *talk* to me. Please—"

"Fine, Rory. *Shit*." He spun toward me. "Do you know that I was left on the fucking doorstep of a church when I was eight weeks old? *Eight weeks* old, I was discarded. Discarded by a mother and father I don't even know. I have no idea who my real parents are. That's how much they loved me. *That's* who I am, the kind of people I came from. That's what I am. I'm not good for you, or for any woman, for that matter. I don't want a family. I don't want the white picket fence, the kids. Hell, Rory, I don't even know what a real family is. Who the hell am I to try to figure it out with someone like you?"

"Like me?"

"With someone who deserves it!" he shouted, throwing his hands into the air. "Someone as beautiful, smart, and courageous as you, Rory. You deserve everything, not some idiot who doesn't even know how to navigate a relationship. Not a guy who can't even admit that he cooked dinner for you. I'm not the guy, Rory. I can't give that to you."

I placed my hand on his arm, but he jerked away and stepped over to the sink, bracing himself on the edge. A long moment passed as I stared at the back of Christian's head, bowed over my sink.

"When I saw you on that cliff," he whispered, "there was a light around you, like an angel. Like I was staring at an angel. That's why I called the painting of the cliff the *Angel in the Storm*. You were my angel. Your perfect, smooth skin glowed in the darkness, your blond hair sparkled in the moonlight. You opened your arms. Rory, you looked right at me."

Tears filled my eyes. "I don't remember."

"I do. I remember every second of that moment. The feeling, the way you drew me to you like a siren. A mythical, beautiful creature beckoning me." He shook his head, and his shoulders slumped deeper. "And then you jumped."

He pushed off the sink and turned his back to me.

"I never saw you again after that. Until the day I stumbled to your house, not knowing it was yours. When no one answered the door, I looked through the windows and saw that damn painting. The painting of the cliff. I saw *you* in that painting. You were the angel. It was like I knew instantly it was you, Rory."

Christian turned to me, his expression tortured. "You've gone through so much loss, so much pain. I'm *terrified* I will cause you more pain," he said as his voice cracked. "That I'll be the cause of more hurt in your life. I don't know how to do a relationship. Love is foreign to me."

Whispering, he choked out, "I'll hurt you, Rory. I will hurt you."

My heart pounding, I closed the inches between us.

"Then hurt me, Christian," I whispered, a tear sliding down my cheek. "Because I know every second I'll get to spend with you before that will be worth it."

His eyes filled with tears and he cupped my face in his hands. Our lips met, and like a tidal wave, the sexual tension that had been vibrating between us was released in one dizzying kiss. Sliding his fingers to the back of my head, he threaded them through my hair and possessively secured me in place as he devoured me. I floated, every sensor in my body numb under his tongue.

He kissed like a man about to lose everything.

Until he pulled away.

Our chests heaving, we stared at each other, acknowledging what just happened between us without saying a word.

His hand fell away from my face. His expression filled with pain and fear, Christian turned and left without a single word.

It wasn't until I stepped outside later that I noticed the new porch swing swaying in the wind under a shade tree next to the porch. Carved into the back rest was a large black butterfly.

41

I didn't wash my face that night. Or my hair. Nothing that Christian had touched.

Him.

It was another sleepless night, but for very different reasons. I'd tossed and turned under the covers with a firestorm of emotions coursing through my body.

One, exhilaration. A dizzying excitement that still lingered on my lips hours after he'd left.

It's too easy, too cliché, to say that the kiss was the best I'd ever had. Because it wasn't—it was unlike any kiss I'd ever had. Incomparable. It wasn't soft. It wasn't tender. It was a raw, feral passion. A hunger with a sense of urgency, as if he had to experience it to the fullest before retreating again behind his armor. It was a kiss that had not been released to anyone else.

It was mine.

Two, anxiety. A restlessness of wondering what might come next. Would he call or text and act like nothing happened? Would he show up unannounced at my house again?

And finally, fear. Fear that whatever was happening between the mysterious Christian Locke and me would end before it really began. Forgotten. Shut down.

Even professionally?

Would I ever see Christian Locke again?

~

The next two days passed like molasses, with thoughts of Christian running on a loop in my head. I won't admit how many times I checked my phone, but let's just say I had to charge it multiple times throughout each day.

The storms had pushed away the heat wave, leaving temperatures steady in the mid-eighties. I'd stayed open late both Friday and Saturday night to cater to the rush of tourists who'd flocked to the lake for camping and fishing. I sold out of everything I had of Christian's but didn't dare call to tell him. The next move was his. His money was tucked in an envelope in my office. I decided to give it a few days before I mailed it to him. I don't know why.

I hadn't hung the *Angel in the Storm* painting. I couldn't do it. So I hung another painting, this one of daisies in a field, the angel hidden in the clouds. It sold within an hour for two hundred dollars. When the buyer asked who the artist was, I choked and told her the artist wished to remain anonymous. And a little light bulb went off.

I received a letter from the fresh-out-of-college attorney I'd hired to represent me in the broken-nose case. Although I planned to plead guilty, I'd been strongly advised to hire a lawyer to work out the details of my sentencing. My court date to face off with Becky Dunks Davies was set for exactly one month from now.

Bring it on.

Cricket's energy was increasing hour by hour, it seemed. The sparkle was back in his milky eyes, although I think he missed Christian.

I was feeling better too. My headaches were becoming less frequent and severe. I was sleeping better, and even napped one day. As much as I hated to admit it, Christian's voice in my head served as the push I needed. I even started a calorie journal to track my progress, recording what I ate for each meal, and would add more food to the day as needed to boost my energy level.

As Christian had suggested, I needed to rethink how I ate. Retrain my brain. I was making a concerted effort to not only consume more healthy calories, but to *not* go for a jog when the extra calories gave me a boost of energy. Instead, I'd force myself to sit at my easel and paint, funneling that energy into my work. Then jog later. Or not. I found that the "guilt" from eating more faded with each painting I completed.

Painting my mother had proven to be extremely cathartic for me. I'd broken down once, collapsed on the deck and sobbed for a solid hour. But this time, the tears weren't rooted in hopelessness. I'd cried simply because I missed her. And in a shocking twist, I felt better afterward.

As if I'd finally released it.

42

*I*t was a beautiful Sunday morning.

Cricket and I had just settled onto the deck, basking in the early morning sunlight, me with my stool, canvas, and paint, and Cricket with his doggy bed and chew toys. I planned to spend the day painting my interpretation of Christian's amethyst lamp, but was interrupted when I heard tires coming up the driveway.

Frowning, I glanced at Cricket. "You order pizza?"

He snorted, and I grinned. The old dog's sense of humor was returning.

Sunlight reflected off the vehicle's windows, blurring my view inside. I glanced down at the silk nightie I was still wearing from the night before. After setting my paint-brushes in the bucket to soak, I stepped inside and quickly crossed the living room.

The tires stopped, and the hum of an engine came to a halt. The thick vines blocked my view of the drive, so very quietly, I pushed open the front door and stepped onto the porch. Peeking through the vines, I watched Christian unfold himself from the cab of his beat-up black-and-orange truck.

He paused, hesitating, and my heart started to pound.

No. Don't leave.

When I pushed aside a clump of vines, our eyes met. Butterflies burst into flight in my stomach.

"Morning," I said softly.

"Good morning." Dark circles ringed his eyes, his skin pale and sallow over a tortured expression.

The silence between us was heavy.

He glanced at the three easels, each holding a painting in various stages of completion, that I'd set up under the maple tree earlier that morning. Painting in different locations had a way of helping me see through my haze. Each painting was of my mother, bright and happy.

Refocusing on me, he cleared his throat. "I came by to say I was sorry."

I dropped the vines and walked to the edge of the porch where I could get a full view of him, and crossed my arms over my chest. "We really need to work on your punctuality, Christian."

His lips curved, but the smile didn't reach his eyes. "And I didn't bring any food. I promise," he said, an obviously rehearsed joke that went over like a lead weight.

"Thank you for my porch swing."

He nodded.

"What exactly are you sorry for?" I asked as I stepped off the porch.

His gaze dropped to my nightie, then quickly to the ground—as if catching himself—then back to my face.

"I'm sorry for snapping at you. For not treating you as gently as I could have. I'm sorry for being an asshole, for everything. I'm just . . . I'm *sorry*, Rory." His voice rose with desperation as if begging me not to ask any more of him. As if to say, *This is it. I'm sorry.*

I nodded. "Thank you. You're forgiven."

Still keeping his distance, Christian dipped his chin, then shoved his hands into his pockets. "How's Cricket?"

"Stronger every day. A lot better than when you saw him last."

"That's good news."

A cool lilac-scented breeze swept past us. My focus shifted to his lips, that mouth that had kissed me into oblivion before he'd disappeared from my life. We stared at each other, neither knowing what to say or do next.

But he was here. And that meant something.

"Well . . ." He kicked a pebble with his boot. "That's it. So. Anyway, I've, uh, got to run to Tractor Supply and the farmer's market for a few things."

"Busy Sunday."

He pulled a postcard from his pocket. "Only day to use my twenty percent off."

"Twenty percent at Tractor Supply? You'd better hold on to that thing." I smirked. "How'd you pull that off?"

"It's my birthday."

I blinked. "What?"

"Yeah. So, anyway—"

"Oh, no, no, no, sir." I stepped off the porch and crossed the driveway. "What birthday is it?"

"The big four-oh."

"What? What the heck are you doing here? Shouldn't you be on a plane to Vegas or something?"

"Just the farmer's market." He glanced again at the paintings, avoiding eye contact.

The man had no plans for his fortieth birthday. That definitely would *not* do.

"Well," I said lightly, "the farmer's market is a fun place, I guess. Are you selling something?"

"I've been given a task." He pulled a long piece of note paper from his pocket. "Tomatoes, squash, carrots, lettuce, and a pink toilet paper holder that reads, and I quote, *shit happens, roll with it.*"

I laughed. "I didn't take you as a pink toilet paper dispenser kind of guy. Or one that uses a dispenser at all, no offense."

"It's for Fatima. She special ordered it from one of her bunco buddies who sells knickknacks—toilet-paper dispensers, apparently—and homemade jelly every Sunday at the market. The veggies are for her too. Sunday brunch, I guess."

"You Sunday brunch?"

"No," he said quickly with a laugh. "I definitely don't Sunday brunch. Fatima, Earl, and Jay, they do it every Sunday. It's a whole"—he waved his hand in the air—"big thing. Sunday brunch, then evening church. Less crowded, for Earl's sake, I guess."

"Have you ever gone?"

"No."

"But they've invited you, haven't they?"

"Every single Sunday. A formal invite right there on my doorstep. You were actually included on today's invite, as was a little cartoon picture of a dog that looks remarkably like Cricket."

"*I* got an invite?"

"Yes, ma'am."

I stared at him, a wicked grin growing on my face. It was his birthday. He needed to celebrate. "We're going."

"What?"

"To brunch. Today. Let's go. Let's do it."

He blinked, his eyes widening as if I'd just asked for his Tractor Supply discount card.

"Let's go," I said again. "My only plan today was to paint and then drop daisies by the cemetery for my mom and dad. Both can wait. Let's go."

"Uh . . ." He scratched the top of his head.

"It's time, Christian. And it's your birthday on top of that."

He shifted his weight.

"Listen." I fisted my hands on my hips, reveling in the flicker of attention he gave my peaked nipples. "I'm going to be the stone-cold one now, and I've got news for you—you need help, and maybe even therapy, just as much as I do, Christian Locke. And I honestly think the first step for you is simply allowing people into your life. You have got to release the fear of letting people down. Someone once told me to believe in myself. I'm saying it back to you now. You're a good man, Christian. Let people see that."

His gaze swept over my legs, then met my eyes with that same spark of heat from the other day. "Only if you wear that, Rory."

I smirked, dramatically sweeping over the silk with my hand. "Oh, this old thing? Well, I would, but I'd hate to steal all the attention at the table."

"Who says we'd even make it to the table?"

I smiled. "The kiss was pretty hot, wasn't it?"

His expression softened as he reached up and lightly brushed his thumb over my bottom lip. I could tell he wanted to do it again, but he was still reserved, holding back.

"Did it scare you?" I asked.

"It didn't scare me, Rory." His thumb swept over my

cheek, his finger hooking my chin possessively. "It obliterated me."

I swallowed hard.

He smiled, that twinkle back in his eye, and stepped back. "You're on. Eleven o'clock. Sunday brunch."

"Sounds good, birthday boy. I'd better get ready. Okay if I bring Cricket?"

"Of course."

"Thanks. All right, then." Blushing now, I turned and made my way across the driveway, my hips with a little extra sway in them.

As I crossed the porch, I stole a glance through the vines.

Christian hadn't moved. His gaze was still following my silhouette through the vines.

My heart gave a little flutter.

Dear God. I'm in trouble.

a couple of hours later, I shot a panicked glance at the clock with one arm hanging out of the collar of the fifth sundress I'd tried on, and two skirts around my ankles.

"*Shit.* Shit, *shit.* I'm late."

Cricket lifted his head.

"Sorry. But what am I supposed to wear to a Sunday brunch?"

A tornado of clothes whirled around me as I ripped off the sundress and kicked out of the skirts. In nothing but a pair of panties, I jogged into my closet and grabbed the only sundress left on the rack. I rarely wore it because of the memories that came with it.

Clutching the dress to my chest, I closed my eyes and inhaled the fabric. Some days, I could still smell her in it. It was a white sundress that hung to mid-calf, colored with bright yellow daisies.

It was my mother's.

I slipped into a bra, pulled on the dress and zipped it,

and turned to the mirror. A smile crossed my face. For the first time, I saw *her* in *me.*

I'd curled my hair, which took up the bulk of the morning, and spent a ridiculous amount of time on my makeup, going for the *barely there but sexy as hell* look that I could never seem to achieve. I'd shaved . . . everywhere . . . and moisturized my skin with a light floral lotion that was supposed to make me "glow." Not so much glow, I decided, as much as sparkle. But that was okay.

I twirled once, checking my backside, and true to form, questioned everything all over again. *Am I overdressed?*

I looked at the clock again. I had to go.

Daisy dress it is.

Bypassing the two pairs of heels I owned, I opted for a more casual flat. Because heels were just too much for brunch. Right?

I closed and locked all the windows—a new measure of security spurred from fears of a Peeping Tom—and bolted out the door, pausing for a moment to do one more safety measure on the way out. After loading Cricket and all his things into the cab of my truck, I jumped in and spun out in a cloud of dust.

When I finally pulled up Christian's driveway, I was exactly sixteen minutes late. And nervous as hell.

Practicing my best yoga breathing, I rolled the truck to a stop under a large oak tree and got out. Voices carried from the open windows of the house. Fatima's laughter, Earl's grunts. The faint sound of a steel guitar carried on the air scented with bread and herbs. Old country music.

I scooped Cricket into my arms, plucked his bed and my purse from the seat, and made my way across the driveway. My heart was racing as I stepped up to the stoop.

I knocked, took a step back, and plastered on my best *I'm*

not nervous at all smile. As a cacophony of incoherent words and shouts drew closer to the door like a slow-motion freight train, my heart started to pound.

What the hell have I gotten myself into?

The door swung open.

"Miss Flanagan, oh, and my dear Mr. Cricket." Fatima bent at the waist and stroked the dog's head. "Sweet baby. He looks good."

Dressed to the nines, Fatima was wearing a blinding-white dress with a lime-green shawl over her shoulders. Her dreadlocks were pulled back into a braid, her lips a sparkly pink.

I let out a silent exhale. I'd dressed perfectly for the occasion.

"I'm so glad you made it," she said. "One is better than none."

"I'm sorry . . . one?"

"Christian hasn't showed, as usual."

"But I'm late." My eyes rounded. "Wait a second . . ."

"No, no, no, you come on in, dear. There's plenty of food, trust me on that. Earl demanded a whole ham today—bone and all. Damn thing was still snorting when I put it on the block."

"Where is Christian?"

"Who knows. Who ever knows? Probably down in that dreadful hole he calls home."

"He didn't tell you we were coming?"

"Well . . . no, dear."

Oh, hell no.

"Hang on." I closed my eyes, shaking my head. "He told me that you invited us to come to your brunch today—that you invite him every Sunday."

"That's a fact. Sixty-seven times now. He's been a no-show to every one."

"*Sixty-seven*?"

"Yes, ma'am. I place an invitation on his step every week —make it real pretty with bows and glitter—and he ignores it. Every time."

I shook my head. "That little . . ."

"Oh, honey, I know. Man's as hardheaded as that horse he lets roam." She exhaled. "It's sad, you know? Just lettin' his life pass him by. Too stubborn and set in his ways to see all the windows God has opened for him."

My gaze shifted to the dirt pathway that led to the basement, then back to Fatima. "Set another placemat, Miss Fatima. Mind if I leave Cricket here for a minute?"

"Not at all. So sweet, little baby," she cooed as I carefully set him in his dog bed just inside the house.

"Give me five minutes." I spun on my heel.

"Don't let him push you around, Miss Flanagan," she called to my back. "Man needs a good kick in the ass, and I've got a feelin' you're just the gal to give it to him."

"Yes, ma'am," I hollered over my shoulder as I rounded the corner, fuming.

I stomped down the gray stone steps, raised my fist, and unleashed hell on the door. Without waiting for him to come to the door, I shoved my way inside, sending the door bouncing on its hinges.

T-Bone and Tater shot up and barreled toward me.

"No! Bad," I said firmly, lifting my hand. "*Sit.*"

The dogs skidded to a stop. And sat.

Christian didn't so much as blink or turn his head from his perch in his La-Z-Boy. His feet were kicked up, his eyes on the television. A half-finished beer was gripped in his hand, an open bag of spicy Doritos on the side table.

"What in the *hell* do you think you're doing?" I demanded.

The dogs tucked tail and disappeared down the hall.

Christian tipped up his beer and sipped.

"I repeat, what in God's name do you think you're doing?"

"Basketball."

"Brunch. *Brunch*, Christian. That's what you're supposed to be doing. Brunch. Not ball."

He grunted, then sipped again.

"Oh, hell no." I stomped across the room, yanked the beer from his hand, and slammed it on the table. Then I did what might be the ballsiest thing thus far—I stepped in front of the television.

"Hey!"

"I am *not* going to this thing alone."

His gaze flicked to the dress, back to the television, then returned to the dress, sliding over me from head to toe.

"Get your sorry ass out of that chair before I drag you out of it."

He heaved out a breath.

I slammed my hands on my hips. "What? What's the deal?" I grabbed the remote and muted the game.

He shot forward, slamming his bare feet on the floor. "Now, wait just a minute—"

"You wait just a minute," I snapped back. "I did *all* this, this morning." I waved a hand over my fancy dress, my curls, my meticulous makeup. "Just for this brunch. If you seriously think you're getting out of this, you are sorely mistaken, pal."

"Pal?"

"Why are you trying to back out?"

He craned his head to look around me. I stepped into his view.

"*Seven* dresses, Christian. Seven damn dresses I tried on. You're not the only one nervous here."

"I didn't say I was nervous."

"Cut the bullshit. You're nervous and you're wimping out."

He thrust a hand at the television. "But the NBA championship—"

"Has been scheduled for months. Record it."

He looked at me, aghast.

"Get up."

He cocked a brow, picked up his beer, and leaned back.

"Get up."

His eyes narrowed to slits.

"Get. Up."

With a guttural groan, Christian rose from the chair. The victory was the sweetest of my life.

"Go change. I look too good to walk in with you wearing that dishrag you consider a shirt."

"It's Hanes."

"It's horrid. Go change. Into something that doesn't have salsa stains and frayed edges. Something with a collar."

"*Woman*—"

"*Now.*"

He flashed me one last glare before disappearing down the hallway and slamming his bedroom door.

T-Bone and Tater crept up the hall, their heads low as they tiptoed to my sandals.

"He's something else, you know that?" I knelt down and ruffled their ears. "But, dammit, he's good to look at, isn't he?"

T-Bone rolled over on his back, his tongue lolling to the side. I laughed, scratching his belly.

A few bangs sounded from the bedroom before the beast re-emerged, and I surged to my feet.

The Hanes had been replaced with a mint-green golf shirt, fitted just enough to emphasize his broad shoulders and thick chest that I loved so much, and bright enough to make his green eyes glow. My gaze drifted to the chinos that hugged his thick thighs, then down to his feet.

"Don't," he said. "I'm wearing flip-flops. It's happening."

"Wasn't going to say a word."

He grunted, grabbed his beer from the table, chugged the rest, and released a Homer Simpson-style burp that rattled the windows.

I shook my head and rolled my eyes. "Is this you when you're nervous?"

"This is me wanting to watch basketball."

"Later. Let's go."

He looked longingly at his empty beer.

I tugged his arm. "Let's go. If she doesn't have beer, I'll sneak down here and get you one."

"Promise?"

"Promise."

44

I pretended not to notice Christian's quick inhale as we stepped out the door. The dogs trailed behind us, tails wagging, excited for whatever was causing such abnormal behavior in their master.

I pulled in a deep breath of my own as I returned to the front door and knocked again.

"It's my house. We don't have to knock," he muttered.

"It's polite."

The whispers inside the house stopped. A moment passed and the door opened slowly.

"Well, Mr. Locke, lovely to see you." Fatima shot me a grin as wide as the Mississippi. Earl was peeking over her shoulder, as if having to see this for himself. "Please, come on in."

"Why, thank you." I winked, stepped inside, and pulled Fatima to the side as Earl greeted Christian with a handshake.

"He's gonna need a beer. A big one," I whispered.

"Lager or ale?" she whispered back.

"Fatima, I'm pretty sure he'd drink a hot PBR right now."

She bit her lip, stifling a laugh. "Got it."

"Also, it's his birthday."

Her eyes bugged out. "What?"

"Yep. Forty. Today."

"Oh my." She gripped her chest in panic. "Okay, I can handle this. You'll have to divert for a bit while I throw something together. Got it?"

"Yes, ma'am."

She placed a hand on my back and gave me a wink. "Nice work, Rory. Welcome, my dear."

"Thank you." I smiled, surprised at the flutter of nerves in my stomach.

When I turned back, Earl was leading Christian through the living room, unabashedly pointing out new cracks in the walls, a dip in the floor, and a hole in the corner that he was certain housed a family of mice. Christian was their landlord, after all.

I knelt down and checked on Cricket, who was exchanging excited sniffs with T-Bone and Tater. It was the most energy I'd seen in him in days.

Glancing up the staircase, I wondered where Jay was.

Luckily, Earl chattered on and on about the house, preventing me from implementing my long list of diversionary tactics.

Ten minutes later, Fatima came back down the hall carrying an icy mug filled to the rim with beer. She winked at me, and I nodded back.

"Dogs, out." Fatima nudged at T-Bone and Tater with her foot, then turned to the boys. "Gentlemen, gentlemen, time to wrap it up. Beer?" she said, offering the mug to Christian.

"Thank you." He crossed the room a bit too quickly, accepted the mug, and took a deep sip.

Grinning, Fatima led the men and me into the dining room. Sunlight pooled onto a long table sparkling with elegant china, crystal glassware, and a row of fresh flowers and candles down the middle.

"Fatima, this is beautiful."

She squeezed my hand. "I know, dear. It's real china, you know. I've been collecting it for years."

My eyes bugged out. "Really? It looks like Haviland. Is that right?"

Her bushy brows popped, mirroring my surprise. "Yes, ma'am. You know your china?"

"I actually collect antiques."

Gasping, Fatima grabbed my arm. "You're *kidding.* Honey, we have got to talk."

"She owns an antiques and art shop in town," Christian said, eavesdropping. "Opened recently."

"Do you?" Fatima asked me. "Whereabouts?"

"Tourist Row. The Black Butterfly." My hand drifted to my pendant, and all eyes snapped to the necklace around my neck.

"I saw that place a few weeks ago and have been meaning to stop by. Oh my goodness, what are the odds? Sit, dear. Let's get started on brunch, because afterward I'm going to show you my dish collection."

"Sounds great. Do you need any help?"

"Yes, for both of my fine guests to sit down. What would you like to drink, Rory? We got the three W's—wine, whiskey, and water—and beer, tea, orange juice, or milk."

"I'll take wine."

"Red or white?"

"Surprise me."

Fatima winked. "You've got it."

Christian pulled out a chair and motioned for me to sit. I smiled and sat. He dipped his chin.

Earl seated himself at the head of the table, and Fatima promptly removed the beer from his hand, replacing it with a glass of sweet tea. She didn't touch the cigarette, I noticed. Limits had been set long ago.

I couldn't help but smile. The couple reminded me of my parents, yin and yang, fire and ice. No reason to work, but for some reason they fit together like two pieces of a puzzle.

I glanced at Christian, still standing as he slowly scanned the room. He was probably making a mental checklist of everything that needed to be fixed.

He and I were also yin and yang. So different from the outside looking in, but so similar once you started peeling back the layers. His layers went much deeper than mine, I was slowly beginning to realize.

"There, boy, sit." Her hands full, Fatima impatiently jerked her chin to the seat next to me. "Good Lord, just sit, Christian."

"Better do as she says, son," Earl gritted out over his cigarette. "Hell hath no fury like my wife during Sunday brunch prep. Trust me."

Christian sank into his chair, his posture mirroring mine. Clearly uncomfortable, we sat stiffly with our backs as straight as rods. I cleared my throat as he sipped his beer, already half-empty, I noticed.

A moment later, Fatima delivered a frosty glass of rosé to me with a couple of ice cubes. My mouth watered at the sight.

Just then, a teenage boy shuffled into the dining room with his shoulders hunched and head down, his face as pale as the tablecloth. The Bradburys' grandson, Jay, I assumed.

He wore all black—T-shirt, denim, and a pair of scuffed combat boots. Patches of scruff dotted his chin in undoubtedly his first attempt to grow a beard. There was a break in his stride when he noticed Christian and me, a brief moment of surprise in his dark eyes.

Christian glanced at me.

"Water or tea, son?" Fatima asked her grandson after making introductions.

"Water." The young man's voice was deeper than I'd expected, and colored with the attitude of a boy coming into his own. Trying to, anyway.

For a moment, I felt sympathy for the kid. I, of all people, understood how hard not fitting in could be.

The air immediately shifted in the room, the sparkle fading from Fatima's eyes, the deep lines of Earl's face hardening. There was something going on in the Bradbury house, and Jay was at the center of the drama. No doubt about it.

Fatima set the water in front of Jay without a word. It appeared that not much was said to the boy. Not for lack of trying, I guessed.

Earl removed the cigarette from his mouth, rolled it into a napkin, and stuffed it safely into the front pocket of his button-up.

We all watched as Fatima gracefully filled the table with a beautifully plated lunch. Honey-glazed ham, sweet cornbread muffins, Tuscan-style broccoli, potatoes au gratin, fresh-cut green beans, and a dish of baked cinnamon apples sprinkled with brown sugar that made my mouth water more than the wine had.

The woman was in her element, taking pride as she served each of us, insisting on doing so. Earl was right—brunch was done as Fatima wanted, no two ways about it. I had a feeling that many things were done as Fatima demanded, despite Earl's macho-man exterior.

She kissed the top of her husband's head after adding an extra scoop of baked apples to his plate. It was Sunday brunch, after all. He smiled up at her and winked.

Again, I smiled.

Fatima and Earl were what I'd consider "old school," still living in the days when a woman was expected to cook for her man, and the man was expected to take care of his woman. Fatima was proud to serve and care for her husband, but she wasn't weak or subservient. The opposite, in fact. Fatima was all woman at her core, innately nurturing, supportive, deriving fulfillment from the quality of her relationships. Offering help wasn't a sign of weakness to Fatima, but one of strength.

I thought of the way my father helped my mother during her many episodes. The patience and commitment he had. The ability to walk that fine line of knowing when to push, and when to simply sit and stroke her hair. His patience and care were the epitome of strength, not weakness. And I'd have words with anyone who said differently.

The love between Fatima and Earl was evident, and it warmed me from head to toe. This was family.

After topping off our drinks, Fatima seated herself at the opposite end of the table from Earl with a glass of chardonnay in hand—double the ice cubes—and a smile on her face.

"Now," she said as she looked at Christian and me. "We say grace at this table. That all right with you?"

"Yes, ma'am," we said simultaneously, as saying no would have surely gotten us a first-class ticket to hell.

With everyone's hands linked and heads bowed, Fatima blessed the food.

"Heavenly Father, thank you for this food and for this time of gathering. Bless this meal with love, light, and laughter. And for our two lovely guests, may the beautiful sun guide their paths, the wind carry them through the darkness, and a rainbow follow each storm. May they find what they're both so desperately seeking. Lord Jesus, give us eyes to see and ears to hear your messages. Amen."

Fatima clapped her hands together. "Now. Let's eat."

Christian's hand lingered on mine. After a quick squeeze, he released it, and my heart skipped a beat.

The table fell silent except for frenzied silverware clattering against Fatima's precious plates. The food was Southern dining at its finest. I glanced at Jay from under my lashes, for the umpteenth time since he'd sat down. Instead of staring at me as he'd done from the windows, he was avoiding eye contact.

Something was there. Yes, *something* was definitely there.

"So," Fatima said over the clatter of silverware. "Is that where you two have been hauling furniture off to every day? The Black Butterfly?"

I nodded, looking at Christian to elaborate, to say anything at all. When he didn't, I realized I was going to be the one to carry the conversation. And that was just fine with me. I didn't get all dressed up for nothing.

"I've been selling some of Christian's pieces in my shop. Selling *out*, I should say."

"Christian." Fatima set down her fork. "Did you make all that furniture I watched you two load up? Is that what you do in that barn all day?"

He nodded. "Among other things, yes."

"Well, *hot dog*." She slapped the table, then gestured to her husband. "See there? I told you, Earl."

Earl grunted in response before aggressively shoving a large bite of ham into his mouth.

Fatima nodded. "Earl was hypothesizing that you ran an illegal meth lab behind those walls."

I laughed.

Christian's lip quirked. "No, ma'am. That would be a fire hazard."

She laughed, then turned to me. "All these years, we wondered what he did in that barn. We've seen him hauling in lumber, this and that. He's given us some furniture— beautiful pieces—and I had an inkling that he'd made it, but of course he didn't tell us that."

She gestured to the other room. "The staircase, wood paneling, cabinetry. We fell in love with it all when we visited for the first time. Such quality work and *pride*." She looked at Christian. "You did all that, didn't you? Renovated this place with your bare hands before putting it up for rent?"

Christian sipped his beer.

"He did," I said proudly. "He's extremely talented. I've already received requests for special orders—"

"That's right," he said quickly. "Special orders to match the *paintings* Rory is going to make to go with each piece."

"What?" Fatima said as she cocked her head, and Earl glanced up.

"That's right." Christian grinned at me with a devilish twinkle in his eyes. "Tell them about it, Rory." He looked at Fatima. "My talent has nothing on Rory's. She's a talented artist. Paints abstract art. Unique, stunning—the kind of paintings that tell a thousand words with colors."

I blushed, his description of my art rendering me speechless.

"Although, she doesn't have the guts to sell her paintings

in her own shop," he said. "In fact, she hasn't even shown a single person her talent—"

"Yes, I have," I said defiantly. "I sold a painting yesterday."

His brows arched. "The *Angel in the Storm*?"

"No . . . not that one." I flicked my wrist, cutting him off before he could chastise me. "One I painted of daisies."

He smiled, his gaze sweeping across my face. He dipped his chin proudly, and I smiled.

A slow smile stretched across Fatima's face. I imagined that Christian and I looked like children, needling each other because we had no idea how else to release the attraction between us.

"Discussing antiques just got pushed to the bottom of the list," she said. "I must see these paintings Christian speaks so highly of."

I shot Christian *the look*, to which he grinned and shoved a piece of ham into his mouth.

"Sounds like you two make quite the team," Earl barked.

We both shoved a bite of the closest things to our forks into our mouths.

Fatima stood and set another roll on Jay's plate, who'd yet to say a word. I watched Christian watch him for a moment.

"Noticed the new ride. Nice truck," Christian said to Jay.

Fatima's attention snapped to Christian.

"V8?" he asked.

"Yes, sir."

Sir.

Fatima cut in. "Jay needed something to tour all these colleges he's going to apply for, isn't that right, son?"

Jay clenched his jaw and stabbed a green bean.

"Kid isn't going to college, Fatima." Earl eyed her over the rim of his glass.

"Other plans?" Christian asked in an attempt to defuse the tension.

"Military." Jay looked up, a spark of defiance in his eyes.

Fatima blew out a breath and looked at me with that heart-wrenching expression of a worried mother.

"That's right. It'll make a man of him," Earl said in a tone that suggested Jay needed some filling out.

Fatima glanced at me.

Jay glanced at me.

I glanced at Christian.

"Which branch are you thinking about joining?" Christian asked.

"Army." Jay wrapped his hand around his drink.

Christian dipped his chin. "I was in the Marines. If you have any questions, let me know. I wouldn't trade my experience for anything in the world. It's a fresh start, gives you a new focus."

"God bless you for your service," Fatima said, regaining control of the conversation. "It's just scary for the families left waiting at home, is all. Anyway . . ." She waved a hand in the air, dismissing the conversation. "How did y'all meet? Because we know it wasn't on Christian's accord."

My back stiffened, a green bean lodging in my throat. I grabbed my wine and washed it down, feeling my heart begin to race. I lowered my hands to my lap, a nonverbal guarding of my soul. Somehow, I didn't think attempted suicide was a Sunday brunch kind of conversation.

Inhaling sharply, I said, "Uh . . . well—"

Christian's strong, warm hand clamped mine under the table, reassuring me.

"We met at the cliff at Devil's Cove four months ago," he

said. "Rory was getting inspiration for her paintings. One of my favorites, actually."

He smiled at me, and I exhaled.

Fatima stared, seeing right through us, but she smiled. "Sounds like you two were meant to find each other." Her gaze cut to her husband across the table, who was leaning on the back legs of his chair, peeking at the muted television down the hall. "Unlike how Earl wasn't supposed to find the remote I hid at the beginning of brunch."

"It's the damn NBA Championship."

"Watch your language at the dinner table, Earl."

"You got the game on?" Christian asked, much too excitedly.

"I got something on. Never learned how to work our latest fancy remote. You into basketball?"

Fatima shot me a wink, and with that, the conversation shifted from the budding relationship of a painter and a carpenter, to the decades-long relationship between men and games that involve balls.

After plates had been licked clean and booze had been drunk, Fatima excused herself from the table. Backlit by the glow of candles, Fatima carried in a frosted Bundt cake decorated with tiny candles and rainbow sprinkles, and a big 4-0 drawn across the side.

Christian was speechless.

I fought the tears in my eyes as we sang "Happy Birthday" to the man who hadn't been sung to in decades.

Somewhere between the last slice of cake and coffee, the men found their way to the television while I helped Fatima clear the table. Jay shot out of the house like a cat on fire the moment dessert was finished, fired up his new truck, and took off. After a quick check on Cricket, I returned to the kitchen.

"Beer?" Fatima paused at the doorway and hollered into the living room.

"Yes, ma'am," Earl yelled back. "Two."

She pulled two longnecks from the fridge while I stacked scraped-off plates next to the sink. "Sounds like the boys are bonding. Won't be long until they start arguing about politics."

"The cement of any Southern man's friendship."

"Exactly." Fatima handed me one of the beers and jerked her chin to the living room. "Take this to him."

"Oh." I looked down at the beer. "It's really not like that. Christian and I are just f—"

"Yes, it is. I can see it written all over your face. His too. Poor kid just doesn't know what to do about it." She took a deep breath. "Men are stubborn creatures, Rory. Primal. Feed them, bathe them, medicate them—that's their measurement of love. They have to be told what to do, how to act, and how not to act. Don't ever assume Christian is just going to suddenly figure it out. If he's worth it, write what you want on a billboard, then he'll finally get the message. Take the beast by the horns—that's what you've got to do with most men."

Raising a brow at me, she said, "We, Rory, are much more complex creatures. We can handle more than men. It's in our makeup. We take care of ourselves, our job, our family members. And when one—or a few—of those go to hell in a handbasket, it's on us to fix it. Which is why it's so important to take care of ourselves so we can take care of everyone else."

Her gaze on me narrowed. "It's easy to forget how strong

you are, I know. But it's on you, Miss Rory, to pull up your big girl panties and take care of yourself. Your brain—and your body."

I felt a weird pull as I looked back at Fatima, her graying dreadlocks twisted in a bun on top of her head, the twinkle in her kind eyes. I realized then that she reminded me of my mother.

Her face softened, her point made. "At the end of the day, dear, family is what really matters. No matter what form it comes in." She shot a look toward the door that Jay had run out through earlier. "Some days are harder than others, but never forget to keep an open heart and mind. People make mistakes and then come back around. Every time."

She grabbed an icy mug from the freezer and thrust it at me. "Now. Let's get these drinks delivered to our men."

My man.

I took the mug. "Thank you, Fatima. For this, for everything."

She winked. "Go on, now. He's waiting . . . for lots of things, if I had to guess."

With a sigh, I led the way down the hall feeling Fatima's grin aimed at my back.

To no one's surprise, the men didn't notice when we women entered the room.

"Your beer, sir," I said with a flourish, but was unable to steal Christian's attention from the TV, which ignited a rush of determination in me. I was up for this challenge.

Bending at the waist, I angled my cleavage toward Christian—and away from Earl—and poured his beer with the delicacy of a seasoned bartender.

Christian's gaze swung to me as if to say, *Basketball game? What basketball game?*

A trail of froth slid down the glass. I swiped the bubbles with my finger and licked the tip.

When Christian's jaw unhinged as he stared at me, I bit back my grin, winked, and sauntered away.

"Oh, child," Fatima whispered as she fell into step with me on our way back to the kitchen. "He's still watching. Make it count."

My hips took on a life of their own as they swayed their way around the corner.

"You should have seen that boy's face." Fatima chuckled as she returned to the sink. "Sexuality is a powerful thing. You've got it in spades. Don't forget it."

My hand drifted to the strand of hair that had fallen into my face. I tucked it behind my ear, catching my reflection in the window, and found myself surprised by it. I did look good. Dare I say, sexy even.

When was the last time I felt pretty and confident? I couldn't remember.

As the final plate was washed and dried, then returned to the china cabinet, hoots and hollers exploded from the living room, followed by heavy boots approaching from down the hall. One man laughing, one cussing—both arguing.

"Game's over." Fatima rolled her eyes.

"Goddamn referee—"

"You watch that language in my kitchen, Earl."

Christian chuckled and tossed back the rest of his beer.

Earl nodded at the empty mug. "Another?"

Christian glanced at me.

"Go ahead," I said with a nod. "I've got to get home. Have a few things to do before opening the shop tomorrow."

"Oh no, come on," Fatima said with a whine.

"I'll take you," Christian said, and the room fell quiet as all eyes turned to him.

"No, I'm fine. You stay."

"I'll take you," he said again, his tone confident despite the attention on him.

"No, really. Stay."

"Let him take you, woman," Earl grumbled, yanking another beer from the fridge.

Fatima grinned. "You heard the man."

"Shall we?" Christian offered me his elbow.

I looked around the kitchen as Fatima wiped the countertop.

"We're all cleaned up," she said with a grin. "No worries."

"Okay, then. Thank you both for inviting me into your home, for brunch."

"Anytime. I look forward to chatting about antiques and looking at those paintings of yours over a cup of coffee one day soon."

"It's a date."

"Next Sunday, then? After brunch?"

"Uh . . ."

When I hesitated, she decided for me. "Next Sunday."

"I'll see you then."

Earl popped the top off his longneck. "Christian, I expect to see you back this week to fix those damn cracks in the walls."

"First thing tomorrow morning, sir."

Earl grunted in approval.

"I'll have coffee and cheese Danishes ready. Go on, kids." Fatima shooed us off from the sink. "Get on home."

45

I glanced in my rearview mirror as Christian pulled into the driveway behind me. A faint flutter of butterflies rippled through my stomach.

To any normal person, Sunday brunch was a relaxing event, a time for indulgence, for letting go of whatever plagued you that week. Not for me. My Sunday brunch had felt like the opposite. Like everything in my life had slowly started spinning, a series of events unfolding around me that I could no longer control.

Maybe it was the wine, or because this brunch was the first time I'd shared a meal with anyone other than my dog in months. Maybe it was the way Fatima had taken me under her wing, reminding me of my own mother.

Or maybe it was the way Christian had placed his hand over mine, and the talk of us—as a couple. There had been a shift between us, and there was no going back. We were a team, there at dinner. Sitting behind a thirteen-pound ham and a pot of green beans, it was him and me.

Christian and Rory. Together.

And it shook me to my core.

I was in deep. My feelings for Christian were past the point of trying to label them as something else, or trying to ignore them.

Of all people, I had fallen for Christian fucking Locke— a temperamental reclusive commitment-phobe with the emotional capacity of a rock.

I'm not good for you, Rory. His words barreled into my head over and over on that drive home. *I'm not the guy.*

A shaky inhale caught me as Christian parked behind my truck, his large, sexy silhouette filling the cab of that beat-up Chevy.

A sharp sting of insecurity sent my pulse skittering. I could really—*really*—get hurt.

Oh hell, what have I done?

Christian hopped out of his truck, then opened my door like a gentleman, doing nothing to help the flurry of emotions inside me. Ignoring his outstretched hand, I climbed out on my own. What had been a mildly warm morning had turned into another steam bath of a day. The air was still, suffocating, no longer tolerable.

Or maybe it was just me.

"You didn't have to follow me home, you know," I said, surprising myself at the sharpness of my tone.

"I know," he replied coolly, unfazed by my sudden shift in attitude. Almost as if he'd expected it. "I'll get Cricket."

"I'll get him."

Before Christian could beat me to it, I jogged around to the passenger door and grabbed my purse, then carefully lifted Cricket, still curled in his doggy bed, from the passenger seat.

Christian lingered beside us, obviously wanting to help. Yes, he'd grown fond of my dog. My dog and my pendant.

I just needed to know if he'd grown as fond of me as well.

"Have you ever thought about trimming these vines?" he asked, following me onto the porch.

"No. It's one of the main reasons I bought the house. You don't think they're pretty?"

"They're a perfect place for someone to hide behind."

He was right, but the idea of cutting the purple blooms, the life of the house, made me feel like I'd be removing another piece of my past.

"If you won't cut them, you need security cameras." Christian gestured to the corners of the roof. "Here, and here. You can sync them to your phone and get alerts when there's movement. That way, you're prepared when you come home. Or don't, and wait for an escort."

As he spoke, I stopped short, staring at the handful of pebbles and leaves I'd left along the porch.

"What?" Christian followed my gaze. "What is it?"

"Someone's been here. Again."

Cricket growled, wiggling in my arms.

Christian took the dog from my hands and carefully set him on the porch. Cricket shuffled to the leaves and began sniffing wildly.

"How do you know someone's been here?"

"I strategically placed a pile of rocks along the porch before I left today. They're scattered now."

Christian knelt down, peering at the stones, then plucked the keys from my hand and approached the door. I lingered back with Cricket. After confirming the front window was still locked, he slid the key into the hole and slowly pushed open the door.

"Is everything okay?" I whisper-shouted.

"Hang tight."

My heart pounded with each second that passed until Christian finally stepped outside again.

"Everything looks secure. Come in."

"Come on, baby." I beckoned for Cricket to come.

Once inside, I tossed aside my purse and took off like a bee, zipping from one room to the next, checking every nook and cranny—and my jewelry tree. Everything appeared to be untouched.

Christian went outside to check the perimeter of the house. When he returned, he asked, "Do you know anyone that might've come by to check on you. Abram, maybe?"

I shook my head, stepping onto the porch. "No. He doesn't even know where I live. And it's Sunday, so no mail."

"No tire tracks on the gravel either."

I glanced at the driveway. I hadn't even thought to check that.

"And this is the second time you think someone has been outside your home recently?"

"Yes. A few days ago, the potted plant I keep on the deck outside the back window had been moved."

"You're sure?"

"Yes." I chewed on my lower lip. "What about Jay?"

Christian gave me a curious look. "What about him?"

"He hauled ass out of there after dessert, a good hour before we left."

"You think Jay's the one that's been creeping around your house?"

"I don't know, Christian." I blew out a breath and dragged my hand over the top of my head.

I watched his wheels turn for a moment. He didn't shoot down the idea. Then he disappeared around the corner of my house again. I blew out a breath, staring into the woods.

I didn't have the energy to follow him. My nerves and emotions were *shot*.

He returned a moment later. "I think cameras will cover every angle of your house. And we need to get you another dog."

"I have a dog," I snapped, annoyed at the implication that Cricket was inept.

"I know you do. I'm talking about a guard dog, professionally trained."

"I'm not ready, Christian. I almost lost Cricket just a week ago."

"Yes, you are. You're ready to take care of shit. We talked about this. You're going to take care of shit, Rory."

"This coming from the guy I had to drag out of his man-cave to go to a damn brunch." I swooped down and picked up the handful of pebbles from the porch.

"The game, Rory. We've been through this."

I rolled my eyes as I hurled the rocks through the air, then turned my back to him and walked into the house, muttering, "I know, I know. The *game*."

"Hey." He scaled the porch railing and strode inside after me. "I went, didn't I?"

Feeling suffocated, I began opening the windows. "Do you know how mad I would have been if you would have left me hanging?"

"But I didn't. That's the point."

"Only after I badgered you." I clicked on the television.

"The badgering isn't what did me in."

I tossed the remote on the couch. "What was it, then?"

Before he could respond, a beeping alert pulled our attention to the television. breaking news, the scrolling red banner read as the newscaster's serious face appeared on the screen above it.

"We have some late-breaking news. Local police have identified a person of interest in connection with the Jessie Miller homicide. While not officially named a suspect, this person is the first to be questioned by BSPD, and remains unnamed at this time. This is the first big break in the gruesome murder mystery that has captivated the entire state. Stay tuned to NAR News for updates in this rapidly developing story . . ."

I looked at Christian, laser-focused on the television. My gaze shifted to the front porch, where someone had been snooping around my house hours earlier.

A chill ran up my spine, and I wrapped my fingers around my pendant.

The alert ended and was replaced by a live-streaming local talk show.

"Can you imagine?" the blond host said to her blonder co-host. "A poor girl murdered, mutilated, and just left in the middle of the woods to rot?"

Christian stilled, and the blood drained from his face, which caught my attention. He was no longer with me, it seemed. Instead, he was somewhere deep in his own tormented thoughts.

Something was wrong. And it had to do with the late-breaking news.

"Christian . . ."

He blinked, then squared his shoulders and turned to me, the intensity in his expression forcing me back a step. "I need to tell you something, Rory."

Oh shit.

"Okay . . ." I tried to keep my tone level and my stance relaxed, but my insides were swirling. Whatever he had to tell me wasn't good.

He sucked in a breath and paused, then closed his mouth and jabbed his hand through his hair. "Goddammit."

I didn't speak, didn't move. Pins and needles tend to have that effect.

Christian began pacing back and forth like a madman. Cricket took notice, his attention sharp on the caged animal pacing the carpet.

Suddenly, Christian shook his head, muttering *no,* spun around, and strode out the front door.

"What the . . ." I looked at Cricket. He looked at me.

I hurried across the living room and onto the porch. "Christian. What's going on?"

Ignoring me, he strode down the porch steps, past the row of paintings of my mother without sparing them a glance. The door of his truck slammed and the engine fired up as I stomped onto the driveway.

"What the hell just happened?" I yelled over the engine as I spread my arms wide.

Christian shoved the truck into reverse.

"Fine!" I flung my arms into the air. "Run. Run again. Run back to your hole in the ground." When he peeled out, this *really* pissed me off. "Run away when shit gets serious—just like your goddamn parents did to you!"

He slammed the brakes, and two red lights appeared in the cloud of dust.

My chest heaved with adrenaline as I stalked down the driveway, my fists clenched. "That's right. Run, but this time —*this time*—don't you come back here. I don't need this bullshit in my life right now. Don't come back, Christian. This is it."

My heart pounded as I stared into the back window. Tears stung my eyes, but I blinked them back.

The grind of the gears sliding broke the silence. The door flung open, and through the dust, Christian's body unfolded from the cab, a dark, menacing silhouette.

The door slammed. He stepped through the dust, his eyes locked on mine, taking long quick strides filled with intent. As if sensing the drama about to unfold, a crow called out before swooping down and disappearing into the woods.

My pulse roared in my ears, but I stood strong with my shoulders squared, just like my mom would have told me to do.

"You want me gone?" Christian's neck was flushed red as he spat out the words, closing the inches between us. "Want me to leave?" His nostrils flared, his eyes wild as he said, "And never come back?"

I realized then that it wasn't anger flashing in those green eyes. It was pain. The kind of pain that is so visceral, so deep-seated, that the only way it releases is in an uncontrollable, messy explosion.

"Take a step back," I said calmly. "Take a deep breath, Christian."

His mouth opened, but the breath held as he stared down at me. A gust of wind blew between us, sending strands of my hair floating over my face. His gaze trailed the tendrils of hair tickling my cheeks, my lips.

He took a step back, his chest rising and falling heavily. Then he looked away and turned his back to me.

"You think you're screwed up?" he said into the wind. "Rory, you've got nothing on me."

"What? Tell me. *Tell me*, Christian, please. My God, you've seen me at my worst. My absolute darkest. Tell me your story. What were you going to tell me in there?"

He spun to face me. "I'm not a good person, Rory."

"I don't believe that."

"Because you *want me* to be good. Good for you." He began pacing. "The woman who adopted me died in a car accident. A pileup on Summit Mountain during an ice storm. The police came to my house, and I knew I was going back into the system. At seven years old. I was so *scared*, Rory." He spat out the word *scared* with such hatred. "I was taken to a children's shelter on the outskirts of town. I didn't sleep, eat, or speak to anyone for days."

I stilled, hanging on to every word coming out of his mouth—because I *understood* it.

"A week later, I was taken to the VanCamps." He took a deep breath. "They tried at first, but I wasn't willing. I didn't know how to handle everything I'd been through. I was a terrible, terrible child, a terrible kid, and a worse teenager."

"That's not your fault, Christian."

"It is. Whose fault is it if not mine? I was a little prick to them the moment they adopted me. Lashing out, feeling like I was being tossed from house to house like a ping-pong ball. Like no one knew what to do with me, but I had to be dealt with."

"Did they treat you badly?"

"No," he said quickly. "But looking back now, as an adult, I think they didn't *take* to me, if that makes sense. They adopted me, and I was such an asshole that they just kind of left me alone."

"Did they take you to counseling? Try to help you through everything you'd been through emotionally?"

"No. It was a cold household. No love, between them or us. Both had affairs their entire marriage. My adoptive mother, Maria, had been their housekeeper for a while— that was her job. I found out years later that the only reason the VanCamps adopted me was because the police had found a letter in our house that Maria had written, a will of sorts, basically begging the VanCamps to take me if anything ever happened to her. To this day, I believe the

VanCamps adopted me to avoid bad press. That didn't set well with an unruly kid, as you can imagine."

He started pacing again, but slower, less anxious now.

"The first time I was arrested, I was eleven. Drinking and fighting. I was in and out of jail constantly after that. The VanCamps threatened to send me away to a boarding school, to which I responded by begging them to. But they never did . . ."

He stopped abruptly. Looked into the woods.

"What happened? What happened that made them cut you out of the family?"

A heavy moment passed before he bowed his head and began again.

"It was January. Ice cold, I remember, the kind of cold that cuts right through to the bone. It happened a few days before one of the biggest snowstorms of the decade. I'd just turned sixteen and had no idea what to do with my life. Arnold asked me to help him mend a few fences before the snowfall. I gave him lip because I was supposed to go to my buddy's house that afternoon, but eventually obliged him with a curse."

Christian pulled in a ragged breath. "We set out on horseback, and true to form, got into a heated argument about what I wanted to do with my life and where I was going with it. I said some horrible things to him. He told me that my father, who had abandoned me at eight weeks, was lucky he didn't have to put up with my bullshit. So I lost it. I was a rubber band finally snapping. I hurled a hammer at him with every bit of strength I had in me, hitting the horse instead. It spooked, started bucking. I was still screaming horrible things at him when the horse bucked him off . . . breaking his back in three places."

Christian went still, his fists clenching. A solid minute ticked by as I waited for him to speak.

"Then what happened?" I whispered.

"I left him." Christian turned to me, his eyes as cold as that January day. "I fucking left him there, Rory. Like the bastard who killed Jessie Miller. I left him for dead in the woods. I left the old man writhing on the icy ground, because I was so mad at him for what he'd said about my father. I dumped the horses in the stable and drove to my friend's house, tossing my phone out the window on the way. I don't know what I was thinking . . . actually, I *wasn't* thinking."

As he raked a hand through his hair and pulled in a stuttering breath, I wondered if this was the only time he'd told this story.

"When I got home, drunk and stoned at two in the morning, no one was there. Arnold was in the ICU, where he remained for the next three days, and hospitalized for weeks after. He'd suffered a heart attack after the fall, and fucking laid there, freezing to death for ten hours—*ten hours* —before Anne found him. They said he was minutes from dying."

The woods had gone silent around us.

"The next day, my bags were packed and left by the door, and I was told to leave and never come back. I lived in my friend's basement for two years until I enrolled in the military. That was twenty-four years ago." He turned away. "We didn't speak again after that day. Twenty-four years. I found out both had died not long ago, on the local news. I never got the chance to apologize."

Christian added distance between us, his shoulders slumped in shame.

"Twenty-four years of this eating you alive, Christian."

"As it should," he said quietly.

"You can't hold on to that guilt. You can't write off yourself and your entire life for this. Your actions were rooted in pain. Leaving Arnold that day was a subconscious fuck-you to your dad that left you, don't you see that? You did to him what your dad did to you. I'm not saying it's okay, but there were reasons. You have to let it go."

"Rory—"

"I tried to write myself off twice—and you wouldn't let me. I'm not letting you now."

Christian turned fully toward me, his jaw clenched. "Why? Why do you want me?"

"Because . . ." I gestured to the maple tree as a beam of sunlight illuminated the row of paintings, next to the porch swing he'd made for me.

"Because, Christian," I said as I grabbed his shirt. "You make me see the colors."

His eyes flooded with tears. Desperately, he placed his hands on my face and kissed me.

46

*A*s Christian hoisted me into the air, I wrapped my hands around his neck, our bodies molding together as if being apart was no longer an option.

The skirt of my daisy dress slid up to my waist as I wrapped my legs around him. He spun me around, kissing, kissing, kissing, the scent of him igniting a feral desire deep inside me, one I hadn't felt in so long.

I heard a click, followed by the creak of the tailgate, seconds before I felt the metal of the truck bed on the back of my heated thighs. He nudged my legs apart, though he didn't need to. The moment he sat me on the tailgate, I spread for him, needing every inch of him against me. A steady throb pulsed between my legs, the heat spreading to the butterflies in my stomach.

Our lips never lost contact. His fingers threaded through my hair as he devoured me like a man about to lose it all. Slowly, he unzipped the back of my daisy dress, making my pulse spike. The dress was pulled from my body, my bra unfastened, the silk sliding from my shoulders and leaving a trail of goose bumps.

For a moment, I'd forgotten about my body insecurities —until his fingertips ran down the bumps of my spine. I stiffened, instantly pulled from the moment and mentally scanning for my bra.

The frantic kisses stopped. Christian pulled away, but only an inch from my face. Our eyes locked, his sparking with a hot, wild need.

I licked my lips, and he kissed them softly.

"You're beautiful, Rory."

I looked down, hating that I'd broken the moment.

"On the cliff that night," he said softly, "you were the most beautiful thing I'd ever seen. You were mine. I felt it in every inch of my body. When I saw you, it was like I've known you my whole life, and you were mine to protect. You're even more beautiful to me now than you were then."

He lifted my chin with the tip of his finger. "If you're not ready, that's okay. But, Rory, this is what I want. This is what I've wanted since the moment I laid eyes on my angel in the storm."

"Kiss me again," I breathed out. "*Yes.* I want this. I want this, Christian."

And in that moment, I surrendered. To *him.* I chose to believe him, to let myself go.

I tugged at his golf shirt, yanking the fabric over his head, desperately pulling him to me so I could run my hands along the body I'd dreamed about every night. His lips met mine again, his hand sliding onto my breast. He groaned as he squeezed—and I loved it.

His five o'clock shadow tickled my cheek as he kissed my ear, then down my neck and onto my chest. My eyes drifted closed, my face tilting to the sky as he took my nipple into his mouth and nipped and sucked, his hands caressing me, gripping me possessively.

His hand slid to my panties, the only piece of fabric left on me. I felt the press of his thumb against my most sensitive spot as he pulled the silk to the side and inserted a finger. I moaned, biting my bottom lip as his thumb pressed against my clit.

"Christian," I whispered in a breathy voice not my own.

His wet finger wrapped around the fabric, now binding and suffocating, and slowly pulled my panties down my thighs, my calves, the silk brushing over my toes before it fluttered to the ground.

"Oh my God." He moaned, looking at me, grabbing my waist and yanking me to the edge of the tailgate, the steel sun-warmed against the slickness between my legs.

His eyes on mine, he lowered to his knees, gripped my waist, and pulled me just past the edge. Gasping, I teetered, grappling for something to hold onto.

"I've got you," he whispered as he placed one of my feet onto his shoulder, then the other. "Relax."

My heart roared as his hands wrapped around me, his lips on the inside of my thigh, teasing, licking, tasting that small crease below my hip.

I closed my eyes, focused on my breathing, and rested my hands on his head. I was nervous. Excited. Exhilarated.

He gripped my hips, forcefully tilted—and suddenly he was *on* me, his tongue sliding through my folds, circling my clit, sending a jolt of electricity through my body.

My breath hitched as I desperately clawed at the edge of the tailgate. The sun slid behind a cloud, and a cool breeze swept over my bare skin. I remember thinking this must be euphoria.

Tingles spread between my legs, the throbbing almost painful. I squeezed my eyes shut—

"Christian . . . *Christian* . . ."

I couldn't control it. Didn't want to. Releasing a guttural moan, I came on his face, on his lips, in wave after delirious wave.

I don't remember him standing, or gently scooting me back. But I do remember the look in his eyes as he stared at me, one hand on my leg as if to keep me in place, the other sliding off his pants.

I didn't think it possible to move—until I saw his erection spring out of his black boxer briefs.

"Come here," I said with a grin. Sated and confident now, I grabbed his forearms and pulled him onto the tailgate.

Christian didn't hesitate, his movements swift and hurried as if he couldn't wait another second. The blankets that had been used to pad the furniture were slid underneath my body, my head. I reached for him as he crawled on top of me, his emerald-green eyes crackling with hunger.

"You're mine, Rory."

I nodded and said yes, because there was no other option.

"I love you," he whispered, his voice cracking.

"I love you too," I whispered back.

He nodded, pressed his lips to my neck, and speared into me, stealing my breath, my heart.

We moved together, riding the wave of pleasure, emotions, the combining of one, under the endless sky until we both came undone. Together.

I opened my eyes, gasping for breath. A duo of clouds drifted over the top of the pines above me, two white wings fading into the sapphire-blue sky.

47

Sometime later, I awoke to a ringing cell phone. Disoriented and dazed, as if I'd taken a sleeping pill, I blinked up at the late afternoon sky.

We'd fallen asleep, right there on the tailgate, buck naked and wrapped in each other's arms. It was the best Sunday nap I'd ever taken in my life.

I turned my head, meeting a pair of relaxed, sleepy green eyes twinkling in the shadows of the shade tree. A warm breeze ruffled his beautifully mussed hair.

I smiled, and he smiled back—a real, genuine smile.

He fit, I realized. His purest self, surrounded by nature. This was Christian. And it was *gorgeous.*

"Your phone is ringing," I whispered.

"No, *your* phone is ringing," he whispered back. "No one ever calls me."

"My phone is in my purse in the house."

He frowned, then sat up. I marveled at the muscles flexing in his back with each movement, and before I knew it, I was wet and ready again.

God, the guy does it for me.

But the phone started ringing again.

He searched through the tornado of clothes around us, tossing his shirt aside, a shoe, my dress. He hooked my thong with his pinky, glanced over his shoulder, and wiggled his brows.

I laughed.

Finally, he found his jeans and pulled out his cell phone from his pocket. His back straightened, his face tightening.

I sat up.

"Hello?" he said.

Thanks to the deaf-old-man volume level Christian had on his cell phone, I could hear the other end of the conversation.

"Christian . . ." It was Fatima, her voice pitched with panic. "I need your help. Oh my God . . ."

"Fatima, calm down. What's going on?"

"They've taken Jay."

"Who's taken Jay?"

"The cops! To interview him about the Jessie Miller murder. They just pulled out of the driveway."

Christian's gaze shot to mine. "Did they arrest him? Put him in cuffs?"

"No. No, I don't know what I would have done if they did that. No, they asked him to come to the station. Christian, my grandson, my baby boy, is being questioned for murder."

The fear in the woman's voice broke my heart. She truly loved her grandson, and her whole family unit. I understood that.

"I'm hoping maybe you have some connections," she said quickly, "or strings you could pull from your connection to the VanCamps? I know I'm grasping at straws, but I don't know what to do. Earl and I have never dealt with anything like this—"

"I can help, Fatima." Holding his phone between his ear and shoulder, he began pulling on his jeans. "I'll be right there. We'll figure this out. Do you know why he's a suspect?"

There was a brief pause.

"Fatima, now is not the time to keep secrets."

"He told me, in confidence, that he'd met up with Jessie Miller a few times, over the last few months."

Shit.

"Were they dating?"

"No . . . I think it was more casual, if you catch my drift."

"Yeah, okay. All right, I'll be right there."

"Thank you. Oh, thank you."

He clicked off the call and turned to me.

"Holy shit," I said.

"Yeah." Christian jerked up his pants, hopped off the tailgate, and grabbed his shirt. "I've still got the contact information for the VanCamps' lawyer—best in the state. She was a huge part in the adoption." He slid into his flip-flops. "Maybe she'll remember me."

"Christian . . ."

"Do I think he did it?"

I slowly nodded.

"Innocent until proven guilty. Come on. Let's go."

"No." I grabbed my dress and flung my legs over the tailgate. Truth was, I did want to go with him, but a bigger part of me wanted him to solidify the budding relationship between him and the Bradburys by handling this all alone. I wanted it to be him—only him—to be there for them. I'd be nothing but a distraction.

"You go, they need you. Besides, I need to lay my daisies at the cemetery for mom and dad, like I do every Sunday."

He glanced up at the sky. "Do it before it gets dark."

"You do understand I've actually slept out in that cemetery, right?"

Closing the inches between us, he gripped the tailgate on either side of me, pinning me in place. He smiled and kissed my forehead. "My crazy little black butterfly."

"Oh. Well, thanks. Does that mean I'm going to die tonight?"

"No." He smiled. "It means you're reborn tonight."

"Time to find that new identity, huh?"

"Or step into the one that's always been hidden behind your mom."

"That's deep." I grabbed his chin and pulled him for another kiss. "I love you, Christian. I do."

"I love you, black butterfly."

I pushed him away. "Go save the day. Keep me updated."

He nodded, finding his keys on the ground. "I'll call when I can, and come over after."

"I'll be waiting."

"Wine? Maybe a movie?"

"Like a real date thingy?" I grinned.

"A real date thingy." He tapped the tip of my nose with his finger. "I'll be back. Don't stay with the ghosts too long."

"I think those days are behind me."

I jumped off the tailgate as he hopped into the truck, clutching my dress to my naked chest as I called out, "See you soon."

The engine turned over, and he leaned his head out the window and winked at me. "See you soon."

A cloud of dust gathered around my ankles as I watched him back down the driveway, a ridiculous grin on my face.

Him.

～

The full moon peeked from behind the treetops, an orb of light pushing through the inky sky and illuminating the headstone in front of me. Six fresh daisies lay at its base, their flawless white petals glowing against the bleak grays and blacks of the cemetery at night.

Once again, I'd lost track of time as I usually did, sitting there under the pines. The sun had set about an hour before, the light dimming quickly.

I mindlessly stroked Cricket, asleep in the grass next to me. I was leaning against an oak tree, my knees up, my bare feet planted in the grass.

It was just after nine o'clock, four hours since Christian had left. I hadn't heard from him, although I was glad. This meant he was putting his full focus on the Bradburys. Although I'd be lying if I said I wasn't dying to get the details on Jay.

I thought of the way Jay had watched me from behind the safety of the windows, and the way he avoided eye contact when we were in close proximity. I thought of the feeling I got under his gaze. And much as I had with Christian, the feeling was like a distant memory tapping at my forehead, trying to come into the light but buried under a haze of darkness.

There was something there. Just like there had been with Christian. And I had to figure it out.

The sound of a vehicle approaching broke the stillness, startling me. Cricket lifted his head. Two headlights shot up from the bottom of the hill. Someone was driving into the cemetery.

I glanced at my truck, a few yards away.

Cricket hobbled to a stance as the headlights popped over the hill, two harsh beams illuminating the trees and rows of headstones. My eyes narrowed in protest to the invasion of light.

In all the times I'd visited the cemetery at night, this was the first I'd been interrupted. A tingle of fear slid up my spine.

The lights bumped over the gravel road, then took a turn in my direction and washed over me and Cricket. I lifted the back of my hand to my face, shielding my eyes.

The truck slowed, then stopped. The engine cut, killing the lights, leaving little white dots bursting in my eyes. I couldn't discern the make or color of the truck, but I was sure it wasn't Christian's.

The door opened, then slammed.

A dark figure emerged through the shadows. Long, lean strides that suggested a man's gait. Although I couldn't see his face through the darkness, I could tell the man was looking right at me. He walked slowly, weaving through the headstones, as if hesitant.

Cricket growled.

"*Shhh*," I whispered, keeping my eyes on the silhouette and shifting into a crouch in case I needed to bolt—or attack.

My heart started to pound.

"Hello there," I said, gaining the upper hand by initiating conversation. There was no hiding at this point.

He didn't speak, and this only increased the anxiety flooding my veins.

I stood and faced the man, with Cricket at my ankles.

"Rory?"

My stomach dropped to my feet.

"Jay?" I said, trying to sound casual despite the blood roaring in my ears.

"Yeah."

Slowly, the teenager came into view. He was wearing the same black outfit he'd worn to Sunday brunch. He stopped abnormally far from me, considering he was obviously seeking me out.

Cricket barked, making me nearly jump out of my skin.

"Hush, Cricket." I focused on Jay. "Is everything all right?"

It was an appropriate question considering we were standing in the middle of a graveyard. One honoring the dead, the other recently being interviewed for dealing death.

"Yeah . . ." He scrubbed the back of his neck, looking down.

"What's going on?" I asked, pretty sure he didn't know that I knew he'd just been interviewed for involvement in Jessie Miller's murder.

"You have a second?" he asked.

What the hell?

"Yes, of course. What's going on?"

Jay took a step closer, then another, the moonlight washing over his pale face and swollen, bloodshot eyes. His dark hair was standing on end, likely from running his fingers through it repeatedly. "I, uh, have something to tell you."

It was the second time I'd heard that sentence today. One ended in an earth-shattering orgasm. This one wouldn't.

We stood a headstone apart, under a large oak tree, its leaves dry and wilted from the heat. As still as statues, we stared at each other, our nervous energy coming off us in waves.

He took another step forward, and said—

"I killed your mom."

48

*M*y insides plummeted, the oxygen in my lungs suddenly gone.

I couldn't speak. Couldn't form a single coherent thought through the buzzing in my brain.

"I . . . I was there that day," he stammered. "My truck . . . I swerved. I didn't mean to. I wasn't drunk or stoned or texting, I promise. I was messing with my windshield wipers. Damn things were stuck, and I swerved. I'm so sorry, Rory. It was me. I'm the one who ran your family off the road. I'm the reason your mom died."

I couldn't breathe.

A flash of memory pulled me back in time to six months earlier, to a big black truck crossing the median. Jay Bradbury.

"I'm sorry, Rory. I'm so sorry."

"Why?" My voice was hoarse. "Why are you telling me this now?"

He took a step closer and swallowed hard. "Being with you at brunch today . . . seeing you . . . just brought it all back. And when Christian talked about the military and mentioned a fresh start, that sounded good."

He kicked a rock. "I sold that truck the next week, you know. Couldn't get behind the wheel again. Then I started having panic attacks. The guilt, I guess. And I've just kind of . . . gone into a dark place since then. That's what Granma calls it, at least."

I thought of Fatima talking about the new truck, saying "it was time." She and Earl obviously knew the real story, and that was why she'd been leery of my presence at first, and so protective of her family unit.

"I'm so, *so* sorry, Rory."

A leaf slowly floated down between us, its surprising vibrant green set aglow by a moonbeam. I watched it silently drift to the ground.

It was the first time since my mother's death that I actually *felt* her presence. An omniscient light next to me, a rainbow of colors against my skin. Goose bumps prickled my arms, and a heavy buzz warmed my chest.

She was with me and Jay. And she was smiling.

I thought of Christian, the guilt he carried from leaving his adoptive dad badly injured on the icy ground. I thought of myself, desperately clutching my old life with bloody fingernails and dying inside because of it.

Just let it go, I heard her say.

We all had secrets and sins. We all made mistakes and needed to be saved. We all needed redemption. And that was one thing I could offer this young man.

"I forgive you, Jay." I smiled, feeling the sting of tears. "Thank you for telling me."

He nodded, and a beat passed.

"I'm sorry I never came forward. The thought of being

thrown in jail . . . charged with murder . . . *murder* . . ." His chest heaved and he began pacing, spurts of breaths escaping in the beginning of a panic attack.

"Jay." I crossed the space between us. "Hey, calm down." I lightly grabbed his arm to still him. "Calm down. Please. Sit."

I held on to his shoulders as he dropped to the ground, pulled his arms around his knees, and buried his head into his forearms.

"That's it. Breathe . . . breathe . . ."

Cricket whimpered.

Once Jay's breathing calmed, I sat on the ground next to him and pulled my knees to my chest, mirroring him.

"I know about tonight, Jay. Did you kill Jessie Miller?" I asked softly.

"No." He shook his head vehemently.

"What happened?"

"Jessie was homeschooled. We met at a bonfire one night, a few months before graduation. She'd snuck out of her house. Got drunk, stoned, you know. Met up a few times after that, but that was it. And then I hear she's dead. And then someone, one of my friends, squealed and told the cops that she'd been hanging out with me."

"Do you have an alibi for the night she was murdered?"

"Yeah. My grandparents. I was grounded on the weekend they say she was murdered. Granma spoke to the cops tonight. They let me go, so I think I'm okay. Except the cops took my damn iPhone."

"That's good."

"Tell that to my bank account."

"No, they'll look at your activity and what cell towers you were pinging on during the dates around Jessie's murder.

That will prove you were home and will one hundred percent prove your innocence. Be grateful."

His brows arched. Then he exhaled loudly, my comment releasing some of the weight on his shoulders.

"Stop worrying," I said. "Fatima and Earl will take care of you. They love you a lot, I can tell. I miss that."

"My mom and dad are drug addicts," he blurted, continuing the evening of confessions.

"Sounds like you're in a much better environment now." I nudged his shoulder. "Don't forget to thank them every now and again, okay?"

He nodded. "Christian's still there at the house with them. They're all having a drink, talking about the eventful evening." He rolled his eyes. "I shot out of there the minute we got home."

"To find me?"

"Yeah."

"I'm glad you did. How did you know I was here?"

"Christian mentioned it when Fatima asked where you were, right before he brought in some fancy lawyer for me."

"Did he?"

"Yeah." Jay chuckled. "You should have seen the cops when she walked in."

"Hell on wheels, huh?"

"Oh yeah. I'm pretty sure she had a sleeve under her suit."

"Of tattoos?"

"Oh yeah."

"Cool."

"Yeah."

"Well, sounds like you've got everything lined up. Please don't worry, okay?"

"I'll try."

We sat in a companionable silence, staring at the head-stones, listening to the wind rustle through the trees while meditating on the binds of guilt. We were at a crossroads, Jay and me.

He glanced at me. "Christian likes you."

"Yeah? How do you know?"

"I can just tell."

"Can I tell you a secret?"

Jay looked at me with a childlike sparkle in his eyes. The kid had so much life ahead of him. So much to learn.

I wanted him to be okay. Not to suffer like me, and like Christian. I wanted Jay to accept everything and simply move on.

"I like him too," I said.

Jay grinned, then shook his head. "Maybe you can get him out of that damn basement every once in a while."

"Maybe with your help? You should talk to him about his time in the military."

Jay nodded, and another minute passed.

"Hey, Jay?"

"Yeah?"

"Have you been by my house recently?"

"No. Why?"

"Not over the last week? Not ever?"

"No."

"Promise? You can tell me."

"No, ma'am. Are you serious? I've been avoiding you like the HPV."

"I think the saying is *the plague*. Avoiding you *like the plague*."

"Not these days. HPV is way worse."

I grinned. Christian would have appreciated this banter.

"I don't even know where you live," Jay said.

I believed him, because how could he?

Frowning, I looked up at the moon as I pondered one more question.

So, who the hell has been sneaking around my house?

49

*C*hristian and I spent the next few days between the Black Butterfly, his bed, and his workshop, where I'd set up an easel and become a creative director of sorts. We also spent time on a very sturdy workbench in the corner of his barn.

Having sex on objects—tailgates, tables, chairs, sawhorses—was becoming our thing. I wasn't complaining. I was walking around with my legs deliciously sore and my head in the clouds.

Christian took me when he wanted me and where he wanted me, each experience pulling me further and further away from the dark hole I'd dug myself in. I was starting to feel sexy again.

Our relationship had progressed at warp speed. It was crazy how quickly and seamlessly Christian and I molded together once our armor had been stripped and we'd both simply given in to each other.

There was an immediate change in Christian after the confession of both his mistake and his feelings for me. A surrender, a new softness in his touch, his voice, the way he moved, the way he looked at me. He was less defensive, less self-loathing and self-destructive. He was lighter, happier, a man I'd never met before. A man with a sex drive comparable to a teenage boy.

Something about us just fit.

Growing ballsier by the day, Fatima began visiting the barn, offering Christian and me a jug of sweet tea and a basket of the latest pastry she'd baked. She'd talk our ears off while watching us enjoy her treats. It made her day, and mine.

I'd gained three pounds in three days. Christian celebrated each pound with extra nibbles. And I celebrated by marking off another day from the calendar without a headache and a bad dream.

The feeling of achievement I'd once gotten from going to bed hungry had been replaced by Christian's admiration of my artistry and my own growing sense of self. I was slowly learning how to feel worthy without my mother's constant reminder that I was. Without relying on her for it. I had to acknowledge my own wins and celebrate myself. It was an entire shift in thinking.

I felt good. Better. Mom would be proud.

Jay had even made his way down to the barn, expressing interest in woodworking, and picked Christian's brain on all things military.

We all spoke freely now that the skeletons were out of the closet. Seeds were being laid, buried, and watered, soon to mature into meaningful relationships.

That afternoon, Christian and I had our first official meeting to discuss the new website for the Black Butterfly.

334 | AMANDA MCKINNEY

We agreed to narrow the focus of the shop to mainly art. It made sense, especially considering I planned to sell some of my paintings there too. Anonymously, of course. After that, Christian bent me over a spindle line boring machine until I forgot my own name, and then we parted ways. Me to drop off a few things at the shop before heading home to begin dinner for us, and him to the lumberyard to pick up pieces for an accent cabinet I suggested would go great with one of my paintings.

It was close to five o'clock by the time I made it to Tourist Row, squeezing my truck into the only parking spot available in front of the Black Butterfly.

Box in hand, I rounded the hood just as the front door of Abram's cigar shop opened. I recognized the man who was leaving as one of Abram's daily customers, the Crypt Keeper, I'd secretly dubbed him due to his uncanny resemblance to the storyteller. I halted, though, when I noticed the lack of lights inside the shop.

"Hello, there," I called out as I pivoted, crossing the small patch of grass between our doors.

The man hobbled around and frowned, scanning me from head to toe with an expression that suggested he knew me, but didn't know where from. Not surprising, considering he spent most of his days smoking cigars and guzzling whiskey inside Abram's office.

"I'm Rory. I run the shop next door."

"Ah. Yes." He frowned at the paint spatter that dotted the T-shirt and jean shorts I'd thrown on for a day of work in Christian's shop. "That's right. You sell art."

The old man refocused on the door, locking it and double-checking the lock, then turned back to me. A faded blue duffel bag hung from his shoulder. "Name's Luther."

"Pleasure to meet you, Luther. Where's Mr. Abram?"

"Sick," he barked out, apparently annoyed that his addiction to free smokes and booze was temporarily unserviceable.

"Sick, you say?"

Luther nodded, shakily descending the stone steps that led down from the door.

"What's wrong with him?" I asked, inching forward to catch him if he fell.

"Vomiting, muscle cramps, chest pain, shaking like a damn leaf. Took him to the doctor."

"Oh my God. When did this happen?"

"Just this morning. The shop was locked when I showed up—same time every day, you know. I banged on the door, called his number." He lifted the cell phone in his hand. "New phone. Grandkids got it for me. Barely know how to turn the damn thing on. Anyway, his truck wasn't around back."

I glanced up at the second story where Abram lived. It was dark.

"Started to worry 'bout noon," Luther said. "So I drove out to his house."

"What house?"

"The lake house he abandoned after his wife died. Never sold it. Just left it to rot, I guess. Bad memories. I offered to buy it from him—we go way back, him and me, all the way to high school—but he couldn't do it."

"And he was there?"

The old man nodded. "Laying on the floor in the front room, 'bout as pale as the sheetrock behind him. Loaded him up and took him to the emergency room." Luther glanced back at the shop. "He gave me the keys to the place to pack up some clothes and toiletries to bring him."

"What's wrong with him?"

"Don't know. Doc was runnin' tests when I left."

I glanced back at my truck. "I was actually going to drop by today. To return some books I borrowed from him."

"You can do it later. I don't want to open it up again."

"Okay." I looked up at the windows again. "Well, let me know if he needs anything. I can take care of the shop, do whatever needs to be done."

Luther pushed past me. "Will do, sweetheart."

As I watched the old man climb awkwardly into his rusted sedan, I couldn't ignore the knot in the pit in my stomach.

50

I pulled up my driveway, inhaling the scent of lilacs on the warm evening breeze. Slanted sunbeams shot through the trees, casting shadows across the front lawn. Crickets sang into the breeze, celebrating the break from the staggering heat.

My thoughts were occupied with the shop and the marketing plan I'd drawn up hours earlier, and of Christian, the man I'd been under hours earlier.

I didn't notice the movement in my house as I parked.

"We're home, buddy." I ruffled Cricket's ears. "Hang tight, I'll be right around."

I'd just stuffed my keys and cell phone in my purse and stepped out of the truck when I paused. A little warning bell went off somewhere deep in my psyche. I listened to the bugs, to the sound of a squirrel scurrying up a nearby tree.

My gaze shifted to the corners of the roof where Christian would be installing security cameras this evening. He'd be there soon.

With that encouraging thought, I rounded the hood and lowered Cricket to the ground. I watched him a moment.

When he didn't bark or start sniffing the ground, I assumed I was alone.

"Need to go potty?"

Ignoring me, Cricket disappeared around the truck.

"Take your time."

Uneasy, I crossed the driveway and stepped onto the front porch. The vines swayed in a breeze I didn't feel. I glanced through the front window as I passed. The house was dark with shadows. I kicked myself for not leaving a light on.

I shoved my key into the lock, the door groaning as it always did when I opened it.

A shadowy movement caught my eye, sending a jolt of fear up my spine. Boots pounded on the hardwood floor. A dark silhouette lunged out the back, sending the door crashing into a few potted plants I'd recently placed in the corner.

"Hey!" I yanked my phone from my purse and sprinted across the room, sending an end table teetering and a lamp shattering on the floor.

"*Hey!*" I burst out the door as the man leaped off the deck, stumbling on the ground.

I froze, my hair whipping across my face from the sudden halt. My mouth fell open as I watched the man dart across the backyard. I recognized the thick snow-white hair, the broad shoulders, the slight limp in his step.

"Walter?" I called out, shock lacing my tone.

I hurried down the steps, confusion replacing the fear.

"Walter!" I yelled one more time as he hobbled into the woods at surely his fastest speed. I considered chasing him —I could easily catch him—but thought better of it. I needed a second to process what the heck was going on.

Blinking in confusion, I stared into the darkening woods.

What the hell was Walter Kelley doing breaking into my house? Had he been the one peeping in my windows?

More importantly, *why*?

I clicked on my phone and made a call, slowly walking to the edge of the woods while it rang.

"Hello?"

"Christian—you are not going to believe what just happened."

"Are you okay?" The phone rustled and I heard heavy footfalls, as if he'd started jogging.

"Walter just broke into my house. I caught him."

"*What*? Walter? Are you sure?"

"Yep. I'm one hundred percent positive."

"Are you okay?"

"Yeah, he ran when he saw me. I'm fine. But get over here."

"I'm on my way."

Seven minutes later, Christian barreled up my driveway, engulfed in a cloud of dust. We were losing light quickly.

The driver's side door swung open as the engine cut off. I met him at the porch steps.

"Did you call the cops?" His eyes were slitted, a steely green, protective testosterone rolling off him in waves.

"No. Wanted you to get here first."

"Are you sure it was him?" Christian stepped onto the porch, striding past me to the door.

I pivoted. "Yes, I saw him."

"Where's Cricket?"

"Inside. Safe."

"Did you have your windows closed?"

"Yes."

"Are any broken?" He knelt down to inspect the locks he'd installed days earlier.

"Not that I could tell immediately."

"Did you lock them before you left?"

"Yes. Christian, what the hell do you think he was doing?"

"Was he carrying anything? Did he take anything from your house?"

"I don't think so. The man took off like a bullet—well, more like a three-legged turtle."

When Christian shot me a frown, I gestured to the house. "Cricket can't hear me. He's inside."

Christian stood, deep in thought as he scanned the door. "Which direction did he go?"

I pointed toward the backyard. "That way."

"Which way, exactly?"

I jabbed my finger into the air. "That way. I just said."

"East, Rory. That's east."

"*East*, Christian," I said, rolling my eyes. "He went east."

"Did he say anything?"

"No. I called after him but he kept running. Whatever he was doing, he didn't want to be caught . . . or didn't want to address it, maybe. I don't know."

Christian pushed open the door and scanned the living room.

"Nothing is missing. I've checked."

I watched as Christian strode from room to room, checking the windows, the door frames. His gaze was hard, his jaw set. He was as confused as I was.

Cricket followed him closely, sniffing the floor.

Crossing my arms over my chest, I leaned against the door frame of my bedroom. "What the hell do you think the old man was doing?"

Christian turned from the jewelry tree he was examining. "Only one way to find out."

51

*D*arkness had fallen by the time Christian turned his truck onto the rutted path that led to Walter's trailer.

"No lights on." I frowned, peering through the windshield.

"He's here." Christian nodded to the heap of rust parked under a tree. "There's no way that old man could have walked all the way back here from your house. He must have parked somewhere in the woods, close to your house, and sneaked up."

I nodded, but something in my stomach twisted. Something didn't feel right.

Christian parked behind Walter's truck and jumped out.

"Wait for me." I jumped out of the truck and jogged around the hood, Christian three steps ahead of me with tunnel vision.

"*Stop*, Christian," I whisper-shouted, unsure why I was whispering. "Let me do the talking."

"The man *broke* into your house. I'm doing the talking."

Christian banged his fist against the door, three loud

booms that echoed through the woods. When there was no response, he pounded again, harder this time, the thin door bowing under the pressure.

Frowning, I shifted my gaze to the woods. "Where could he be?"

Leaving Christian to his snoop around the trailer's windows, I crossed the yard, being pulled like a magnet to the trees. He mumbled something to me, but between the screaming cicadas and my tunnel vision, I didn't hear it. My attention was locked on a lump on the ground between two pines, just past the tree line, barely visible in the darkness.

My heart suddenly racing, I broke into a jog.

I dropped to my knees, placing my hands on Walter's limp body as I screamed for Christian. Footsteps thundered behind me as I frantically pulled my cell phone from my pocket and clicked on the flashlight.

Walter's eyes were closed, his skin waxy and pale, a line of foam trickling from the corner of his mouth. Blood matted the side of his head, and also colored a large rock lying next to his ear.

"Call nine-one-one. And move."

As Christian took my place, I surged backward, stumbling before scrambling up. Watching Christian slowly roll the old man onto his back, I made the call.

"Ten minutes," I said after finishing the call, then repositioned the light above the body. My hand was trembling.

"No pulse."

"*Shit.*" Blood roared in my ears.

"Keep the light there."

Christian lifted from his haunches and straddled the body, lacing his fingers over Walter's chest. Tears welled as I watched Christian pound Walter's chest, breathe into his mouth, and start again. And again.

And again.

My stomach rolled. There was no life in the old man. With each thrust of Christian's fists, Walter's eyes fluttered open with the movement, revealing a lifeless gray around dilated pupils that were rolled back into his head. A horrifying sight.

Still, Christian didn't give up. He continued CPR, occasionally rolling Walter onto his side, then back again and starting over.

The man was dead.

"Christian," I whispered, my voice shaking.

He didn't look up, didn't hear me. His eyes were wild as he kept pounding the poor man's chest. Although it probably didn't matter at this point, I was afraid he would break Walter's rib cage.

It felt like a lifetime passed until the eerie wails of sirens broke the silence. Red lights flashed across Walter's body.

"Over here!" I yelled.

Two EMTs jogged across the yard.

"Get back, sir," one said crisply to Christian, but he didn't move.

I wasn't sure he'd heard them. His face, red in the light, was contorted with strain, his focus solely on Walter's chest.

"Sir. Please, move."

Still no response. It was as if Christian were somewhere else entirely.

"Christian," I shouted.

His head shot up at the sound of my voice, and he blinked, returning to the present.

"They need you to get back," I said breathlessly. "They're here. Let them work."

His gaze shifted to the medics, and he surged up and jumped back.

With Christian at Walter's head and me at his feet, we watched in silence as the medics went to work.

My heart thundered inside my chest, not only from the scene unfolding around me, but at the look in Christian's eyes. I knew he was thinking of Arnold, his adoptive dad, and how he'd left him to die in the woods. The past muddled with the present in a pain so raw, it crackled off him like sparks of electricity. Although this time, Christian couldn't push it aside or run away and hide in his cave. It was right there in front of him.

"Got a pulse," the medic informed the other.

Our eyes met in a flash. Christian's chest heaved, as if he'd been holding his breath.

The next few minutes were a blur. Everything switched to warp speed, a rush of urgency now as the medics loaded Walter into the back of the ambulance. Although I couldn't hear much of the chatter between them, one thing about Walter's pulse stood out.

"It's faint, but it's there."

Christian and I watched the ambulance speed down the dirt road, leaving behind a cloud of dust that rose into the darkness.

He turned abruptly, making long, quick strides across the grass.

"Where are you going?"

"To the hospital. The old man has no one. Someone should be there."

52

*I*n the small waiting room we'd been ushered to when we arrived at the hospital, I watched the second hand of the clock slide from one second to the next, the loud *tick, tick, tick* breaking the excruciating silence.

Christian stood motionless in front of the single window in the room, his arms crossed over his chest, staring unseeing at the darkness outside. We hadn't spoken since arriving at the hospital. Not a single word.

I tossed the *Parenting* magazine that I'd mindlessly flipped through three times onto the table and stood, unable to sit any longer.

The door opened and a young, bright-eyed nurse with braided hair and blue scrubs walked inside. "Hello," she said, her gaze flicking to Christian.

He turned and crossed the room in two swift steps.

"You're both here about Mr. Kelley, is that correct?"

"Yes. How is he?"

"The doctor will be in shortly to talk to you. I'm sorry I don't have any details right now, but I know Mr. Kelley has a team working on him as we speak. He's in good hands."

Working on him didn't sound good.

"Are you family of the patient?" she asked.

"No," Christian and I replied in unison.

She nodded as she flipped open the folder in her hands. "I have his clinic information here. It's a bit dated—he hasn't been here in a while—but we'd like to contact the person he noted as his emergency contact." She searched the papers. "Do either of you happen to know a Christian Locke?"

I frowned, then looked at Christian.

He blinked. "That's me."

"Oh," she said, surprise in her tone. "Oh. Well, Mr. Kelley has here," she tapped the file with the tip of her finger, "that we should contact you in case of an emergency."

A line formed between Christian's brows as he tried to process what the woman was saying. "Me? Are you sure?"

"If you're Christian Locke, then yes, I'm sure."

"Why me?" he said quietly, as if the private thought accidentally slipped free.

The nurse lifted the paper, scanning another page. "Well, Mr. Locke, according to the paperwork he filled out, you're his son."

53

*S*wiping a tear from my cheek, I pivoted and retraced the six-foot line I'd paced exactly seventy-two times since Christian was ushered out of the room—to speak with the staff and complete paperwork.

Because Walter Kelley was Christian's father.

I was an absolute mess about it, overcome with joy that Christian had finally found his father, but also riddled with fear that he might lose him—only minutes after finding him. Because I knew what it was like to lose a parent.

Memories swamped me of standing in that very room six months earlier, waiting to hear if they were able to bring my mother back to life. I remembered the tile with the stain that resembled a bird, and the one with a crack zigzagging through the middle like lightning. The nicks in the sheetrock, where so many relatives of loved ones had surged from their chairs at the sound of footsteps coming to the doorway.

I remembered the moment the doctor walked in. I'd been staring at the door in a weird daze that felt like a dream.

I remembered his face when he looked at me. The feeling in my body. The hole that was never repaired.

When the door finally opened again, I was beginning round number seventy-three. The same nurse from earlier stepped in.

"Rory Flanagan?"

"Yes, ma'am."

"You can go in now."

"Go in?"

"To Mr. Kelley's room. Mr. Locke is in there."

"He's okay?" My heart stammered.

"He's in ICU. The doctor, or Mr. Locke, can give you details on his current condition. But I will say he's an extremely lucky man. The doctors believe the CPR you administered not only brought him back to life, but kept him alive until the medics got there." A soft smile lifted her mouth. "Good job on not giving up on him."

As she turned to leave, I whispered breathlessly, "It wasn't me. Christian didn't give up on him."

She turned back. "What?"

I shook my head, unable to form another word.

Christian had saved his father's life—in the sweetest twist of redemption.

"Are you okay, ma'am?"

I nodded, blinking back the tears.

"Okay. Follow me, please."

My knees felt stiff as I walked down the same hall I had six months earlier, under harsh fluorescent lights that reflected off the little gold specks in the tile floor. I remembered the smell—bleach, antiseptic, and sickness. The pale faces that watched as you passed and the pity in their eyes.

I balled my hands into fists to hide the tremor in my bones.

"Room one-twenty-two." The nurse gestured to the closed door.

I stumbled to a halt. It was the same room my father had been put in for observation after the doctor confirmed to me that my mother didn't make it through the accident—but that my father did.

When the nurse disappeared down the hall, my gaze shifted to the IV stands that lined the walls, the carts, trays, the other rooms occupied by people clinging desperately to hope.

A deep breath expelled from me, something that felt like a circle coming to a close.

I knocked lightly on the door. When there was no answer, I knocked again, but this time I cracked it open.

"Christian," I whispered before poking my head in.

I will never forget that moment for the rest of my life.

With his head bowed and his eyes closed, Christian sat in a chair pulled as close to the bed as possible, praying over his father. Walter's eyes were closed, an oxygen mask on his face and a bandage around his head, speckled with blood. IVs ran like wires out of both arms. His pale gnarled hand was tightly enveloped by his son's.

Sensing me, Christian opened his eyes.

I quietly stepped inside and closed the door behind me. After a moment, I tiptoed across the room, careful to keep my distance, a part of me feeling like I was intruding on an extremely personal moment.

Staring at them both from the other side of Walter's bed, I could see the resemblance in the men. The size and mass of their bodies, the sharp nose and jawline. Thick, unruly hair. And their eyes, with dark brows and dark lashes over bright irises that pulled you in and never let go.

Christian had the spirit of his father in him. I could see it now.

A few minutes passed as we watched the rise and fall of Walter's chest.

A nurse—one that I hadn't seen—bustled in, breaking the moment. She sent me a quick pitying smile, then went about her business, checking the monitors, recording stats. Christian didn't acknowledge her. His watchful eyes remained fixed on his father.

I stepped out of the way, closer to Christian. When the nurse left, I placed my hand on his shoulder.

"What did the doctor say?" I asked quietly.

A moment passed, and Christian's rigid demeanor finally faltered, his vise-like grip releasing his father's hand. He sank back in the chair with an exhale. While keeping his gaze on Walter, he gave me the update.

"He went into cardiac arrest—from the running, we assume—then tripped and fell headfirst into a rock. He has a concussion and stitches, but that's fine. That will heal."

Christian's Adam's apple bobbed with emotion. "Walter has severe coronary artery disease, according to the doctor, and needs open-heart surgery immediately if—*when*—he's stable enough. He's sixty years old. This is a lot for his body."

He inhaled deeply. "His heart has suffered a lot of damage. They'll run tests in the morning to see if, or how much, his brain suffered." He looked at me, childlike panic and pain in his face. "He died, Rory. He died. Before we got there. They say he died."

"You saved his life, Christian. You saved your father's life."

He sniffed and leaned forward, turning his face away from me.

"Would you like me to—"

"No." His voice cracked, his shoulders hunched. "No. Please. Stay."

~

And stay I did, for the next forty-eight hours.

Although still not awake, Walter had improved greatly, and the doctors hoped to do surgery within the next few days. Christian and I took turns to eat, shower, and check on Cricket. Despite the nurses' and doctors' advice, Christian wouldn't leave the hospital to get a solid night's sleep.

I'd called Fatima, informing her of the events, and asked her to feed and water T-Bone and Tater, and let Ishka out of the barn to stretch her legs. Two hours after that, Fatima delivered a four-course meal to the hospital for not only Christian and me, but the entire nursing staff and doctors in the ICU unit.

She'd pulled me outside for some fresh air, and to my utter humiliation, I fell to my knees and had a full-blown mental breakdown, right there in her arms. She let me cry and cry, never asking a single question.

The woman was a saint. An angel, right there on earth, sent by someone that day. Just for me.

Other than comments and observations about Walter's progress, Christian and I barely spoke. He was an absolute wreck.

As I sat there with Christian as he watched his father for all those hours, I couldn't imagine all that was going through his mind. His father was a real, tangible person now, right there in front of him, no longer a phantom of his past.

Was Christian replaying every moment he'd seen the

man, and all the times he'd left food on the old man's doorstep. Did he wonder how they were alike? What characteristics and personality traits he might have gotten from Walter?

And where was Christian's birth mother? Was she alive?

Did he have grandparents? Were they alive?

Where was he from? His ancestry, his roots?

There were so many unanswered questions. Walter obviously knew Christian was his son, according to his medical records. So, why hadn't he said anything?

And the most haunting question of all was, why did Walter leave Christian on the steps of a church all those years ago? What had brought him to that moment?

Why did he have a wind chime exactly like the pendant my mother gave me?

And why, decades later, did the man break into my house?

Like father, like son, indeed.

I was on my bi-hourly walk around the building to clear my brain and my lungs of the antiseptic smell when I saw the Crypt Keeper himself hobbling down the sidewalk. I realized I hadn't even thought of Abram since finding Walter running from my home.

When our eyes met, a flicker of recognition came to his.

"Luther, right? Abram's friend?"

He nodded and stopped. "Rory."

"That's right. How's Mr. Abram?"

He shook his head. "Died. This morning."

My breath caught. "*What*?"

"Yep. They thought it was a heart attack when I first brought him in, but then they found it."

"Found what?"

"The bite."

A pair of eyes milky with cataracts met mine, and a chill ran up my spine.

"A bite from what?" I asked, although I already knew.

"A black widow. Slowly poisoned the old man to death."

54

*A*fter retrieving the spiral-bound notebook from my truck, I spent the next twelve hours sneaking peeks at it while trying to get comfortable on the hospital room couch. Christian took up the other half of the couch as he waited for Walter to wake up.

Sometime in the middle of the sleepless night, I decided the half-completed manuscript wasn't fiction. It was the work of a madman, a lonely widowed veteran who'd lost it somewhere along the way.

There were too many coincidences to ignore in the handwritten letters from the girl who'd been held captive, compared to the girl I'd found in the ditch—and Abram.

Such as the girl's red hair, pale skin, and tall height. Her comment about the lingering scent of cigar smoke, her captor's stained teeth, and his obsession with knives. All could pertain to Abram. And how she could hear the lake outside her window—a home on the lake, exactly as Luther said Abram had.

And finally, the black widow spider.

At sunrise the next day, Detective Darby met me in the hospital parking lot at my request. After giving him the notebook, I told him everything. Whether he'd look into it or not, I didn't know. But I had more important things to focus on.

55

I'd just returned from the hospital's "café"—otherwise known as an overpriced version of the Git 'N Split—with nothing more than gas station food. Balancing two seven-dollar cups of coffee in one hand, I pushed open the hospital room door and halted at the sound of low, deep voices.

Christian looked up at me, his eyes bright, a small smile lifting the corner of his mouth.

Walter was awake, sitting up and talking.

"Well, hi, there." I smiled widely at Walter, then shifted my attention to Christian. "Do you want me to—" I tilted my head toward the door.

"No," Walter croaked out. "If that's coffee, get over here."

I snorted out a laugh and crossed the room, holding out the cup without the floating grounds. "Just brewed, sir."

"Wait." Christian snatched it from my hands. "You're not supposed to be drinking caffeine. Doctor's orders."

Walter scoffed. "Damn doctors. No coffee? That's bullshit."

"You want a decaf?" Christian asked, unfazed by the spitting discontent.

"I want a shot of whiskey."

Christian's gaze flicked to mine with a flash of amusement.

I wasn't sure what to say, how to address the dynamic in the room. Obviously, Walter was aware that his secret was out now, considering his son was standing next to him. I could only assume that in the short time I'd been gone, questions hadn't been asked or answered. It would probably take much more than a shot of whiskey for that. For now, both men were carrying on, nimbly avoiding the elephant in the room as men so easily do. And I figured that might go on a while.

I lowered myself to the edge of the plastic couch and tried to disappear. A minute passed.

Finally, Walter sighed. "So, what happened? Did I pass out or what? I want to hear it from you, not the doctors."

"You went into cardiac arrest."

Walter grunted, seemingly unsurprised.

"You have heart disease," Christian said in his ever-so-blunt way, which I now know means that he cares. "Did you know that?"

"I'm an old man, Christian. Many things aren't working like they used to."

Christian opened his mouth, probably to demand—in his typical emotionless delivery, of course—that the man start taking better care of himself. But he hesitated and closed his mouth. Apparently, I wasn't the only one unsure how to navigate these murky waters.

"When do they cut me loose?"

"After you have surgery."

"Surgery? On my heart?"

Christian nodded.

"No." Walter's eyes narrowed in defiance.

"Yes," Christian snapped back. "You'll die if they don't fix your heart."

Walter worked the muscles of his jaw, his mind racing. A long, heavy moment passed in the room, and I knew it was coming.

Walter shifted his gaze to the window. His expression softened with surrender as he closed his eyes.

"I'd just joined the Navy," he said quietly, already losing himself in the story. "I was young, stupid, immortal —or so I thought. I asked Marian to marry me, and she said yes. She was the love of my life." He paused, gathering himself. "She was seventeen when you were born. I'd just turned twenty. Six weeks later, she fell down the stairs, broke her neck, and died. Two weeks later, I got word that I was getting deployed. The next day, I left my son on the church steps. And I've regretted it every day since."

It was as if the world had gone still. The air had been sucked from the room, the only sound my beating heart. Such a simple, short story, yet the actions had carried decades of pain, guilt, and regret. Had shaped both men before me.

Christian stood frozen in place, as still as a statue. The only sign of life was the heavy rise and fall of his chest.

Still avoiding eye contact with his son, Walter continued.

"I left a note in your bassinet with your name and birthday. I used Marian's maiden name, Locke. She was almost full-blood Irish. She would have loved . . ." He swallowed deeply and shook his head, unable to go there. "I heard you were adopted by a nice lady while I was overseas. I returned months later and never left. All my life—all your life—I've never been more than a few miles from you, Christian, you know that? Your entire life, I've been here."

He coughed, his face wrinkling in pain. The confession seemed to have drained the little energy he had.

"I thought about reaching out to you, especially when Maria died and the VanCamps adopted you. But I could never give you what they could. You were in better hands with the VanCamps, trust me."

My gaze shot to Christian, but he still didn't move. Didn't speak. He simply stared down at his father, trying to process the words coming from the man's mouth.

Walter's eyes opened on me. I set the coffee on the floor and stood. Squinting, the old man looked me over, his attention settling on the pendant around my neck. When I lifted the necklace, he nodded and opened his calloused hand.

Pulling the chain over my head, I crossed the room and placed the pendant in his calloused palm. He released a deep exhale the moment the metal touched his skin.

Walter's craggy face softened as he lifted the pendant, examining it, losing himself in it. "It's been so long," he whispered, studying the pendant. Then he frowned, bringing it closer to his face. "Should've cut deeper."

"What?" I asked.

"It's fading. The Caim prayer." He looked at me. "What's your name?"

"Rory. And you know my necklace, don't you, Walter?"

He nodded. "This is Marian's. Christian's mother's."

He continued examining the pendant as if a bomb hadn't just exploded in the room, or maybe he was simply too tired to care anymore.

"I made it for her when I asked her to marry me." With the pendant clenched in his hand, he looked at Christian.

"And she gave it to you when you were born. I tucked it in the bassinet when I put you on the church steps."

My lips parted in shock. My conversation with Christian by the barn flitted through my head . . .

"Why did you ask about the pendant?"

"Just caught my eye is all . . ."

I now understood why Christian had such an interest in the pendant. He had a deep-seated memory of it, exactly like I had with him. The pendant had brought us all together.

A full circle.

Walter turned his focus to me. "And now you have it. Where did you get it?"

"I . . . My mother gave it to me."

His eyes drifted closed, a soft smile spreading across his face. This pleased him, but I wasn't sure why.

"Where did she get it?" he whispered.

"A flea market."

"Must've got lost, or stolen, during the shuffle." He smiled again. "But it looks like it found its way back, didn't it."

Mouth agape, I looked at Christian.

"Yes . . . found its way back," Walter whispered, closing his eyes.

Christian blinked, his breathing short, quick inhales now. He spun away from his father's bed and strode out the door, unable to hear another word.

I turned and took a step to follow. "Christian—"

"No," Walter croaked. "Let him go, Rory. Let him go."

Unsure, I stopped, turning back to Walter.

"The man needs a minute."

I looked at the door, then back at Walter, and stepped to

the side of his bed. "Walter, is this why you broke into my house? Why you'd come by?"

His lips pressed into a thin line. "Sorry about that, kid."

"It's okay."

"I recognized the pendant right away when I saw it around your neck. It was . . . the past, right there in front of me. Around your neck for the world to see. For the world to figure out. I wanted it gone—no, I wanted it back."

"Why didn't you just ask for it?"

"Well, I came by your house twice to do just that. You weren't home each time. I figured that was for the best, because you would have probably put the pieces of the puzzle together at some point. I didn't want that. It's been so long." He paused. "And then I got desperate. I haven't been able to sleep . . . I just wanted it back."

"I would have given it to you."

"Then I would have had to explain."

"Well, it's out now, Walter."

He nodded, turning over the necklace in his hands.

"What does the tree symbolize?" I asked.

"It's the Celtic tree of life. I added a cross base with our birthstones down the middle. Marian's, Christian's, and mine. Red, pale green, and blue. It's ours, forever."

"And the back?"

"Is the prayer Marian and I recited at our wedding. And the black butterfly . . ." His voice wavered. "That was my nickname for Marian."

My heart tripped. Christian had called me the same thing.

"She was a beautiful black butterfly," Walter said. "With hair as black as a raven's wing—like Christian. She gave me a new life from an old one, set me straight and made me a father. She symbolized rebirth in me. New beginnings." Our eyes met. "And the pendant found you, Rory—brought Christian to you, you to me, and now him to me."

He closed his eyes, the words lingering in the air.

But Walter had left out one link in the chain of the pendant—my mother.

My mother had gifted me the necklace that united Christian and me, and him with his family—hours before she left this world.

The pendant wasn't a curse. No, it was my mother, guiding me to my new life. My new identity. Rebirth. New beginnings.

She's always with you.

There were still many questions to be answered, many conversations to be had. But in that moment, one thing became as clear as day to me.

My mother is still here.

Still very much watching over me.

Two weeks later...

"Get your hands off me, boy."

"Then move a little faster, old man."

"I would if you'd level the ground back here, like the landlord you say you are. My backyard is like the damn Rocky Mountains."

Christian released the handles of the wheelchair and glanced at me with a gleam of amusement in his eyes. Happy for him, I grinned back.

Taking a step back from his independent father, Christian stayed close by as Walter rolled across his backyard, slow and steady, and hating every minute of it. He'd insisted he didn't need the damn wheelchair and wanted the canes and walker he'd stored in his barn.

A cloud drifted over the sun, providing a momentary reprieve from the late afternoon heat. The summer was getting cooler, with temperatures holding steady and comfortable in the low eighties.

A trio of blackbirds settled onto the edge of the metal

building on Walter's land as we approached. Walter had trouble angling his chair so he could reach the combination lock that bound the rickety wooden doors. His gnarled, arthritic hands trembled as he spun the dial.

A minute passed. Then two.

The old man cursed under his breath.

"Here . . ." Christian reached out. "Let me."

Walter swatted his son's hands away. "Stop. I got it."

Another minute passed. In an attempt to rein in his patience, Christian closed his eyes and inhaled deeply.

Waiting, I grinned, but I didn't have to wait long.

"Walter." Christian finally snapped, lunging forward. "There aren't enough hours in the day to accommodate your goddamn pride. Move." He wrestled the lock from his father's hands. "What's the combination?"

Walter huffed out a breath. "It's oh eight, oh four, eighty-one."

As Christian froze, Walter looked down, fidgeting with his hands. I sucked my lower lip between my teeth, biting back tears.

The combination was Christian's birthday.

Regaining his composure, he tried again and popped open the lock, and the metal building's doors swung open. Dust spiraled up the pinpricks of sunlight that shot through rusted holes in the roof.

Walter nudged Christian away and rolled inside.

The sharp scent of metal and oil permeated the cool, musty air. My gaze locked on the back wall, which was lined with dozens of wind chimes and iron wall hangings.

"The Celtic tree," I said breathlessly as I stepped inside. "Just like the pendant and your wind chime."

Awestruck too, Christian surveyed the walls and the rusty old machinery that was tucked under the awnings, safe from the holes in the ceiling. The metal building served as a workshop for Walter—almost exactly like Christian's. Except Christian worked with wood, and his father, metal.

I gestured to the metal wall hangings. "Did you make all these?"

Walter smirked at me. "I don't just sit around and watch TV all day."

My lips widened into a smile, and I gaped at Christian as our eyes met.

"You know," I said with a grin as I looked at Walter. "Christian has a shop, just like this. He makes furniture. You work with metal, and he works with wood."

"I know."

"You do?" Christian asked.

"I've seen it. You work outside on sunny days."

Christian nodded. "I do."

Their eyes met briefly, and as two men unaccustomed to dealing with emotion generally do, they looked away.

"Anyway, the walker and canes are over there." Walter wheeled over the dirt floor, deeper into the building. "Ain't used them since I broke my ankle a few years back. I just want out of this damn wheelchair."

Christian and I remained by the door, taking it all in.

"Have you made other necklaces or pendants?" I asked.

"A few." Walter nodded to a stack of boxes in the corner.

"Those are filled with pendants?"

The old man shrugged as if it were no big deal.

Christian walked to a large rolling toolbox covered in rust. "Where'd you get this equipment?"

"Here and there. Works just fine for me, despite the appearance."

Christian's gaze lifted to the rusty roof, his brow pulled

in concentration as he noted all the holes. Mapping out his renovation that would begin immediately, if I had to guess.

I wondered how Walter would take that.

"May I?" I stepped to the boxes in the corner.

"Go head, young lady."

I carefully opened the flaps of the first box. Inside lay hundreds of necklaces, pendants, and pendants hanging from silver and gold chains. Colorful gemstones sparkled off brushed silver or gold, each engraved with the same Celtic tree cross. Each unique and beautifully flawed. Just like Christian's furniture.

"Walter, this jewelry is exquisite."

The old man snorted out a laugh.

"I'm serious. I see where Christian gets his talent and creativity."

"Careful, old man. She's about to ask you if she can sell it in her shop," Christian said, rolling his eyes.

"It's yours," Walter said quickly, as if he'd already considered it. "Take it all."

"All?"

"Take every bit."

"Not unless you make me a deal, Mr. Kelley."

Walter turned his chair, a twinkle in his eyes. "What kind of deal?"

"You agree to replenish what I sell, and I'll give you one hundred percent profit." My gaze flicked to Christian. "But I get to set the retail price of each piece."

A smile quirked Walter's lips. "Deal."

Christian's gaze met mine. He inhaled deeply, then dipped his chin, his message clear. *Thank you for giving him purpose.*

I winked, my message just as clear. *You're welcome.*

"I can display them with Aaliyah Buhle's paintings—the bright colors will play off the darkness of the jewelry."

"On schedule to arrive this week?" Christian asked as he examined a rusted piece of . . . something.

I nodded, a little tingle of excitement shooting up my spine. After a few emails and phone calls, up-and-coming artist Aaliyah Buhle agreed to not only sell her art in my shop, but to also do an in-house meet-and-greet. It would help put my store on the map. I'd already begun working on the fliers to advertise it.

"Well . . ." Christian looked around the shop. "Looks like we're gonna need to get you some new equipment, old man."

"This equipment is fine. Don't touch that, son." Walter jerked his wheelchair over to Christian. He shooed away his son's hand from his precious machine and warned Christian he'd lose a finger if he touched anything else.

It had been a week since Walter's heart surgery, and the old man had been champing at the bit to get back to normal —whatever that looked like for a family reunited after a lifetime apart. We'd made a pact before leaving the hospital to keep the news that Walter was Christian's father to ourselves until he fully healed from his surgery.

It had been difficult keeping it from Fatima, who was more interested in why we were suddenly so invested in the old man's life. But, being Fatima, she was willing to help however she could. Walter had been ordered by his doctor to use a wheelchair and ease back into his daily routine— something proving to be very difficult for the proud, stubborn old man.

Like father, like son.

I smiled from across the barn, watching the men bicker. Their mannerisms were so similar. The way each held their head when speaking, the twitch of their jaw when they were biting their tongue.

There was pride in Walter's eyes as he looked at his son, and a spark of life in Christian's as he looked back. I'd reveled in watching the slow progression of ease between the two.

"You collect guns?" Christian asked his father, noticing a row of gun cabinets tucked against the far wall.

"A few. Rifles, mainly," Walter said as he wheeled himself over to a cabinet and opened it. Pulling out a rifle, he laid it in his lap, running his hands over it.

"You hunt?" Christian asked.

"Used to."

A moment passed.

"Season starts up soon." Walter looked up, his questioning gaze meeting his son's.

Christian slowly nodded, and Walter dipped his chin, in unspoken agreement of plans made. A big step forward.

To my knowledge, not another word had been uttered about the past since that day in the hospital. And I had a feeling it might never be. Walter's binds of guilt had been released with his admission, and decades of questions had been answered for Christian. He'd finally gotten the closure he so badly needed.

They were both free, and wanted to stay that way . . . together.

Our attention was pulled to a tall, lanky figure standing in the doorway. Hands in his pockets, Jay hovered awkwardly in the shadows.

"Come on in, boy," Walter called out.

"Granma said I should help."

"We could use an extra set of hands, come—"

"Whoa, is that a Sauer 202?" Jay hurried across the shop

in the quickest movement I'd seen from the kid. He seemed lighter and happier. Like he suddenly had less weight on his shoulders.

"You like guns?" Walter asked Jay.

The teenager nonchalantly shrugged, eyeing the rifle.

"Here." Walter thrust it at him.

Jay slid a glance at Christian, asking permission. Christian dipped his chin.

Jay took the gun gingerly from Walter's hands, cooing over it as one might a newborn baby.

"You know how to shoot?" Christian asked.

Jay shook his head, a touch of embarrassment in his eyes.

"Takes practice, like anything else." Christian stepped over and positioned the rifle against Jay's shoulder. "Hold it here."

"I've got some old targets in the back." Walter jerked his chin to the corner of the shop. "You can use them."

"I can? This weekend, maybe?"

"Why the hurry, son?"

Jay tested the weight of the rifle in his hands. "I'm planning to enlist next month."

Walter and Christian exchanged glances of pride.

"Then I guess we better start working on that aim, son," Walter said.

Christian stepped back, a smile on his lips as Walter stumbled clumsily into a mentor role. The one he probably wished he'd had with his own son decades earlier.

Christian slung his arm around me, and together we watched the beginning of Walter's redemption.

The sound of tires crunching on gravel pulled our attention to the shop doors, where Fatima rolled to a stop in her dented blue Chevy. We watched her step in the doorway, her height blocking the light.

"Load up, team. Sunday brunch."

Walter scowled, taking his time to warm to the strange woman who kept delivering him food.

She spotted Jay and her eyes lit up. "Did you tell them?"

"Naw." The kid shook his head.

She clucked her tongue, then focused on us. "Rumor is, they've made progress on the Jessie Miller case. BSPD received a tip that led them to Cecil Abram's lake house. They're searching it now. Apparently, he's been selling minors, including Jessie, whiskey from the back door of his shop. Lured her to the lake one weekend, and that was that." Fatima's frown turned to a smile. "So Jay's cleared, of course. It's all in the past. Onward," she said with a wink.

I exhaled, closing my eyes. The family of the poor girl I found in the ditch would receive closure and justice. Thanks to my pendant, yet again.

Thanks to my mom.

"Come on, team." Fatima clapped her hands. "Let's go. I didn't cook all morning for nothin'. Get a move on."

As Christian rubbed my back, he asked Walter, "Hungry?"

"Got pumpkins?" he muttered back.

"No pumpkins," Fatima barked from the doorway. "Your son made it clear you don't like the flavor."

I halted in midstep, and everyone's shocked eyes focused back on Fatima.

"Oh, give me a damn break." She impatiently waved her hand in the air. "Earl and I knew it the moment we first saw the old man years ago." She jabbed a finger at the men. "You both got that same look of steel in your green eyes."

"You *knew*?" I asked.

"Guessed, is all. Ain't my business to tell, so I kept it to myself." She focused on Christian. "I knew something would make you come around, open those eyes of yours to this beautiful world around us." She glanced at me. "Just didn't know it would be in the form of a woman. Funny how things work like that, ain't it?"

Christian squeezed my hand.

"Come on, let's go," Fatima said again. "I brought the trailer."

Christian wheeled Walter outside, and he began sputtering.

"Whoa, whoa. You expect me to ride on a damn trailer?"

"I expect you to watch that tongue of yours at my dinner table, and I ain't got time for Christian to push you all the way up the hill. I have exactly four minutes until my puff pastries are ready. Let's go."

"Giddyup," Christian said with a grin as he pushed the wheelchair onto the trailer.

"What am I? Livestock now?"

"Oh, come on. Just think of it as a chauffeur."

Christian locked the wheels of the chair and then helped me onto the trailer. Jay hopped in the car with his grandmother.

"All saddled up?" Fatima yelled from the driver's seat.

I bit back my laughter as I squatted down, holding on to the spare tire in the back. Christian squatted behind Walter, gripping his chair.

"All good," he hollered.

"Yeehaw!"

When we took off with a jerk, sending me stumbling, I burst into laughter. Christian grabbed my arm to steady me, laughing too. A smile cracked Walter's face as we rode up the hill.

Christian tilted his head up to the sky, closed his eyes, and inhaled. My hand found his again, and he gave it a squeeze. He opened his eyes, emotion zipping between us as he stared at me. Butterflies erupted in my stomach as I stared back.

When the truck crested the hill, I gasped at the long wooden table set up beneath two shade trees. Vases of fresh flowers lined the center over a long red runner that dangled from the ends. Elegant china glittered in the light, sunbeams catching in the glass stemware.

Fatima rolled to a stop and turned off the engine.

I glanced at Christian, a flicker of understanding—appreciation—passing between us.

Fatima had set up brunch outside because she knew Walter would have a difficult time navigating the narrow hallways of the old farmhouse in his wheelchair. It had been planned and well thought out in Fatima's ever subtle way of bringing people together.

Christian wheeled Walter across the grass as Earl slowly made his way from the house with an unlit cigarette hanging from his lips and a bottle of beer in his hand.

Jay jogged to the table, a new man now.

Fatima ushered us around the table, demanding we sit and drink.

A breeze picked up, rustling through the canopy of leaves above us. It was a beautiful afternoon—scripted, as Fatima might say.

Over plates of fried chicken, roasted vegetables, bread, and rice, we fell into comfortable, smooth, easy conversation in the same way we had at the last Sunday brunch we'd enjoyed together. Earl and Christian talked basketball, Walter took Jay down memory lane with stories of war, and

Fatima and I discussed my marketing plan for the Black Butterfly.

Seconds were served, and drinks were refilled. Laughter echoed through the woods.

As Fatima set a slice of apple pie in front of me, I looked around the table, a warm tingle spreading through my chest.

This was family.

Christian's hand slid on my leg, under the table. I reached down and squeezed.

Our eyes met and he smiled, his thoughts matching mine.

57

After licking my finger and picking up the last crumbs of pie crust from my plate, I leaned against the back of the chair with a loud exhale.

"More?" Fatima nodded to the single remaining slice of apple pie in the center of the table.

"Fatima, if I put one more thing in my mouth, I'm going to have to roll out of here on the back of Walter's wheelchair."

He scoffed. "Take it. Take the damn thing."

"A few more weeks, Walter," Christian murmured over the rim of his coffee.

The old man groaned, then turned back to his conversation with Jay and Earl, which had slid into politics. A good sign.

We turned as a black Porsche sped up the driveway. Frowning, I glanced at Christian as he stood. He was the man of the house, after all.

The car rolled to a stop, and a bulky blond woman with tattoos peeking under her silk shirt wrestled her way out of the front seat.

"Sorry to interrupt." The woman slid her sunglasses to the top of her head as she rounded the hood. Her gaze locked on Jay, and he blushed and smiled bashfully.

And that's when it hit me—the woman was the lawyer that Christian had called when Jay had been taken in for questioning. She was the VanCamps' former lawyer.

She waved a hand in greeting. "Hi, y'all. I'm Jennifer Kessler from Kessler Law, Inc. Again, sorry to interrupt. Christian, you have a second?"

Christian rounded the table and crossed the grass, dwarfing the woman as he approached. Everyone at the table stilled to eavesdrop, hanging on to every word between the two.

"Mr. Locke, we meet again." Jennifer lifted the black leather folder in her hand. "I apologize that this is a little late."

"What's late?"

"You just had your fortieth birthday, right?"

"'Bout three weeks ago."

The lawyer nodded. "Great. I'm here to deliver the details of your trust—"

"My what?"

"Your trust."

"Trust?"

She frowned. "Yes. The VanCamps set it up years ago with the caveat that the funds become available to you on your fortieth birthday. Again, I apologize, my assistant just brought it to my attention yesterday."

"I'm sorry . . ." Christian shook his head. "Funds?"

"That's right. Five point five million dollars, ready to be transferred to you immediately to spend as you see fit."

My jaw dropped.

Jennifer continued. "I have some paperwork to sign, and

I'll need the bank account number that you want the funds transferred to. Also, there's this . . ." She opened the folder and pulled out an envelope. "Arnold requested I deliver this to you with the paperwork."

Christian opened the envelope and pulled out the handwritten note, which he shared with me later.

Christian,

We all make mistakes. Mine was never opening my heart to you. My wish for you is that you don't make the same mistake I did. Please accept my apologies on the late arrival of this inheritance. Past experience suggested you might mature later than the average kid. No offense.

Sincerely,
Arnold VanCamp

58

Six months later...

I took one final sweep of the floor and leaned against the broom, a puff of dust settling around the piles of lumber, cans of paint, and the sawhorse in the corner.

Progress.

Taking a moment to soak it all in, I grabbed the jar of peanut butter from atop a stack of boxes and wiped off the sawdust before unscrewing the lid, then found a spoon from the small plastic container I'd dubbed "snack box." I spooned a man-sized glob into my mouth.

Heaven.

Sighing, I leaned against the counter and shoved in another bite, gazing outside.

Frost blurred the edges of the beveled window that framed a rolling hill, shimmering white under the sun. We'd had our first snowfall of the winter the night before, with plenty more on the way, according to the weatherman. Trees glistened in the morning light, their ice-covered branches sparkling like diamonds. My gaze shifted to the floor at the two bundles of fur curled up in matching fluffy beds adorned with printed paws.

A smile came to my lips.

"Daisy," I whispered, not wanting to wake Cricket, who was sleeping.

Two big brown eyes popped open, followed by a toothy smile. The puppy surged off the bed and wiggled its way across the room, its body vibrating with instant excitement at the mere mention of her name.

Oh, to have that kind of energy again.

I carefully lowered myself to the floor, plopping onto my butt like a beached whale. Daisy jumped into my criss-crossed legs, using her tongue to attack the smear of peanut butter on my chin.

Laughing, I stroked her ears in an attempt to push her away, failing miserably when the German Shepherd-mix pounced onto my chest. With a yelp of laughter, I fell onto my back. This only excited her more.

Cricket looked up, and with the closest thing to an animal eye roll I'd ever seen, repositioned in his bed, his butt facing us. I grinned. The old dog was definitely taking his time to warm to his new baby sister.

I straightened my legs, dropping to "dead-man's pose" on the ground. I'd taken up yoga and discovered I wasn't half bad at it. Daisy wove between my legs like an obstacle course. I turned my head and smiled at the painting leaning against the counter, soon to be hung above the windows. The focal point of the room would be the *Angel in the Storm* painting. I'd never put it up for sale. It had become too special to me—to us.

Daisy crawled her way onto my belly.

"Okay, all right, all right . . . Get off, Daisy—"

Suddenly, the puppy froze, her ears perking up. I stilled as a low growl escaped her throat, and she took off like a rocket to the front door.

Cricket didn't stir.

Frowning, I gripped the countertop and pulled myself off the floor as the front door opened.

When the growl turned into excited yips and barks, I smiled—beamed, more like.

"Good girl, Daise. Good baby." Christian ruffled the puppy's ears, but his gaze settled on me. He smiled. "Get down, girl. You're not supposed to jump up."

I rolled my eyes and shook my head. Although Daisy had been *my* Christmas gift from Christian, the two had been inseparable since the moment she'd bounded out of the box under the tree. The puppy had Christian wrapped around her furry little paw—and she knew it.

"Mac's coming to pick her up this afternoon."

I groaned, snapping my fingers for her to come back to me. "Does she really have to go for a full week? How long does guard-dog school take?" I ruffled her ears.

"It's obedience school, and yes, a full week. He's going to start training her to track too."

"Like a sniff dog?"

Christian grinned. "Yep. A *sniff* dog."

"Having her professionally trained to guard me is enough, you know."

"No, ma'am. Only the best for my baby. On that note, it's time to take a break." Christian leaned against the doorway, a smile below the sudden twinkle in his eyes.

"Whatcha got behind your back?"

His grin widened. "Close your eyes."

"You know how I feel about surprises, Christian."

"Close your eyes."

With a *tsk, tsk*, I did as I was told and sensed him move through the room, adding a crackle of electricity with each step.

"Okay," he said. "Open."

I opened my eyes and gasped, closing the inches between us. "*Christian*."

"You like it?"

"I *love* it."

I traced my finger along the ornate letters centered on the long wooden sign with a large black metal butterfly in the corner.

Black Butterfly Art Studio

I grinned. "Walter made the butterfly?"

Christian nodded. "I made the rest."

"You two make a great team."

"We'd better, since we're in business together now." He softly snorted, then smiled as he leaned the sign against the cabinet. "Now that I've got your approval on that, let's talk through a few other things."

Christian pulled a pocket notebook from his jeans, one of many he'd been keeping in his pockets lately. The man liked his lists, which was a good thing, because lately I'd been putting my shoes on the wrong feet.

"Okay, first thing, window treatments . . ."

Christian and I fell into step together with Daisy at our heels, discussing lighting, fixtures, and the finishing touches of the new art studio he'd built almost single-handedly. His touch was everywhere—in the sweeping windows, the vaulted ceiling with thick mahogany logs running parallel against the white paint, everything crisp and clean with earthy accents that pulled the outdoors inside.

It was him, and it was me. It was my mother. My tribute to her, a way to carry on her legacy, her dream, her in me.

We discussed the placement of the painting stations, eight excluding my own, each including an easel, a chair, and a rolling paint cabinet. We'd decided to add a long table on the opposite side of the room to allow for overflow students. Christian informed me that the plumber would be in the next day to check the sinks that ran below the cabinets that lined an entire side of the building.

It was all coming together, and I'll be damned if nerves didn't flutter in my stomach. I was excited. Nervous.

Ready for this new chapter in my life.

Shortly after the visit from Jennifer Kessler from Kessler Law, Christian had begun renovations on the farmhouse with Fatima and Earl leading the charge, and construction on a two-bedroom, two-bathroom log cabin to replace his father's trailer. At the bottom of the hill, Christian had added a massive workshop to house the business he and Walter had started together—Kelley and Son, LLC—a custom furniture and metalworks shop.

Although Christian had yet to refer to Walter as "Dad," their relationship had blossomed slowly but surely. They were two stubborn, bull-headed men treading lightly through the murky waters of forgiveness and healing. Walter was out of his wheelchair and walking two miles a day, and considering the fifteen pounds he'd lost, in the best shape he'd been in years. The man had discovered the freedom and joy that came with releasing your secrets to the wind.

There had been a change in Christian too. He was finally

free. Free of the anger, guilt, pain, the feeling of abandonment, and he was embracing this new identity of his.

Aside from showing me the letter he'd received with his inheritance, Christian hadn't spoken about it. He didn't need to. The letter served as closure and forgiveness, for not only his actions that icy day in the field, but for the VanCamps' loveless home as well. He'd kept the letter, though, in his closet, secured in a metal box Walter had made for him.

Walter had taken Jay under his wing, becoming somewhat of a father figure to the young man who was desperately seeking a hero. He gave the boy guidance at what could be the most pivotal time in a man's life—breaching adulthood and everything that comes with it. They'd bonded over their mutual interest in the military, and he'd helped Jay train before his departure for basic training a few months ago. While hesitant, Fatima and Earl were proud their grandson had finally found direction in his life and was passionate about something.

Passion was something that Fatima had also found when I'd hired her as manager of the Black Butterfly. Decades of pent-up energy and untapped creativity had been focused into a marketing campaign that had more than doubled my revenue goal for the year—in six months.

Christian had purchased Abram's building after it went up for sale weeks after the old man's death. Detective Darby had not only read the notebook I'd given him, but dispatched a crime scene unit to search both Abram's apartment above the Back Porch, and his lake house. At the house, they found the DNA of Jessie Miller, along with the remains of two other missing women, both in their mid-twenties, Caucasian with red hair.

The police also found several half-written manuscripts,

presumably written by Abram, each depicting horrifying tales of murder, rape, and torture. The working assumption was that Abram kidnapped the women and observed each as research for his latest masterpiece. The captives were given journals, which he would then incorporate into his manuscripts. The estimated time of the death of all three victims was after Abram's wife's death.

Old stories of unreported sexual assaults by Abram began to surface from local young women—now older and more willing to talk about the experiences—painting a picture of a cheating husband with a sadistic sexual fetish. But now, a madman was dead, and three families had finally received the closure they so badly needed.

Christian knocked down the wall that separated the Back Porch and my shop, and was actively renovating the entire first floor to expand the Black Butterfly, which now featured furniture, metal decor, and art—including my paintings. Everything we sold was handmade locally by Christian, his father, or me.

Business was booming, both indoors and online. The Black Butterfly had not only become one of the top tourist destinations in Berry Springs, but one of the top custom furniture stores in the state. With Fatima's marketing savvy, Kelley and Son was bringing in more business than Christian and his father could keep up with. They were currently interviewing for an office manager and a carpenter.

And me? I was about to open my second business, an art studio that offered free afterschool programs for children, in addition to group and one-on-one lessons.

Christian and I had purchased the small patch of land behind the brick building that we now owned. The land backed up to vegetation that extended to the city park. We'd preserved the trees as much as possible, constructing the studio between the soaring oaks and maples, giving it a bungalow kind of feel. Once a week, the Black Butterfly would lead art classes at the local elementary school, which also served as my community service for breaking Becky Dunks Davies' nose. A win-win for everyone.

The studio was a little oasis in the middle of town, an escape, an outlet for creativity and dreams. But it was also meant to honor my mother.

It represented acceptance. My acceptance of the past, of the circle of life. Of the ebbs and flows that come with it, and the realization that everything is interconnected. Woven like a thick tapestry of color, our paths run along and across others, every decision we make leading us in a different direction. Everything has a reason and leads somewhere . . . you just have to be open to see it.

On Christmas Eve, Christian had asked me to marry him. To my delight, he gave me a diamond solitaire haloed by our gemstones, and a little black butterfly etched into the band. We were surrounded by our new family—Walter, Fatima, Earl, Jay, Cricket, Tater, T-Bone, Ishka, and our new puppy, Daisy. The next day, Christian moved out of the basement and into my house—where he had also begun renovations.

Because more space was needed.

We paused in front of the sweeping window that overlooked the woods. The warmth of sunlight pooled around us.

"Last, but not least." Christian flipped a page in his notebook. "Fatima wants you to take one last look over the menu for the grand opening next week."

I laughed. "I already have, a million times. I told her she can do whatever she wants."

"I know, I know." Exasperated, he shook his head. "She

needs to hear it again—and she needs to hear it's *enough*. The woman has added three more finger foods since we last spoke about it. A fancy cheese-on-a-stick thing that required me to drive to three different specialty stores and one goat farm to get the ingredients. And for the local hippies, she's doing some sort of vegan, gluten-free brush-something with roasted *jam*." He wrinkled his nose in disgust. "And some sort of beef pie."

I laughed. "Bruschetta, and beef tourtieres."

"Tourtieres?"

"Yeah. She made them for brunch the other day. You didn't touch them."

"I don't eat meat pies. The point is, you need to rein her in. She's making enough food to feed an army."

"And she's loving every second of it, isn't she?"

"It's all she talks about. Aside from the Black Butterfly, of course." He shook his head. "I could barely make it out of there this morning. The woman had lured in a local book club with homemade cookies and coffee."

"And how many of these women requested a meeting with Kelley and Son, LLC?"

"Two. One wants me to design her entire house. And one wants a date with Walter."

"Ah. How do you feel about that?"

He shrugged. "Whatever makes the old man happy."

"You're running a background check on her, aren't you?"

He cleared his throat and looked away.

I laughed. "That's very sonly of you."

"I don't think sonly is a word."

"And I don't think you're as detached as you pretend to be with him."

"I'm instantly detached from this conversation."

I laughed and bit my tongue.

Since the day Walter was released from the ι. Christian had been micromanaging every aspect of his ᵤ from his doctor's appointments, his medications, his food, ensuring he was getting adequate exercise and that he didn't get overworked in the shop. Christian thrived in a caretaker position. Because he'd spent his entire life caring only for himself, he found happiness in caring for others, and took pride in it. And Walter eventually took the help graciously, his happiness lying in finally having a partner again in his life.

It was quite something to watch from the sideline.

"Oh, one more thing." Christian glanced at his notepad. "Along with the mini cream puffs, chocolate-covered strawberries, and caramel-apple bites, Fatima also wants to know if you want oatmeal or chocolate chip cookies. Or both."

"Both. And lots." My eyes lit up. "Oh . . . with little peanut butter chips in them. And Reese's chunks."

Laughing, Christian lightly grabbed my waist and pulled me to him. His hands swept down my sides onto my stomach. Goose bumps rippled over my skin.

Slowly, he took a knee and then another, lifted my T-shirt, and kissed my growing belly. I threaded my hands through his hair. He closed his eyes and inhaled, the sweetest smile crossing his face.

"I'm almost done with the bassinet."

"Is this your second or your third?" I smiled down at him.

"The last one, I promise."

"You know there's only one baby in here."

"I figured we'd get a head start on Charlotte's brother."

Yes, we were expecting a little girl, which thrilled me. My mother's name would live on in her.

out first," I said, "then start working on

ed my belly again before he stood and
ds around my cheeks. "You promise, my
e?"

"I p⋅

"I love you, Rory."

"I love you, my future husband."

Under the warm sun, he kissed me, slowly, softly, one hand in my hair, and the other on his baby girl in my belly.

A new beginning in this crazy, beautiful circle of life.

ABOUT THE AUTHOR

Amanda McKinney is the bestselling and multi-award-winning author of more than twenty romantic suspense and mystery novels. Her book, Rattlesnake Road, was named one of *POPSUGAR's 12 Best Romance Books,* and was featured on the *Today Show.* The fifth book in her Steele Shadows series was recently nominated for the prestigious *Daphne du Maurier Award for Excellence in Mystery/Suspense.* Amanda's books have received over fifteen literary awards and nominations.

Text **AMANDABOOKS to 66866** to sign up for Amanda's Newsletter and get the latest on new releases, promos, and freebies!

www.amandamckinneyauthor.com

If you enjoyed REDEMPTION ROAD, please write a review!

Made in the USA
Las Vegas, NV
15 April 2024

88682022R00236